ROUND 'BOUT MIDNIGHT

For Aunt Valerie

ACKNOWLEDGMENTS

There are so many to thank for the birth and rebirth of *Time Will Tell*, and now its sequel, *Round 'Bout Midnight*. I first want to thank God for trusting me with this gift and for Divine inspiration.

To my parents, Juanita and the late Thomas McDonald, I thank you for your love, support and encouragement and for inspiring me to pursue my passions. To my brother, Lenny, thank you for believing in me and for sharing your knowledge with me. To my cousin Kaye Hill Hawkins, thank you for your continued support.

To my support team: Risi Ademola, C.B. Cotton, Irene Hill, Shirley Hunter, Anne Johnston, Toya Littlejohn, Diana Monroe, Greta Oliver, Kiara Palmer, Gilda Thompson, Lisa Villamil, and Russ Woods, thank you for your comments, criticism and inspiration which helped me make *Round 'Bout Midnight* a better book than I ever imagined.

Special thanks to Jordan Fieulleteau, Roxy Slay, James Sanders, Don Miskel, Dr. Elizabeth Motyka, Mark Tulloss, Livis Freeman, and Tricia Robinson for sharing your expertise with me and for critiquing respective sections of the book. Your insight made *Round 'Bout Midnight* more authentic.

To Patricia Haley, thank you for convincing me to step out on faith and self-publish *Time Will Tell* back in 1999. During that journey, I found a very supportive community of countless authors who were willing to share and uplift each other.

I also found immense support among Delta Authors on Tour, which I started in 2000 along with Stephanie Perry Moore and Victoria Christopher Murray. Through the years and through visits to many chapters we were able to promote literacy and encourage a new generation of writers of all ages.

To Karen E. Quinones-Miller, you will never know how much your words at the Delta Centennial Convention in 2013 mean to me. They never left my mind and in fact, stirred my spirit. I am happy to say that I am writing again.

To Jacquelin Thomas. Where do I begin? I remember meeting you early in my writing career. Thank you for all of your inspiration and encouragement through the years, and for being a midwife in helping me birth this new project

To the booksellers, book clubs, and readers, thank you for believing in me enough to buy my books. I hope that you will enjoy reading them as much as I enjoyed writing them.

1

IT NEVER ENTERED MY MIND

I *t never entered my mind that the world I spent ten years building would come crashing down around me at once,* Hope thought at a time when she should have been basking in the afterglow. She looked over at the red glowing numbers, which illuminated the silhouette of the condom wrapper on the nightstand. The only glimmer of light was from the full moon over the Atlantic Ocean, which peeked through the tiny crevice between the curtain and balcony door of the hotel room. Hope calmly arose from the king-size bed and glanced over her shoulder at the unfamiliar face of the unfamiliar man who slept so peacefully after their encounter. *Typical.* The time was 11:55 p.m. It was only three hours ago that she sat quietly at a table in the hotel lounge nursing her new baby, rum and Diet Coke. She knew he had been watching her from across the room, but she didn't care. Before long she knew he'd serve his only purpose in her life. To try to help heal the wound made by Jason's sudden rejection of her, of their five-year marriage and their relationship, which dated back to freshman year of high school.

I spent my life with Jason, for Jason and this is all the thanks I get, Hope thought as she slipped on her red dress. Night after night, she didn't work the dress. The dress worked her. But like the man she picked up in the hotel lounge this evening, the dress had served its purpose tonight, as it had so many other nights. Only neither tonight, nor the countless nights in previous weeks had served their purpose—to heal her pain.

She quietly picked up her small clutch from the floor where she haphazardly dropped it when she entered the room. *In like a raging lion and out like a meek lamb* she thought while gentle and careful steps carried her out of the room and into the hallway of the upscale, ocean-front hotel.

Before this recent drama of her life, Hope would have happily spent her midnight in the hotel room indulging in the offerings of the room service menu, but now food didn't matter to her. Nothing mattered, but trying to pick up the broken pieces of her life. It didn't matter to her that she had relegated her last days in Kalamazoo to frequenting clubs and bars armed with rum and Diet Coke, to have careless, yet safe sex with a variety of men in places that never entered Hope's sheltered mind. It didn't matter to her that her friends felt she had a new lease on life.

She had an opportunity to make a fresh start, which was assisted by her new position as Chief Incentive Officer with Vantarca Health System in Virginia Beach, accompanied by a six-figure salary. This position allowed Hope to combine her years of experience as an accountant, with her newly minted Masters of Healthcare Administration. It was what she wanted when she was with Jason, but now that he was no longer in her life and had filed for divorce, it didn't matter.

The decision to go to her room alone faced her. Since Jason packed his belongings and had Hope served with divorce papers, she endured many restless nights. She often spent them questioning her life, questioning her mistakes, and wondering where she went wrong. The temporary solace of a novel sexual experience sometimes lulled her to sleep, but tonight she had too much on her mind.

Instead of pushing the up button for the elevator which would take her to the club level suite known as her temporary home, courtesy of Vantarca Health System, Hope pressed the down button, as it signified how she felt.

❧

IT NEVER ENTERED my mind that I would be calling Patrick six years after our breakup Rachel thought as she tried to muster up courage once again to pick up the phone and face the truth. Just days earlier, after she finally located the right Patrick Long and had gotten up the nerve to call him, their conversation was deferred by distressing news about two of the most meaningful men in her life—her estranged father and her estranged husband. The appearance of her living room reflected the anxiety that consumed her. A backlog of mail and unfolded laundry covered her sofa and coffee table. Silently, Rachel sat in the corner swirling vodka and orange juice in her glass. "This will take the edge off," she said as if someone were in the room with her.

With Martin and Malcolm safely tucked into bed, sleeping peacefully, Rachel felt free—if just for a few hours. Her summer respite had been quite eventful—high school reunion, the discovery of her father, and her husband's tragedy. But her biggest shock came when she and Sina spent a week at the beach. It was then that Rachel shared her memorable breakup with Patrick with her friend. It wasn't exactly the break-up itself that was memorable. It was that one last kiss which led to one last, well you know, which may have led to Martin. And while Rachel spent the last five years as if Martin were her estranged husband's son, that curl of his upper lip and left hand catch put too much of a question in her mind.

Rachel careened to the sofa in search of the phone. Amid a stack of bills hid the patriotic airmail envelope postmarked Sydney, Australia. Rachel stared at the postmark, took a swig of her cocktail, and decided to allow her anxiety to grow yet another day.

IT NEVER ENTERED *my mind that I would wake up to find the man of my dreams sitting across the aisle from me.* Sina smiled, stretched her arm across the aisle, and touched Rodney who slept like a baby. *Surely, I must be dreaming.*

Sina gently tapped his shoulder. "I hope you were dreaming about me, Sugar Cane."

Rodney's smile was so bright it would chase the darkest of storm clouds and the accompanying rain away. "Excuse me, sir," Rodney said to the gentleman in the seat next to him. "Would you mind switching seats with this beautiful woman across the aisle from me? I can arrange a pair of courtside seats for you the next time the International Basketball League's Windy City Gale Force plays in Sydney."

"Why certainly, mate." The man gathered his belongings from underneath the seat in front of him as Rodney stepped into the aisle to allow the change. Just then, the flight attendant came down the aisle with Arrival Cards for each passenger to complete for Customs and Quarantine.

"Did you plan to surprise me all along?" Sina asked as she and Rodney completed their Arrival Cards.

"We'll just say I was very determined," emphasis on very. Rodney wrapped his arms around Sina and kissed her intensely. They ate dinner, while sipping Hunter Valley wine, then fell asleep in each other's arms for the duration of the flight.

2

DREAMIN'

Blue and white banners welcomed the new arrivals to Sydney Kingsford Smith Airport. Groggy, travel weary passengers shuffled slowly through Immigration Services after their fourteen-hour flight, which made the line through baggage claim seem like an eternity. An anxious brigade of beagles swarmed around the carousel sniffing out fruits, meats, and plant material. After successfully finding undeclared food, they were richly rewarded for their hard work.

"I can't believe you came halfway across the world with only your gym bag." Rodney took Sina's suitcase as they exited the Customs and Quarantine area.

"Like I said, I was very, very determined." Rodney took Sina's hand. "And I meant what I said last night, or was it two nights ago?"

"We did cross the International Date Line and lose a day," she chuckled, then yawned.

"I love you, Sweetie Pie, and I have a confession to make." Rodney recounted his journey to the airport, from getting pulled over for speeding, to calling the travel agent to book him on Sina's flight to Sydney, and calling his pet sitter to take care of Zack while he was away.

Sina put her arm around his waist. "I have to say this is the sweetest thing anyone has ever done for me. You thought of every-thing—even ground transportation. This means the world to me."

✦

"THE VIEW IS BREATHTAKING," Sina said of the nearly panoramic view of Darling Harbour from their Full Harbour Junior Suite at the Four Seasons Hotel Sydney. The dark, clear sky was bisected by bright specks of lights from Sydney's skyline in the distance. Up-close, blue lights beamed from the Harbour Bridge like rays from the sun. Shim-mers of gold light danced across the water, perfectly reflecting the bridge's pylons on either end, sandwiching a subtle hint of green which swayed in between. The glow of the full moon down the center seemed to be reaching out to her. "This is much nicer than the hotel I stayed in when I was here five years ago. I feel like a queen."

"You are my queen." Rodney put the phone receiver down, walked across the room, wrapped his arms around Sina's waist, and gently kissed the back of her neck. He led Sina to the chaise in their lounging area, then pulled the cord to open the curtains of the corner floor to ceiling window which revealed an even more breathtaking view of the Sydney Opera House. Taking Sina's hand, he guided her to him as he rested on the chaise. Encircled in silence, together they became inebri-ated from the view. Their reverie was punctuated by the intense rumbling of Sina's stomach. Rodney chuckled. "Don't worry. I ordered a snack from room service. Should be here soon." Rodney gazed into Sina's eyes as she leaned in to kiss him, and together they savored the moment, before devouring their snack, and then each other.

✦

STRETCHED out in a chaise lounge at the edge of the well-lit hotel pool, Hope sipped her rum and Diet Coke. *Why am I doing this to myself?* She looked out at the Atlantic Ocean, only buffered by a neat row of palm trees and a wooden railing. A gentle breeze gave her a slight, momen-tary chill. Another sip, actually a gulp. A tear began to form in the corner of her eye. *How did all of this happen? And how did it happen so fast?* Released from its captivity, the tear slowly trickled down Hope's right cheek, just as a joyous couple walked hand in hand for a midnight swim. She watched as he stepped into the shallow end of the pool, and tenderly guided his beloved to join him.

Radiant, subtle pastel hues gleamed from the fountain in the center of the pool. The colors seemed to change to the rhythm of a slow, sweet melody. Hope's perception about the couple's relationship made her pine for Jason even more, or at least the dream she had of their relationship. She watched as their midnight swim, a waltz synchronized to the changing colors of the fountain, connected them. Tears began to form in her left eye, and she could taste the salt in them as they fell down her face. The couple exited the pool, and he wrapped her in the plush towel, before taking his to dry himself off. Although there were numerous empty chaise loungers stationed around the pool, the couple chose one near Hope.

"Is everything alright?" The woman asked her.

Hope took a short sip of her drink, the last one, as what was left of the ice clinked in her glass. "Yes. I'm fine." Hope stood up and began to walk towards the ocean.

"You be careful, Hun." The woman said to Hope as she exited the gate surrounding the pool.

Hope stood at the railing overlooking the Atlantic Ocean, and stared into the bright glow from the moon which was surrounded by dark, endless water. While the palm trees behind her offered an easy breeze, the floodgate which held her tears back for so long broke, unleashing a sea that raged like a breaking dam in the aftermath of a hurricane. Hope didn't know or care if the couple by the pool could hear her. Her pain was too intense, and she had held it in for so long, looking for solace in the wrong places. This pain cut her deeply, and she felt it each day, in her heart. Her shoulders heaved as she continued to release, with her lip quivering and nose running. And when there were no more tears left, at least for that night, Hope turned away from the ocean and made her way back to her suite.

৯৯

RODNEY SMILED as he looked at Thomasine sleeping so peacefully next to him. Carefully, he slid out of bed and tiptoed to the bathroom, grabbing his gym bag on the way. He was so pleased that he kept a light jacket in his bag. With another month of winter left in Sydney, Rodney would need it this morning. He placed an order for room service from a house phone in the lobby in an effort to not wake Sina. It was scheduled for delivery an hour and fifteen minutes later.

"Morning, mate," the bell captain said to Rodney as he stepped outside the hotel. The sky was layered with an array of delicate colors. Periwinkle blue overshadowed a slight sliver of coral which peeked from behind the lower level of buildings in the distance. Rodney stood on the sidewalk, rotated his ankles on each foot, created circles with his knees, then hips and torso, in preparation. The brisk walk insulated him from the cool, crisp morning air, fully warming his body. Rodney set the stopwatch on his Ironman. When he turned right onto Cumberland Street, he began to pick up the pace, easing into a nice jog as he approached the Harbour Bridge. The coral ribbon in the lower horizon began to grow, and Rodney noticed how the sky and water were a mirror reflection. Rodney's heart fluttered, and he embraced his happiness at how he and Sina reconnected at the Piney Hill High School Class of 1987 ten-year reunion weeks earlier. He picked up his pace, his breath synchronized with his stride. And to think, a misunderstanding kept them from being together ten years earlier. Rodney made his way to the bridge's pylon and prepared to reverse his steps. The coral ribbon was now behind him, as the shades of blue above him began to brighten.

Rodney had always been immensely proud of Sina. She was smart, talented, and beautiful, but the cold shoulder she had given him during their college internship caused him to keep his distance. Although he had dated other women, and even had a long-term relationship during his college days, Sina was always imprinted on his mind and in his heart. Every now and then his long-time buddy, Jason, would mention her latest accomplishment. Rodney checked his watch to monitor his pace as he found his way to Argyle Street and rounded the corner at the Museum of Contemporary Art Australia.

The past few weeks revealed that Sina was everything Rodney imagined, and more. His heart warmed as he ran through Circular Quay, turning left onto Macquarie towards the Sydney Opera House. Boats drifted by as a ray of light shimmied on the water. Just beyond the bridge, sharp beams of light directed below grew in intensity, and seemed to flow directly to him. As Rodney neared the Sydney Opera House, and the end of his run he wished that he had a camera with him to capture this perfect moment so that he could share it with Sina. He found a bench and stretched his calves and hamstrings before he began his cool down walk back to his temporary home with Sina.

Rodney grabbed a bottle of water before making his way back to their suite. As he quietly opened the door, Sina turned over and cracked her eyes open to a sliver. She wasn't quite prepared for the morning sun that Rodney so enjoyed on his run. "Good morning, Sweetie Pie." Rodney walked towards the corner window to close the curtains.

"Leave them open, the sunrise is so beautiful," Sina stretched her arms. "Morning run?"

"Yes. Training camp is a week away," he smiled. "And I didn't want to wake you." Rodney walked across the room, kissed Sina on her forehead. She reached up to hug him. "Uh, I'm kind of sweaty. Let me take a shower first." Rodney grabbed his gym bag and tossed Sina one of the bathrobes in the closet. "Oh, and I ordered room service from the house phone downstairs just before I left for my run. Should be here soon."

Sina heard the bathroom door close, and seconds later the shower. The plush bathrobe caressed her skin. She climbed back into the bed, the drizzle of the water came to an abrupt halt. She smiled and savored the thought of how lucky she was, and how Rodney was so different from the men she dated before, she only hoped that she would continue to feel this way, that their love would continue to grow, and that she would trust him and most of all, herself.

"I don't believe this!" Rodney exclaimed from the bathroom.

"What's wrong?" Sina yelled to him.

Rodney exited the bathroom and rounded the corner near the bed.

"Rodney, why are you wearing swimming trunks? Do you run AND swim every morning? Aren't you supposed to wait forty-five minutes after eating before you swim to avoid leg cramps? Didn't you say that breakfast would be here soon?" She shot questions to him in a rapid-fire sequence.

"This is so embarrassing." Rodney sat on the edge of the bed. "I always have a change of underwear in my gym bag. I can't believe I would go clear to the other side of the world without any. These swimming trunks are all that I have."

"Well, it wasn't like you packed your gym bag to come clear to the other side of the world." Sina began to laugh. "Baby, you have to admit that this is pretty funny." She pulled Rodney to her, he joined her in laughter. "And they're green." She began to laugh louder. "But you do have very nice legs, and a cute butt." She kissed him just as she heard a knock on the door. "I'll get that," She looked at him again and laughed.

Rodney couldn't help but laugh. *This will be a funny story to tell our grandkids one day.* "One thing I know for sure is that we're going shopping today."

Sina signed the breakfast receipt and the waiter placed their smorgasbord of berries, omelets, waffles, sausage, bacon, yogurt, and coffee on the table nearest the corner window. Rodney pushed the chairs together and they enjoyed their breakfast and the view. Sina stretched and rubbed her eyes.

"Are you still sleepy?" Rodney asked.

"I am. The travel, the time change, the season change, and then last night," a sly smile crossed Sina's face.

"Get back in bed," Rodney said. "It is still very early, and the stores don't open for a few hours anyway. I can live with these swimming trunks a bit longer."

Sina climbed back into the bed. Rodney wrapped his arm around her waist and snuggled up to her, his knees in the back of her knees. Before long they were both fast asleep, despite the sunlight that flooded their room.

§

"HAVE A GREAT EVENING, MR. MCCOY," Melissa, the receptionist said. "And welcome to Zandt, Monroe, & Cates."

"You have a great evening as well," Jason smiled. "And it was a pleasure to meet you." Jason walked briskly to the door, briefcase in hand. He pushed the button for the elevator, and walked closer to the window overlooking Grant Park to admire the view of Chicago's lakefront, which extended from the Museum Campus to the south to the big Ferris wheel at Navy Pier to the north.

"When you make partner, you will have this view from your office. Two floors up." A very fit, middle-aged, bespectacled man with hints of gray around his temples extended a firm handshake. "Ed Campbell, Trademark Agreements."

Jason firmly shook his hand. "Jason McCoy, Licensing."

"Oh man, it's so nice to meet you." Ed said. "You were such a great running back. I've been a fan of yours since you were at Piney Hill."

"Really?" Jason replied as the elevator doors opened.

"I was devastated when you were injured in that game against Lake Effect. I thought you gave up too soon. Dude, you were a Heisman hopeful." He paused while the elevator doors opened and a short, stocky woman with a mushroom haircut and freckles joined them. "And Duncan University Medical Center has the best orthopedic surgeons in the region. They've made major innovations in ACL surgery in the past few years."

Jason wiped his left hand across his brow as the elevator reached the first floor."I'm sorry for rambling on and on, and I hope you aren't offended." Ed said. "I just think you were one of the best, no, the best college running back who ever played the game."

"Thanks, man."

"And I'm glad you're at the firm."

When Jason stepped outside the high-rise office building in the 900 block of South Michigan Avenue, all he could do was exhale. Ed's comments put a lot on his mind, almost too much. Jason headed north on Michigan towards the Van Buren Metra Station, bobbing and weaving his way through the avalanche of neatly groomed and well-suited people flooding out of office buildings up and down Michigan Avenue. As he paused at the corner of Balbo and Michigan when the light changed, he observed a man walking in his direction nearly run over by a cab. His attention was focused on his newspaper, not his surroundings. Buses and cars idled by and Jason was really happy he decided to take the train to work rather than drive. *It would take me forever to get out of the Loop, and I can't even imagine how backed up the traffic is on the Ryan.* With that in mind, Jason decided to hang around downtown to avoid the mad rush.

Kelly green and ivory Tiffany-style lampshades hung from the ceiling adorning the brick veneer, which lined the walls of the bar and the section dividers. New adult contemporary music from the 70s and 80s could be heard faintly beneath the cacophony of chatter throughout the Irish pub. Jason scanned the bar as he approached the hostess line. He observed a man signing his receipt, so he made his way through the crowd in perfect time to retrieve the seat the man was leaving. "I'll have a Heineken," he said as the bartender approached him to clear the glass and plate from the patron who preceded him. "Oh, and an order of buffalo wings," he added.

Jason set his briefcase on the floor, then steadied himself on the bar stool, his feet firmly on the floor. "Thanks," he said as the bartender placed his beer before him. *Gave up too soon.* Those four words resonated and reverberated in his head. He took a sip of his beer. The chatter all around him became more and more faint.

☙

"JASON, I have to be honest with you," Naomi drew closer to him, her left leg entangled with his right, her breasts nuzzled at his ribs, her head rested on his bare chest. "I think you're giving up too soon." She tilted her head up and kissed his neck.

"It's too late."

"It's only October. You just need to give yourself a chance to heal."

"I'm out for the rest of the season." A week had passed since Romanizak's hit took Jason out of the Homecoming game his senior year at Duncan.

"But you have another year of eligibility, and you can make a comeback next season as a fifth-year senior. Surgery, PT. You'll be ready for practice and workouts in the spring. Jason, you'll be on top of your game. And you can apply for the draft next year."

"I don't want to get my hopes up too high. The only thing I'm going to apply for is Law School."

"Law School?" Naomi sat straight up in the bed. "Uh, where in the hell did this come from? I've known you for three years and you ain't never said a word to me about wanting to be a lawyer."

"It's a good career and I'll make a lot of money."

"Jason, that don't even make sense." Naomi's legs dangled over the edge of the bed. "Good career. I'll make a lot of money," she said mockingly. "That don't even sound like you. And where are you applying?

"Lake Effect."

"Aw hell no. Lake Effect. That ain't got a damn thing to do with you and everything to do with Hope." Naomi stood up. "And Lake Effect is in Kalamazoo where Hope lives. I don't believe this shit! Hope don't give a damn about you. Where in the hell was she when you got injured? She didn't even step her behind on the field. And where is she now? Not here. But I am, just like I've always been the past three years."

"This has nothing to do with Hope."

"This has everything to do with Hope," Naomi searched on the floor for her clothing. "I know she was your high school sweetheart and all, but that chick don't give a flying flip about your welfare and well-being." Naomi pulled her panties up around her waist. "It's all about appearances for her. What she thinks will look good to someone else who don't even matter."

"Naomi, how can you say that?"

"Jason," Naomi faced him, arms akimbo. "Would you listen to yourself? Why are you giving up on your dream so easily? This," she picked up his football, "Is your dream, not no damn Law School."

"I'm not giving up. I'm just being realistic."

"Realistic is this," Naomi pulled her Henley shirt over her head. "You are the best college running back in this conference, heck, maybe even the country. You're throwing it all away to live some fantasy Hope has created. And the sad part is that this isn't gonna make you happy, and she isn't gonna to make you happy. You still have time, Boo. You have a window of opportunity. Take advantage of it. That's all you have to do."

Jason clenched his jaw. "I didn't invite you over for all of this."

"Jason, when have you ever known me to just go along or just tell you what you want to hear? This ain't about me or anyone else but you."

"Naomi, I've made my decision."

"You are not in an emotional space right now to make this serious of a decision. This is a major life decision, and if Hope really cared about you, she would give you the time and space you need to make the decision that is best for your heart, your health, your life, and your highest good, and not just protect what she thinks are her interests. And I promise you this. You'll regret this decision forever." The last word was drawn out and unforgettable, like a flat note.

"It is my decision, and it's final. Discussion over,"

"Over is right." Naomi buttoned her jeans and stepped into her flats. "Jason, I certainly hope you had just a little bit of happiness with me, and that I was more than a stadium whore for you these past three years."

"I never thought of you like that."

She grabbed her purse. "And don't even think about calling me until you get the courage to stop living your life for your momma and Hope. Learn to live your life for you, Boo." She walked to the door. "I'm out!"

"ONE ORDER OF BUFFALO WINGS." The bartender placed the food in front of Jason.

"Could you please bring me a box? And the check?" Jason was no longer hungry.

3

TAKE FIVE

"You'll need a jacket," Rodney reminded Sina. "Don't forget it's winter here." Sina buttoned up her jacket, and Rodney held the door open for her as they left the room. He placed the "Do Not Disturb" sign on the inside of their hotel room door.

"I can't believe we slept through lunch." Sina said as Rodney pushed the down button for the elevator. "But amazingly, I'm not hungry just yet."

"It will take you a while to get used to the time change." Rodney extended his arm, directing Sina to get onto the elevator first. "When I started my IBL career, adjusting to the travel and time changes were brutal. But after six seasons of spending a month on six different continents for six months, it's old hat for me."

Rodney put his arm around Sina and they walked across the granite floors of the hotel lobby, which wore the color of red clay and had a spit shine polish. The glass doors that lined the hotel entrance offered a glimpse of guests arriving in shuttles and limos.

"G'Day, Mr. Harris." The afternoon bellman said as they stepped out of the hotel's doors. "I hope you and the lovely lady are enjoying your stay."

"We are, Peter." Rodney shook his hand. "It's good to see you again. Have a great day."

Rodney and Sina made a right onto George Street. "Wow! He knew you by name." Rodney walked around behind Sina and took her left hand, so that he was on the curb side of the street.

"I've known Peter for years. Well, since I've been playing in Sydney. This is the team hotel."

"So, you know your way around here pretty well then, I mean, after six seasons. Where should we go?"

"The Strand Arcade and Queen Victoria Building are just down the street. About a ten-minute walk."

"Those sound familiar." They stopped at the corner for a passing car. "I was here for about a week five years ago." Sina looked up at Rodney, and faked a smile as they crossed the street. She knew that she should live in the moment, stay in the present. But mentioning her brief time in Sydney reminded her of why she cut her trip short five years ago. She was anxious to get back to Kenneth, her fiancé. She had buried herself in her master's thesis, leaving him feeling very ignored. Making an outstanding convention presentation was so important to her, as was her career. Sina had laser-sharp focus on meeting her goals and was less interested in wedding planning. She remembered how much she left Kenneth out of her decisions, to postpone having children so that she could pursue her Ph.D. first. She also remembered how doubly painful the end was when she found Kenneth cheating on her in the townhome they purchased to start their life as husband and wife. To make matters even worse, he was cheating with Sophronia, the woman she later learned had spread a lie around Piney Hill High School that prevented her and Rodney from being together ten years earlier.

Sina put her arm around Rodney. She wanted to hold him close and knew that she would have to be very open with him. She really wanted this to work.

The Victorian era building held shops on four levels. The floor was a tile mosaic that reminded Sina of Native American art with the terra-cotta, turquoise, goldenrod, and white color scheme. As always, it was crowded, with tourists scurrying to the lower level for Duty-Free shopping or browsing many of the ground floor shops for anything and everything Australia. The floor-to-ceiling windows in each of the shops gave passersby a good look at each store's offering. "Let's stop here," Sina said, observing the vast array of menswear. Once inside, she held up a sweater. "I think this would look nice on you." Rodney found a pair of pants and socks to go along with the sweater, and told the clerk he would like to wear his new purchases now.

"It feels so good to get out of those clothes," he told Sina as they left the store. "Now I'm dressed appropriately for the season."

"But we need to do something about your shoes," she smiled. "And a jacket."

"My favorite shoe store is in the Queen Victoria Building," Rodney looked up at the glass atrium. The sky was a deeper shade of blue. "We should head over there now so that we'll have time to shop before the stores close."

With the sun a bit lower in the sky, the late afternoon winter chill was a bit more intense. The two Chicago natives made the brief walk to the Queen Victoria Building in record time. The expansive Romanesque Revival building, which took up a city block, had a mosaic floor at ground level. Stained glass domes and an indoor court-yard provided natural light to the shops below. Cast iron railings kept shoppers on upper levels safe. Sina's eyes were wide like a child's at Christmastime when she saw a red dress in a store window.

"Do you like it?" Rodney observed her interest.

"Yeah, but I want to shop around for a while. I may find something else."

After finding the perfect pair of shoes for his remaining days in Sydney, Rodney purchased winter jackets for both of them, and choco-late from Haigh's. "Taste this," Rodney put a dark chocolate walnut cream into her mouth as they rode up the escalator. "It's my favorite."

Sina's eyes rolled back into her head as she savored the sweet, coffee flavored cream, which perfectly offset the bitter dark chocolate. "Mmm, mmm, mmm. This is so good."

They made their way to the second level and scanned the windows of shops as they walked by. "I've been to this one before," Sina said of the jewelry store. "I bought a loose solid white opal here. I really wanted a black opal, but I was a broke graduate student and couldn't afford it. I wish I had splurged."

Rodney smiled and made a mental note. "Did you see the Royal Clock?"

"I don't recall."

"Let's go up, it's almost time."

"Time for what?"

"You'll see."

The Royal Clock was on the upper level of the Queen Victoria Building. The clock resembled a castle. Just as they reached it, puppets of trumpeters playing classical music popped up from each turret. The portal was a window which displayed a diorama of six different scenes.

"Pretty cool, isn't it?" Rodney asked as they watched the execution of King Charles I.

"Yeah, but."

"But what?"

"I didn't see anything about the history of Australia before Captain Cook came in 1788. You know the Indigenous Australians have been here for 50,000, maybe 60,000 years."

"Very true." Rodney turned to Sina. "And aren't you here to do research on Aboriginal women."

"I am. I'd love to tell you about it over dinner."

"The Sydney Tower isn't far. Let's have dinner there."

They made their way back to the building's ground level. "The dress?" Rodney asked as they approached the store where the window display caught her eye.

"We'll have to come back." Sina observed the closed sign on the door.

❧

THE SYDNEY TOWER RESTAURANT revolved and gave patrons a 360-degree view of the city. Sina and Rodney arrived at sunset for a perfect ending to the day. The restaurant's buffet was enormous, offering cuisines from across the globe. Sina took a bite from one of her prawns. "So, have you heard of the Stolen Generations?"

"Yes, I have," Rodney replied. "It's horrible that children were removed from their families in an effort to get rid of Indigenous

Australians. Have you read the report, *Bringing them Home?"*

"I have." She took a sip of her wine. "When I was here five years ago, I met two women in Redfern. They told me about their childhood. I was in shock."

"Such a human rights violation."

"I'm doing field research with some of the women who were stolen from their families."

"I'm so happy you're doing this research. Their stories need to be told." Rodney said. The sun had set and the night time view of Sydney was spectacular.

"Will you excuse me?" Sina stood up from the table. "I'll be right back." She stopped and asked a waitress a question which was inaudible to Rodney. The waitress pointed her toward the restroom.

She hadn't turned the corner before two young chatty women made their way to the table. "Say, you're Rodney Harris from the IBL, aren't you?" Her blonde hair was pulled back into a ponytail and her jeans were so tight they looked like they had been painted on.

"He sure is," replied her friend, she put her plate down on the table. "I'm from Houston, and I've been a fan of yours since your rookie season. Can I get a picture with you?"

"Sure." Rodney began to stand up from the table when the blonde's friend pushed him back down in the seat, then sat on his lap.

"Wait, Wait!" He tried to get up. Before he knew it, the camera flashed in his face, and unknown to him, Sina was rounding the corner on her way from the restroom.

&

SINA STOOD at the corner window of their suite. "This view is so beautiful." She snapped a photo with a disposable camera she picked up during their shopping excursion. "I'd better savor it. I move into my rental in Haberfield tomorrow." Rodney walked over to her and reached out to hug her. She stepped back.

"Is everything okay, Sweetie Pie?" he asked. "You've seemed a bit different, almost distant since dinner."

Sina exhaled deeply. "Actually, it isn't. I'll just cut to the chase. Do you make it a habit of letting your little fans sit on your lap to pose for pictures?" Her words had edges so sharp they could cut. Sina turned from Rodney, looked out at the Harbour, inhaled deeply, and silently counted to ten.

"I can explain," Rodney replied. "That is if you let me, this time. I haven't heard that tone from you since we were in high school."

Sina sat on the chaise, reflected on her past assumptions and mistakes, closed her eyes and took a deep breath. "Yes Rodney," she said softly. "I was surprised when I returned from the bathroom to see this chick sitting on your lap, all up in your grill."

Rodney sat across from Sina, held his head in his hands. He took a deep breath, then looked up, directly into Sina's eyes. "Sweetie Pie, know that you are the woman I love. I made an unplanned trip halfway across the world, first class ticket, to make sure you knew I meant the words I said the night before you left Chicago, the night we first made love."

Sina closed her eyes momentarily and nodded.

"And you are in a relationship with me, not the guy everyone across the globe sees on the court, or in TV commercials, but the real Rodney Joshua Paxton Harris. Me, your Sugar Cane."

Sina listened patiently.

"And like all athletes and celebrities, some people hate me, some love me, some are secretly married to me in their heads. I can't control any of that. Everywhere I go, I meet fans who want autographs and want to take pictures with me. I agreed to take a photo with that woman from Houston, I was standing up to take the picture and before I knew it, she was on my lap. She actually pushed me back into the chair. I was caught off guard. I was eating my dessert for goodness sake! It meant nothing to me, she means nothing to me. Heck, I don't even know her name."

"So, you expect me to get used to women just throwing themselves all over you all of the time?"

"Actually, I don't." He reached out and took her hand. "Sweetie Pie, I want you to feel secure in this relationship. I love you," he paused after each word to add emphasis. "I'm not interested in skirt chasing, groupies, or the like. I can't control what other people do, but I will make a promise to you to be more firm in the future. I don't want you to ever get the wrong idea. Ever! Do you forgive me?"

Sina walked over to Rodney and sat on his lap. She held his face in her hands and kissed him. "I do, Sugar Cane. And I love you too."

"Now let's not let this last night of our view go to waste."

4

WHAT IS HAPPENING HERE (NOW)?

Patrick sat on the edge of his bed in his dimly lit room, thumbs firmly at his cheeks, index fingers between his eyebrows, elbows resting on thighs. He was still in shock that Rachel called him nearly a week ago. How did she find him, what did she want, and why on earth would she call him now? His head felt like it would explode from the confusion. He didn't know how to feel about her call. Should he be happy or pissed off? She totally caught him off-guard just like she did on the best and worst days of his life—the day they met and the day she broke their engagement. An array of emotion, mostly of pain, had consumed him. He exhaled deeply. *Why, and why now?* He asked himself again. *It couldn't have been too important,* he thought, *if it were, she would have called back by now.*

Patrick stretched out on his bed, grabbed his remote control from the night stand, flicked his television set on, and stared at it passively. For the past few days he was barely able to eat, had restless nights, and was almost numb to everything around him. *I've got to get back on track.* He changed the channel to his favorite TV show, but even that didn't work.

Patrick picked up the remote to turn off his television when his phone rang. He looked at the caller ID before picking up. "What's up, Phil?" he asked his older brother.

"I just wanted to remind you about this weekend."

"What's happening this weekend?"

"Duh, I'm, no we're helping Jessica move into her first apartment on Saturday."

"That's right," he paused. "I can't believe our baby sister is starting her junior year at Vanderbilt."

"I know. That's crazy, isn't it." Phil replied. "Here's the plan. Jessie and I will roll into Nashville around lunch time. We'll get her moved in and set everything up for her, grab dinner, I'll crash at your place Saturday night and fly back to St. Louis on Sunday morning. Sound good?"

"Yeah." Patrick's response was dry, almost melancholy.

"Say bro, is everything alright? You don't sound yourself. How are things with you and Veronica?"

"Everything's good."

"Are you sure?"

"I swear, it is." Patrick stared into his nearly dark room.

"Sounds good. I'll see you then."

"You all drive safely. And please get Jessica and her stuff here in one piece. Dad always called you a speed demon."

Patrick hung up the phone, then turned the television off and pulled the sheet up to his shoulders. He couldn't find a comfortable position in the bed. He stared up at the ceiling and hoped that for the first night in many, sleep would eventually find him.

§●

"Huh, Huh, Huh, Huh, Huh." Brothaman gasped for air. He was cornered.

While he easily could have scaled the fence towards freedom, the Rottweiler and pit bull in the adjacent yard would have eaten him alive. He put his swollen hands up in front of his face, shoulders down and back. "I'm sorry."

"Sorry my ass." Dee-Mo was so close that he could hear Brothaman's heart racing. He leaned in as Brothaman cowered down, then raised his thick, muscular right arm. Brothaman jumped backward, fell into the chain link fence and drove the dogs wild. "A smart man would have learned his lesson last time."

Brothaman turned and didn't take his eyes off Dee-Mo in hopes that he could distract him long enough to get a running start toward the opposite end of the alley or a gangway or anywhere but here. "I —I—I."

"I. I. I. Don't want to hear your bull." Dee-Mo was close now that he could smell the fear surrounding Brothaman. "You think you can get away with stealing from me, not once, but twice?"

Brothaman slid to the side. "Where you think you goin'?" Dee-Mo kicked Brothaman in the groin so hard he levitated a bit before landing on his knees. "Is that what you think?"

Blood flew from Brothaman's head in slow motion after catching a front kick, as he fell backwards, flat on the ground. Dee-Mo straddled him. "You punk ass crackhead." Blows to the left and right side of Brothaman's face sent more blood flying, this time spurting in the air like a firework show. "I'm so sick and tired of you dumb ass crack-heads." Dee-Mo slammed Brothaman's head into the concrete, harder and harder with each word. Dee-Mo stood. "You ain't gon' do this no more are you?" He stomped Brothaman in his side. "Are you?" This stomp almost went to his head. Brothaman was silent and motionless, face unrecognizable. Just then, the coach lights on the garage behind him came on, casting a spotlight on Brothaman's lifeless body. Dee-Mo scrambled away just as he heard a door close.

❧

"I WAS TAKING my garbage out, and there he was lying in the alley," Mrs. Jackson, a middle-aged lady, told Tommy and Jesse as they took notes. A shallow pool of blood stood beside them. "I don't know how long he's been out here."

"Was anyone here with him?" Jesse asked.

"I didn't see anyone," she replied. "Is he still alive?"

"He's still breathing, but he has a weak pulse," the EMT replied as she and her partner put the gurney into the ambulance. She climbed into the back of the ambulance, her partner got behind the wheel and sped off. Sirens blared.

"You know, this was a nice neighborhood when I moved here," Mrs. Jackson's voice was shaky. "But ever since Mrs. Adams passed away and left her house to that shiftless son of hers, I'm liable to see anything around here. He has turned that beautiful home into a crack house. People coming all times of night and day. Just a few weeks ago, I turned down the alley to go to my garage one night and saw a woman down on her knees servicing someone, probably for crack." She shook her head. "I'm so glad my five-year-old grandbaby wasn't with me." She sighed. "Man, I'm so glad."

"Did you report it?"

"I was so shocked at what I saw, in the alley, right by home, that I didn't know what to do. Umph, umph, umph." She wiped her brow. "By the time I thought to call you all, they were long gone."

Tommy gave her his card. "Please call whenever you see anything. If the community works with us, we can move this element away from here."

"I will, because I don't want my property value to decrease," she turned to go into her backyard. She closed the gate, then put a chain around the gate and the fence post just before she padlocked it.

&

"WE HAVE ONE DAVID BROWN, DOB April 13, 1967, patient is breathing, weak pulse, unconscious." The EMT wheeled him into the ER. "One, two, three," she said as she, her partner, and the ER doctors lifted him onto a hospital gurney.

"Anyone with him?" the chief ER resident asked?

"He was found alone in the alley," Tommy replied.

"Hey Tommy, "Hank said as he walked into the room. "What do we have here?"

"Beating victim, one David Brown." Jesse replied.

Hank walked to the gurney, looked down at Brothaman's hands, and let out a deep sigh. "Brothaman. He's my brother-in-law." He said to the chief resident. "He was just here last week. Somebody busted his hands with a hammer."

"Wow!" Tommy said. "I never knew Brothaman's name was David."

"Bilateral breathing, airway intact, pupils dilated. Let's send him up for a CT Scan. STAT," the chief resident said as they wheeled Brothaman away.

"I don't get it." Hank shook his head. "I had a long talk with him, for my sister's sake, just a few days ago. And now this." He and Tommy walked down the hallway. "This time it's much worse than before. He'll be lucky to survive."

"I don't understand either. This guy has it made. Beautiful, smart, hard-working wife. Two sons," Tommy said.

"He should want to make them proud, but he loves that crack pipe more than he loves his wife and kids. And once again, I get to call my big sister with bad news."

Tommy shook his head.

"I never liked this guy, but I wanted to give him the benefit of the doubt after my sister up and married him. Now I curse the day she met this loser. He has ruined her life." Hank exhaled deeply. "She would have been so much better off with Patrick."

"Man, I would feel the same way if it were Sina," he said of his little sister. Air hissed through Tommy's clinched teeth as he first inhaled, then exhaled. "Shoot, you and Rachel, and even Hope are like my younger siblings." Tommy patted Hank on the back. "Man, if there is anything, anything at all that I can do, please let me know."

"I'll keep you posted on any developments.

5

MY FAVORITE THINGS

"Good morning, Sweetie Pie." Sina rubbed her eyes and walked groggily past the kitchen on her way to the bathroom of her tiny sabbatical home in Haberfield. "I just brewed a pot of coffee."

"Morning."

Rodney poured a cup for Sina, placed it alongside his on the tray, and carried it to the living area. He set it on the coffee table beside the *Sydney Morning Herald*, took a sip from his cup, looked out the window into the courtyard, then turned his head and smiled. "You're so cute first thing in the morning," he said to Sina as she came out of the bathroom. "Cream and sugar, but not too sweet, right?" he motioned to her cup of coffee.

"Ah, you're a fast learner." She joined him on the sofa.

"Am I?" He kissed Sina.

"Yes," Sina kissed Rodney, "you," she kissed him again, "are." She took a sip of her coffee and smiled. "How was your run this morning?"

"Very nice. Haberfield is a quaint, little suburb. Most the homes are single story, but they're all different. Not cookie cutters." He took a sip from his cup. "Oh, and some of the walkways to the houses are tessellated."

"Tessellated?"

"Oh baby, the tile work is just beautiful. They are works of art in and of themselves. Beautiful, colorful mosaic patterns."

"Sounds nice."

Rodney picked up the newspaper and turned to the sports section. Sina walked across the room and grabbed the stack of papers from her desk.

"Can you believe I had all of this in my mailbox when I stopped by the university yesterday?" Sina sat on the sofa and put the stack on the floor.

Rodney looked down. "That's quite a bit. Your box must have been stuffed."

"It was, and I was so busy with the tour and meeting everyone, that I didn't get a chance to look through the mail, so I brought it all home." She took a portion of the stack, placed it on her lap, and flipped through it as Rodney read the newspaper.

Sina picked up her coffee cup and took another sip. "I really like this coffee. Tastes chocolaty."

"Yeah, it is good. I picked it up yesterday when I went to the Central Business District while you were on campus. It's a new local company, Bay Coffee." Rodney bit his bottom lip. "I think it's their house blend."

"I'll have to remember that." Sina put the first stack on the coffee table, placing half of it on the floor to the right of the sofa, then she picked up an envelope. Inside she found a newspaper article. "I don't believe this!"

"What?"

"The Australian Attorney General has ordered bureaucrats that "stolen child" is a forbidden term to use with regards to the Stolen Generations."

"What on earth?"

"Listen to this," she said. "Instead, he wants them to say relocated."

Rodney shook his head. "Revisionist history at its best—or maybe its worst."

Sina went through the rest of the stack. She placed some items on the floor and others on the coffee table. She picked up the stack from the floor with her right hand, and the stack on the coffee table with her left. She walked across the small living area to her desk. The items in her right hand went straight into the trash, while she neatly stacked the items in her left hand on the desk. She looked out into the courtyard from the window just above her desk. "Sugar Cane, come here—quick."

Rodney made the seven-step journey from the sofa to the window.

"Look at the parrot couple. They are so colorful."

"Eastern rosellas." Rodney put his arm around Sina. "He just kissed her," he said of the male parrot feeding his mate.

"That's how she knows he'll be a good provider." Sina smiled.

Rodney leaned down and kissed her. "Like this?" he kissed her again. "Or like this?" He wrapped his arms around Sina and held her tight and long, savoring the moment. "I really don't want to leave you, Sweetie Pie." Rodney loosened his embrace just enough to look Sina in the eye.

"But you have to get back for training camp."

"I do." He squeezed her, then kissed her nose.

She tilted her head up towards his face. "Is there anything special you want to do on your last day here?"

Rodney gently guided Sina to the sofa, sat down, and pulled her onto his lap.

"I made reservations for a dinner cruise for us this evening."

"I like," Sina said, then bit her bottom lip. Her face wore a sly smile. "I need to go to Redfern today to pick up something from Melba this afternoon. Want to come along?"

"Why certainly, mate."

Sina kissed Rodney's forehead, then nose, then right earlobe, then left earlobe, then a lingering kiss on the lips, and he carried her to the bedroom.

೩

A PAINTING OF PEMULWUY, an eighteenth century Aboriginal warrior who led raids on European settlers, welcomed Sina and Rodney to The Block as they turned onto Eveleigh Street from the Redfern train station. An Aboriginal flag was just beneath his image. Sina remembered meeting Denise and Melba during her first visit to Sydney. They gave her a miniature flag and explained the meaning of the colors.

"Black at the top is for the people, red at the bottom is for the earth, and yellow is for the sun" that stood so boldly in the center of the flag.

They walked slowly, surveying the block long mural, while locals hung out in Pemulwuy Park. Kids were riding their bikes, playing on the swings, and playing basketball. They could have been in any city anywhere in the world, but for the unique detail of the mural. "This wasn't here when I was here five years ago."

They continued down Eveleigh Street, past the mural of the Aboriginal Flag on the side of the gym across the street. It covered the entire wall. Terrace style row houses lined the block. A litany of raucous laughter erupted from one unit as a man ran outside and nearly bumped into Sina. Rodney braced Sina from falling while the man apologized. In the middle of the block, graffiti covered the front of another. "I've never been to this area of Sydney before."

Sina looked up at him, "Melba's home is just a few blocks over."

They turned the corner and the sun's warmth emitted a brighter vibration. Rodney loosened his grip on Sina's hand. Sina reached into her pocket to double check the address. "We're here." She rang the doorbell.

Melba, a stout, dark woman of Torres Strait Islander descent, opened the door. "Hey love," she said to Sina as she gave her a big hug. "Welcome back." She stepped back, and looked at Rodney. "Is this your bloke?"

"Yes, this is Rodney. Rodney, Melba."

Melba gave Rodney a hug, then put her arm around Sina and whispered, "He is one fine blackfella," as she ushered her inside. She turned to Rodney, "Come on in. Can I fix you a cuppa?"

"Sure," Sina replied as Melba led her to the living area before going into the kitchen to start the kettle.

An abstract painting on the wall caught Rodney's attention. He walked over to it, his gaze intently fixed upon it. A sea of dots in complementary colors were overlaid on vibrant shades of blue and yellow in unique shapes.

"Does it strike your fancy?" Melba asked when she returned with the tea.

"Yes. It is interesting. Very detailed with all of the tiny dots," Rodney replied. "What is the significance of the dots?"

"There are sacred symbols in our paintings, and artists use dots and abstraction to conceal the sacred meanings from Westerners and members of other tribes."

"Interesting," Rodney replied. "Not exactly the same, but kind of reminds me of the symbols in the Underground Railroad Quilt Code." He sat beside Sina on the sofa.

"We can't stay long," Sina picked up her cup of tea. "This is Rodney's last day in Sydney."

"I'll be back in about six weeks."

"And he's taking me on a dinner cruise tonight."

"Oooh, how lovely!" Melba responded.

"And there's a dress in a shop in the Queen Victoria Building I want to wear tonight, so we don't have much time."

"The QVB is only about ten minutes away by train." Melba handed an envelope to Sina, then gave her another hug. "You all have a great time."

"I'll give you a call next week."

SINA AND RODNEY made their way back to the Central Business District. Their walk to the Queen Victoria Building was brief and hurried. When they arrived at the store, the dress was no longer in the window. They went inside to inquire. The face of the petite salesclerk with vibrant blue eyes and blonde hair lit up like a thousand-watt daylight bulb when she saw Rodney.

"You had a red strapless dress in the window a few days ago, but it's gone now. Can you show me where the others are?"

The salesclerk wore a puzzled look on her face as she guided Sina and Rodney to the rack with the red dresses. Sina browsed through the rack, checking the tags on each of the dresses. "I would need the equivalent of a US size eight."

"Then you'll need an Australian size twelve." The sales clerk glanced quickly at Rodney.

Sina breezed through the rack a second time. All the dresses were either too large or too small for her. "Do you have any in the back?" Sina asked.

"I'm sorry, we don't."

Sina's face grew long.

"But we can order one for you."

"Never mind. I wanted to wear it tonight."

"Does anything else catch your fancy?" The salesclerk asked. She held up a black dress. "This one is lovely."

"No." Sina replied. "But thanks."

❧

THEIR JOURNEY back to Haberfield was quick and quiet. When they arrived at her home, Rodney went straight to the bedroom and Sina went to the kitchen, opened the fridge, and poured a glass of water. "I really wanted to wear that dress this evening." She sat on the sofa, "Now I don't know what I'll wear."

Rodney joined her on the sofa. "Why don't you look in the closet? I'm sure you have something perfect to wear."

She put her glass on a coaster on the coffee table, and ambled into the bedroom. Rodney sat on the sofa with a big smile on his face. "Rodney!" Sina called from the bedroom. She ran from the bedroom and gave him a big hug.

"I saw the look on your face when you first saw the dress and knew that you just had to have it. So, I bought it yesterday while you were on campus."

"How on earth did you hide it from me in this tiny house?" She covered his face with kisses, took his hand, and pulled him towards the bedroom. "And how did you know my sizes?" The dress was spread out across the bed, beside it was a pair of shoes.

"I did a little bit of sleuthing so that everything would fit you perfectly. I hope you don't mind."

"Mind? Are you serious?"

Sina sat on the edge of the bed and tried on the jeweled pump as Rodney went into the closet and removed a suit bag. He unzipped the suit bag, removed a smaller bag, and handed it to Sina. "I'll get dressed in the bathroom."

"What's in here?" Sina asked before he left.

"Take a look." His face glowed. "And surprise me." He closed the bedroom door behind him as he left.

Sina opened the bag to find a strapless bra in her size, thigh high stockings, and red lace bikinis with a matching thong. Her heart warmed and her aura vibrated at a high frequency. She carefully, but quickly got dressed, well almost.

Rodney knocked on the door. "How are you coming along? The car will be here soon to pick us up."

"Come on in. I need a little help." Sina called to Rodney. Rodney entered the room and was frozen at the sight of Sina. He could see her reflection in the mirror. Her hair was swept into an updo, the dress fit her perfectly, and hugged each curve in her body.

"I can't reach the top of this zipper." Rodney stood behind Sina and zipped the top of her zipper, then removed a box from his jacket pocket. He carefully placed a necklace with a black opal pendant around Sina's neck just before kissing it. He handed her a pair of black opal and diamond earrings. "You're so beautiful." Rodney wrapped his arms around her waist from behind.

"Thank you for everything," Sina put the dangling earrings on, then turned, tilted her head, and kissed his cheek, just before applying her lipstick. Rodney placed a wrap around her shoulders, then straightened his tie, and they departed.

❧

"Dinner was great," Sina said as they returned. "The Harbour is so beautiful, especially at night."

"It is." Rodney closed and locked the door. He placed 8 x 10 photos they took on the cruise on the table.

"I had a wonderful time."

"I did too." Rodney loosened his tie. "And when you told the waiter that what you wanted for dessert was not on the menu I nearly spit out my wine. I knew exactly what you meant." He took the wrap off her shoulders and gently placed it beside the photos. "Now let me help you out of this." Sina turned her back to him. Her dress fell to the floor when he unzipped it. "And I see that you have pleasantly surprised me." Sina had chosen the latter in the bag of items Rodney gave her before she got dressed. Rodney grew flush as a warmth enveloped him. He looked at her from head to toe, with a clear focus on her pleasant surprise. She turned to face him.

"And let me help you with this, Sugar Cane," Sina slid the jacket off Rodney's shoulders and it fell effortlessly to the floor. Carefully, she removed his cufflinks, placed them on the table, then unfastened each button on his shirt slowly. She unbuckled his belt, unzipped his pants, and stood back to watch them slide to the floor. He stepped out of them as she took several steps back, almost posing for him.

He took one look at her, in four-inch heels, thigh high stockings, a red lace thong, and strapless bra, then swept her up into his arms, carried her to the bedroom, and gently placed her on top of the bed. She lost her shoes along the way. Rodney kissed Sina's right thigh, then rolled the stocking down her leg. He kissed the toes on her right foot, then swirled his tongue around the big toe. His lips wrapped around the tip of her toe, then his mouth slid down fully enveloping it. A charge moved through Sina's body like a bolt of lightning. The other stocking made a much quicker exit. Rodney planted hot kisses up and down her thighs, giving them equal attention. She lifted her hips as he slid the thong off them, then down her legs. Rodney inhaled deeply when he made his way back to the top of her thighs

Rodney swirled his tongue in Sina's navel, then due South, just to the top of her hips. Her body trembled with excitement as his tongue made its way back up to her ribcage. Her back arched and he unfastened her strapless bra, then cast it aside. Sina gazed down at him, the look of love in her eyes. He sowed kisses like seeds, on her lips, across her cheek, neck, and collarbone, before caressing her breasts. The tip of his finger circled her right nipple while he cupped the left in his hand. His tongue followed a similar, yet not identical pattern of movement on the left. Sina exhaled deeply.

Rodney kissed her navel once again, his breath left a trail of heat as he moved downward. Her anticipation grew, like the desire for something cold and wet on a hot, humid summer day. He grazed her, gently, before nuzzling her with the tip of his nose. Each swirl of his tongue sent shockwaves through Sina's body. Sina arched her back in response and savored each nanosecond. "Rodney," she drew his name out in a deep, breathy whisper.

His firm, yet gentle pressure gave her great pleasure. And this was only the first course. His neatly manicured fingers massaged her, his tongue flicked, teased, then danced on the tip of her essence. "Ohhhh," emitted in a higher pitch from Sina as Rodney massaged her. The tips of the fingers on the other hand waltzed gently like a feather on Sina's right inner thigh. She reached down, caressed his head, then swirled her finger inside his ear. Her body vibrated, then shook as Rodney's tongue tickled her inner depths. She buried his head in her thighs, her eyes rolled back in her head.

She relaxed her legs, and Rodney rose up. His eyes scanned her body, then gazed into hers. He reached into the nightstand drawer, then carefully tore the condom wrapper open with his teeth. Sina caressed Rodney's hip, then rolled the condom onto him. He entered her slowly, gently, slightly, massaging her a little at a time. She moaned in ecstasy, letting him know her enjoyment. Slowly and methodically his strokes grew, deepening with each thrust. Rodney gazed into Sina's eyes, looking deeply into her soul. Her gaze mirrored his. Together, they floated to another plane, another realm of reality. "Oh, Sweetie Pie," he said, throaty with pleasure.

They were a work of art. A detailed masterpiece. Not abstract, but realist. Not blurry or fuzzy, but crystal clear like a painting by Pedro Campos or a drawing by Kelvin Okafor. They moved together, in sync, in unison. Their tempo increased, and their timing was perfect. They reached a crescendo together, then held each other tight, not wanting that moment to end. Ever. "I wish we could stay like this forever." Sina whispered in Rodney's ear.

"Forever and a day, Sweetie Pie," he replied. He kissed Sina deeply, and lay on his side. She turned to face him. They gazed into each other's eyes and gently stroked and caressed each other before embracing deeply. Their bodies and souls vibrated at higher and higher frequencies, as they held each other tightly, Sina's breasts pressed against Rodney's chest. Her right leg entangled his left. She wrapped her leg around his even more tightly at the realization that she would not see him again for at least six weeks. Sina rested her head in the center of Rodney's chest, synchronizing her heartbeat with his. And they drifted off to sleep.

Rodney rubbed his eyes, then looked over at the clock on the nightstand. He woke Sina with a kiss. "I have a little more than an hour before I leave for the airport," he swung his legs over the side of the bed. "I'm going to hop in the shower." Sina watched as Rodney got up. A glow from the moon through the bedroom window cast onto Rodney's body. Sina looked at his strong legs and thighs, and how they connected with his firm, chiseled butt. Strong like a warrior, he was a monument in motion. When he opened the bedroom door, the light from the living area gave her an even better view of him. She sighed as he walked down the hall to the bathroom, which was just beside the kitchen next to her bedroom. She heard the drizzle of the shower.

Rodney stood underneath the showerhead, water firmly beating his face, eyes closed deep in thought. He was swaddled in its steam. Then he felt a momentary cold gust. "How about I help you with that?" Sina joined him. She washed his back and worked her way down. He turned around to rinse and she took great delight in giving the front of his body even more attention, which brought him to attention. Full attention.

He had to have her, just one more time before he departed, and he had to have her now. He picked her up, she wrapped her legs around his hips and he entered her, firmly and fiercely this time. Almost primal. She moaned as each thrust was deeper, more frequent. "Oh, Sugar Cane," a guttural whisper.

"Oh Sina," he sang as he released inside her.

Tears dropped from Sina's eyes as Quantas called for first class passengers to board the nonstop flight to LAX. Rodney wiped them with the tip of his thumb. He snatched her up into a tight, deep, lingering hug. They looked into each other's eyes and kissed deeply. "Rodney, you've made me a very happy woman." More tears fell from her eyes. "And I'm going to miss you so much." She squeezed him as tightly as she could.

"I'll be back soon." His eyes were long and sad like a puppy's. "I'll be back before you know it."

"I know." Sina kissed him. She went into her totebag and removed a boomerang. "Call me superstitious, but I'm giving you this to make sure you come back." They stood still in time, holding each other tightly one last time before Rodney picked up his gym bag and boarded the plane.

Sina stood in the window, and watched as Rodney's flight taxied from the gate, made its way to the runway, then took off into flight.

6

AUTUMN LEAVES

W hen Sina opened the door to her sabbatical home the remnants of last night greeted her. Rodney's jacket, pants, and shirt were on the floor near the dining table. Her dress and shoes weren't far from them. She draped her dress over her arm, then picked Rodney's clothing up item by item, jacket, pants, shirt. She took a moment, inhaled Rodney's scent on his shirt and smiled. After going into her room to hang them in the closet, she brewed a small pot of coffee and booted up her computer. A week's worth of e-mail awaited her.

She poured a cup of the Bay Coffee House Blend Rodney purchased for her, and warmed a blueberry muffin in the microwave. Sina went to her desk, took a sip of her coffee, then began to scroll through her e-mails. The first she chose to open was from Tommy informing her about Brothaman's beating. He told her to reach out to Rachel as soon as she could, and that he would keep her posted on any new developments. Sina took a bite of her muffin and said a quick prayer. She replied to Tommy, and gave him her phone number on campus and in Haberfield. Sina reached for the phone to call Rachel, and tried to figure out what time it was in Nashville. As she pondered making the call, her AOL Instant Messenger chimed.

RACHELCB: Hey girl, are you settled in Sydney?

DRSINA: I am. I heard about Brothaman. I'm so sorry.

RACHELCB: Oh, my goodness, Sina. The past week has been so rough.

DRSINA: I'm sorry to hear that, and sorry that I'm not there.

RACHELCB: This is the second time Brothaman has been beaten since the reunion.

DRSINA: Wow!!!

RACHELCB: Hank said they had to remove part of Brothaman's skull because the swelling was so bad.

DRSINA: Oh my goodness!!!!

RACHELCB: And on top of that, my Mom found out that my Dad had been alive all these years.

DRSINA: What?!?!?

RACHELCB: In Australia.

DRSINA: No way!!!!!

RACHELCB: I can't believe it either.

DRSINA: Are you going to connect with him?

RACHELCB: Can't. Too late. He's dead.

DRSINA: My goodness, Rachel. I'm so sorry to hear all of this.

RACHELCB: It's hard, but I have to stay strong for my boys.

DRSINA: Yes you do.

RACHELCB: How have you been? I hope things are going better for you.

DRSINA: Rachel, I've just had the most amazing week of my life with Rodney.

RACHELCB: Oh?

DRSINA: I woke up on the plane and Rodney was seated next to me. We spent the whole week together. Rachel, he told me he loves me. And I'm in love.

RACHELCB: Sina. I'm so happy for you. After all you've been through, you deserve a man who really loves you. I had that with Patrick, I never should have ended it.

DRSINA: Did you ever find Patrick?

RACHELCB: I did, but got interrupted with calls about my father and Brothaman. I never called him back. I've been afraid to. Actually, I'm terrified.

DRSINA: Rachel, if he is Martin's father, he needs to know. And you need to know the truth. I know you're going through it right now, but you have to call him. Call him tonight.

DRSINA: No, sign off and call him now.

RACHELCB: You're right. I will. Say a prayer for me.

DRSINA: I already did.

RACHELCB: Ciao.

DRSINA: Catch you later.

JESSICA and her brothers pulled side-by-side in the parking spaces marked "V" in front of Veronica's apartment. A crepe myrtle with magenta flowers stood beside the short, concrete walkway to the front door. Neatly trimmed boxwood and barberry hedges topped out just beneath the windowsill. "This seems like a nice area," Phil said to his younger brother, Patrick, who unlocked the door.

"Mmm, sure smells good in here." Phil walked into the living room.

"You all finished earlier than I expected." Veronica appeared from the kitchen wearing an apron over her T-shirt and denim shorts. She was short, yet had an athletic build, and her brown hair was pulled back into a ponytail. She hugged and kissed Patrick, then gave Phil and Jessie a group hug. "Dinner will be ready in about ten minutes. Just have a seat. I'll get you something to drink."

"Let me help you," Jessica said. "They've been doing the heavy lifting all day." Jessica followed Veronica into the kitchen. Patrick sat on the sofa across from the fireplace, and reached for the remote control to turn on the television on the corner TV stand.

"That is such a nice photo of you two," Phil said, referring to the 11 x 14 photo of Patrick and Veronica taken in Howe Wildflower Garden at Cheekwood Botanical Garden in April. It stood in the center of the mantel. "And it smells like she can really cook, too."

Patrick flipped through the channels on the remote.

"Patrick, did you hear me?" Phil asked after getting no response from his brother.

Jessica returned carrying a tray with two glasses of sweet tea. "I'm going to set the table for Veronica." She turned and walked toward the kitchen.

"What's going on?" Phil asked, barely moving his teeth, in an effort to not be overheard.

"Nothing," Patrick turned away from the television. "Everything is fine," his voice was an intense, don't ask me that shit again tone.

"Trust me, we'll deal with this later," Phil replied as Veronica called them to dinner.

"The bathroom is right here," Patrick instructed Phil on his way to the kitchen. Phil went in to wash his hands, and Patrick followed when he was done.

"Everything looks so good," Phil said of the platters of barbecued chicken, macaroni and cheese, mixed greens, and cornbread.

"Well, I tried to put my foot in it." Veronica said as they fixed their plates. She took off her apron, hung it on a hook in the kitchen, and joined them. They held hands, and Patrick led them in blessing the food. Bright orange rays from the setting sun filtered through the vertical blinds of the patio doors, making a promise for a beautiful tomorrow.

"Thank you for fixing dinner for us," Jessica told Veronica. "That was really nice of you."

"This sauce on the chicken is slammin." Phil licked his lips.

"It's my mother's recipe." Veronica smiled. She looked over at Patrick who was playing with his food. "Is everything alright?" She felt his forehead with the back of her hand. "You've been so quiet and you've barely eaten a thing."

"I'm okay," Patrick replied. "I'm just exhausted."

"I should be the one exhausted," Phil said. "After driving the U-Haul from St. Louis. That thing shook the whole way."

"Yeah, Phil wouldn't let me drive," Jessica smiled. "But that's what big brothers are for, right? And I'm so lucky to have two."

Phil got another serving of greens, while Patrick continued to pick at his plate. "Veronica, these are some of the best greens I've ever had. Only second to Grandma Odessa. I didn't even have to put any vinegar on them."

"Oh, shoot. I almost forgot," Jessica said. "Grandma Odessa sent one of her pound cakes. It's Patrick's favorite. See Grandma Odessa is

thinking of you." She patted Patrick on the back. "It's still in the car. I'll
go get it."

"Now you didn't tell me that, "Phil said.

"Nope, because most of the cake would have been gone by now if I
had," Jessica replied, making the group laugh. "I'll be right back."
Jessica got up from the table, grabbed her car keys, and went outside.

⁚

"I'm sorry I'm so late," Patrick said. It was late afternoon on a crisp
autumn day and the sun had begun to lower in the sky. The leaves on
the trees on Aunt Mary's block had changed into beautiful shades of
red, rust, and gold. Some had fallen to the ground and were crunchy
when you stepped on them. "Grandma Odessa sent you this. I had to
wait for her to take it out of the oven. She's looking forward to
teaching you to make her award-winning pound cake when you get
everything settled here and move to St. Louis. I can't wait." He
grinned like a Cheshire cat.

Rachel took the cake. Patrick set his overnight bag in a living room
chair and followed her into the kitchen.

"Please tell her I said thank you."

Patrick hugged Rachel. She was stiff. He squeezed her tighter and
rubbed her back. "I know this has been a difficult time for you, probably the most difficult of your life."

"There is so much I've had to deal with," Rachel replied. She sat at
the dining room table where they had Easter dinner with Aunt Mary
six months earlier. A tear fell from her eye. "Just so much. And there's
no instruction manual."

Patrick rubbed the back of Rachel's hand.

"I'm just so overwhelmed."

"Baby, that's what I'm here for," Patrick grasped her hand. "I know
I'm not here all of the time. But," he looked into her eyes and caressed
her cheek. "I come as often as I can."

Rachel withdrew her hand, turned away from him, and broke into
a long, loud sob.

"Patrick, I can't do this anymore."

"What? What can I do to help you? I'm here."

"I need space," Rachel got up from the table and ran upstairs. Patrick was stunned. Speechless.

❧

"PATRICK! DON'T YOU WANT A SLICE?" Jessica asked. Everyone else was at the kitchen counter getting slices of cake. Patrick sat still at the table, fiddling his fork over his plate. The other plates had been cleared.

"No," he got up from the table, walked over to the trashcan, and raked his plate. "I'm not very hungry." He went into the living room.

Phil stared at him like he was crazy. "I'll cut a few slices for us to take back to your place."

Veronica opened the drawer beside the stove and handed Phil the foil. Jessica took it from him.

"I'm going to have to take mine to go," she said. "I got a transfer to the Penney's at Cool Springs Galleria."

"That's wonderful," Veronica said.

"Since I have an apartment now, I have to make my own money."

"Which department do you work in?" Veronica asked.

"Children's."

"That's great."

"And I have to work tomorrow," she folded the foil around her cake. "So, I have to run."

Veronica walked Jessica to the front door.

"If you ever want anything at Penney's, just let me know." She hugged her. "I get a discount."

"Be safe, Jessie," Phil called from the kitchen. Veronica joined Patrick on the sofa.

"Is everything all right, Baby?" she asked. She touched his forehead again, and then felt his neck for swollen glands. "I hope you aren't coming down with something."

"I'm just tired. That's all." Patrick kissed her. "I promise I'm not contagious. I just need some rest." He hugged her, then stood from the sofa. "Come on Phil. We'd better roll."

Phil followed Patrick to the front door, gave Veronica a big hug. "Thanks for dinner."

"This is just the first of many," she smiled. "You all have a good evening." She hugged Patrick again. "Now you get some rest. I'm ordering it!"

As Patrick and Phil walked across the parking lot, Patrick unlocked the car with his remote key fob. They got in, Patrick started the car, turned on the headlights, and backed out of the space. Dru Hill's *Never Make a Promise* played on the radio. Patrick turned the volume up. When they stopped to turn onto Bell Road, Phil turned the radio off.

"Hey," Patrick started, as he made his right turn.

"Hey nothing. What in the hell is wrong with you Patrick? You on your period or something?"

"Nothing's wrong."

"I ain't buying it," Phil replied. "You've been distant for about a week. You didn't eat that bomb ass food your fiancée fixed. That chicken, those greens. My goodness!

"And then you turned down Grandma Odessa's pound cake! There is definitely something wrong with you, little brother. You sure everything is okay between you and Veronica?"

Patrick sighed. "It's not Veronica." Patrick stopped at the red light. "Rachel called me."

"Aw, hell no! What in the hell did she want?"

"We really didn't talk. She said she had something important to tell me, but she just didn't know how."

"Oh really! That seems to be the pattern with her," Phil was fuming. "So, what did she tell you?"

"She didn't. She got another call." Patrick accelerated as the light turned green. "Said she'd call me back, but she hasn't."

Phil shook his head.

"I don't believe this. But then again, I'm not surprised. You were engaged to her. You proposed to her at graduation in front of everybody. I mean everybody! You even got the commencement speaker to write your proposal into his speech. You all were on the freakin' Jumbotron in the football stadium for goodness sake! She promised to move to St. Louis for you two to get married, yet she was running around Chicago with some other dude, pretending like she was so into you, and probably screwing dude, 'cause she married him really fast."

"That's not fair, Phil. She was grieving. Her aunt who raised her had just died suddenly. No one expected that, especially not Rachel."

"Don't even go there. You were grieving too. You just lost your closest cousin. Mario was like our little brother. But did you go off and screw some chick, or jump up and marry someone else?" Phil shook his head again. "That's no excuse.

"And then she didn't even have the decency. Not one shred of decency to tell you. She took the punk's way out with that 'I need some space,' crap."

They turned into the parking lot for Patrick's apartment complex.

"And it took you so long to get over her. She was your first love, I get that. But you don't need her. You have Veronica now and you all are getting married next month."

Patrick parked, turned off the lights, then the ignition.

Phil sucked air through his teeth. "Man, if I were you I wouldn't want to ever see or talk to Rachel again." Phil was so mad that he almost dropped the pound cake when he slammed Patrick's car door.

The brothers climbed the steps to Patrick's second floor apartment. "Man, focus on your future," Phil advised as Patrick brought him pillows for the sofa bed. "Veronica is perfect for you. She's smart, she got a slammin' body, she can cook in the kitchen so I know she's working it out for you in the bedroom. Most of all, she loves you Patrick. I mean she really loves you. Heck, she healed your broken heart."

Patrick went into his room, sat on the edge of his bed, and picked up his phone. There was a voicemail message from Rachel. "Hi Patrick, this is Rachel," the recording began. "I really need to talk to you. It's really important..." she left her number.

"RACHEL." Patrick followed her into the bedroom. "It's okay. I understand." He hugged her while she cried on his shoulder, then pulled her onto his lap as he sat on the bed. He wiped her tears and held her tight. "It's gonna be okay." He was assured. He kissed her forehead and Rachel paused to take a breath. He smiled at her. "Now let me kiss your tears away."

Patrick held Rachel's face in his hands. He looked into her tear-filled eyes, and kissed her. She was still, actually stiff. "You don't have to cry." He kissed her cheek, then caressed her right cheek with his left hand. She relaxed a bit. "Rachel, I love you." He kissed her lips. "I really do." The tension in Rachel's shoulders eased. He kissed her nose. "I really, really do." This time, her lips.

Rachel exhaled all the built-up tension. Her face softened. She kissed Patrick, mouth open and relaxed. "Everything's gonna be all right." Her eyes fixed on his. She could no longer hold back. Their mouths met and she gave into her unleashed desires. Their tongues danced together, joining, then separating, then joining again first slowly, then growing in intensity.

Patrick stood still, then stepped back and looked intently into Rachel's eyes. He scanned her tear-stained face. "I want you to feel better." He pulled her to her feet and hugged her, then kissed the top of her head. "Don't hold back."

Those three words ignited Rachel. She pulled him close to her as she fell back onto the bed. Patrick unhooked Rachel's bra and removed it and her shirt in one fell swoop. He paused and admired her natural beauty, while removing his shirt. He loosened his belt buckle before burying Rachel in kisses.

His tongue engaged in a variety of ballroom dances. A Viennese waltz on her neck and breasts. A foxtrot to her navel. A tango down below. He forged a trail of kisses interlaced with gentle brushstrokes with his tongue from the point of her ankle to the apex of her thighs. Rachel responded in delight.

Patrick gently rested Rachel's leg on the bed, reached up and caressed her face. He was fully immersed in her. They glided to great heights, and together they reached the stratosphere, before softly and slowly floating down, like a feather, to their current reality. Patrick held Rachel's face and kissed her. "Rachel, I love you with all of my heart. I am fully committed to you, no to us. Everything's gonna work out for us. I promise I will do whatever it takes to make you happy for the rest of your life."

Rachel sat up, turned her back to him and started crying again. He leaned over to comfort her. "It's okay."

"No, it's not Patrick. There's someone else."

Patrick grabbed his clothing and left the room. He dressed as fast as he could, and put his shoe on the wrong foot at first. He grabbed his overnight bag, and slammed Aunt Mary's front door so hard on the way out that he nearly shattered the glass in the bay window. Patrick sped off into the dark of the clear, biting late night, on his way back to St. Louis.

Rachel had just stomped all over his heart, with golf cleats. He was angry, full of rage, to the point that he was pulled over for speeding.

The trooper approached and shined his flashlight into the window. Carefully he scanned the back seat, the passenger's seat, then Patrick's face.

"License and registration please."

Patrick provided them.

"Patrick Stephen Long, you headed home to St. Louis?"

"Yes sir."

"I clocked you going thirty miles over the speed limit?"

"I'm sorry officer," Patrick said. "I've never been pulled over for speeding before. It's just, it's just," his voice grew weaker and his shoulders heaved.

The trooper stood still, head turned slightly to the side.

"It's just," Patrick started again, fighting tears. "I just lost a loved one."

"I'm so sorry to hear that. Losing a loved one is always hard. You'll always miss them, but I'm sure you have great memories." The trooper handed back his license and registration. "I'll let you off with a warning."

"Thank you," Patrick sniffled.

"Now, I want you to get home to St. Louis in one piece. So, slow down and be careful. And try to take it easy. It'll get better, I promise."

Patrick drove to the nearest rest area, which was two miles down the road. Enveloped in solitude, his tears were big and intense. A sharp pain developed across his head, that matched the one in his heart. He was alone, in darkness, in complete isolation, in the stillness of night. The only brief interruption was from the occasional buzz of a tractor trailer zooming by. When Patrick had no more tears left, he started his car, turned his lights on, and made his way back onto the interstate for the remainder of his journey. His eyes were sore and swollen and his head was throbbing, but neither was nearly as painful as the hole in his heart.

❧

PATRICK WAS SEETHING. He replayed the voicemail message and wrote down Rachel's number. Frantically, he pressed the buttons on his phone so hard that some of them nearly stuck. After the second ring, Rachel picked up. "Hello Rachel, this is Patrick. I got your message, and I want you to know this. I never, and I mean never, want to talk to you again as long as I live. Do not ever call me again. I'm getting my number changed tomorrow so don't even bother." He slammed the phone down without letting her utter a word.

7

WHAT'LL I DO?

"I had a really nice time last night," Hope barely cracked her eyes open and turned in the direction of the voice. "I'll let myself out."

Fully dressed, he walked to the French doors of her bedroom in her executive suite, stepped into the living area, then closed them. Hope rubbed her eyes and then her throbbing head. She looked at the door, then at the space in the bed next to her. A fragment of light came through the small opening in the bedroom curtain. She looked up as he cracked the French doors open, peeked his head in and said, "I'm really sorry the condom broke." Hope sat straight up in bed, brain full of fog, and tried to process what she just heard.

She slipped on her dress from last night, then stood on the balcony of her hotel suite, reflecting on what she just heard, what happened last night, her behavior of the past few weeks, and how she could end the pain she was feeling. On the one hand, she had a great start for a bright future. She had her dream job as a top administrator for a major health care system and was in the executive suite at this ocean front hotel, courtesy of them. They had rolled out the red carpet for her, wanting her to feel wanted, she assumed. *At least somebody wants me, even if it is a company.* On the other hand, she wondered how much worse going through this divorce would be if she were still in Kalamazoo, in the place and space where she and Jason made so many memories. She looked out at the ocean, and studied the rhythm of its waves.

Hope went back into the room, brewed a small pot of coffee, sat on the love seat, stared into space, and sipped it—black, no sugar or cream. *What on earth am I doing? Wait a minute. Broken condom. I need to find a church. Oh hell. I have to get a prescription for the morning after pill. Oh shit, shit, damn, damn, shit. I have to go someplace other than Vantarca. Oh my God! What am I doing?*

Hope set her cup on the table, jumped up, and ran into the bathroom to shower. *But I'm not supposed to take a shower. Wait a minute! Last night was consensual. I can take a shower.* She was a big mass of confusion.

Hope tied the belt of the bathrobe around her waist when she got out of the shower, then found the Yellow Pages in search of an urgent care not in the Vantarca Healthcare System.

She made the hour-long drive through Norfolk and the tunnels into Hampton, and hoped that she would not run into a colleague. Hope was pleased when she arrived to find only one person in the waiting room. With it being a Sunday morning, she didn't expect it to be crowded.

She filled out the paperwork, and listed her former address in Kalamazoo. With a floppy hat and sunglasses, as a disguised tourist, she even claimed to not have health insurance and stated that she would pay cash. When the nurse called her name, and took her vitals, she thought about the mistakes she had made, and even more how she had unfairly judged others through the years. She was embarrassed for putting herself in this position as the doctor asked her questions about the date of her last menstrual period and her sexual behavior. After Hope shared with reluctant honesty, the doctor recommended that she also be tested for STDs. This had never crossed Hope's mind. She was informed that the test results would be mailed to her home in Michigan. Hope was thankful that she had her mail forwarded to a post office box in Virginia Beach, rather than her job.

The doctor handed her the prescription for emergency contraception. "You may become nauseous. If you vomit within two hours of taking the pill, please call us so we can decide if you should repeat the dosage. You may also have headache, dizziness, breast tenderness, or fatigue. Do not have sex again until you start another method of birth control. This will not protect you against a future pregnancy."

Hope nodded.

"And I have to be honest with you. The morning-after pill is not as effective on overweight women as it is on normal weight women, so be mindful of that." He pushed his glasses up on his nose. "Your period may be delayed by a week after taking emergency contraception. If your period doesn't start in three to four weeks, then you will need to take a pregnancy test. If you experience spotting that lasts for more than a week, or severe abdominal cramping three to five weeks out see your doctor immediately."

Hope put the prescription in her purse, stood, then put her purse on her shoulder. She trudged out of the examination room and to the front desk. "Where is the nearest pharmacy?" she asked the receptionist, as she counted her cash to pay for her visit, rather her nightmare.

I've got to change my behavior, and I've got to lose weight. I'm going to join a gym after work tomorrow. She started her car and carefully backed out of the space, then turned right onto Mercury Boulevard.

RODNEY PUNCHED IN HIS CODE, and the black iron gate slid open. He turned right, then left, then left again before punching the button on his garage door opener. He backed his SL 500R into the garage next to his Chevy Blazer, put the top up, then unlocked the door leading to his basement. He punched in the code on his alarm keypad, then made his way past his exercise room, guest bedroom, and pool table. After climbing the stairs to the main level of his house he found a pile of mail awaiting him just beneath his mail slot. He gathered it and then went upstairs.

Rodney dropped the pile on his breakfast bar, and went into his bedroom. He set his gym bag on the bed, looked up at the skylight in the vaulted ceiling, and smiled. His unplanned trip, and parking bill for staying long-term in short-term parking had cost him a fortune, but the memories he made with Thomasine were priceless.

Rodney pressed the button on his answering machine. "Hey Dude, where are you? We were supposed to go for a run this morning. This is

Kenny. Call me." Kenny had been one of his teammates since college. *I'll see him tomorrow,* Rodney thought.

"Hey Rodney. Jason. I really need to talk. I know your training camp starts next week. But maybe we can grab a bite to eat. Give me a call. I'm staying at my Mom's. You know the number." Rodney looked at the time on his digital clock and figured that Jason wasn't home from church yet. He'd call him later.

"Hey Rodney, this is Kimmy. Dinner at my house on Sunday. You know what time." Rodney smiled before he heard the next message.

"Rodney Joshua Paxton Harris. This is your mother." When his mother used his full name, he knew that he was in trouble.

Rodney walked into the kitchen and thumbed through his mail, separating endorsement checks from bills, and tossing the junk mail aside. He had a ton of letters from attorneys wanting to represent him for the speeding ticket. He watered his houseplants, now droopy from neglect during his unplanned vacation. Rodney stood and stared inside his refrigerator, then regretted not picking up something on the way from the airport. He didn't feel like thawing anything out to eat, and in a few hours he would have a gourmet meal prepared by his sister, Chef Kimmy."

Rodney went back into the bedroom and stretched out on the bed. He calculated the time difference in his head and decided not to wake Sina at four-thirty a.m. Sydney time on her first full day on campus. He unzipped his gym bag, removed the boomerang and the framed photo he took with Sina on the dinner cruise, and put them on his nightstand. Stretched out on his bed, he turned on his side, rested his head in his hand, elbow bent, smiled at his pleasant memory, and drifted to sleep.

SINA REACHED over to the nightstand when she heard the phone ring. Slivers of sunlight had begun to peek through the blinds, and although the alarm woke her up fifteen minutes earlier, she continued to rest in bed, holding on for dear life for a few more minutes of sleep. "Hello," her voice was throaty, hoarse. She cleared it, "Sugar Cane!" Sina smiled from ear-to-ear.

"It's so good to hear your voice," his lips parted into a toothy smile.

"How was your flight?"

"Good, baby. I slept most of the way to LAX."

"Are you back in Chicago?"

"I am," his voice was soft, mellow, and sensual.

"I miss you already."

"I miss you too."

"What time is it there?"

"Three-thirty Sunday afternoon. I wanted to give you a call before you started your day. I'm about to head over to my sister's for family dinner."

"That's so nice. Give your Mom and sister my love," Sina stretched.

"I will. I love you."

"I love you too." Simultaneously they ended the call with a smooch into the phone.

❧

"SURE SMELLS GOOD!" Rodney entered his sister's split level ranch in South Holland. The fragrant aroma of rosemary wafted down from the kitchen. The low-key mix of New Edition's "Boys to Men," played on the stereo in the living room. "What's for dinner?"

Kimmy gave her younger brother a hug. "Perhaps a permanent menu item." Kimmy had been testing different recipes and preparing a menu for the restaurant she planned to open within the next two years. Rodney started up the stairs to the living room/dining room combo and stopped dead in his tracks.

"Rodney Joshua Paxton Harris!" His mother, slender with salt and pepper hair, and hazel eyes stood tall with her hands on her hips. Her glare was so sharp and pointed that it would bore a hole into the wall. "Where have you been? And why didn't you pick up the phone and call your mother?"

Rodney stalked towards her, bent down to give his Mom a hug and kiss. "I took a little vacation," he replied. "I was out of the country, it was sudden. I'm sorry I didn't let you know. Everything happened so fast."

Kimmy always kept her dining room table dressed with the finest linens and china. A vase of fresh cut red roses and Oriental lilies stood in the center. Her home décor was simple, yet elegant. Serving bowls held garlic roasted potatoes, Swiss chard, and a large platter held the pepper crusted grill roasted beef. Rosemary chimichurri sauce was on the side.

Kimmy sliced the beef, and plated their meals, Rodney blessed the food.

"I called your father. He said he hadn't heard from you either," Carol Paxton said as her son held the chair out for her. After her divorce, she went back to her maiden name since she was the last person in her family line. "I was really worried about you."

"Where out of the country?" Kimmy asked.

"I went to Sydney." Rodney took a bite of his roast beef. "Kimmy, this is really good. And the rosemary chimichurri! I'd say you have a winner."

His Mom chimed in, "What would take you to Sydney for a week on such short notice?"

Rodney revealed a toothy smile. "Thomasine."

"Thomasine from Piney Hill?" Kimmy asked.

"Yes."

"Isn't she the one who dumped you before the senior prom and you ended up going with that Amonia, Samonia, or whatever her name was chick?" his mother asked.

Rodney chuckled. "Sophronia. Thomasine and I connected at our ten-year reunion. We talked about that. It was all a misunderstanding." Rodney tasted his Swiss chard. "Kimmy, what did you put in this chard? Is it from your garden?"

"Hold up. So why is Thomasine so interested in you now? You're an international basketball star, you have endorsements up the wazoo." She was being an overprotective big sister.

Rodney cut Kimmy off. "It's not like that. She's not like that."

"Why didn't you let anyone know that you were going to Australia?" his Mom asked.

"I didn't know myself."

"What?" his Mom and sister asked in unison.

"I promised Sina that I would meet her at the airport before her flight. I overslept, got pulled over for speeding, and missed her. So, I called my travel agent and she booked me a seat on Thomasine's flight from LAX to Sydney." He ate a potato. "They actually held the plane for me."

"Wait a minute. You just up and got on a plane on impulse and flew I don't know how many thousands of miles away? Spur of the moment!"

"A little over nine thousand miles. Yeah, I guess I did."

"You didn't have toothbrush, change of underwear, nothing."

"Got everything I needed when I got there." Rodney took a sip of his tea. "I did have my gym bag though."

"Wow. I sure wish someone would do something like that for me." Kimmy said. "Thomasine is a lucky woman."

"And just what did you do in Sydney for a week?" his mother asked. The smile on Rodney's face told it all.

"Mom, what do you think they did in Sydney? Look at his face. I haven't seen that kind of smile on Rodney's face evah," Kimmy drew out the last word. "My little brother is in love." Kimmy drew out the last word again.

"I am. Mom and Kimmy, she's the one. I'm so sure of it."

"So why didn't you bring her to family dinner? Why isn't she here right now so that we can meet her?" his Mom asked.

"Because she's still in Sydney. But I called her just before I came here. She sends her love."

"What? Why?"

"You mean you called her and you didn't call your Mother?"

"I'm sorry Mom." Rodney shrugged his shoulders. "Thomasine is a professor at Steeplechase University, an anthropology professor. She got her Ph.D. from UNC-Chapel Hill when she was only twenty-five."

"Oh!"

"And she got a very prestigious study abroad grant to do research on Aboriginal women in Australia who were removed from their families during the Stolen Generations."

"Wait a minute," his mother paused from eating and scratched her head. "Thomasine, Thomasine. What's her last name?"

"Mintor."

"Rodney Joshua Paxton Harris," his mother said each of his names loudly and slowly. "You were running around clear on the other side of the globe with your pastor's daughter!"

Rodney nearly choked on his food. That thought had never crossed his mind.

§▲

"I KNOW it's a sad story, but don't cry Mommy," Martin said to Rachel as she closed the book. Martin walked across the room, took a tissue from the box on his dresser, and handed it to Rachel, then wrapped his arms around his mother's legs.

"You are so sweet," she smiled. A single tear trickled down her face. She rubbed the top of his head. "It's time for bed, boys. You have school tomorrow." Rachel walked to the closet, and hung a pair of pants and a shirt for each of her sons, one on the doorknob outside the closet, the other on the doorknob on the inside of the bedroom door. "Go get in bed now so that I can tuck you in."

"Okay Mommy." Malcolm jumped into his bottom bunk, while Martin started the climb to his top bunk. Rachel sat on the side of Malcolm's bed, tucked him in, gently brushed his face with her right hand, and kissed his forehead. "Sweet dreams." She did the same for Martin, another tear trickled down her face as she watched his upper lip curl, just like Patrick's, as he smiled.

"Mommy, I have a question. How come me and Malcolm won't go to the same school anymore?"

"Because you're starting Kindergarten tomorrow. Malcolm will start Kindergarten next year, and then you'll go to the same school again." Rachel folded the safety rail up, and locked the hinges into place. "You'll get a new teacher and you'll meet new friends. It will be fun," she assured him. She rubbed his left cheek with her hand. "Now get some sleep, so that you'll be ready for your first day." She smiled at her son, then turned out the lights and closed the door.

Rachel let out a deep sigh as she fought the inevitable flood of tears. Although it had been nearly twenty-four hours since Patrick told her that he never wanted to talk to or see her again as long as he lives, the pain was still raw. Very raw. Her shoulders shook, sadness stifled, as she walked down the hallway to the kitchen. She did not want Martin or Malcolm to hear her crying.

Although she rarely drank when she had to go to work the next day, she felt that she needed something to help her sleep. Rachel poured vodka into her glass, then diluted it with orange juice, only slightly. She reached into the freezer and grabbed three ice cubes from the bin. Rachel swirled the ice in the glass as she walked down the hallway to her bedroom, leaving a trail of tears behind her. She sat on the side of her bed, set her alarm for five-thirty a.m., took a swig of her drink, slid between the covers, and buried her face in her pillow. An attempt to silence her sorrow. *What'll I do? What on earth will I do?*

8

CONFIRMATION

R odney had to regain his focus. He had never been late for practice or training camp. Well, he wasn't really late, but he always arrived early. If he hadn't been so distracted by his trip, Sina, and then his mother's admonishing reminder that Sina is indeed the daughter of his pastor, he might have remembered to ask his mother to deposit his endorsement checks into his accounts when she went to work the next day—the cause of his delay. She was an Executive Vice President at First Federal Bank, and started there as a teller long before she met Kimmy and Rodney's father.

Rodney cruised north on the Kennedy Expressway, top down, sun beaming on his head. He sang along with "Sun Goddess 2000" from Ramsey Lewis' *Between the Keys* CD. That album usually moved him into the zone. The syncopated drum beat on the next track, "Cold and Windy," brought back fond memories of his moves during a play on their journey to last season's world championship. He bobbed his head in sync to the beat. As Rodney made his way up the exit ramp, a highlight reel of his game-winning baskets played in his head. He saw himself making that half-court shot that provided a photo finish to their season and was picked up by newspapers around the world. *Stay focused*. The title track played as he turned onto the street leading to their practice facility. In the distance, he could see the masts from the microwave dishes of at least six news trucks. *It was a nice long break. Back to my reality.*

Rodney slowed, and turned into the parking lot of the practice facility. Windy City Gale Force was emblazoned on the front of the building in their team colors, red and white, like the gale warning flag. Kenny was getting out of his black Porsche Boxster when Rodney parked beside him.

"Man, I can't believe I beat you here." Kenny laughed as Rodney got out of his car. Kenny's hair was cut in a smooth and wavy fade, his goatee neatly groomed.

"There's a first for everything." Rodney took his bag out of the trunk.

"Where on earth have you been?" Kenny asked. "I called you last week."

"Hey, I'm sorry. Something came up suddenly. I was out of the country."

"Out of the country?"

Rodney's grin was wide and bright, putting his pearly whites on full display.

"Aww man. There could only be one thing responsible for a smile like that," Kenny rubbed his chin. "So, what's her name?"

"Thomasine."

"Dude, I'm happy for you," Kenny patted Rodney on the back. "You have been single for more than a minute. It's about time."

Before they made it halfway to the door, news cameras and microphones from two different stations were stuck in their faces. The questions posed were similar, what are their expectations for this season and will the team repeat a championship win?

When Rodney finished talking to reporters and made his way into the locker room, Kenny had already changed into a jersey and shorts and was lacing up his shoes. Rodney put his bag on the bench beside Kenny, unzipped it, and removed a photo he took of Sina at Darling Harbour to put on the inside of his locker door.

Kenny looked up. "Oh man, she's beautiful Rodney." He tied his shoe. "So why did you take her to Sydney?"

Rodney gave Kenny the abbreviated version of his last week.

"Look at you," he gently punched Rodney's bicep. "Flying all the

way to Sydney just to let her know you cared. Your ass is sprung,"
Kenny drew out sprung, and said the last letter so hard that it almost
sounded like a k instead of a g. "But on a serious note, I'm really, really
happy for you."

"Thanks, Kenny." Rodney put his bag inside his locker and closed
it. As they headed to a meeting with the coaches, Rodney had an aha
moment. "You know Kenny, I just decided to dedicate each game this
season to Thomasine."

"Oh man, that's serious," Kenny's eyes looked up and around.
"Shh, shh, shh. Do you hear it?"

"Hear what?" Rodney asked.

"Have you bought the ring yet? Because surely I'm hearing
wedding bells."

❦

HOPE HAD EATEN every peppermint she put in her jacket pocket in an
effort to soothe her upset stomach long enough to make it through the
meeting with the Community Teams Leader and the Director of the
Employee Wellness Program. She was still learning the ropes of her
new position as Chief Incentive Officer. As much as she wanted to
reschedule the meeting, go back to her hotel room, and camp out in the
bathroom with her head over the toilet, she was too new in the position to call off. Unfortunately, the sweet candy made her upset stomach
feel even worse.

Hope pushed the chair to the conference room table, turned off the
light, and walked across the hall to her office. The fluorescent lights in
the hallway as well as in her office, combined with the bright sunlight
from her large office windows intensified the dull pain in her head.
Upon entering, she closed the blinds on the glass walls near her office
door, and did the same for the blinds at her window. The only light
was the slight glow from the computer on her desk.

She removed her jacket and hung it on her chair. Hope sat, rested
her head on the back of her chair and closed her eyes, then exhaled.
With arms folded across her chest, she breathed slowly, deliberately.
The cool gust from the central air soothed her only slightly. Hope
continued to breathe deeply, and was nearly in a meditative state when

her moment of peace was interrupted by the shrill ringing of the phone. She was shaken, nearly jumping in her chair, and jarred as she reached for it. The call was from her assistant, letting her know that she was taking her lunch break a bit late and would be gone for the next thirty minutes. As Hope stood at her desk, her stomach did a handspring vault. Fortunately, today she stuck the landing, unlike yesterday when she had to leave work early. Two days had passed since her nightmare sent her to urgent care.

She walked slowly and carefully, and decided that saltine crackers and ginger ale might help her make it through the day. She didn't know what would be worse, the stairs or the elevator. Hope chose the latter.

The elevator doors opened and it was crowded. She had to hold her breath as she stepped on to prevent the harsh aroma from the overperfumed woman next to her from further nauseating her. When they reached the first floor, Hope walked briskly and turned left, right, then left again and down the long and narrow hallway to the cafeteria. Once again, she had to hold her breath, this time due to the scents of the food.

The chatter and activity in the cafeteria nearly turned her dull headache into a throbbing one. She walked straight to the refrigerated case near the cash registers and grabbed a ginger ale. Near the condiments, she picked up a few packages of crackers. "Hope? Is that you?"

She turned around and looked up. "Dana! It's so nice to see you." Now butterflies joined the disruption in her stomach. "I haven't seen you since college in Savannah." She had been his statistics tutor. "How have you been?"

"Things are going great for me," he placed his tray on the counter near the register. "I'm in my first year of a psychiatry fellowship here at the hospital."

"Really? That's wonderful," Hope put two packages of crackers and a bottle of ginger ale on the counter next to his tray.

"Is that all you're having?" he asked. "Doesn't look like much of a lunch."

"Upset tummy," she replied.

He looked down at her hand, "Hey congratulations! How long have you been married?" he asked. "Expecting?"

"I'm afraid not." Hope replied. "I've got to get back to my desk. Lots of work to do. Still learning the ropes."

"You work here? How ironic." Dana took two steps forward as the line began to move.

"Yes. I just got my M.H.A." She smiled. "I'm the Chief Incentive Officer."

"Oh, you're big time," Dana smiled. "Congratulations, again."

"Thanks Dana." The line progressed a bit more. "We have to get together for lunch one day when I'm feeling better. My extension is 3769."

"Three seven six nine. I'll remember that," Dana paused to pay for his meal. "And I hope you feel better soon."

"Thanks, me too," Hope said as he walked away and she paid for her items. *I've really got to get it together,* Hope thought as she walked back to her office. She was a mass of confusion, and wasn't yet ready to accept that in a short while, she would be a divorced woman. She wasn't ready to take off her ring, and definitely not ready to tell anyone that her marriage was over.

❧

MELLIFLUOUS STRAINS of subtle drum beats, piano chords, and saxophone riffs from the smooth jazz station overpowered the constant beeps and tones of the EKG, ventilator, and ICP monitor in Brothaman's room. Over a week had passed since Dee-Mo brutally beat him, and he was still in ICU. His head was bandaged, the ICP monitor probe was in the right side of his head, and an endotracheal tube provided extra oxygen. Brothaman was truly a fighter.

Hank held a photo of Martin and Malcolm up for Brothaman to see. While his eyes were open, he was nonresponsive. "Today is Thursday, it is three-forty-five in the afternoon." Hank said. "Look at Martin. He started Kindergarten on Monday. He misses being at the same school with Malcolm, but he said he has made a lot of friends."

Hank reluctantly sat by his bedside. As much as Hank hated Brothaman, he knew that in spite of his chemical dependency, his brother-in-law did love his children, and even his wife. Reflecting on his own life without his father, who came up missing in Vietnam months before he was born, then learning that his father had been alive all of these years changed his perspective. He really wanted Brothaman to pull through, not for him or Rachel, but for Martin and Malcolm, who he loved like his own. He wanted his nephews to have what was missing from his own life. A bond with their biological father.

"Hey, Rachel will call you Saturday, and the boys will tell you all about their week." Hank touched his hand. "Rachel and the boys are really praying that you get better."

"And so am I." Conrad walked into Brothaman's ICU Room. He was wearing a black short sleeved clergy shirt and collar. He reached out to shake Hank's hand.

"Well, he's improving, a little at a time."

"That's good to hear," Conrad replied. "And I'm glad you're playing his favorite radio station. It's much better than him listening to machines all day and night."

"Yes, familiar sounds, voices, and even smells will help in his healing process."

"You know, when I came to see him a few days ago, I walked in on Lorenzo from our block. He was dressed like an orderly. Dude was about to fire up a joint."

"You have got to be kidding!"

"He said that Brothaman will get well faster if he's around familiar smells."

"Thank God you arrived when you did. Unbelievable!"

"Yeah, I had to put him out of the room. I should have called security."

"That definitely should have been reported."

"Well look, I came to pray for our friend."

"Yes, let's do that."

Conrad walked on one side of the bed, Hank on the other. They each touched one of Brothaman's hands, then reached over the bed to join hands. With their heads bowed and eyes closed, Conrad asked God for a miracle. He asked to not only heal Brothaman's body, but to heal his life, and his broken relationships with Rachel and the boys. And that Brothaman's life be transformed so that he can use his gifts, talents, and skills to one day heal others.

9

REVELATIONS (FIRST MOVEMENT)

A lthough the life she had with Jason was far from her dreams, Hope never imagined that life without him would be this painful. In fact, she never imagined life without him.

She placed her room service tray on the coffee table in the living area of her suite, and put the silver metal warming cover on top. She had barely touched the food. Jason had not only been in her life since freshman year of high school, but he had been her man for fourteen years, half of her life. However, the past month started to put things into perspective for her, especially the near tragedy last weekend. Since that time, Hope gave up one-night stands and her nightly intake of rum and Diet Coke.

Over the past two weeks, Hope's days consisted of work, evenings in the hotel suite with room service, and a few days of emergency contraceptives. She felt so lonely, no she was lonely. Hope used this time to reflect on her life. She felt horrible that she had been such a crappy friend to Thomasine and Rachel, judging them both for their choice in men and what she perceived as their youthful mistakes— Thomasine's pregnancy during her freshman year of college and Rachel's decision to marry Brothaman instead of Patrick. She wanted to reach out to apologize to both of them, yet she found it difficult to own up to the choices she made over the past month with the men she encountered in clubs in Kalamazoo just before she left, then at the lobby bar of this hotel—she stopped counting after a dozen. She could remember their faces, but their names, at least those she got, were all a blur. *How could I do this to myself?* And to make matters even worse, how could she ever face her friends again after Jason revealed her biggest secret? The fact that he had not proposed to her, that she was jealous that her friends were engaged to men they knew a fraction of the time she knew Jason, and that she bought the ring herself.

Hope felt humiliated, dehumanized, and embarrassed beyond imagination. At the same time, she had such a great opportunity. New job, much higher salary, new city. It was a great chance for her to start over with people who knew nothing of her mistakes, and most of all knew nothing about the fourteen years she gave to Jason for it to end this way. She felt like such a fool.

Hope picked up a magazine on the opposite end of the coffee table. She passively flipped through it, first perusing the ads, then skimming the articles. She sighed deeply and continued to turn the pages. Midway through the magazine, her gaze fixed upon one quote in the center of the page. "Sometimes it's hard to move on, but once you do, you'll realize it's the best thing you ever decided to do." She tore the page out of the magazine.

Hope steeped a cup of chamomile tea, climbed into bed, and sipped it while she plotted and planned for her next day. She realized that what she most needed was to get out and meet people, outside of the hotel bar. Her first move would be joining a gym and getting into shape.

$\approx$

RODNEY TOOK a sip of his iced tea with a splash of lemonade. He sat at a wrought iron table on the north end of the patio. The tilted green umbrella slightly shielded him from the setting sun. Though all the patio tables were occupied, the occasional buzz of a passing car post-rush hour on South Western Avenue was much calmer than the commotion inside the bar on a Friday night. As usual, Joe Bailey's was crowded.

Training camp was over, and the exhibition games against other IBL teams in North America would begin in a few days. His season opener in Sydney was weeks away. He smiled at the thought of reuniting with Sina. He looked up from the menu briefly, and spotted Jason as he approached the front door. Rodney stood and waved to his long-time friend.

"Sorry I'm late," Jason said when he finally made his way to the table. He looked around the patio. "I'm glad you were able to get a table out here. It's crazy in there." He was wearing long mesh shorts and a jersey.

"No problem." The pair shared the secret handshake done by athletes from Piney Hill.

"I'm coaching a youth football team my firm sponsors. Today was the first day of practice." Jason sat at the table.

"How did it go?"

"It went longer than I expected. I've got my work cut out for me. I have nine-year-olds," Jason picked up the menu as he saw the waiter approaching. "I'll have a Heineken and a cheeseburger, medium well." Rodney ordered the grilled chicken sandwich and a side salad.

"I remember that age. Hey, isn't that how old we were when we played on the youth team years ago?"

"It sure is. Then we both went to Piney Hill."

"I can't believe we've been friends for almost twenty years."

"I know. Doesn't seem that long."

"That was also the age I fell in love with basketball and dreamed about playing professionally. I sucked at football."

"You weren't that bad, you just didn't stick with it long enough. How was training camp?"

"Training camp is, training camp. I passed all medical tests with flying colors. I'm looking forward to the season, and getting back to Sydney."

"Oh?"

"Yes," Rodney smiled. "Season opener is in Sydney, and it's going to be a great game."

"Wait a minute," Jason set his beer on the table. "Uh, didn't I see you dancing with Thomasine at the reunion?"

"Yes."

"And, isn't Thomasine in Sydney doing research?"

"Yes." Rodney's smile grew monumentally.

"Wait, wait. Did I hear you say get back to Sydney? When were you last there?"

"I got back Sunday before last." Rodney showed nearly all his perfectly straight teeth.

"Oh. Oh. Ohhh!" Jason reached across the table to give Rodney a high five. "I'm happy for you man. I don't know the details, but I know from Hope that she's had it a bit rough in the love department. She had a broken engagement about five years ago."

"Yeah. Sina understandably doesn't talk about that much."

The waiter arrived with their food orders. They bowed their heads and blessed the food.

"Hey. I'm sorry to hear that you and Hope didn't work out."

"It's really for the best," Jason took a bite of his burger. "The truth of the matter is that I can't give Hope what she deserves and desires, so I have to release her."

"That's a positive way to look at it."

The waiter came back around and lit a citronella candle near the center of the table. "Can I get you anything else?

"I'll have another Heineken."

"I'm good, but you could please bring me the check?" Rodney asked as the waiter left the table.

"Look Rodney, I need your honest opinion on something."

"Sure," Rodney leaned in closer to the table. "What is it?"

"I've been thinking lately about my football career." Rodney was silent, he listened intently. "Do you think I gave up too soon?"

Rodney leaned back in his chair and inhaled deeply. "To be completely honest, I thought your decision was a bit hasty. Surgery, rehab. Some of the best orthopedic surgeons in the country were right at your fingertips."

"Yeah, I thought about surgery, but I didn't want to get my hopes up too high."

"You might have made it to the NFL, but at the end of the day that is a question that only you can answer." Rodney rubbed his chin. "And you can't second guess yourself."

"Well, I've been thinking about it a great deal lately. And I'm seriously considering having ACL surgery. Can you recommend anyone?"

"I'll ask my trainer."

❦

RACHEL TURNED the key in the lock, and pushed her front door open. She felt free, if just for the afternoon, while her boys were at a playdate and dinner with their friend Joey. They were celebrating their soccer team's 3-0 record.

Her freedom floated away upon entering her apartment. She had been so consumed by her current life experience that she didn't realize how much she had neglected her home. It looked like a pig sty. "My goodness!" she exclaimed. "I never live like this." Sadly, it was the first thing she saw when she opened the door.

Rachel walked over to the sofa. It was covered with a mix of clean and dirty clothing, and there was a backlog of mail on the coffee table in front of it. She picked up a shirt and smelled it, then a pair of pants. The funk almost knocked her down. She decided that it would be more time efficient to just wash it all. Quickly, she separated the items by color. When she got to the bottom of the pile of clothing, she found a pair of Martin's school pants with the tag on them. She remembered that they were too short for him and that she needed to return them to JC Penney's. Rachel draped them over the arm of the sofa.

This is inexcusable she thought as she walked down the short hall-way. The laundry closet was right next to her bedroom. *I have no excuse for letting things go like this.* She changed the water temperature on the machine, then loaded the clothing into the washer. Once she added her Downy ball, she was able to tackle the stack of mail.

She sorted the stack with the efficiency of a postal clerk nearing retirement. Junk mail to the left, magazines in the middle, and bills on the right. "Oh shoot," she said when she saw the big red letters on her phone bill. They read DISCONNECTION NOTICE. "I've gotta pay this. No phone means no dial-up Internet." She looked at her watch. She had an hour left to pay the bill before the payment center closed for the weekend. Rachel reached for her purse on the left edge of the coffee table. An air mail envelope postmarked Sydney fell onto the floor. From the opposite side of the table, the handwriting did not

remotely resemble Sina's. Curiously, she picked it up, ripped the envelope open with her finger tip, and got the shock of her life.

When Rachel opened the letter, a photo she took with her father as
an infant fell to the floor. She bent down to pick it up and her purse fell
from her shoulder. Perched on the edge of the sofa with the photo in
her right hand, a tear fell from her eye. She flipped it over and saw in
her mother's handwriting *Henry and Rachel at 6 months, May 1970.* The
photo was taken shortly before her father deployed to Vietnam. Rachel
pondered over how different her life might have been had her father
not disappeared in Vietnam. Then she learned twenty-seven years later
that he had been alive all along. She wasn't sure if she should be sad or
mad. But what hurt her to the core of her being was the fact that he
disappeared before her brother was born. No one knew if Henry, Sr.
even knew there was a Henry, Jr.

Rachel slid back on the sofa, sighed audibly, and unfolded the
letter.

DEAR RACHEL,

*I know this letter may seem a bit strange and shocking to you, but I felt
that I had to reach out. I hired a private investigator to find you. I hope you
don't mind.*

*I don't know how to say this any other way, but to share that I'm as gobs-
macked as you will be once you finish reading this. I won't beat around the
bush. My name is Heather and I am your younger sister. You also have two
younger brothers, James, Jr. and Shane. I found this photo I am sending you
among our Dad's things which I found after three weeks of Sorry Business
(what we Indigenous Australians call funeral services), along with his dog
tags and his draft card. I never knew he was from the States. What a clanger! I
always thought he was a Murri just like my Mum and the rest of my mob.*

*I don't know how he came to Sydney, or why. Nor do I know why he
changed his name. Had his reasons I suppose. I guess he was afraid someone
would dob him in. I do know that he was fair dinkum, loving, a good provider
and a great Dad. He was one-off.*

*There is so much more to say, but I don't want to overwhelm you any
further. I do hope that, in time, you and me can build a relationship. I've*

always wanted a sister all of my life. A big sister. I'm happy to have found you
and I look forward to meeting you one day. I really hope we can be mates.
  Your little sister,
  Heather

RACHEL WAS PARALYZED WITH EMOTION. She sat still on the sofa, reflecting, deep in thought, and ignored the buzzer indicating that her first
load had finished washing. She looked around the room through sting-
ing, tear-filled eyes. Rachel pulled her knees to her chest, and curled
herself into a ball. A multitude of thoughts flooded her mind. *What*
happened to him? Why were me and Mom a secret? Did he ever try to come
back to us? Did he ever want to come back to us? What on earth would lead
him to estrange himself from everyone he ever knew, and assume a new life?
Did he love Mom? Did he love me? Rachel draped the afghan she kept on
the back of her sofa over her body. This would take Rachel a while to
reconcile, and she knew she couldn't do it alone. She needed to talk to
someone, but wasn't sure who she would call first, her Mom or Hank.
All of this made her realize just how important getting to the truth of
Martin's paternity was. She knew that she would need to talk to
Patrick, but after his hurtful rejection of her, she was afraid. She knew
what she had to do, but she didn't know how.
    Rachel stretched her legs out in front of her, and put her feet on the
floor. She reached for the phone on the end table. Bridled with a noth-
ing-to-lose type of courage, she picked up the phone, and the line was
dead. *Damn! It's too late. I'll have to stop by the payment center on my way*
to work on Monday. Until then, Rachel decided to focus on the mess
right in front of her, well the physical mess her living room had
become, because that was all she could handle at present.

❧

A PEACEFUL ENERGY and tone permeated Front Street African Christian
Church. The ushers, dressed in navy blue suits and white shirts or
blouses, began to take up the offering after a small group of presum-
ably well-heeled members took their walk to the tither's box. The
organist played "You Can't Beat God Giving." Rodney placed his five-

figure check in an envelope in the collection plate when the usher made her way to his pew. Rodney believed in tithing, but not in an outward display of that part of his inward walk.

The choir sang a medley of hymns as Rodney took slow steps on the plush crimson carpet while he waited in line behind other members who desired to leave their burdens at the altar while the choir sang, "My Faith Looks Up to Thee."

When he made it to the front, the assembly had thinned. He looked to his right. Martha Mitchell and her niece, Janae stood beside him. Martha nudged Janae so hard that she had to brace herself to keep from bumping into Rodney. Martha's actions did not escape the eyes of Crystal Mintor who sat on the front pew, her floral down brim hat tilted to the side, partially covering her right eye. When a space became available, Rodney motioned for Janae to take it.

Rodney took to his knees, folded his hands on the chancel rail, bowed his head, and closed his eyes. He had a conversation with God about his life, his career, Thomasine, and his next move. Most importantly, he didn't just ask, he listened. When Rodney was done, he stood, smiled, and nodded. He made his way back to his seat, as the last person to leave the altar.

The choir selection, "Total Praise," enveloped him in the warmth of peace. The tempo was slow and steady. The choir sang in perfect harmony. The fifty-voice choir combined with chamber quartet accompanied by piano left him entranced. While he didn't hang onto every word, Rodney drank in the underlying message of Reverend Mintor's sermon—not partial, not fifty percent, but when you do something, give it your all.

Rodney sat momentarily after Reverend Mintor gave the Doxology and Benediction, and the choir recessed down the center aisle. He was deep in thought. When most of the congregants made their way through the line, he walked down the center aisle, his feet left no imprint in the well-cushioned crimson carpet. He felt as if he were walking on air. His focus was fixed straight ahead, yet he heard light chatter behind him.

There were now only five people ahead of him to greet Reverend and Mrs. Mintor. "Excuse me, Rodney," Martha Mitchell stood behind him. "Let me introduce you to my niece, Janae." Rodney cordially shook Janae's hand. The line moved forward.

"You and Janae are about the same age. She's new to Chicago, she just started a job in banking."

"That's nice." Rodney tried to be friendly, but there was only one thing on his mind.

"With you being around the same age," Martha continued. "I thought maybe you could show her around, since she is new and all. You all can hang out."

Crystal Mintor took a step forward. "Now Martha, I'm sure that your niece is a nice young lady, but Rodney doesn't have time to show her around the city. His basketball season is about to start, and," Crystal put emphasis on and, "He is in a relationship." She emphasized the words is and relationship.

"Oh!" Martha replied with a mixture of astonishment and disappointment.

Crystal turned to Janae, "Now Janet, is it?"

"Janae," she responded.

"Janae, if you call the church office tomorrow, I'm sure that Mrs. Winters, our Church Administrator, will be more than happy to connect you with our Single's Ministry. That would be a better fit for you. I'm sure your Aunt Martha knows the number to the church."

Martha was speechless.

Rodney extended his hand to Crystal, she pulled him closer and gave him a hug, then placed her hand on his arm.

"Rodney, it's so nice to see you." Reverend Mintor extended his hand.

"I really enjoyed your sermon," Rodney said as they shook hands. "It really touched me."

"Glad to hear that, son. I just ask God to work through me." Reverend Mintor smiled. "I hear your season opener is in Sydney."

"Yes," Rodney replied, a monumental smile dressed his face. "But I have to get through the exhibition season first, all stateside."

"I'm sure you'll do well, Son."

"Say, Reverend Mintor, I need to get on your calendar soon. In fact, I would like to meet with you and Mrs. Mintor."

"Oh," a smile began to brighten Crystal's face.

"That shouldn't be a problem. I'll be in all week," Reverend Mintor replied.

"And I'm certain I can make myself available for whatever time you schedule." Crystal's smile grew to match Rodney's.

Rodney had something big in mind. Really big!

10

EVERYTHING HAPPENS TO ME

Thomasine went into the kitchen and put the kettle on. She opened the canister, sniffed it, then set it on the countertop. Sunlight filtered through the kitchen window as she walked across the room, opened the cabinet, and grabbed her favorite mug along with a saucer. In the kitchen drawer, she found her infuser. Thomasine scooped the peppermint tea into the infuser, placed it into the mug, then when the kettle whistled, she filled the mug with hot water.

Thomasine inhaled the fresh peppermint scent as she walked back to her bedroom. She placed the mug and saucer on the nightstand and climbed into bed since she hadn't been feeling herself lately. There was no way she could make the three-hour flight to Cairns, then the hour-long drive to Yarrabah the way she was feeling. She picked up the phone and dialed her research assistant, Evonne.

"Good morning, love," Evonne said when she answered the phone. She was scheduled to travel with Thomasine.

"My morning's not so good," Thomasine said. "I feel horrible."

"Are you knackered?" Evonne asked.

"I am a bit tired, and feel a little faint, but it's more than that. My stomach is upset as well."

"Have you eaten this morning? A good brekkie might make you feel better."

"I don't know," Thomasine responded. "I'm hungry, but when I get food, I'll eat a little of it, and I'm full very fast."

"Strange."

"And I've been feeling like this the past few days. I think we need to postpone Yarrabah for a while. I'll just rest today. I have been working very hard."

"I'll call the airline and cancel the flight, then I'll contact the director in Yarrabah to see when we can reschedule."

"Thanks, Evonne."

"No worries, mate. I'll check on you later. If you need anything, please let me know."

Thomasine removed the infuser from the mug and placed it on the saucer. She took a sip of her strongly brewed peppermint tea, believing that it would ease her discomfort. She sank into her bed, hoping to find the pillows and linens comforting. Her stomach still felt queasy, the comforter gave none. *I feel horrible.* Thomasine thought. *I haven't felt this bad since. Oh my goodness!* Thomasine struggled to a seated position. Slowly, she put her feet on the floor and somehow managed to drag herself out of her bedroom and to her desk. She eased herself down into the chair and thumbed through her planner until she found the calendar section. She scanned the calendar for this month, as well as the previous month in search of the tiny "T" which marked the arrival of what she called the landing of the red cardinal. She flipped from page to page, back and forth, this time looking more carefully. *But we always used protection* she thought, recalling the night before she left Chicago, and the week that followed. Then she remembered. The morning Rodney left. The shower. The spontaneity. The. *Oh! My! Goodness!*

Her deep moment of reflection was interrupted by the high pitched double ring of her phone. She looked at the clock on her desk. It was nine-thirty a.m. Sydney time. Sina picked it up on the second ring. "Hello," her voice was a bit faint.

"Hello Sina," the way he said her name was refreshing, melodious, and comforting. "I wanted to catch you before you head up the coast."

"That's so sweet of you," Sina replied. As much as she tried, the usual joy she exuded whenever she talked to Rodney was absent from her voice. She had too much on her mind.

"Is everything alright?" he asked. "You don't sound your usual self."

"I'm a little under the weather," Sina walked back to the bedroom. "I've been pulling all-nighters to get these interviews transcribed and organized."

"Don't you have a research assistant? Why don't you hire a transcription service?"

"I've heard rumors that the agency won't be able to fund my grant for a second year, so I've been trying to budget wisely and get as much done as possible this year."

"If you need any money to make this easier for you, let me know. I'm here." It was the first time Rodney had ever offered Sina money.

"I think I'll be good. But if I run into a rough spot, I'll let you know." There was momentary silence.

"Sweetie Pie, is everything really alright?"

"Yes, Rodney. I just need some sleep."

"You sound a little worried. Is there something you aren't telling me?"

She sighed. "I guess I'm just concerned that not being able to go to Yarrabah today will put a big delay in my project. That's all," Thomasine put another pillow behind her back. "Say, how are Kimmy and your Mom? How was dinner?" As soon as Thomasine posed the question, she regretted it, the mere smell, thought, or mention of food formed somersaults in her stomach.

"Everyone's fine. I saw your parents today as well. Your Dad really preached today. Great sermon."

Thomasine smiled. "Daddy sure can preach. Say, when do you head out for your first exhibition game?"

"We leave for Atlanta day after tomorrow, mid-morning. I'm having a late lunch with my Dad shortly after I arrive. I can't believe my little brother is in high school already."

"Tell your Dad I send my love."

"I will. And Sweetie Pie, please take care of yourself. I'm here. Know that you can always come to me about anything, and I do mean anything."

"I will, darling. I'm in bed right now," she stretched. "I'm sure I'll feel better after I get some sleep."

"I certainly hope you do. I'll be back on Wednesday. I'll call you then." Rodney paused. "And remember, I love you."

"I love you too, Sugar Cane."

Thomasine gently placed the phone in its cradle. She slid down underneath the comforter. Her gaze fixed on the ceiling. Her reflection from before Rodney's call made a rapid return. *Maybe I should have told him. Why? You don't know for sure?* Thoughts competed in her head.

Thomasine struggled to sit up. She knew there was no way she could walk to the pharmacy to purchase a pregnancy test. She didn't have the energy. An array of notions danced through her mind. The last thing she wanted to do was call Evonne and ask her to bring a pregnancy test. That would be too embarrassing. *I've got to get my mind off this for now, direct my thoughts elsewhere.* Sina picked up the folded newspaper on the night stand and began to read yesterday's news. As she flipped through the pages, she saw an ad for Ramsay Street Pharmacy in Haberfield. They deliver.

Thomasine placed a call and requested a pregnancy test, as well as a few other items. She was informed that there were several orders ahead of hers. She went into the kitchen and toasted some bread. She remembered that her Mom gave her dry toast whenever she had an upset tummy. She also added water to the kettle and turned it on to make more tea. Thomasine turned her head and raised her arms to stretch. She quickly decided that a hot shower and clean clothing might help her feel just a little bit better. It was also needed. She turned the pilot off underneath the kettle.

Steam rose as the hot water beat her body with a relaxing vigor. Thomasine turned around to rinse her back. When she faced the wall, her mind flashed momentarily to the day Rodney left, their urges, and their urgency. *How could we be so careless?* She stood still in reflection. A tear formed in Thomasine's eye. She was alone, once again possibly pregnant, and still single. She exhaled deeply. She was sure of Rodney's love for her, but were they and their relationship ready for a baby? Going through her first pregnancy alone was in her mind, a necessity, a requirement actually given the circumstances. But although she was much older now, how could she do this again with everyone she knew and loved almost ten thousand miles away? There was no way she could burden her friends who were going through their own personal hells with this. Sina rinsed the soap off her body, toweled off, put her underwear on, then tied the belt of the bathrobe around her waist. She cracked the bathroom door open when she heard the doorbell ring. Her eyes opened wide in astonishment. She didn't expect her delivery this quick. "Hold on," she called through the front door. "Let me grab my purse so that I can pay you."

"It's been paid for already," she heard from the other side of the door. This frightened Sina a bit. *How could that be?* Sina opened the door to a huge bouquet from Lucy's Florist in Summer Hill. A mylar balloon with the words "Get Well Soon," stood in the center.

"I just need your signature," the delivery man said. Thomasine signed and he handed her a stuffed animal. "You might want to put this underneath your arm. You'll need both hands for this bouquet."

Sina carried the bouquet of lilies, roses, and orchids over to her dining table. She set the stuffed animal beside it, then opened the card.

Sweetie Pie,

I know that Renoir is your favorite artist. While this isn't one of his masterpieces, I hope this "Renoir" bouquet can lift your spirits and your energy. And here's a little something for you to cuddle the next few weeks until I return. I'm counting the days and hours.

I love you with all my heart.

Sugar Cane.

❧

Hope was amazed at how crowded the gym was on a Monday night. When she joined on Saturday, she decided to delay her first workout until there were fewer people around and more access to the equipment. At least that's what she told herself. She was pleased that the gym had locations both near her job, and near the new corporate apartment she rented. Hope had to get out of the hotel. There was far too much access to too many temptations.

She walked through the door, gym bag on her shoulder, ID card in hand. The glass display case at the counter contained a variety of protein bars and jars of protein powder large enough for a month supply. The wall behind the counter held socks, swim goggles, and padlocks, all of which were for sale. To the right there was a countertop refrigerated case containing water and sports drinks. The tall, lanky woman who scanned her ID was as thin as a blade of grass. "Welcome to Fit and Healthy," she told Hope. The name Eva was printed on her nametag.

"Thank you," Hope smiled. "I have a five-thirty appointment with Ernie. My first personal training session." Hope wasn't sure if she should be pleased or afraid by the smile on Eva's face. "Could you please direct me to the locker room?"

"Straight ahead, then turn left at the first hallway."

"Thank you, Eva."

Hope was nearly mesmerized by all the activity. People of all races and ages were using the treadmills, stair climbers, ellipticals, and bikes. Many of them were thin. To her right was a variety of weight machines, along with an area for free weights. And when she reached the hallway, she noticed a functional fitness area for stretching and other calisthenics.

Hope entered the locker room and found an unoccupied area. She was very self-conscious about her size, and didn't want to dress in front of anyone. She opened three lockers without locks before she found one empty. She put her bag on the bench in front of it, unzipped it, and removed her sports bra, T-shirt, and spandex biker shorts. Hope dressed one part of her body at a time. She removed her jacket, and hung it neatly in the locker, then followed suit with her blouse. She wanted to take good care of her work clothing. After she hung her skirt up in the locker, she put her right leg into the spandex biker shorts, then her left. She nearly lost her balance when she began to pull them up her legs. Hope sat on the bench and pulled them up to the bottom of her thighs. She stood, and pulled, one side at a time. Her struggle was so intense that she broke a fingernail in the process. Just when she thought she was home free, and the shorts were around her waist, she exhaled, and they began to roll down her stomach. *Thank goodness for my long T-shirt.*

Hope scanned the exercise floor. When she noticed a tall, reasonably fit, middle-aged man with a clipboard, she assumed that he was her trainer, and she was right. Hope walked up to him, extended her hand and introduced herself.

"Ernie Foster," he shook her hand in return. "Tell me about your current workout routine."

"Well," Hope started. "I just moved to the area about a month ago, so I'm getting started again. But, when I lived in Michigan I used to exercise with my husband." She paused. "We're separated." There, she said it for the first time. And as much as it hurt, she felt a little lighter. A sense of freedom.

"What brings you to Virginia Beach?" Ernie asked.

"A new job, with Vantarca Health."

Ernie took copious notes on nearly everything Hope told him. He put his pencil behind his ear and directed her toward the fitness floor. "I want to introduce you to some strength training as well as some exercises for balance and flexibility." He stopped at a stationary bike. "But first, you'll need to warm up." He adjusted the seat for Hope's height, then helped her climb on. "Start pedaling," Ernie instructed. Hope did as she was told, and was stunned when he punched in fifteen minutes. *Warm up? This is a workout.* Hope knew if she wanted to lose weight she had to start somewhere, however intense, but she had never been a fan of the stationary bike. It made no sense to her to pedal and exert energy and not go anywhere. To get through this, Hope had to imagine that she was riding a bicycle on an oceanfront path, and it was then that she got the bright idea to purchase a bicycle and do just that.

Ernie got Hope started on a whole-body strength routine and instructed her to gradually increase the number of sets and the amount of weight. He also gave her a class schedule. "Yoga will help you increase flexibility, and relax as well. Oh, and make sure you do thirty minutes of cardio at least three times a week."

"Will do."

"But most important in your weight loss program, is what you put in your body. Some of the best nutritionists in the area are at Vantarca Health. You should make an appointment and a lifestyle change. Notice I didn't say diet. Diets are temporary, lifestyle changes focus on your total wellness."

"I will do that," Hope replied. "Thank you, Ernie."

"Just keep up the good work. I'll see you same time, next week."

Hope made her way back to the locker room. She was pooped. She decided not to go through the struggle of getting the spandex biker shorts off. Instead, she neatly folded her work clothing and put them inside her gym bag. *Thank God for my long big T-shirt.* She walked to her car.

Hope swung by the post office on the way to her new apartment. Her box was full of mail. She put it on the passenger seat of her car, then made the short drive to her new home. She opened the door to her fully furnished apartment. It looked like a model home. Hope put the stack of mail on the table and went to her bedroom to hang up her suit and blouse. She returned to the kitchen, sat down, and sorted through the mail. When she saw the letter from the lab, she ripped it open, then exhaled a big sigh of relief. Her test for sexually transmitted diseases came back negative. The next letter she opened was from her attorney. A date had been set for her divorce hearing. It was six weeks away. Hope walked to the refrigerator to get some cold water. When she reached to open it, she saw the quote from the magazine, "Sometimes it's hard to move on, but once you do, you'll realize it's the best thing you ever decided to do."

❦

THE MID-AFTERNOON SUN had been chased away by dark storm clouds. It wasn't a downpour yet, but a fine, misty rain that annoyed Rachel to no end. Rachel circled the aisle when she saw a lady walking to her car with a little girl. She was in the third space, right next to the disabled parking space at Cool Springs Galleria. "Boys, put on your rain hats. I don't want you to get wet."

She got out of the car and opened the door for Martin. Together they walked around to the other side and she did the same for Malcolm. Rachel kept the child safety locks activated on the back doors of her car, so she always had to open them for the boys. She opened the trunk to retrieve the bag containing the pants that were too short for Martin. "Boys, hold hands," she told them, as they approached the end of the parking aisle. They paused briefly to let a car pass by. "Step up,"

Rachel told the boys once they reached the curb. She held the door open for Martin and Malcolm, and then put her umbrella down. The threat of severe weather must have kept many shoppers at home. The mall was unbelievably empty for a Thursday afternoon. When they reached JC Penney, Rachel and the boys walked around the children's section for a while before they found a salesclerk. An instrumental version of "Wind Beneath My Wings," played throughout the store. The salesclerk was folding boys' T-shirts on a lay down table. "Excuse me miss. I'd like to return these pants. They were too short for my son." The sales clerk turned around, her dark brown hair fell over her shoulder. She looked at Rachel and her two boys and was frozen in place. "Rachel?" she said inquisitively.

Rachel stared for a moment, then looked down at her name tag. "My goodness, Jessica. Is that you?" Rachel's voice was high-pitched from excitement. She gave her a hug. "I haven't seen you here before? Have you worked here long?"

"No. I just transferred from the store in St. Louis. I worked there this summer. I'm a junior at Vanderbilt. I just got my first apartment, so I have bills to pay."

"Wow! You're all grown up now."

Jessica smiled, then looked down at the boys. "Are these your sons?"

"Yes. Boys introduce yourselves."

"Hi, my name is Malcolm." His rain hat covered most of his face.

"Tell her how old you are."

"I'm four years old." He held up four fingers with his right hand.

"Hi, I'm Martin and I'm five years old." Martin turned up the brim on his rain hat and extended his left hand. Jessica squatted to his level to shake it and stifled a gasp. She was face-to-face with the image of her older brother's Kindergarten picture. That smile! Speechless, Jessica rose and her hand began to shake. She didn't know what to do or what to say to Rachel. She stood still.

"The return?" Rachel asked. With all she was going through, she was in another world. "I really want to get back home before the storm hits. And the boys haven't had dinner yet."

"Oh, right," Jessica led them to the register. She checked the SKU number on the tag, made sure that it matched that on the receipt, and circled the item. Jessica printed the return receipt and nervously gave it to Rachel. She handed Rachel a pen. Rachel signed the receipt, completed the section stating the reason for the return, and included her phone number. "The refund will go back on your Penney's charge." She handed Rachel a refund receipt which she had stapled to the original.

"It's so good to see you, Jessica. You've grown into a very beautiful young lady, and a smart one at that. A junior at Vanderbilt. Wow!"

"It's good to see you too, Rachel." She bent down to the boys' levels. "And it is nice to meet you Malcolm and Martin." She could barely take her eyes off Martin.

"Say goodbye, boys," Rachel instructed her sons.

"Goodbye," they said in unison.

Jessica stood at the register and waved to them as they walked to the door. Martin waved back with his left hand. Her eyes followed him to the door, and his mirrored hers.

Jessica was chomping at the bit. She was the only one in the department so, as much as she wanted to, there was no way she could leave early. She needed to talk to Patrick. Now! But, Jessica was covering for her coworker Eileen who had to study for an exam. It was only five-thirty and Jessica had to close. *How on earth will I make it through the next four hours?* Jessica retrieved Rachel's return receipt. She tore a piece of register tape, and wrote Rachel's number on it, then folded it and put it in her pocket. Jessica immediately called Patrick, but got no answer. *Where on earth could he be?*

About twenty minutes after Rachel and the boys left the store, the intensity of the rumbling thunder in the distance began to grow. *I hope they made it home in time.* Jessica thought.

With the store near empty, Jessica passed the time folding clothing and organizing the racks, to expedite closing. From a distance, she could see the rapidly falling rain through the glass doors. It was torrential.

She exhaled, releasing the built-up tension that permeated her entire body. *This is crazy. What are the odds of this happening? And now? I don't usually work on Thursdays.* Jessica switched shifts with Noelle so that she would be off on Saturday for Patrick and Veronica's wedding.

With every item on the racks and tables neatly organized, she sent the batch, and closed out her register. The manager counted her drawer, then looked through her purse before telling her good night.

Once Jessica hit the door, she ran to her car. She put her purse on the floor of the back seat of her car and fumbled with the keys. They fell on the floor in the center. When she bent over to pick them up, she saw a card between the passenger seat and the center console. With the precision of slant tip tweezers, Jessica pulled it out. It was an invitation to Patrick's Bachelor Party. "Phil must have dropped this when I picked him up from the airport last night," she said as if someone were there with her. Jessica picked it up and looked at the address. On the opposite side, she found directions. It was at Gary's house in Goodlettsville. Gary was one of the first people Patrick met when he moved to Nashville to get his doctorate.

A straight shot on I-65, Goodlettsville took Jessica past the exit for her off-campus apartment near Vanderbilt. The mixture of the rain from the evening storm and oil made the roads as slick as owl's shit. Although she had an eight-o'clock class in the morning, talking to Patrick was a priority. She drove carefully.

Jessica turned onto Gary's street and automatically knew which house was his, although she parked a half-block away. It was lit up. She walked down the street, then up the long driveway. Gary's house was far back from the street on a half-acre lot. Laughter, talking, and heavy bass from the music flooded the front porch. She rang the doorbell twice before she heard Gary announce, "The strippers have arrived," from the other side of the front door. The porch light glowed directly above Jessica's head, fully illuminating her. "Come on in, come on," Gary paused. "Jessica, what in the world are you doing here?"

"I really need to talk to Patrick. It's important!"

"Uh, you can't come in here, Jessie."

"Hey man, what's taking so long?" Phil staggered to the door and peeked his head over Gary's shoulder. "Jessie, what on earth are you doing here?"

"I have to talk to Patrick, immediately." She was antsy by now, anxiety had not just consumed her, it overwhelmed her. Phil stepped outside and pulled her aside. They walked towards the street.

"Jessica. This will have to wait. Patrick's in no condition—."

"Rachel was in the store this evening, with her two boys," she interrupted. "Phil, when I looked at the oldest, it was like," she paced. "No, I was looking at Patrick's Kindergarten picture, in 3D."

"Slow down!"

Jessica paused to catch her breath, they continued to walk towards her car. "Rachel came in tonight with two little boys. She had to make a return. I got her phone number off the return receipt." She pulled it from her pants pocket, then put it back in.

"Jessica, don't worry. That has got to be a coincidence," Phil replied. "There is no way. No way! Rachel broke up with Patrick six years ago."

"Phil. Martin is five years old and IsweartaGod he looks just like Patrick."

"Oh shit!" Phil exclaimed, the butts of his palms on his forehead.

"And he's left handed, too." Jessica turned and started back towards the house. "I've got to tell him. And I've got to tell him now." Phil stood directly in front of her.

"Jessie. We can't do this tonight. This is Patrick's bachelor party. I promise you that in the morning, when we're both sober, I will talk to Patrick and we'll sort this out."

Jessica opened her car door and pulled the phone number out of her pocket. She retrieved a pen from her purse, and wrote Rachel's number on the bachelor party invitation sitting on the passenger's seat. "Here is Rachel's number. Put it in a safe place. I just wrote it down for myself, so if you lose it tonight, call me."

Phil put the slip of paper with Rachel's number inside his wallet, then nodded.

"And, there's a lab that does paternity testing near the mall where I work. I'll call after my eight-o'clock class and make an appointment for Patrick. Do you think one-o'clock will work?"

Phil nodded again.

"I'm going to call you after my class to make sure that you handle this." Jessica started her car.

"Jessica," Phil began. "What I am about to say is very important. Do not, and I repeat do not, say anything to anyone, and I mean anyone. I will talk to Patrick. It is Patrick's responsibility to talk to Veronica."

She nodded.

"You are not to talk to Mom and Dad, Grandma Odessa, or anyone else about this. Do not tell a soul. Promise?"

"I promise."

"Now you be careful," he kissed her cheek. "Drive safely, be aware of your surroundings, and park as close as you can to your apartment." He closed her car door and she rolled the window down.

"I'll talk to you in the morning." Phil stepped to the curb and Jessica drove off.

❦

PATRICK FINALLY SHOWED signs of life around nine-thirty on Friday morning. Phil had been up most of the night, restless and pacing. Patrick held his head as he sat at his kitchen table. "Let me get you a cup of coffee," Phil said. "I've already had three."

Patrick rested his head on the table, his chin was perched atop his folded hands. He squinted, then opened his eyes. "Phil, what is Rachel's number doing on my table? And why is it in Jessica's handwriting?" Patrick stood up. "Are you playing some sort of cruel joke on me?" Patrick asked. "You were the one who told me I should never want to talk to her again."

Phil placed Patrick's cup of black coffee on the table. "Patrick, you need to have a seat." He placed his hand on Patrick's shoulder and gently pushed him down into the chair.

"What in the hell is going on?"

"Do you have any idea why Rachel kept calling you a few weeks ago?"

"No," Patrick stared at Phil. "When we got home after helping Jessie move and dinner at Veronica's, I listened to my voicemail. Rachel had left me another message. It just said to call her. I called her back and told her I never wanted to talk to her again as long as I live."

"I never thought I'd ever say this, but you need to call her."

"Why?"

"Jessie was working last night. Rachel came in with two boys. Jessie's all frantic because one is five and one is four, and she thinks that the oldest one resembles you. She called here twice already this morning."

"What? I haven't talked to or seen Rachel since she broke up with me back in 1991, and we always used protection," he paused. "Except."

Phil interrupted, "What are the chances? You know, that probably ain't your kid."

"How old did you say the boy was?"

"Jessie said he was five."

Patrick rested his elbows on the edge of the table, forehead in his palm. "Oh boy!"

"Let me give you a little bit of brotherly advice. Here is what I would do if I were you. Go on and do the paternity test, it will prove that you're not the father. Then Rachel will leave you alone, and you'll never have to be bothered with her again." Phil tried to reassure Patrick, but he was really trying to convince himself.

Patrick shook his head. "I can't believe this is happening. I have to call Veronica." He walked towards the phone on the kitchen wall and picked it up.

"No. I can't let you do that, Patrick." Phil took the phone from him. "It is highly unlikely that this is your child. You haven't seen Rachel in years! There is no use in getting Veronica, her family, and everyone who has flown in from across the country for the wedding upset. We have the rehearsal dinner tonight. The wedding is tomorrow afternoon."

"You're right."

"You have an appointment at Clinical Lab Testing at one-o'clock today. Call Rachel and let her know so she can have the kid tested."

Patrick picked up his mug of coffee and walked to his bedroom. Rachel's number was in his other hand. He set the mug on the nightstand, picked up the phone and dialed Rachel's number. On the fourth ring, he heard the voicemail recording. "Hi Rachel, this is Patrick. Look, I'm sorry I blew up at you when I called last time. I'll cut to the chase. I know you ran into Jessica at the mall last night and you have a son who was born the year after you broke our engagement. I'm having a paternity test done at Clinical Lab Testing near Cool Springs Mall today. I'm just letting you know so that you can have the boy tested too. If he is my son, I will contact you when it is confirmed and I promise to be a good father to him. If he isn't my

son, well, then there's no reason for us to ever speak again." He
hung up.

11

STRAIGHT, NO CHASER

J ason walked between the rows of boys on the practice field at Abbott Park. They were in lines of four and two arm lengths away from each other. It was an early autumn afternoon, and the stifling heat of the summer had departed for a more refreshing humidity level. "Now count," he said to the boys who were doing their stretching exercises. Every time they reached ten, they clapped in unison.

"Move in." The conditioning coach took over. "High knees," he instructed for the warm-up. Jason continued to walk between the rows of boys until he found an empty space.

"Where's Christopher?" Jason had a special interest in Christopher, one of the running backs. The players continued with kickouts, back pedals, and sprints then moved to a rotation of conditioning stations before Christopher showed up, running across the field. His mother, Zuri, was walking behind him.

"Christopher, you're twenty minutes late," Jason said, looking at his watch.

"I'm sorry. My Mom is having car trouble. We had to take the bus."

"Make sure you're on time for the game tomorrow." Jason patted him on the shoulder. "Go to the crabs conditioning station." Christopher waited in line. Two players were ahead of him. When it was his turn, he lay prone, then crawled on his hands and feet. His knees never touched the ground.

Jason smiled. Christopher was quite athletic, and in many ways reminded him of himself at age nine.

"I'm so sorry we were late," Zuri began. "I promise it won't happen again." She wore her mahogany hair in a sassy pixie haircut. The sides and back were tapered. It perfectly framed her sun-kissed caramel colored heart-shaped face. Her jeans hugged her hips, she had a tiny waist, and her smile was bright and sunny. "My car is in the shop, and we had to take the bus. I'm sorry. I'm Zuri Hicks, Christopher's mother." She extended her hand.

"Nice to meet you." He shook her hand, then glanced at her left. He saw no ring. "Jason McCoy. Excuse me a second." He blew his whistle, then yelled, "Water break," to the players.

"Jason McCoy. Say, didn't you play at Duncan?" Zuri asked. "I went to U of I in the eighties. I was a cheerleader."

"Then you probably know Rodney Harris? He was on the basketball team. He's my boy. We were on the same youth football team. We started when we were nine."

"I've met him before, but I didn't get to know him well. I quit the cheerleading team in the middle of football season in 87 when I found out I was pregnant with Christopher. I left Urbana at the end of that semester, then transferred to UIC after he was born."

"I hope you don't think I'm getting too personal, but, are you single?"

"I am."

"I have the utmost respect for single mothers. I was raised by one," he winked at her. "My Dad passed away when I was eleven."

"Sorry to hear that."

"Yeah, it was rough, but my brother and I made it through." Jason blew the whistle again. "Get into your teams," he told the players.

"Christopher's father lives out-of-state. He's in Racine. He tries to make every game."

"Oh."

"He's married now and has a four-year-old daughter."

"Oh." Jason repeated himself. "Well, I've got to get back to coaching, but it's been nice talking to you." Jason began to walk away, then turned.

"Hey, I can give you and Christopher a ride home. Since your car is in the shop. Do you know how long the repair will take?"

"I'm not sure. It will be several days. It's an older car, and they had to order parts."

"In that case, I'll pick Christopher up for the game in the morning. That is, unless you want to come too. Then I'll pick you and Christopher up in the morning."

"That's so nice of you. I really appreciate it."

Jason winked, then turned and ran towards the practice field.

❧

RODNEY OPENED THE DOOR. Brushstrokes of red and orange in the sky had been pushed out for cornflower blue and a rising waxing crescent moon. "You made it just in time. The game is about to start." Jason's hands were full. He had buffalo wings in his right hand and a six pack of Heineken in his left. Jason climbed the stairs behind Rodney, then set the food and beer on the breakfast bar. Rodney's black lab, Zack, was on his heels.

"I hate that corny song," Jason said of the Monday Night Football Intro. The New England Patriots were playing at Denver. Rodney washed his hands and handed Jason a plate, before fixing his own. Jason walked over to the couch in the open living area. Rodney sat in the recliner right next to him. Zack sat between them before lying down.

Scott Bentley kicks off for 70 yards, the announcer said.

"Who are you pulling for?" Rodney asked Jason.

"Denver. Hey, they have, Elway, Terrell Davis, and now our home boy Howard Griffith. They have the best offense in the NFL. How about you?"

"I'm a diehard Bears fan, so I don't have a dog in this fight," he ate a chicken wing. "So, how's coaching going?" Zack tilted his head upward and twitched his nose. Rodney tossed him a French fry which he caught in his mouth.

"Great. Really great. We're 4-1."

"Off to a great start."

"Really, really great." The smile plastered on Jason's face was huge.

"Okay. Something tells me that there's a little more than football involved. What's going on?"

"For the first time in a very long time in my life, things are just really going extremely well. I love my new job. My passion for football has returned. I have an appointment with the orthopedic surgeon you recommended. It's six months out, but I'm on his calendar. Oh, and I love working with the kids and interacting with the parents."

"Do you mean the parents, or one parent in particular, like in a female parent."

"I can't hide anything from you. Her name is Zuri Hicks. Her son Christopher is a running back. She was a cheerleader at Illinois just before you started playing."

"Un huh, I see!"

"Well, it's nothing yet. I mean, I just met her Friday, then drove her and Christopher to the game on Saturday. We just grabbed a bite to eat after the game."

"Is there more?"

"Not really, not yet at least. She just seems really nice. And she's cute, especially the way her nose wrinkles when she smiles."

"Dude, you're looking at her facial features that closely. You must really like her."

"Like I said, we just met. But as long as I'm living with my mother, there's not a lot I can do. At least until this divorce is final. As much as I want to have my own place, the last thing I'm going to do is buy any property right now."

"I hear you," Rodney turned his attention to the game. *Ball is snapped in the Denver end zone. Bledsoe throws. Pass intended for Glenn, intercepted by Mobley. He scores. Denver is up thirteen nothing.*

"And that should happen in another month."

"Wow. That soon!"

"Well, there are no assets to divide, so I expect things to go smoothly. And once the ink is dry, I'll start looking to buy my own place. I believe I'll be in Chicago for a while."

"I'm seriously considering putting this house on the market."

"Really?"

"Yes. I think I want, no, need something bigger."

"Oh!"

"I'll be right back." Rodney walked down the hall to his bedroom, and returned to show Jason just a small part of his something bigger.

"So, when do you leave for Sydney?"

"Day after tomorrow."

ॐ

VERONICA OPENED the vertical blinds on her patio door. It was a sunny early October afternoon, and her second day back to her first shift job at the hospital since returning from her honeymoon. She took the flowers she picked up at the grocery store out of the bags, trimmed the stems underneath running water, and arranged them in her favorite vase. Veronica stood back and looked at the vase in the center of her table. She moved it two inches to the left, then stood back again. *Perfect.* She took the candlesticks out of the drawer, and put a taper in each of them. They went perfectly beside the vase.

Veronica washed and cut up the vegetables for the salad while the meat sauce simmered. She beat an egg, and mixed it with ricotta cheese, parsley, and salt in a bowl, then set it aside. She rinsed, then dried, two crystal red wine glasses, opened a medium bodied Cabernet Sauvignon and poured it into a decanter. Her new Diana Krall CD, *Love Scenes* played in the background. A few days post-honeymoon, Veronica was really enjoying married life.

After layering the lasagna, then covering the top with foil and putting it into the oven, Veronica rinsed the dishes. She looked down at the marquise cut diamond with diamond wedding band on her finger and smiled, then loaded the pots and pans into the dishwasher. The chocolate covered strawberries were in the fridge.

She took her apron off, then decided to check the mail which had been held while they were on their honeymoon. She stopped and smiled at photos of her and Patrick on the mantel. Their engagement photo was on the right, a framed snapshot from their honeymoon in Jamaica to the left. A large empty space in the center was reserved for their wedding portrait.

The bundle of mail in her box was larger than expected. Veronica forgot that Patrick's mail was now being forwarded to this, his new home. She sat on the living room sofa and sorted through it and smiled as she looked at the cards she and Patrick received from guests who were unable to attend their wedding. She set those aside so that she and Patrick could open them together after dinner. In another pile, she placed the bills, household and personal, that arrived while they were away. Then she stopped. A letter addressed to Patrick from Clinical Lab Testing. She became worried. *Why on earth would Patrick need to have lab work done* she wondered.

She heard the click of a key going into the lock, then the tumbler turning. "Hey Baby," Patrick said as he started in the door. "How was your day?" Patrick's face wore a wide smile as he walked towards the sofa.

"Patrick. You have some mail here, and I'm a bit concerned." Diana Krall's "I Don't Know Enough About You," was playing.

"Oh," he reached down to hug her. "What is it?"

"You have a letter from Clinical Lab Testing. What's going on?"

Anxiety flooded him. His heart sank to his toes. Patrick took the envelope from Veronica and opened it. What he was feeling inside now showed on his face.

"Oh my God!" Patrick said as his eyes scanned the envelope's contents.

"What is it?" Veronica asked, a mixture of excitement and anxiety in her voice. "Are you sick?"

He closed his eyes and took her hand. "I'm fine Veronica. But I don't know how to say what I'm about to, have to tell you now."

"What is it?"

He put his face in his hands and fought back tears. A range of emotions surged through his body. It wasn't so much about the test results, but about the prospect of how hurtful this news would be to his new bride.

"Long before I ever met you, I was engaged to a woman named Rachel."

"Yes, you told me that before."

"And Veronica, I swear I have not seen or talked to Rachel in six years. She broke our engagement in 1991 and it was very painful for me. I didn't have a serious girlfriend for a long time," he managed a smile. "Then I met you three years ago."

"Patrick, what is going on?"

"Veronica. I swear I did not know. I swear to you before God that I did not even find out that she had a son the year after we split until the day before our wedding."

Veronica gasped, "Patrick, what exactly are you saying?"

"I have a son. His name is Martin Brown. He's five."

Veronica rose to her feet. Tears rolled down her face like a flash flood. Patrick walked over to comfort her. "Do not touch me!" she screamed. "Do not put your hands on me!"

"Veronica. I haven't been in contact with Rachel in six years. The last time I heard from her was about two weeks after our break up. She sent a package of everything I ever gave her via UPS, including the ring. There was a note too. She said that she had eloped. Then she started calling me in August, but we never talked. The weekend that Jessie moved into her apartment, I called Rachel and told her that I never want to talk to her again as long as I live and to never call me again."

Veronica looked puzzled.

"Then, I swear to God, two nights before our wedding Rachel came into Penney's with two little boys. Jessie said she was returning some pants. Jessie met them. She said that Martin looks just like me. Phil said Jessie even showed up at the bachelor party to tell me. I didn't know until the next day."

"Why didn't you tell me then?" Her tone was brazen.

"I didn't want to ruin our wedding. We'd been planning it for a year. All of the guests were in town."

Veronica wiped her tears. "So instead, you chose to ruin our marriage." She ran upstairs and slammed the bedroom door.

Patrick sat in the wing chair in the corner of the living room. He stared in disbelief at the letter. *How did this happen? And why is it happening now? How could Rachel do this? This is ruining my marriage.* Patrick looked up when he heard a thump at the top of the stairs. Veronica trudged down the stairs, suitcase in tow. Patrick ran over to her. "Veronica, baby! We can work through this." He tried to take the suitcase from her.

"Do not touch me and do not touch my suitcase!" she screamed, not caring if the next-door neighbors heard her.

"Wait," he said as she opened the door. "Where are you going?"

"To my parents, at least I know I'm loved there," she stepped outside. "Do not, and I mean do not call me either." She slammed the door. Patrick looked out the window while Veronica threw her suitcase in the back seat of her car and sped away.

He stood in the window and stared. A tear trickled down his face. He walked over to the sofa and began to reflect on how all of this happened. He began to feel bad for shutting Rachel out when she called him weeks ago, and also for following Phil's advice. Phil used to get Patrick in trouble often when they were growing up. Very often. He should have known better than to listen to him. Patrick didn't know what to do, or who to turn to. Who could he trust? Who would give him sage advice? Ahh-Grandma Odessa.

Patrick picked up the phone and dialed. She answered on the second ring. "Hi Grandma Odessa."

"What's the matter, honey?" she asked. "Because you surely don't sound like a happy groom who just got back from his honeymoon with his beautiful bride."

"I don't know where to start."

"Just tell me. You know that you can always come to me for anything."

"Grandma Odessa, everything's such a mess," Patrick began to cry. "Veronica just left, she packed her things and left me."

"What happened, baby?"

"This is so hard."

"Just give it to me straight."

"Remember Rachel?"

"Yes. I was quite fond of her, sad when she broke up with you. But I really like Veronica," she didn't want Patrick to think she favored his ex-fiancée over his new wife.

"Well, Rachel called me about a month ago. Long story short, I just learned today that I'm a father of a five-year-old son."

"My word!" Grandma Odessa replied. "I can understand why Veronica is upset. How do you feel about this, baby?"

He sighed. "Right now, I'm shocked by it all." Patrick was in such a state of shock, and deep in conversation that he didn't hear the oven timer go off.

"Wait. If the boy is five, then why are you just finding out?"

Patrick recounted the events that led up to the discovery, then the paternity tests to Grandma Odessa. "And I didn't tell Veronica about the test."

She interrupted, "Because you didn't know for sure if that child was yours, and you didn't want to upset her that close to the wedding."

"Exactly."

"I know that you don't see it now baby, but that child will be a blessing to both you and Veronica. The only bad thing in all of this, is that you have missed out on the first five years of your son's life. Patrick, that child is part of you, and if Veronica truly loves you, she will love your son too. You just need to give her time."

"You think so?"

"I know so," Grandma Odessa said. "And I'll keep our conversation to myself. You can share this with the family when and how you see fit."

"Thank you, Grandma Odessa."

"You know I love you, baby."

"I love you too, Grandma Odessa." Patrick hung up the phone, then heard the smoke detector near the kitchen go off, he went into the kitchen, turned off the oven, and opened the oven door. Smoke billowed throughout the kitchen and dining area. Veronica's lasagna was burned. The bottom of the oven was a big mess. He opened the sliding glass patio doors and the window to let the smoke escape. It was then that he saw the beautifully set table, the decanting wine, and the stunning floral arrangement. His heart sank.

§&

Veronica opened the front door of her parents' split level ranch. Her mom walked into the living room, and looked down at the landing by the front door. She wiped her hands on the apron. "Veronica?"

Her dad stood at the bottom of the stairs, shocked to see her with a suitcase. "Baby Girl, what's going on?"

Veronica's face was red and crusted over from crying. "I've left Patrick!" she announced, "and my marriage is over." She ran up the stairs into her childhood bedroom, closed and locked the door, climbed on her canopy bed, and buried her face in the pillows. *How can I ever trust Patrick again? How can I ever trust any of the Longs?*

In between her cries, she could hear her father knocking gently on the door and asking what happened.

JANAE SMOOTHED HER SKIRT. She had been waiting to see Ms. Paxton for twenty minutes now, fifteen past her appointment time. "Let me apologize for the wait," the receptionist said. "Ms. Paxton is on a global conference call. It went longer than expected."

Janae nodded.

"She should be available shortly."

Janae sat on the leather sofa and flipped through the current issue of *Forbes*. The colorful painting on the wall offered a nice counterbalance to the earth toned walls and fluorescent lighting. Instrumental jazz played faintly in the reception area. The phone buzzed, then the receptionist walked towards Janae.

"Ms. Mitchell, Ms. Paxton will see you now. Right this way," she directed.

Janae placed the magazine on the table, stood up, smoothed her skirt and jacket, then followed the receptionist down the short hallway.

Through the large window of Carol Paxton's office, the Sears Tower seemed within reach. Carol's desk was to the left. Two black leather banker's armchairs were right in front of it. Behind her desk there was a hutch which contained her computer and photos. Carol stood and shook Janae's hand. "Please have a seat, Ms. Mitchell. I'm Carol Paxton."

"Janae Mitchell. I really like the arrangement of the furniture in this office."

"Feng Shui. Never place your back to a door or a window. This way I get the best of both worlds. Please have a seat." Carol motioned to one of the banker's armchairs in front of her desk. "I see you're interested in the Financial Analyst Training Program."

"Yes, I am," Janae handed Carol her résumé.

Carol placed it on her desk, and scanned it.

"Typically, that program is for graduating college seniors. You've been out of college for six years."

"Although I majored in Finance, I just started working in banking a year ago. I want to open myself up to new opportunities."

"I see there is a gap in your resume. What did you do the first three years after college graduation?" Carol asked.

Janae's eyes scanned the room. She was nervous. She looked at Carol, then to the window, then diverted her eyes back toward Carol. On the right side of the computer, Janae noticed a picture of Rodney.

"Ms. Mitchell?"

"I'm sorry. Is that Rodney Harris?"

Janae walked to the side of Carol's desk to get a closer look.

"Yes. He's my son." Carol was a little taken aback that Janae seemed more interested in Rodney's photo, than the training program for which she applied.

"Who is that in the picture with him?"

Carol looked at her watch. "His fiancée." Although that wasn't true, Carol said that hoping to stop Janae's inquisition about her son. "Now Ms. Mitchell, can you explain this three-year gap in your résumé?"

"Oh. I'm sorry." She sat back in the chair. "I was working retail, and sometimes I helped with the books. I didn't think it was relevant to banking."

"It is better for you to include it, rather than leave gaps on your résumé." Carol put the résumé on her desk, and folded her arms. "Janae, let me give you a little advice. Don't ever sell yourself short. Don't be afraid of self-promotion. And expect the best."

Janae took notes. "Thank you so much Ms. Paxton. I really appreciate you taking time out for me."

"We'll be in touch regarding the training program." Carol stood and escorted Janae out of her office.

ﻬ

When Veronica woke up it was pitch dark in her room. She turned on the lamp and stretched. She sat still for a few moments in reflection. The only sound was the intense rumbling of her stomach. Just a few days back from her honeymoon after Nashville's wedding of the century, and now this. Veronica was hurting. She felt betrayed. She didn't know what she would do next. She climbed out of bed and opened the bedroom door. Nightlights in the hallway guided her to the kitchen. Her mother had left a plate on the stove for her. Veronica opened the fridge to get something to drink.

"Baby Girl!" Her father rose from the living room sofa. His walk, a slow limp, carried him into the kitchen. He hugged his daughter, then kissed her forehead. "It hurts me that you're hurtin'," he said. "And I don't know how to make it better, because I don't know what happened." He walked toward the breakfast bar and sat down on a stool. "I hate to see you cry."

"This is my biggest nightmare Daddy," she began to cry again. "Patrick is not the man I thought he was." She sat next to him.

"I don't understand, Baby Girl. You all had that beautiful wedding. You promised before God that you would be there for each other through better or worse. Then you had a two-week honeymoon in Jamaica. What happened?"

"Daddy, Patrick has a son." Her tears and cries distorted the words.

"Come again."

Veronica took a napkin, wiped her face, blew her nose. "I found out tonight that Patrick has a five-year-old son."

"Wait. And he didn't tell you this before? You haven't met the child? I don't understand."

"He just found out today," Veronica recounted the romantic dinner she planned for the two of them, the trip to the mailbox, the letter, and then the circumstances that Patrick told her led to the discovery. She also shared Patrick's reason for not telling her about the paternity test.

"I see," her father started. "But let's put this into perspective. First, have you ever known Patrick to lie to you?"

"No."

"Patrick is a respectable young man. If he had known about the son from the beginning, would you have still dated him?"

"Yes."

"Because I'm pretty sure if Patrick had known, he would be a big part of his son's life."

Veronica nodded.

"How would you feel if Patrick knew he had a son, but did not take care of him?"

"I wouldn't be married to him. I would have kicked him to the curb."

"How would you have felt if Patrick came to you the day before the wedding and told you that he just found out he might be a father?"

"I would have been as devastated as I am now. I probably would have called the wedding off."

"And your mother and I would have had to tell all the guests that the wedding was canceled," he rubbed his beard. "I have another question. If Patrick had known for sure that he was the father of the child, or let's say he found out a few weeks ago, or a month ago, do you think he would have been honest with you about that?"

"I do." She took a sip of her juice.

"Do you love him."

"I do. I'm mad as hell at him right now, but I do love him."

"Why are you mad, Baby Girl? He didn't have all the facts. Didn't he tell you as soon as he did?"

"Yes, but it just hurts."

"Why? When was the last time he saw the mother of the child?"

"Six years ago."

"And when did you meet Patrick?"

"Three years ago."

"And they have been the happiest three years of your adult life. Haven't they, Baby Girl?"

Veronica sat still, arms folded across her chest, lips pursed, and nodded.

"You've been much happier with Patrick than you ever were with Tyrique."

"It's just, It's just."

"What?"

"I wanted our first child to be special. The first child for both of us. The first grandchild on both sides of the family. Our realtor is taking us out this weekend. We plan to build our first house."

"And why wouldn't your first child, and every child after that be special for you, Patrick, and the rest of the family. I know that Patrick will have financial obligations now that weren't expected, but why should that prevent you from moving towards your dreams? This will work out, Baby Girl. You and Patrick are made for each other."

"You think so, Daddy."

"I know so," he smiled. "I know with absolute certainty that Patrick loves you. I can see it in the way he looks at you, and especially in the way he looked at you when he first laid eyes on you on your wedding day."

Veronica smiled.

"And remember. Although Patrick's son is a surprise. Consider him a pleasant surprise. Children are a blessing. He is part of the man you love, and you should love this child as well."

Veronica hugged her father.

"Now I want you to get some rest. Give Patrick a little time to himself. He has a lot to sort out. But take tomorrow off, go home to your husband, and work this out, if you know what I mean."

"Daddy!" Veronica gently hit her father's arm.

Veronica did as her father instructed. When she opened the front door to their apartment, Patrick was sitting in the wing chair in the corner. His eyes were swollen, and he looked like he hadn't had a moment's rest. The scent of burnt lasagna lingered in the air. He looked up, saw Veronica, and a smile infused his face. He ran over to the door and carried her suitcase inside. With the door barely closed, he pulled her into his arms and hugged her tightly. "The hours you have been away seem like an eternity," he kissed her forehead. "I'm so sorry, Veronica. I really want this to work."

"I do too." She kissed him back, then pushed the door closed. He took her hand and guided her to the sofa. "I'm sorry for storming out yesterday."

"I understand." He sat beside her. "I fully understand. So, what's next?"

"I've thought about it, and it's really important for you to be in Martin's life."

"No, it is important for us to be in Martin's life." She nodded in agreement.

"Have you talked to Rachel yet?"

"I haven't. You are my wife, and I want you to be involved with these decisions. Nothing impacts me solely any more. This has an impact on both of us. I know that I'll be responsible for child support."

Veronica nodded.

"And that will have an impact on our household budget."

"We'll make it work."

"And, if it's okay with you, I want weekend visitation. Just two weekends a month."

Veronica nodded. "I'm fine with that."

"And we should probably start an educational savings account for college. On a small level."

"We should definitely start a 529 account for Martin."

Patrick leaned in and kissed Veronica, then embraced her tightly as if he never wanted to let her go. He inhaled deeply. "I love you, Veronica. Thank you for understanding." He kissed her again. A quick peck on the lips. "Hey, you're late for work."

"I called off today," she stood and stretched. "I wanted to straighten things out between us."

"Then I won't go into the office today."

"Are you gonna call Rachel?"

"Not today. Today is just for you."

Veronica walked towards the stairs. "I'll be up in a minute." Patrick said. He went into the kitchen and put the decanter, a wine glass, and chocolate strawberries on a tray. When he reached their bedroom, Veronica had already closed the blinds and lit a candle. Patrick set the tray on the side of the dresser. He poured wine into the glass, then stood behind Veronica, his arms around her waist. Slowly, carefully, and attentively, he swept her long hair over her right shoulder and kissed the back of her neck. His fingertips grazed the small of her back, the small of her waist, the curve of her hip. He lifted the sides of her skirt to her hips. His fingertips lightly brushed the outside of her thighs. He reached around to the back and unbuttoned, then unzipped her skirt. It fell from her hips. He pulled her closer, then caressed her breast while his tongue gently danced inside and behind her ear. Patrick methodically released each button in her blouse and slid it from her shoulders. He inhaled deeply, and became drunk from her scent.

Veronica turned to face him, planting kisses on his lips, cheeks, neck. She felt his firm shoulders, chiseled chest, perfect biceps. She pulled his shirt out of his pants, and unfastened each button, giving Patrick a kiss in between. She pushed it off his shoulders and unbuttoned each sleeve. She grabbed the end of each sleeve and pulled the shirt off in one movement. Veronica massaged Patrick's chest, and held him close.

He sat on the bed, and pulled her to his lap. With Veronica's chin between his thumb and index finger, he kissed her lips, first lightly brushing her lips with his lips, then her tongue with his tongue. He paused, and reached for a strawberry on the dresser. He placed the tip of the strawberry between her teeth. She bit gently, just enough to crack the chocolate. Then she sucked the strawberry, before biting it, eyes closed, head arched back. And that is how they spent the entire day. With each other, in each other. Feasting on each other. And becoming intoxicated by each other.

12

MOOD FOR THOUGHT

R odney was captivated as the driver turned the corner onto
Thomasine's street in Haberfield. The purple canopy provided
by the Jacaranda tree-lined street was alluring. "Could you please
come back in an hour and a half?" he asked the driver as he stepped
out of the car onto a carpet of the lavender flowers shed by the tree on
the curb and lawn. He opened the gate and walked towards the courtyard. Near the door, red bell-shaped flowers on the Illawarra Flame
Tree had just begun to bloom. Rodney embraced the natural beauty of
Spring in Sydney.

He paused at the door. He had big plans. After the team's arrival,
then practice and meetings, Rodney had checked into the team hotel.
He requested the same suite he and Thomasine shared weeks ago
when she arrived in Sydney. The driver would return to take them to
dinner, then a stroll through the Royal Botanical Gardens, and a short
walk back to the hotel. Rodney smiled as he reached up to ring the bell,
a single red rose was in his left hand.

His pearly whites were on full display when he heard Sina
unlocking the deadbolt and turning the knob. "I'm back," he started.
And as the door cracked, his happy expression became one of deep
concern. Thomasine's hair was shot all over her head, and although
she was bundled up in her bathrobe, it was clear to Rodney that she

had lost at least ten pounds. "Oh, Sweetie Pie! You don't look well at all." Rodney hugged her, then closed the door and walked her over to the sofa. "Have you seen a doctor?"

"I haven't found one here yet."

"I'm taking you to see one today. I'll call our team doctor for a recommendation," he rubbed the back of her hand. "And I'm sure when I drop his name, they'll squeeze you right in."

Thomasine gulped, a dry heave. "Rodney, help me to the bathroom, quick." Rodney picked Sina up, carried her to the bathroom, helped her to her knees, lifted the toilet lid, and pulled her hair back. "Are you okay?" he asked, just before she started again.

Sina tore a piece of toilet paper and wiped her mouth. She flushed the toilet, then put the seat down. "I need you to leave the bathroom right now," she said as she began to sit on the toilet.

Rodney went into the bedroom, and took his hotel key out of his back pocket to get the number off the key folder. It fell to the floor. He bent down to pick it up, and saw the corner of a box sticking out from underneath the bed. He picked it up. At first, he was startled. Then it all made sense to him. Thomasine wasn't sick. She was pregnant. *I'm going to be a father*. He beamed with pride.

Rodney called the hotel and asked for the team doctor's room, then for a recommendation for the best OB/GYN in Sydney. As expected, by dropping his name and the team doctor's, he was able to get an appointment that afternoon.

He walked into the bathroom as Thomasine was spraying air freshener. "Sina, why didn't you tell me Sweetie Pie? I'm so excited." He held up the box for the pregnancy test. "I made an appointment for you at Taylor & Khan, the best OB/GYN practice in Sydney."

When Thomasine saw how happy Rodney was, she felt even worse. "Rodney, I'm not pregnant."

"But the, the test! I don't understand."

"A few weeks ago, I realized that I was late."

"Why didn't you tell me?"

"I didn't want to upset you."

"Upset me! Thomasine, if you weren't so sick right now, I'd be really mad at you."

"The test was negative." Thomasine put the toilet lid down and sat on it. "And I've been on my cycle now for ten days. I'm normally only on for five."

"Oh no! This doesn't sound good" Rodney touched Thomasine's cheek. "Then you really need to see an OB/GYN, stat!"

When the car returned to pick them up, Rodney was so attentive to Thomasine that he did not notice the man in the car parked across the street taking pictures of him, nor did he notice the car following them.

℘

RODNEY TAPPED his foot rapidly as he waited in the reception area. Thomasine returned after her examination with a quart sized cup of water. "We'll be here a while," she said as she took big gulps of the water. "The doctor wants to do an ultrasound." She sat beside Rodney.

"Ultrasound? I don't understand."

"The doctor said my uterus felt large. She wants to find out exactly what's going on, but first I have to have a full bladder."

Rodney put his arm around Sina, then kissed her forehead.

Click. The photographer had been watching from the vestibule all along. *Taylor & Khan OB/GYN* was etched on the glass entrance.

"I don't want you to worry about me, Sugar Cane." She drank more water. "You have your season opener tomorrow."

"Baby, I've got this, and I've got you." He kissed her again. *Click.* "I need you to know that I'm always here for you. You're not single anymore. You don't ever have to go through anything like this alone. Ever." She drank the rest of the water, then rested her head on Rodney's shoulder and fell asleep.

"Ms. Mintor," the nurse's voice woke Thomasine and Rodney. "It's time for your ultrasound."

"Rodney, will you come with me?"

"Absolutely," he helped Thomasine to her feet, then followed her and the nurse down the hall. Thomasine was directed to a small changing room. She was given a hospital shirt and pants with a draw-string to put on.

They went into the ultrasound room. Rodney sat in a chair on the side, Thomasine's purse in his lap. The technician helped Thomasine onto the table and instructed her to lie back. "This ultrasound gel is going to be a bit cold." She squeezed it onto Sina's abdomen, then moved the transducer around on the gel. When the technician was done recording the images, she wiped the gel from Sina's stomach and helped her to a seated position. Rodney helped her down from the table, and she returned to the changing room to dress.

"It looks like you have two fibroid tumors in your uterus." Dr. Taylor sat behind the desk in her office. Through the window behind her, stood the Australia Square Tower. "One the size of a plum and one the size of a navel orange."

Sina sighed. "My Mom had fibroids."

"We're not certain, but there may be a genetic connection. Truthfully, not much research has been done on the causes of uterine fibroids." She handed Thomasine a pamphlet. "But this is the reason for your irregular menstrual cycles, the cramping, and the heavy bleeding, and other symptoms." She pulled out her prescription pad. "I'm prescribing an anti-inflammatory, as well as an iron supplement. You have lost a lot of blood in the last ten days."

"Yes, I have."

"It is not life threatening, but you have a few options. You're young, and by the look of things, in love," she smiled at Rodney, "so I would only recommend hysterectomy in a life or death matter."

They both nodded.

"If you want to have children, myomectomy, where we remove the fibroids is the best option. But sometimes there are smaller fibroids that we don't see, and they grow after myomectomy, so I would recommend the surgery when you are ready to have children. Your uterus would need about three months to heal, and then when those three months are up, you should start trying to conceive."

Rodney looked at Thomasine and smiled.

"There is a new procedure called Uterine Artery Embolization, but honestly, we aren't yet certain how it impacts pregnancy, so I don't recommend it.

"Right now, watch and wait is probably your best option. In some instances, the fibroid will outgrow its blood supply and begin to degenerate. That can be pretty painful." Dr. Taylor handed the prescription to Thomasine. "And here's a menstrual calendar to keep track of the length of your periods, the amount of flow, and the number of days in your cycle."

"Thank you." Thomasine stood.

Rodney stood behind her, then shook Dr. Taylor's hand. "Thank you so much. I really appreciate you fitting us in today."

"No worries."

Rodney held the door, and followed Thomasine out. While they were checking out at the front desk, the photographer caught sight of them, and walked across the street, into position. Rodney held the door for Sina as they left the Taylor & Khan OB/GYN offices, then put his arm around her shoulder while the photographer clicked away across the street.

RODNEY UNLOCKED THE DOOR, and placed the bags from the pharmacy and the store on the dining table. He helped Thomasine take off her lightweight jacket, then hung it up in her closet. She sat at the table, while Rodney went into the kitchen, put some water in the kettle, and turned the fire on. He opened the refrigerator and poured a glass of water for Thomasine, then handed her the water, and opened her prescriptions. "I'm making a cup of ginger tea for you. Kimmy swears by ginger root. It is one of Mother Nature's best anti-inflammatories. That should help alleviate the cramps."

Thomasine took the iron pill. "Says here that I need to eat something with this other prescription."

"I'll heat some soup for you. I don't think you should eat anything heavy, just yet."

"Thank you, Rodney."

Rodney made Sina a cup of ginger tea, which she found soothing. "Kimmy was right," Thomasine said after drinking half of the tea, "My cramps aren't as painful." After the light dinner Rodney prepared for Thomasine, they retired to the bedroom like an old married couple. Thomasine got into bed first, while Rodney looked in the closet to see if he had left something he could sleep in. He climbed in beside her, then kissed her forehead.

"Do you think you'll be able to come to the game tomorrow? I reserved a courtside seat for you."

"I wouldn't miss it for the world."

"Let's grab a late lunch/early dinner before the game," Rodney said. "I have meetings and practice in the morning, but I'm in the same suite we were in the last time I was here."

"You are?" Thomasine smiled.

"Yes. I'll probably head out early in the morning, but I'll leave a key to the suite here for you. You can come by at any time. I should be back to the hotel around two."

"Sounds good."

"Say, have you been to the Royal Botanical Gardens?"

"I haven't."

"The weather should be nice tomorrow. How about a picnic lunch there? The fresh air will be good for you."

"I'm looking forward to it," Sina yawned, "I'm going to get some rest." She turned over on her right side and Rodney wrapped his arms around her waist, gently massaged her tummy, and they both fell fast asleep.

❧

RODNEY SPREAD the picnic rug on the grass near a palm tree at Flower Bed Lawn 39, and set the picnic hamper to the left side. The grass was a rich shade of Kelly green. He helped Sina to a seated position. "We have a nice view of the Harbour," he said. Sina turned to drink in the view. Rodney kneeled on the side of the hamper, then opened the lid toward Thomasine.

"We can see part of the Opera House from here," she pointed in the direction. Rodney handed Sina the plates and cutlery. She set them on her lap. Then he took the boxes with the lunch items, bread, cheeses, cold meats, diced fruit, and beverages out and set them on the blanket beside the hamper. Rodney looked into Sina's eyes and smiled as he pulled out a bouquet of flowers, "These are for you," and handed them to Thomasine, then closed the hamper and sat next to her. He placed the hamper between their outstretched legs with the clasp facing Thomasine, then placed their lunch items on top of the hamper.

"Thank you for everything, Rodney. I feel so much better since you got here." Thomasine put the flowers on the blanket beside her.

"I'm glad to hear that." He smiled. "I ordered food that isn't too heavy." He opened the boxes containing the picnic items.

"That's so thoughtful of you. I really do appreciate everything you've done for me," Sina fixed Rodney a plate and handed it to him, then fixed her own. Freesia, irises, sweet peas, and tulips were all in bloom. To their left was a pond. "And I'm excited about the game tonight. I've never sat courtside." She ate a spoonful of her diced fruit, then some of the roast chicken on a piece of bread. "I'm hungrier than I imagined."

"I'm glad you're enjoying it." As happy as he was to see Thomasine, and as much as he loved her, he was very nervous. "I can't believe I'm starting my seventh season." He poured the sparkling water into the champagne flutes, and handed one to Thomasine.

"That's a blessing," Sina took a sip of the water, then another bite of her cold meat and bread. "You've been able to see the world on someone else's dime, and have a career you thoroughly enjoy that pays you well enough to give back to the causes that mean the most to you."

"I have." He ate a few bites of his meal. "And during the off season I was able to get my executive MBA too and make plans for the future.

"I'm blessed. Really blessed," Rodney noticed that Sina's plate was almost empty. "I hope you have room for dessert."

"Dessert?"

"Yes. Open the picnic hamper."

Thomasine opened the hamper and felt around, then she lifted the lid and looked inside. "Rodney, what is this?" she pulled the box out of the hamper, opened it, and looked up to see Rodney down on one knee.

He took her hand, gazed lovingly into her eyes, and became full. "Thomasine, two months ago when I went to our ten-year reunion my only expectation was to catch up with old friends. Then I saw you, and you've exceeded my greatest expectations. When we danced that night, I knew then that you were the woman I wanted to spend the rest of my life with. These have been the happiest two months of my life, although right now work keeps us in different parts of the world. But baby, that is only temporary. I want to watch the sun set and rise in your eyes each day. I want to build a life with you, give life to and raise children with you, and grow old with you.

"I've already met with your parents and asked them for your hand in marriage. I also talked to Tommy. We already have their blessings. Mom, Kimmy, and my Dad have given us their blessings as well. Right now, I just need yours. Thomasine Mintor, my Sweetie Pie, will you marry me?" Rodney put the six-carat emerald cut diamond with side baguettes on Thomasine's finger.

"Yes," Thomasine said as she flooded Rodney's face with kisses through tear-filled eyes.

❧

"ARE you sure you don't want to celebrate your win with the team, Sugar Cane?" Thomasine asked Rodney. She sat in a chair near the corner window in the Full Harbour Junior Suite at the Four Seasons. "This is your first game of the season."

Rodney sat beside her and reached for the remote. "I'm on the road with those guys for five, maybe six more months," he turned the TV on. "I'd rather be here with you." He leaned over and kissed Thomasine's cheek. "We don't get to spend a lot of time together."

Thomasine looked down at her left hand, "Right now. But we'll spend the rest of our lives together." Thomasine gazed into his eyes. "I was so surprised when I reached into the basket. And I'm very happy."

There was a knock at the door. "Room service," they heard from the hallway.

Rodney walked across the suite to the door. "I didn't order anything," he opened the door. The waiter wheeled in a bucket with a bottle of chilled champagne, two flutes, and two chocolate covered strawberries. Rodney read the card. "Congratulations on your big night, but more importantly your big day. Wishing you and Thomasine many years of happiness. From Kenny." The waiter popped the cork, and poured the champagne into the flutes. Rodney tipped him, then placed the flutes and the plate with the strawberries on a tray and carried it across the room.

"Rodney, they're talking about the game on the news." He put the tray down on the table in front of Sina and sat on the arm of her chair. *What a season opener for the Windy City Gale Force's Rodney Harris, who scored a career high sixty points for the reigning world champions!* Sina looked up at him with pride in her smile. *And sports fans wonder if this was his motivation.* The video cut to a shot of Thomasine kissing Rodney just before tip-off. *If tonight's game is any indication, and if Harris and the team stay motivated, they may have another world championship run this season. In other sports news...*

Rodney leaned in and kissed Thomasine's lips. "I may need to bring you to all of my games."

"Where do you play next?"

"Melbourne this weekend."

"I think I can make that."

"Then Wellington and Auckland, then on to Cairns next weekend, and then back to Melbourne and Sydney."

"I'm not sure about the New Zealand games. I don't have a visa. But I can attend all the Australia games. In fact, I have to go to Yarrabah next week to conduct interviews. It's near Cairns. My research assistant Evonne will be with me."

"Then I'll get two courtside tickets for that game." Rodney raised his glass. "To us."

"Our past, our present, and our future." Thomasine lightly clinked her glass with Rodney's, then they each took a strawberry and fed it to their beloved. They kissed, then walked over to the corner window to enjoy the view.

❧

RACHEL SET the tray in front of Martin at McDonald's. Malcolm was visiting his friend Joey so that she and Martin could have time to themselves. "Ooh, French fries," Martin said, then picked one up and ate it. "You want some Mommy?"

"You're so sweet, honey, but no thanks." She looked at her son, eyes fixed, lips still. She didn't know how to tell him, but her time was running short. They were meeting Patrick by the dragon sculpture in Fannie Mae Dees Park in forty minutes. "Martin, I have something really important to tell you."

He looked up from his food. "Is it about Brothaman?"

"Well, kinda."

"Did he have to go back to the hospital?"

"No, son," Rachel exhaled again, as Martin ate another French fry. "This is very hard, Martin. And if you were older, it might be a bit easier for you to understand."

He looked up from his food. "What is it Mommy?"

"Before Mommy met Brothaman, she was very much in love with another man named Patrick."

"What happened Mommy? Did Patrick yell at you like Brothaman does sometimes?"

"No, Martin. Patrick never yelled at me."

"Then why didn't you marry Patrick?" That was a question Rachel was asking herself quite often lately.

"Things didn't work out between me and Patrick. It's something you'll understand better when you get older."

"How old Mommy?" Martin took a sip of his drink. "Everybody always tells me that I'll understand when I get older." He shrugged his shoulders. "But I'm not sure how old I have to be."

Rachel chuckled, then her tone became serious. "This is very hard for Mommy, Martin, but I just learned that Brothaman is not your father, Patrick is."

"Really, Mommy? I don't like Brothaman, but you always said that I have to respect him because he's my father." Martin took a bite of his cheeseburger. "Is Patrick Malcolm's father, too?"

"I'm afraid not, Martin. Brothaman is Malcolm's father."

"But you said that Patrick never yelled at you. Does that mean that he's nicer than Brothaman?"

"Patrick was very nice to me."

Rachel smiled at the pleasant memories.

"Then he'll be nice to me too?"

"Yes, he'll be nice to you, too."

"Will I ever meet Patrick?"

"Yes," Rachel replied. "Your father really wants to meet you. In fact, we're going to the park to meet him as soon as you finish eating."

Martin smiled broadly, then began shoveling food into his mouth.

"Slow down, Martin. He will wait for us if we aren't on time."

Martin took a sip of his drink then belched. "Excuse me, Mommy." He wiped his mouth with the napkin. "I'm finished. Can we go now?"

❧

PATRICK SAW the turquoise blue mosaic sculpture up ahead. He was a bit early. He heard the laughter of children as they ran underneath the arches, while others climbed atop the dragon's scales. The sculpture of a mother dragon and her baby emerging from the sea was the focal point of Fannie Mae Dees Park. The tail curved around the playground area and provided a long bench for parents and children to rest their feet.

Patrick heard the words of Grandma Odessa in his head. *Martin will be a blessing to you and Veronica. The only bad thing in all of this is that you missed the first five years of your son's life.* Patrick had the full support of Veronica, Grandma Odessa, and the rest of his family, in fact, Jessie had already left a few toys at the house for Martin, and his mother sent a box of Patrick's old toys and favorite childhood books. Patrick sat on the bench facing the park. He and Rachel talked earlier in the week, and it was important to both of them that he and Martin begin to bond, even if it had not yet been ordered by the court. Patrick sought legal advice before he talked to Rachel, and agreed to a Voluntary Acknowledgment of Parentage for Martin. In spite of his thorough preparation, Patrick felt a mixture of excitement and fear. *What if Martin doesn't like me? What if he doesn't like Veronica? How will I feel seeing Rachel for the first time in six years?*

In the distance, he saw a woman holding a child's hand. His heart began to race. When they got closer, he saw the little girl's ponytails. He leaned back and stretched his arms out on the back of the bench beside him. Behind him he heard a familiar voice say, "Martin, don't climb too high."

Patrick stood up and turned around. "Rachel?"

Rachel turned her head to the left and upward. "Patrick?" She stood up and turned around. The years hadn't been as kind to Rachel. She had put on some weight, and was beginning to gray at her temples. In comparison to the last time he saw her, Rachel looked haggard.

"I'll come around to your side." Patrick walked briskly around the end of the dragon's tail where Rachel met him. They sat beside each other. "So, are you still teaching?"

"I am. How about you? Are you still a school counselor?"

"No. I just finished a post-doc about a year ago. I'm teaching at Vanderbilt, clinical psychology, but I'm doing research this semester."

"Wonderful."

"And I just got married. Three weeks ago."

"Oh Patrick. I'm so sorry. I had no idea. I hope that this hasn't caused any problems for you and your wife."

Patrick looked at the ground, then turned to Rachel. "She loves me very much, and she's very supportive."

"Patrick, I'm sorry." Rachel looked at the ground. "I found out I was pregnant three months after I married David. I had no idea that Martin could be your son, especially since he favors me. I'm just sorry. And I'm really, really sorry about our breakup. You didn't deserve that."

As difficult as this conversation was, Patrick tried to find the silver lining. Besides, he wasn't there to rehash or relive his past with Rachel. "That was a very painful time for me, but what's most important is that we now have the truth. To be honest, I'm very upset that I've missed out on Martin's first—everything. But now we have to deal with the present and move forward from this point on." He sat up straight. "So, when do I get to meet my son?"

"How about now? Martin!" Rachel called.

Patrick's eyes watered when Martin ran in his direction. His left dominant slew-footed gait was a dead giveaway. "Yes, Mommy," Martin said when he reached Rachel.

Rachel placed him on her lap and turned to face Patrick. "There's someone I'd like for you to meet."

Martin smiled broadly, his upper lip curled. "Are you Patrick?" he asked. "I mean Daddy?"

Patrick folded his hands over the bridge of his nose and fought back tears. "Yes, Martin. I am your father." He smiled, then reached out to hug his son. A tear trickled from his left eye. He released the embrace, then looked into Martin's eyes and smiled.

"Hey, you look like me when you smile." Martin giggled. "Mommy said that you were very nice to her."

Patrick smiled more broadly. "Your Mom tells me that you're quite the soccer player. I played soccer when I was younger."

"Really?"

"Yes, me and my brother, Phil."

"I have a brother too. His name is Malcolm. He's four years old. He's at our friend Joey's house right now."

"I have a sister too. She's your Aunt Jessie."

"Really? I have another aunt. Cool! But T-Sina and T-Hope aren't my Mommy's real sisters. Mommy only has a real brother. My Uncle Hank. He's a doctor in Chicago."

"I remember your Uncle Hank," Patrick smiled again. "I also have a wife. I got married recently."

"Really? What's her name?"

"Miss Ronnie."

"Is Miss Ronnie nice?"

"Yes, she is. She's very nice. In fact, she can't wait to meet you."

"Really? When can I meet her?"

"How about next weekend. Maybe you can visit us next weekend," Patrick smiled. "Would you like that?"

"Yes. I would like that."

13

MERCY, MERCY, MERCY

The hour-long drive through the mountains and along the coast from Cairns to Yarrabah was picturesque. Although Yarrabah seemed like a direct shot from Cairns, the mountain range and an inlet of the Coral Sea made the journey require an indirect route. Originally the home of the Gunggandji people, Yarrabah later became a mission after European colonization. Now it was again an Aboriginal community in coastal Queensland. When Evonne and Thomasine parked in front of Cardinia's house, she was sitting on the verandah. It was a sunny Spring afternoon with a temperature of about seventy-five degrees Fahrenheit.

"G'day, I'm Evonne, I spoke to you last week."

"Well, Hello," Cardinia hugged Evonne. "And you must be Sina." Cardinia hugged Sina like a long-lost sister. "You're the first Black American woman I've ever met."

"Really? It's so nice to meet you."

"Please have a seat," Cardinia said. She motioned to the sofa on the verandah which sat atop a red and white area rug. "Can I fix you a cuppa?"

"Certainly," Evonne replied.

"I'll have one as well."

While Cardinia was inside making tea, Evonne set up the tape recorder and Thomasine pulled out consent forms and her interview protocol.

"Cardinia has already completed the consent forms," Evonne said as she plugged the microphone into the recorder. "I sent them to her and Pangari while you were out sick. They mailed them back. I have them right here." Evonne went into her briefcase and removed a folder, then passed the signed form to Thomasine.

"You rock, Evonne. You're always on top of things."

Cardinia returned with a tray of tea and set it on the table near the sofa. "I'm so glad that you have agreed to be interviewed. I'm Thomasine Mintor, a professor of anthropology and women's studies at Steeplechase University in the States. North Carolina specifically. I'm very interested in learning more about the impact of the Stolen Generations on the women who were removed as children, as well as the mothers who had their children taken from them by the Australian government."

"I think it's great that you're doing this. Maybe then the whole world will see what really happened to us."

"So, I'd like to begin the interview by asking you about your life before you were removed. Are you originally from Yarrabah? Evonne, are you recording?"

"Yes, I'm recording."

"I was the fourth of five children born to my Mum in a small rural area down in Victoria. My Dad was an Irish farmhand. He was here and there. Probably had children all over the state. The Australian government was removing Indigenous children with white fathers, and they made that determination merely by the color of our skin. Mum tried to hide us, but I got caught. I was only four years old. And I forever lost my connection to country."

"Could you please explain what you mean by connection to country?"

"I was disconnected from family, our land, and my people. It was my identity and my legacy. I was forced to assimilate into white culture and lost my native tongue."

And Thomasine and Cardinia continued the interview—a conversation about her harsh childhood in an institution, the poor education she received, how the curriculum of the school only prepared them to be domestics, and the physical and sexual abuse they suffered.

"The goal of the government was to rid the world of Blackfellas, through breeding us with white men. And this is our land. Our ancestors were here 50,000 years ago.

"But what is most painful is that I had a childhood without love. I never felt loved as a child. After I was kidnapped and taken from the people who knew me, I never got a hug, nor a word of encouragement.

"I was in my late teens when the government ended the removal policy. That's when I came to Yarrabah. Yarrabah was the closest thing to home for me. Now it is home."

"What is the one thing that would bring you the greatest sense of relief?"

"An apology. An apology from the Australian government."

&.

THOMASINE AND RODNEY held hands as they walked down the Esplanade Boardwalk to Wharf Street. They had dinner at a nearby restaurant with some of Rodney's teammates and their significant others. It was a beautiful spring evening. Thin wisps of cirrus clouds stood still in the cobalt blue sky. The Coral Sea swayed softly as they turned onto a brick sidewalk near the Hilton Cairns. Torchlights bordering the lawn cast a warm red glow on the palm trees stretched in a wide zig zag pattern. In the center, three rectangular tables for twelve were dressed with white linens, and set with fine china. Each chair wore a matching slipcover adorned with a red bow. A sign near the first table said *Congratulations Mr. & Mrs. Stephens.* Through the glass windows of the Hilton Blue Horizon Wedding Chapel, Rodney and Sina could see the happy couple sharing their first kiss as husband and wife.

Rodney put his arm around Thomasine's waist and pulled her closer. She looked up at him and smiled. "That will be us next Summer, Sugar Cane."

Rodney bent down and kissed Sina's lips. "What's stopping that from being us right now?"

Thomasine smiled. "I really do like the intimacy of the small wedding—the water and the backdrop of the mountains," she kissed him back, "but none of our family is here. If our parents, siblings, and close friends were here, I would be all in."

Rodney wrapped his arms around Sina and hugged her tightly, then took her hand. They continued towards the hotel. "How's your field research going?"

"It's going well, but it's emotionally draining. I interviewed Cardinia and Aunty Pangari today. Aunty Pangari talked about how her children were taken away from her. One of them was only three years old. All because of the color of their skin."

Rodney shook his head. "It's just atrocious." He held the door open for Sina.

"And the government has never apologized."

"I thought I read about an apology earlier this year."

"Most of the states have issued an apology, but the Australian government has yet to do so."

"And this happened for how long?" Rodney pushed the button for the elevator.

"For over seventy years. It just ended in 1970. It's really horrific. All of that culture lost forever."

"Sad. Just sad. But that's what also happened to the Africans who were enslaved in America, heck, all over the world."

"Very true." The doors opened, and they stepped inside the elevator. "The good news is that I was able to get all of my scheduled interviews done for this trip. So, from now until I return to Sydney, I'm all yours."

The executive spa suite overlooked Trinity Inlet, offering a water view sandwiched between a backdrop of palm trees and mountain ranges. Mellow, smooth jazz and R & B music played on the in-room Bose system. The blinds on the bathroom wall were open, revealing that a bath with floating flower petals had been drawn. Thomasine looked up at Rodney. "What did I do to deserve this?" She smiled.

"No, the question is, what did I do to deserve you?" He put the privacy lock on the door, then pulled Sina close and kissed her. He teased her bottom lip, first with light brushes from his lip, then gently with the edges of his teeth. Their bodies swayed in rhythm to Tony Toni Toné's "Slow Wine." Rodney kissed Thomasine again. A quick

peck on her lips. "Now we don't want that bath to get cold." He
guided Sina into the bathroom. "Let me help you with this." He
unzipped her dress, it fell to the floor and she stepped out of it.
Rodney unhooked her bra, then pulled her close and slid her panties
down her legs. She stepped out of them and into the deep garden tub.
"The water is still warm," she said. Red and yellow rose petals floated
at the surface. "Aren't you going to join me?"

Rodney bent down and kissed Sina, "In a second." Rodney was
back in a flash, wearing only his boxers, and armed with protection.
He lit the candles on the vanity, and on the corners of the tub, slid his
boxers down, and joined Sina in the tub. They took turns bathing each
other and basking in each other.

§♣

A SUBTLE BREEZE sent slight tingles down Thomasine's spine as she and
Rodney sat on the balcony of their suite in chaise loungers. The chatter
from the wedding party below was dwindling. Palm trees swayed ever
so gently. Thomasine took a sip of her Waverly Estates Chardonnay.
The cut of cheddar cheese on a table water cracker provided the perfect
balance to offset the buttery apple flavor and smoky finish of the
Chardonnay. Thomasine looked at Rodney and smiled.

"What?"

"I'm just sitting here reflecting on the last two months. You're
amazing, Rodney. Not like any guy I ever dated before."

"Baby, we aren't dating. We're getting married."

Thomasine looked down at the emerald cut diamond on her finger.
"Yes, we are, and I can't wait."

"So, have you thought about who will be your maid of honor?"

"This is going to be tough to figure out. My cousin Kelsey will be
my matron of honor. For maid, it's a toss-up between Rachel and
Hope. Strangely they are both going through divorces."

"That's right. Oh gosh. You know that Jason and I have been
friends for almost twenty years. Hmm."

"That could be sticky, especially for Hope. But then I don't know,"
she took another bite of her cheese and crackers. "I haven't talked to
Hope, dang, since the reunion."

"Jason stopped by a few days before I left for Sydney. He's doing quite well." Rodney sipped his wine. "He's working at a law firm downtown and coaching a youth football team."

"That's great," Thomasine smiled. "I'm sure Hope's busy with her new job in Virginia Beach." Thomasine topped another cracker with cheese. "I just hope they both find happiness, like we have."

"Yes."

"And I'm happy. Very happy," Thomasine continued. "After Kenneth, my ex-fiancé, I was single. For five years. I've really grown accustomed to being alone and doing everything for myself," Thomasine smiled. "Everything.

"A lot of little things I always took for granted. I watch my neighbors and how they divide household duties, like the trash. I've noticed that for many of the couples, the wife never touches the trash cart. It is the husband's responsibility to put it by the curb, and his responsibility to bring it back into the garage, even if he doesn't get home from work until after ten p.m. I know this sounds silly, but I look from my home office and think why is that trash cart still outside? I bring mine in as soon as Waste Management picks it up."

"It's not silly. I understand. So right now, I guess that means I'm signing up for trash patrol." They both laughed.

"It's so good to have you in my life, Sweetie Pie. I know that I can trust you. That we love each other, and most of all that we will inspire each other to achieve all of our dreams." Rodney ate a cracker. "Early in my career I met all sorts of women."

"Oh."

"You would be amazed at the groupies, the stuff some women do."

"I'm not sure I want to hear the details, Sugar Cane." Thomasine looked horrified.

"I've never been interested in chasing skirts. I always try to treat women the way I would want my Mom or Kimmy to be treated. And when I went to college, my Mom gave me the best advice ever. She told me to always make sure that whomever I deal with has as much to lose as I do."

"That's great advice," Thomasine yawned.

"Yeah, it's getting late. We should go to bed."

Thomasine stretched, then walked into the suite. Rodney came in behind her and secured the balcony doors. She slipped her robe off and draped it across the armchair, then slid underneath the covers. She reached for the remote control while Rodney climbed beside her.

Will the IBL's Rodney Harris be endorsing diapers and baby formula soon? According to the tabloid Global Query, Harris was seen leaving an OB/GYN office in Sydney with the same mystery woman who has been giving him game winning kisses courtside. We reached out to Harris' publicist but she was unavailable for comment.

"Goodness!" Thomasine sat straight up. "Thank God I talked to my Mom and she knows I went to the doctor due to the fibroids."

"This is the part of my world that I hate you have to be exposed to, Sweetie Pie," Rodney shook his head. "These people will stop at nothing."

"I don't believe this!"

"Don't let it worry you," Rodney said. "I'm just upset that a photographer was following us and I didn't even know."

"Don't beat yourself up," She hugged him. "You were focused on me and finding out why I was sick. And I appreciate it."

"Well, by this time tomorrow, no one will even remember this story on this silly show. They'll be trashing someone else."

VERONICA SAT near the window at the small diner. Photos of local celebrities, mostly musicians, lined the wall. Corrugated metal wainscoting covered the bottom half of the wall throughout the restaurant, while a mix of country and adult contemporary music played throughout. Every time the door opened and she heard the bell ring Veronica looked for someone who matched Patrick's description of Rachel. The waiter refilled her water. When she saw a woman with her hair pulled back into a bun, gray at the temples enter, she stood and waved to her. "Yoo hoo. Are you Rachel?"

Rachel sat across from Veronica, her back to the door. "I'm sorry I'm late."

"No problem. I've only been here a few minutes. Thank you for coming across town, close to my job, to meet with me on my lunch break."

Rachel looked like a bundle of nerves. She was even shaking.

"Rachel, relax. I know this is awkward, but let's call it for what it is. We are two women who loved the same man at different times. Your love for him produced a child, and that is who we're here to talk about."

"I just felt so horrible when Patrick told me that you had just gotten married."

"Would you have felt less horrible if we had been married, a year, two, four?"

Rachel shook her head no.

"Look Rachel, I don't harbor any ill feelings towards you." Veronica looked Rachel in the eye. "None at all. I asked to meet you because I know if I was sending my five-year-old child to spend the night with his father who I hadn't seen in years, I would want to get to know the woman who's sharing in the parenting duties."

"You're right, Veronica. I've just had a lot to happen to me lately. But like you said, we're here to talk about Martin."

The waiter took their orders, then Rachel provided a list of Martin's favorite foods and drinks, his morning and bedtime rituals. "This is going to be an adjustment for all of us," Rachel told Veronica. "Martin has never been apart from Malcolm, except at school."

Veronica nodded.

"But it is so important that he builds a relationship with his father. That is something I missed out on."

"I'm sorry to hear that."

"My father went missing in Vietnam when I was an infant." Rachel ended her discussion of her father right there.

The waiter brought their salads, and they laughed and chatted, not quite like old friends, but like two adult women who had a common interest, Martin's welfare.

∮

A SMALL CADRE of sports reporters gathered in the press room of the Cairns Arena Queensland. The Windy City Gale Force had just finished practice and team meetings. Kenny was already at the press table when Rodney arrived in his practice uniform, a towel hung around his neck.

"The Windy City Gale Force had an amazing season last year. What game philosophy do you attribute to your successful season?"

"I'll answer that," Kenny said. "Just good, old-fashioned team work. From looking at film, to making strategic modifications, to working together as a team but most of all, recognizing that everyone brings something to the court, and making sure that each contribution is valued. That is what has made us cohesive and helps us win games."

"And scoring as well," the reporter said. "Rodney, we're still fairly early in the season, but you've scored over forty points each game thus far this season. What is your secret?"

"Well, I'm coming off the World Championship high, and I have laser-sharp focus."

The reporter interrupted. "Does that beautiful mystery woman who kisses you courtside before each game have anything to do with it? Is she your girlfriend?"

"She's actually my fiancée," he beamed with pride. "Dr. Thomasine Mintor. She's a professor at Steeplechase University in anthropology and women's studies and in Australia on research leave." He said proudly. "We went to high school together, and reconnected last summer at our reunion."

"So, now, for the million-dollar question. Will we soon see your faces in ads and on commercials for diapers and baby formulas, as reported in the *Global Query*?"

Rodney chuckled. "Not in the next nine months. As you know, I'm a very private person, so questions about our relationship are off limits, but I did want to address the article in the *Global Query*."

"Speaking of articles," a reporter from the back of the room started. "Does your fiancée, uh, Dr. Mintor, always keep such big secrets? According to an article in the *International Observer*, which just hit the newsstands today, she kept a college pregnancy a secret, as well as the father of the child."

Rodney was speechless. He forced himself to exercise restraint. Veins began to bulge on his arms, on his head.

"This press conference is over!" Kenny pulled Rodney from the seat and ushered him to the locker room. "Man, I'm so sorry," he whispered to Rodney as they walked. "Neither you nor Thomasine deserve that."

Rodney paced back and forth in front of his locker, then let out a deep grunt. He was so angry he didn't know what to do. He opened his locker, grabbed his personal belongings, and headed towards the door. "I'll see you tonight at the game."

"Keep your head up man," Kenny called to him. "What is that you always tell me? Tomorrow they'll be talking about someone else."

RODNEY SAT in silence in the dark hotel suite. Although it was sunny and bright outside, he closed the curtains when he arrived. *Is it true? Why would Sina keep a secret like this from me when others knew? Why won't she open up to me? How well do I know this woman I'm about to marry?* A vast array of questions flooded his head.

Thomasine opened the door to the dark room. "Why would house-keeping close the curtains when I left them open?" she asked aloud as if someone else were in the room with her. She was wearing flip flops, a beach hat, a swimsuit, and cover up. She walked across the dark room and began to slide the curtains open.

She jumped, then put her hand on her heart. "You scared me Rodney. I didn't know you were back." She looked down at him with fearful concern at his facial expression. "Rodney, what's going on?"

"I thought we agreed to put everything on the table."

"We did."

"I did, but did you?"

"Rodney, what are you talking about?"

"Thomasine, is it true that you had a child while you were in college?"

Thomasine turned and faced the corner, her shoulders shrank. "Yes Rodney," she turned to face him, "it's true. I gave birth to a daughter the summer after my freshman year. I decided that a closed adoption was best for me and the baby."

Rodney stood and began pacing. "Why didn't you tell me about this? Can you even begin to imagine how I felt hearing about your child for the first time from a reporter?" his tone was biting.

"Thomasine, why weren't you honest with me? Why didn't you tell me?"

"Because I didn't tell anyone, Rodney. I wish that it never happened and I wanted it to go away."

"I can understand with you being a preacher's daughter, the judgment, I totally get that part. But that was so long ago. Why didn't you feel that you could tell me now?"

"Because I couldn't tell myself that it happened. Rodney, I was raped," she cried. "It was my first time. I wanted to forget that it ever happened, so I did nothing. I denied to myself that it happened, I denied to myself I was pregnant. Hell, my parents didn't even find out until they came to pick me up for the summer, and by then I was six months and a half months along." She paused. "When I gave birth to that baby girl on August 13, 1988, I couldn't even look at her."

"Oh my God, Sweetie Pie, I'm so sorry, I had no idea," Rodney walked towards her and held her.

"I never told anyone, not my cousin Kelsey, not Rachel and Hope, not even my own mother." The built-up tension and pain inside Thomasine erupted in tears, like a volcano. She sat on the bed.

"Oh baby, I'm so sorry." Rodney sat beside her and pulled her into his arms. Her head rested on his shoulder and her tears streamed down his back. "I can't believe you never talked about this to anyone, I think your mother would have been very supportive."

"Rodney, it wasn't my mother I was worried about. I didn't want to see an even bigger family tragedy. My brother carries a gun for a living. He would have killed Conrad, and would probably still be in prison today."

Rodney released Sina from his embrace and shook his head from side to side as tension and anger built up in him. "Conrad Thompson! That motherfucker is lucky I'm not in Chicago right now, Oooh is he lucky!"

"I saw him the day before the reunion and confronted him about it. Rodney, I didn't just say no. I begged him not to. He had some excuse about drugs and alcohol impairing his judgment, but I begged, I screamed, even cried. And when I saw him a few months back, I told him and myself that I forgave him, but what I'm feeling right now, I don't think I really meant it."

"That punk ass motherfucker." Rodney paced the floor. "I don't even understand how a man can get and keep an erection when a woman is crying and screaming." Rodney punched the air. Thomasine got up and walked behind him. "If I were in Chicago right now I'd find him and choke the fucking life out of him." Rodney grunted again, balled up his fist, and began to swing.

"No Rodney," Thomasine jumped up and grabbed his arm. "Baby, I know you're mad, but you can't put your fist through the wall. If you mess up your hands you won't be able to play tonight, or for the next several games. This rage and anger that you feel for what happened to me, take it out on the court. Go score sixty points tonight, get all the boards you can. Please, please, try to channel it into something positive."

Sina sat on the edge of the bed again. "That is what I tried to do with my master's thesis on acquaintance rape. I thought it would heal me, but it didn't. Some of the women I interviewed said that they were blamed for their rapes by relatives and some had boyfriends and husbands throw it in their faces during arguments."

"That's awful."

"That's why so many women are silent. It happens more often than we'll ever know."

"You, and all these other women need some justice. Thomasine, you need to seriously consider reporting it."

Thomasine shook her head. "I'm afraid it's much too late for that. I thought about it when I was writing my thesis, but the statute of limitations for reporting rape is only two years in the state of Illinois. This happened ten years ago."

Rodney pulled Sina close again, and hugged her tight. "Thomasine, I love you, and I feel just horrible. I feel sick inside." He looked into her eyes. "This has all come out because of your relationship with me, and you don't deserve this. I hate that you are having to relive this now, and I don't want you to have to relive it again. Ever. I really need to know, Sweetie Pie, you have to tell me what's off limits for us." He wiped her eye and kissed her cheek. "Because I don't ever want to be responsible for conjuring any unpleasant memories for you, or causing you any pain."

Rodney followed Thomasine's advice and scored a new career high of sixty-four points that night.

ॐ

MARTIN STOOD at the living room window, still waving, more than ten minutes after Rachel dropped him off at Patrick and Veronica's. It was his first overnight visit with his Dad and Miss Ronnie, and also the first time he and Malcolm had ever been apart aside from school. Rachel dropped him off after his Saturday morning soccer game.

Veronica and Patrick glanced at each other. Veronica went to the toy box in the corner of the room and picked out one of the items. "Martin, I heard that you like *Power Rangers*."

Veronica sat on the arm of the chair near the window, "Your Aunt Jessie got you a Rescue Megazord."

Martin turned and looked at it, "I don't want to play with it right now. But please tell her I said thank you." He remembered his mother telling him to always be polite and to always say please and thank you.

Veronica put the toy back into the toy box, then looked at Patrick and shrugged her shoulders. She kissed Patrick's forehead, "I'm gonna start dinner."

Martin walked over to Patrick. "Miss Ronnie is nice, but I just don't feel like playing right now. I hope I didn't hurt her feelings."

"No," Patrick said and reached out to take Martin's hand. "You didn't hurt her feelings at all. Your Mommy told me that you really like fish sticks. Miss Ronnie is making you homemade fish sticks."

"Homemade fish sticks? I didn't know there was such a thing."

"Yes. Miss Ronnie is a good cook. She can cook anything."

She overheard them from the kitchen, and smiled.

"Let me show you around," Patrick said. "Here is the downstairs bathroom. And you have a bedroom and bathroom upstairs too."

"A bedroom just for me?" Martin asked.

"Yes, it's just for you. Would you like to see it?"

"Yes." Martin turned towards the stairs, and began to climb. He tried to take two steps at a time, but his little legs wouldn't let him. He reached the landing.

"Keep straight, son," Patrick's heart warmed when he said that word. "Your bedroom is straight ahead when you get upstairs." Patrick followed.

"Oooh, Power Rangers covers," Martin said with excitement about the comforter set.

"Yes. Miss Ronnie and I thought you'd like it."

"I do!" Martin smiled. "I really do!" Martin walked across the room. "What is this door for? Is it the closet?" Martin asked.

"No, it is your own bathroom."

"My own bathroom?"

"Yes son."

Martin hugged Patrick's leg. "At home I have to share a bathroom and a bedroom with Malcolm. We have bunk beds. I sleep on top. But Mommy has a bathroom in her bedroom just like I do here."

"Do you like it, son?"

"Yes, I love it." Martin squealed with delight. "Thank you, Daddy."

Patrick's eyes watered just a little bit at hearing Martin address him as Daddy.

"You're welcome son," Patrick said and gently patted Martin on the top of his head. "Hey, how about we go back downstairs. We can watch TV, or play checkers. Have you ever played checkers?"

"No, Daddy."

"Then I'll teach you. Let's go back into the living room."

Martin started at the top of the stairs. "Be careful, Martin. Hold on to the railing."

Martin took very careful steps down the stairs. Patrick set up a card table in the living room, and placed the checkerboard on top. Martin walked around and stopped at the end table near the window. "Daddy, is this Miss Ronnie?"

"Yes. That's Miss Ronnie's college graduation picture."

"She's very pretty on this picture.

"That's you and Miss Ronnie in Ja, Ja," Martin said when he reached the fireplace.

"That's from our honeymoon, in Jamaica."

"Jamaica," Martin repeated. "And there you are again with Miss Ronnie. Are you in a garden?"

"Yes," Patrick replied. "We're at Cheekwood Botanical Garden.

Miss Ronnie and I will have to take you there in the Spring when all of the flowers are blooming."

"I would really like that."

Martin walked over to the other end table near the opposite end of the fireplace. "Hey, wait a minute. This picture looks like me."

"It sure does. But, it's my kindergarten picture. I was five years-old when this picture was taken."

"That's why you're my Daddy. Because we look alike." Martin turned his palms up and tilted his head to the side when he said the word alike. "So, I guess that means I'm going to look just like you when I get older."

"You probably will." Patrick smiled back. "Have a seat, Martin."

Martin climbed into the chair across from Patrick and looked in puzzlement at the board. "Now do you like red or black?"

"Red." Patrick gave Martin the red checkers.

"Starting with the row closest to you, put a red checker on each black square."

"Okay, Daddy." Martin followed Patrick's instructions. "Daddy I don't have enough for the next row."

"That's okay, son. You leave these two rows between the black checkers and the red checkers empty. That's how we play. Let me show you." Patrick showed Martin how to move the pieces diagonally, and then how to jump. After a practice game, Veronica brought Patrick a glass of tea and Martin a cup of juice.

"Thank you, Miss Ronnie," Martin said, then he picked up his juice and took a sip. "Grape juice is my favorite."

"You're welcome, Martin." She smiled back at him. "Dinner will be ready soon."

Martin was a quick learner, and although Patrick let him win the first game without instruction, he won the next game on his own.

"Dinner's ready," Veronica called from the kitchen.

"Can we play again after dinner?" Martin pushed his chair back from the table.

"I thought you, Miss Ronnie, and I would watch a movie after dinner?"

"Oh, that will be fun. Will we have popcorn?"

"Yes, son," Patrick's heart warmed every time he used that three-letter word, son. He smiled, and Martin smiled back as a mirror reflection.

"I have to wash my hands before dinner," Martin said.

"Do you remember where the downstairs bathroom is?"

"Yes, right there," he pointed.

Martin washed his hands, and Patrick followed. They walked into the dining area together.

"This is your seat, Martin," Veronica said. Patrick sat at the head of the table, and Veronica sat beside Patrick, directly across from Martin.

"These fish sticks are really big, Miss Ronnie." Martin said when he looked down at his plate. "But we have to say grace first."

"Would you like to do that?" Veronica asked.

"Yes. Me, Mommy, and Malcolm hold hands when we say grace. We bow our heads too." Martin instructed.

"We can do that, son."

"Okay, is everyone ready," Martin asked, with his head bowed. "You have to close your eyes, too, that's how God knows you really mean it." He closed his eyes tight. "God is great, God is good, and we thank him for this food, Amen!"

"Amen," Patrick and Veronica said in unison.

"And you made me broccoli too," Martin said, "I really like broccoli. Mommy says I should always have something green on my dinner plate."

"That's right," Veronica said. "It is always important to eat a well-balanced diet."

Martin took his fork, and cut one of his fish sticks. He lifted the fork to his mouth and tasted. "Miss Ronnie. Daddy was right. You are a good cook. These are the best fish sticks I've ever had." Martin ate another bite, then chewed. "Please don't tell Mommy, but they taste much better than the ones she gets out of the blue box she keeps in the freezer."

Veronica chuckled.

"I'm really happy," Martin continued. "I'm really happy that you are my Daddy, and you are my Miss Ronnie Mom."

"I'm glad to hear that, son."

"Yeah," Veronica paused from eating. "Me too."

"I never liked Brothaman. He's Malcolm's father."

"Oh," Patrick replied.

"No, he's mean to Mommy. He yells at Mommy, he pushed her down, made her fall, and made her cry. Mommy cries all of the time now when she goes into her room by herself. Almost every night."

Patrick put his fork down and stopped eating.

"And Brothaman used to live with Uncle Hank, but Uncle Hank made him move out. I don't know why. But Brothaman have, has." Martin corrected himself. "Brothaman has an apartment now where he lives at. Me and Malcolm spent the night there once."

"Really?"

"That was a long time ago. It was cold outside." He paused to think. "It was right after Christmas when Mommy took us to Chicago. Mommy won't let us go back, I don't want to, and since you're my Daddy, I don't have to because Brothaman is mean. He don't cook breakfast for me and Malcolm. Mommy cooks us bacon and eggs every day, oh and toast with butter, too. And she makes us pancakes that look like Mickey Mouse ears and sausage every Saturday. But Brothaman don't cook us any breakfast. So, me and Malcolm try to cook ourselves. We watch Mommy do it all the time. But it caught fire."

"Oh my!" Veronica's heart leapt, she put both of her hands on the table.

"And I think that's why Brothaman pushed Mommy down. She was mad at him about the fire. She came to pick us up and she had to put out the fire.

"And then Brothaman had this lady over there. Her name is Shaniqua, and she have, has five different colors in her hair." Martin held up five fingers.

Patrick looked at Martin with his head tilted to the side.

"And Shaniqua is thirsty all of the time. She has this long straw. It's made out of glass. And when she drinks from her straw it sounds just like when the curtain gets caught in Mommy's vacuum cleaner."

A mixture of fear and panic was painted on Veronica's face.

"Martin, I need to ask you a question."

"Yes, Daddy." He looked up at Patrick.

"Do you know the difference between the truth and a story—make believe?"

"Yes, I do. The truth is something that happened for real. A story is something you make up."

"So, everything you just told me is a story, right?"

"No, Daddy. I'm telling the truth. Shaniqua has five different colors in her hair." Martin held up five fingers again. "Five. I counted them. Twice."

A tear fell from Veronica's eye.

Martin looked across the table. "Don't cry, Miss Ronnie. It makes me very sad to hear my Mommy cry." Martin ate some of his broccoli.

"But my Mommy says she'll be okay. She doesn't want to be married to Brothaman anymore. I heard her tell T-Sina that she was getting a, something that starts with a duh sound."

"Divorce?"

"Yes, that was before T-Sina left the country. She is in Aus, Aus, it's another country, I can't pronounce it. It is a big word."

"Austria?" Patrick asked.

"I think so. They have kangaroos there, and T-Sina sent me and Malcolm boomerangs."

"Oh, Australia."

"That's it," Martin smiled and drank a sip of his juice. "Australia."

"Miss Ronnie, are you a teacher like my Mommy?"

"No baby, I'm a nurse, a nurse practitioner."

"Do you work in a hospital?"

"I do."

"Brothaman was in the hospital. Mommy said he was in a coma. We would call him every Saturday after the soccer game and Mommy said that he could hear us but he couldn't talk back to us. I don't understand that. Mommy said it was almost like he was asleep. But, Mommy said that maybe hearing our voices might make him get better. I heard Mommy talking to Uncle Hank about somebody beating him up.

"But Uncle Hank worked at the hospital where Brothaman was in the coma. He just graduated from medical school. I went to the graduation. So, I guess Uncle Hank helped Brothaman get well," Martin wiped his mouth with the napkin. "Daddy, where do you work?"

"I'm a teacher too."

"Like Mommy?"

"Kind of, but I teach older students. College students."

"Like T-Sina. She teaches in North Carolina and Mommy took us to her house when it was warm outside and we went to the beach. She has a dog named Sparky. I like to play with Sparky." He put his fork down on the table. "Mommy said that when I finish high school, I'll go to college. And that I have to make good grades in school so that I can go to college. So, I always do my homework, and pay attention to the teacher."

"That's good son. That is exactly what you should do."

"I'm all done. Miss Ronnie, the fish sticks and broccoli and French fries really tasted good. Thank you for making me fish sticks."

Veronica stood up from the table to clear the plates. "You're welcome, Martin," she bent down and kissed his forehead.

"Can we please go watch the movie now?" Martin pushed his chair in, and he and Patrick walked towards the living room. Martin turned his head. "Miss Ronnie, aren't you coming too?"

"I'll join you soon. I want to wash the dishes first."

"Okay. I can help you like I help Mommy. Mommy says that many hands make work easier."

She smiled. "That's okay, Martin. You and Daddy can go start the movie. I'll be in there soon."

Hearing Martin describe Shaniqua smoking crack stirred a mixture of anger, fear, and sadness inside her. Veronica put the stopper in the kitchen sink and turned on the water to cover the sound of her sobs. Dealing with a crack addict was hard for an adult, something with which she unfortunately knew about firsthand. Veronica was twenty-three, out of college, and an independent woman, but Martin was only five. A baby!

IT STARTED AS A MID-SUMMER ROMANCE, but ended in horror. Veronica, a recent college graduate, had just moved to the East Coast to work as a registered nurse. She was new in town and attended a cultural festival with a friend of her cousin who was showing her around. "Girl, he's looking at you," Monica said. "And he is fine." She said the last four words slowly, with emphasis.

Tyrique wore a tight-fitting T-shirt and jeans with ripped knees. His skin was a soft tan, and it complemented his neatly groomed mustache and beard. His hazel eyes were inviting, and his close-cut hair wore waves. "Hi," his voice was deep, mellow, and warm. "I'm Tyrique, and you are?"

"Veronica."

"Well," he rubbed his chin and winked. "I saw you standing over here with your girl, and thought I'd come and talk to you. I'd like to get to know you better."

Tyrique, an account executive, swept Veronica off her feet in ways a recent college graduate had never imagined, let alone experienced. She happily took him home to Nashville during a late fall visit. Everything went smoothly at first, then Tyrique became irritable. His pupils were often dilated. When Veronica held his hand, his fingertips were rough, as if they had been burned. He became restless, lost his focus, and began to lose his temper over the most mundane things. This started happening about a year after they first met.

Although she knew the signs, at first Veronica did not want to believe that Tyrique had a problem, especially since she had never seen him with drugs or drug paraphernalia. She believed him when he told her that his change of behavior was due to work-related stress and the pressures of having a new boss.

It wasn't much later that whenever Tyrique visited, money was missing from Veronica's purse. First it was small amounts, like her lunch money, then one week it was the money she put aside in an envelope to pay her electric bill. Veronica confronted Tyrique about it, but he convinced her that she misplaced it. Sometimes the money would miraculously return, but often it didn't.

Then just before Christmas, Veronica invited Tyrique over for a special holiday dinner. She had to work on the holiday, so she wanted them to celebrate early. She had roasted a turkey breast, and put garlic slices and rosemary underneath the skin. She also sautéed spinach, and mashed sweet potatoes. She even made homemade rolls. In the corner of the living room in her tiny, one-bedroom apartment, Veronica had a tabletop Christmas tree with a color wheel. The table was set, soft music played throughout the apartment, and Tyrique arrived —on edge.

Every little thing seemed to bother him, and especially the choice of food Veronica prepared. When she took the rolls out of the oven, he threw them across the room. He called her all sorts of names, and she could not understand what she did to provoke such anger from him. It didn't make sense. Then his rage intensified, like a power surge.

"Tyrique, I think you need to leave now," Veronica had become very afraid. Tyrique was wired. His pupils were wide, and when he reached out and grabbed Veronica's collar, she felt the coarse, rough, burnt tips of his fingers. He shook her hard, then pushed her into the wall. She was terrified.

"Tyrique, you need to leave now," she said again, this time screaming, "Or I will call the police." Veronica reached for the cordless phone at the end of her kitchen counter. He snatched it out of her hand, threw it against the wall, and Veronica screamed before his fists pummeled her into that same wall. That was the last thing she remembered before she woke up in the hospital where she worked with her next-door neighbor, who called police, by her side. As soon as the physical bruises healed, Veronica packed her things and moved home to Nashville, then decided to pursue her graduate degree and become a Family Nurse Practitioner.

"I HAD A GREAT DAY, DADDY," Martin told Patrick as he tucked him in. "Would you please read me a story?"

"Sure," Patrick said. He picked up Ezra Jack Keats' *Snowy Day*. It was among the childhood books his Mom sent him when he told her about Martin. "This book was my favorite when I was your age."

"Where's Miss Ronnie?" Martin asked. "I want her to read part of the story to me too."

"She's getting ready for bed, but I'll go get her." Patrick set the book on the nightstand. "I'll be right back."

Patrick walked down the hallway to the master bedroom of the townhome apartment. "Martin wants you to join us." Veronica tied the belt on her robe, and followed Patrick into Martin's bedroom. They sat on the side of his bed and took turns reading Patrick's favorite childhood story to Martin.

"Now let me tuck you in," Patrick said.

"But Daddy, I have to say my prayers first."

"OK." Martin climbed out of bed, knelt beside it, and bowed his head. Patrick and Veronica knelt on either side of him.

"Remember to close your eyes so that God knows that you really mean it."

They did.

"Now I lay me down to sleep, I pray the Lord my soul to keep, If I should die before I wake, I pray the Lord my soul to take. God bless Mommy, Malcolm, Daddy, and my Miss Ronnie Mom. Also, please make Mommy happy and make Brothaman stop making her cry. Amen."

Martin stood, and climbed back into bed. Patrick tucked him in, then kissed his cheek. Veronica did the same. Veronica turned on the night light, as well as the light in the bathroom, before turning the light out in Martin's room.

"Goodnight Daddy and Miss Ronnie Mom."

"Goodnight, Martin," they both said, not quite in unison.

Veronica climbed into bed while Patrick changed into his pajamas. "Martin is such a sweet boy."

"Yes, he is," Patrick buttoned his pajama top, then climbed into bed. "He really warms my heart."

"He has your warm spirit." Veronica said, and pecked Patrick on the lips.

"He does, but I can't believe what he told us at dinner."

"I can't believe that Rachel married a man named Brothaman."

Patrick shook his head. "Did I actually hear my five-year-old son describe someone smoking crack?"

"Yes, you did, Patrick. My heart goes out to Rachel, and I've only met her once. You know what I went through with Tyrique. But, I am glad that she seems to be getting out of that situation. It's just too bad that she will forever be tied to him through Malcolm, and I'm so upset that Martin has witnessed so much sadness at such a young age. It broke my heart to hear him talk about his mother crying. No child should have to deal with that."

"I agree."

"You know you're gonna to have to talk to Rachel."

"I was thinking that we should talk to her together."

"No Patrick. We had lunch one time, and as a woman, I would not take a conversation like that too kindly from another woman I barely knew, who is now married to my ex."

"You're probably right. I'll talk to her when I take Martin home tomorrow afternoon."

14

STREAMS OF CONSCIOUSNESS

"**D**addy, I had a really good time with you and my Miss Ronnie Mom," Martin said when Patrick parked beside the silver maple tree in front of Rachel's apartment. Its leaves had begun to turn red and a few had fallen to the ground. "I wish you were Malcolm's daddy too, so that he could come next time and eat Miss Ronnie's homemade fish sticks and play checkers."

"I'm glad you had a good time, Son," Patrick opened the door for Martin, then went to the trunk and got Martin's overnight bag. Martin ran ahead of Patrick and knocked on the front door.

"Mommy, Mommy!" Martin said with excitement in his voice when Rachel opened the front door.

"Did you have a good time?" Rachel asked.

"Yes. Daddy taught me how to play checkers and we watched a movie and Miss Ronnie made me fish sticks for dinner and pancakes for breakfast this morning and they read me a story." Martin was so happy that once he started telling Rachel about his visit, he couldn't stop. "Where is Malcolm?"

"Malcolm's in the bedroom." Martin ran down the hallway to see his younger brother.

"Checkers. How nice!"

"The little guy beat me in two games," Patrick smiled. "Well I let him win the first, but he beat me fair and square in the second." Patrick stood at the front door.

"Come on in and have a seat."

Rachel's living room was now presentable. She had stayed on top of keeping that area of her apartment clutter-free. "I need to get the boys a checkerboard."

Patrick handed Martin's bag to Rachel, then sat on the sofa. "I can drop one by later this week. I'll call first."

"Thanks, I appreciate it," Rachel set Martin's bag in the corner of the room.

"Rachel, there's something I really need to talk to you about. Something Martin told Veronica and me yesterday over dinner."

Rachel looked at Patrick. Her eyes squinted slightly, left brow ruffled. She tilted her head to the side and turned it slightly in his direction. "Oh!"

"Yes. This is pretty serious. I wouldn't want the boys to overhear this."

"I'll let them play outside on the patio." Rachel walked to the toy box and retrieved their soccer ball. She took Martin and Malcolm to their fenced in patio and told them to practice their drills, then closed the glass patio doors. From across the room they could both keep an eye on the boys.

"Just what did Martin say to you?" She sat on the sofa.

"He talked about your husband. Rachel, has he used drugs in front of the boys? Because I swear, what Martin described to me was someone smoking crack. Someone named Shaniqua. This is going to sound crazy, but Martin insists that she has five different colors in her hair. I know children can have very active imaginations."

Rachel's face fell to the floor. She got a sick feeling in the pit of her stomach, and anguish pervaded her face.

"There was one time, at the beginning of this year, that I let the boys stay overnight with their, I mean Malcolm's father, and when I got there I had to put out a fire. They were trying to cook their own breakfast. Patrick, they were only three and four years old. When I confronted him about it, he pushed me down in the hallway and I know that Martin saw it. I couldn't believe it. I had to fight the tears. And since that day I've never let them stay with him again." Rachel shook her head. "But I never knew about any drug use in front of the boys. I'm shocked. My ex-husband hid his addiction from me for years. I only found out about it after he moved back to Chicago for a job. He was living with Hank in Aunt Mary's house. One evening Hank came home from a rotation and the house was full of people smoking weed and doing lines of coke."

"Martin said that Hank put Brothaman out but he didn't know why. Wow!"

"I'm shocked. I'm really shocked."

"Martin also said that you've been very sad lately."

"Patrick, so much has happened to me in the last few months. The first time I called you, I got two phone calls. The first was about my soon-to-be-ex-husband. He was in the hospital. Someone beat his hands up with a hammer. Hopefully, there's no permanent damage because he's an artist and needs his hands to work. A few weeks after that, Hank called and said that Brothaman was in a coma and had been beaten within two inches of his life." Rachel began to cry. "Patrick, Sina's brother, Tommy said that a lady found him in the alley when she went to take her garbage out. Tommy was the officer who responded to the call." Rachel shook her head. "Patrick, an alley!"

"Oh my! So, what Martin said about the coma was true."

"Yes. Miraculously he is now out of the hospital now, but he was in a coma for a few weeks."

"And then I got another call. It was about my father."

"Your father was missing in Vietnam since you were a baby."

"And my mother received word that he had been found in Australia, and had recently passed away.

"Twenty-seven years he lived there. And then I got this." She got up from the sofa, went to her bedroom, and returned quickly. She handed the Air Mail envelope to Patrick, he unfolded the letter and read it.

"Shoot, I'm gobsmacked as well." Patrick folded the letter and handed it back to Rachel. "Rachel. I'm so sorry to hear that you are going through all of this. And I feel really bad that when you called me back my attitude didn't help things at all. I had no idea! I was only thinking of myself." He rested his head in his hands, elbows braced to his chest. "How are you surviving? This is heavy! And on top of this you have work and two young boys to take care of."

"And I also direct two choirs and play the organ at Well of Salvation African Christian Church."

"Wow," Patrick shook his head. "How do you do it all?"

Rachel relaxed her shoulders. "It's really hard, at least when I was in Chicago, I had family there. I have no one here. I only moved here a few years ago because Brothaman got a job at an advertising agency. And he didn't last a year on that job. I didn't see it then, but I'm pretty sure he was using then, which is why he lost the job."

"Wow," Patrick shook his head again. "Please let me know what Veronica and I can do to help you."

"No Patrick, I can't impose on you two. You're newlyweds. You're still honeymooning."

"Now Rachel. I will never see my son as an imposition. Neither will Veronica." Patrick smiled. "I think Martin stole her heart yesterday. You've done an outstanding job with him. He's so polite."

"Thank you."

"I tell you what. I'll talk to Veronica, but I'm sure she'll be on board. Maybe next time Martin and Malcolm can stay for the whole weekend. That will give you a little break and time to relax a bit. Go do something fun, just for you."

"Really?"

"I'll talk to Veronica as soon as she gets home from work this evening. I'll call you and let you know what she says."

"Thank you, Patrick," Rachel reached out to hug him. "I really appreciate it."

Patrick looked at his watch. "Look, I'd better run. I'd like to say goodbye to Martin."

Rachel walked across the room and slid the patio doors open. "Martin, come say goodbye to your father."

Martin walked into the living room, Malcolm was behind him. "Do you have to go now Daddy?"

"Yes, son."

"I had a really good time. Tell Miss Ronnie I said thank you for the pancakes. I think I forgot to tell her."

Patrick smiled, "I will, son." He reached down to hug Martin, Malcolm joined them.

"Can I come next time and learn to play checkers and watch a movie?" Malcolm asked.

"I'll ask Miss Ronnie, but I'm sure it'll be okay."

"Yay!" Martin said. "Malcolm can come next time!" He and Malcolm jumped up and down, full of excitement. Then he turned to Rachel. "But will you be lonely, Mommy?"

"I'll be just fine, Martin."

Patrick gave both of the boys big hugs. When he stood, he smiled at them. Martin smiled back, and Patrick's smile grew even bigger. "Both of you be good, and do everything your mother tells you to do."

"Yes sir!" Martin and Malcolm said.

"I'll see you next time."

"Thank you for everything," Rachel said as she walked Patrick to the door.

When Patrick started his car, he could see Martin and Malcolm waving to him from the living room window. He waved back.

§♣

THOMASINE WALKED TO HER COMPUTER, coffee cup in hand. Outside she could hear a high pitched three-note trill. She looked out the window at the bright orange breast of a male flame robin perched on the fence, a white stripe crossed his beak. She placed the cup of coffee and her mid-morning snack to the right of her keyboard, then sat in the chair. This was her second cup of the day. Sina was trying to stay ahead of the game by typing field notes, but took Rodney's advice and instructed Evonne to dub the interview tapes before she sent them out to a transcription service.

Thomasine squinted, as she tried to make out what she wrote hastily, when attempting to record the mood and tone of the environment for her interview with Aunty Pangari. The trill from the birds continued. It was a beautiful spring morning, and she typed vigorously while contemplating taking an afternoon flight to Melbourne so that she could attend Rodney's evening game. She pinched a bit of her muffin and it melted in her mouth. She heard the double ring of her phone. "Good morning," she said once she put the receiver to her ear.

"What on earth is going on down there Thomasine?" her mother asked. "Do I need to hop on a plane and come down there?"

"Good morning, Mama. I know that it seems like a big mess, but Rodney and I are working it out. I just can't believe that a photographer followed us to the doctor's office."

"Sina, have you read the paper or watched the news today?"

"No, I got in yesterday afternoon, had dinner with Evonne, came here and crashed. I've been typing field notes all morning. Mama, you're scaring me. What happened?"

"Rodney was arrested for assault at his hotel last night."

"What? No! That has to be a mistake."

"I just saw a story about it on the six o'clock news here."

"Oh my! I should have gone to Melbourne, but after all the stories in the tabloids, especially the one in the *International Observer,* I'm lying low. I can't imagine why someone who went to college with me would talk to the tabloids about my pregnancy. I really kept to myself. I know that Deborah or Measha wouldn't betray me. And Gwen, well, she's been gone for years." Thomasine said of her college roommate who died tragically a month before their college graduation.

"That doesn't make sense, either. None of this makes sense." Crystal paused. "Wait a minute," she said, making three words sound like one. "Do you remember Martha Mitchell from church?"

"Yes."

"Well, I had to lay her and your friend Hope's Momma out when I overheard them talking about you when you were pregnant."

"Really?"

"And that Martha Mitchell was trying to push her niece off on Rodney. She almost knocked the girl down at Altar Call when she nudged her towards Rodney with her shoulder."

"No way!"

"And after church that Sunday I heard her ask Rodney to show her niece around Chicago, but you know I nipped that in the bud."

"Are you serious?"

"That heifer! 'Bout to make the First Lady cuss. I'd bet a million dollars that she is the anonymous source. And you know your mama don't gamble. Just wait 'til I see her!"

"Mama, do you really think it was her?"

"Sina, the report in the tabloid is almost identical to what I over-heard her saying to Phyllis Jones almost ten years ago."

"I don't believe this!"

"Yeah, I'll take care of her. Sunday after next is the Church Anniver-sary. I invited your future mother-in-law to be my guest."

"I think that's wonderful. From the way Rodney describes her, I think you two will get along well," Sina looked at the clock on her desk. "Look Mama, I need to find out what's going on with Rodney, so I'll talk to you later."

"Before you go, I've been meaning to ask you the name of the lady who did your hair for the reunion. It looked so pretty, and it's so healthy. Sister Newton is moving to North Carolina and she's looking for a stylist." Sina looked through her planner and gave her Mom Regi-na's number and the address to the salon.

Sina called Rodney's hotel, but was unable to reach him. Thoma-sine paced the floor, then remembered that it was time for the morning news. She found the remote control underneath a stack of papers on the coffee table. *All charges have been dropped against Windy City Gale Force forward, Rodney Harris, who was arrested for assault last night in Melbourne. According to IBL officials, he will play in tonight's game. This is not a good look for Harris, the team's leading scorer, who has been in the news quite a bit of late.* Sina breathed a sigh of relief. At least he was out of jail. But she needed to find out what happened. She picked up the phone and called the airline to purchase a ticket on the next flight to Melbourne.

❧

AND JUST LIKE THAT, the lights were back on. Hope looked at her watch. It was nine-thirty on Sunday evening. A Nor'easter blew into Hampton Roads and ruined her weekend plans which included a Friday evening bike ride along the Boardwalk Bike Path, Saturday morning at the gym, then on to the Town Point Wine Festival, and a peaceful and relaxing evening recuperating from the wine tasting. Peaceful and relaxing is what she got, if you could call it that.

When she saw the weather forecast about the storm, her survival instincts from college kicked in. She bought non-perishable food items, bottled water, and filled all her large pots with water. The one thing she forgot to purchase was a flashlight. *How could I be so stupid? No flashlight!* She was glued to the television on Friday, and had just gotten news of Thomasine and Rodney's engagement from an entertainment show when her power went out. Since it was dark and she had no flashlight, that meant she had to go to bed.

The first night she tossed and turned. She was thankful for the fall weather. Had she experienced such a long power outage in the summer, she would not have been able to handle it. Hope spent that night staring at the ceiling. And for the first time in her life, she began to think about what she really wanted. Here she was, not yet thirty, accomplished in her field. She could do anything she wanted, go anywhere she wanted. She needed hobbies, a way to get out and meet people. Hope asked herself what she really liked. Beautiful things. Art! While she wasn't a great singer, Hope loved listening to music, and when she was younger she wrote poetry. *Hmmm.* The word birth kept popping into her head when she finally drifted fast to sleep.

She started Saturday with a sugar overload. Lukewarm bottled Frappuccino since she was not able to make a hot cup of coffee, and a blueberry muffin. She sat by her patio door and watched the rain, blank notebook in her hand. *Birth* she wrote at the top of the page. *Who says it only happens once? Surely, I'm not a dunce. We were born into this world, Bodies tiny, fingers curled, around that of one we trust, loving feelings are a must, then we get older and we grow, and everything we think we know, and then we learn we're not so smart, we haven't yet been guided by the heart. But the beauty is the second chance, we must first take a firm stance. If we advance we must enhance, and give another chance at romance. See, birth is not a one-time occurrence. It is actually more of a daily transference. And each day we live we have an opportunity, to have peace and love and most of all unity.*

"Whew," Hope said when she got up from her chair. "That worked up an appetite for a cheeseburger." Then she remembered that she was in the midst of a storm, dangerous flooding was expected, and she was without electricity. And her stove was electric. *Back to the non-perishables.*

Hope snacked and wrote in her notebook until sunset, and only took a break for a quick, barely lukewarm shower. By Sunday afternoon, she was craving all her favorite meals, just because she couldn't have them. When the power was restored Hope realized just how much the weekend was like life. We often crave what we cannot have, instead of appreciating what is right in front of us. And of course, that inspired yet another poem. But most importantly, this weekend Hope learned to enjoy her own company.

♫

"G'DAY RODNEY AND THOMASINE," Peter said as they entered the Four Seasons Sydney. They just had lunch at a restaurant in Sydney's Central Business District.

When Rodney stepped onto the polished tile floor in the lobby of the Four Seasons Sydney after he and Sina had lunch, he stopped dead in his tracks when he saw his publicist, Lauren Dixon, waiting for him in the lobby. She wore a navy-blue pantsuit, gold blouse, and navy-blue pumps. Her dark auburn hair was cut in a shoulder-length bob and her sand colored skin was lightly dotted with freckles. "What on earth is going on with you Rodney?" she asked without even greeting him. That is when Thomasine realized that Rodney had stopped walking alongside her.

"Well, hello Lauren."

Sina turned, walked back to Rodney, and cleared her throat.

"Let me introduce you to my fiancée, Dr. Thomasine,"

"Mintor." Lauren completed the sentence, then turned to face Rodney. "You're all over the tabloids, and arrested? What on earth is going through your head?"

"Lauren, it's nice to meet you, but I don't think we should discuss this here."

"Yeah, let's go up to the suite," Rodney said.

The lobby was full of convention attendees. Chatter and laughter could be heard throughout. Sina was right, that was no place for a discussion, and especially not one as serious as the one Rodney was about to have with his publicist. After the photos of them at the OB/GYN office were published in an international tabloid, Sina understood the importance of playing it safe. The doors for the elevator opened, and it was packed, so neither Sina, Rodney, nor Lauren said a word.

Rodney unlocked the door to his room and ushered Sina then Lauren inside. "Can I get you something to drink?" Sina asked, offering hospitality.

"Sure, I'll have sparkling water." She sat at the table near the far window. Rodney sat across from her after pulling up a chair beside him for his fiancée. Sina placed the tray on the table, and sat next to Rodney.

"Assault! Really, Rodney?"

"Let me explain."

"Please do, because I've been your publicist for six years, and this does not sound like you at all."

"I can explain." Sina placed her palm on the back of his hand. "When I was at the hotel in Melbourne, I went down the hall to get some ice, and I heard a woman scream. I dropped my ice bucket and ran in the direction, and saw this tiny woman, barely five feet tall, trying to fight off a drunk man who had to be at least a foot taller than her. I spoke up for her, and he came at me, so I let him have it." Rodney held Sina's hand.

"Rodney, let him have it is an understatement. He has a fractured jaw and broken nose."

"And she might have had much worse if I hadn't stepped in. That's why charges were dropped against me. The one thing that I will absolutely not tolerate is violence against women," he squeezed Sina's hand. "I have a mother, a sister, and soon I'll have a wife, then maybe a daughter. I know how I would feel if anyone ever violated them. That lady is someone's daughter, and I would want someone to stand up for mine."

Lauren bit her lower lip and raised her eyebrow. "You know, I'm thinking. We can turn this into a positive to make you an even bigger hero."

"It wasn't about being a hero for me," Rodney said. "It's about doing what's right."

Lauren slid the small hotel notepad in front of her and wrote down the last words that Rodney said. She pursed her lips, "Hmmm, this could be something really big. Global even."

"Lauren, what's going on in your head?" She nodded her head up and down. "You know how I work. I'll fill you in when I have all the details, but not until then."

❧

"Did you ever find out what Lauren was cooking up?" Sina asked Rodney after giving him a quick peck on the lips, careful not to touch his clothing since she was cooking dinner when he arrived at her sabbatical home. It was his last night in Sydney and the Windy City Gale Force had swept the games they played in Australia and New Zealand. This was the start of another winning season.

"I'm not exactly sure," Rodney sat at the dining table. "But I heard she met with the league's VP of Communication."

"Wow. I wonder what she's up to." Thomasine wiped her hands on the dish towel, then removed her apron. "Oh, I heard from Hope, finally. She sent a virtual bouquet of flowers congratulating us on our engagement."

"That was nice of her."

"She said she loves her new job and she really likes Virginia Beach."

"That's not far from your house in North Carolina."

"Just a three-and-a-half-hour drive."

"It'll be nice for both of you to be that close to a long-time friend. You'll both be road tripping."

"You know, I didn't think of that, but you're right." She touched Rodney's shoulder. "Hope also wrote a poem for us. I printed it." Sina walked over to her desk and took the printed sheet from the top tray, then handed it to Rodney. He read it silently while Thomasine stood over his shoulder, then he looked up at her and smiled.

"That was really nice of Hope!"

"Yes, it was. I didn't know she wrote poetry."

"Sina, it smells so good in here. What's on the menu?"

"Well," Sina walked across the room, retrieved a covered plate, then placed it on the table in front of Rodney. She removed the warming cover. "I thought we'd start with an appetizer of roasted shrimp, or prawns as they say here, with garlic, lemon, and marjoram."

Rodney bit his lower lip, then gently licked it and smiled.

"Oh, and I picked up a baguette as well."

Thomasine placed the crusty bread in front of Rodney, who then broke off a piece. He ate a shrimp and dipped the bread in the buttery sauce. "Thomasine, this is really good." He paused to chew. "I didn't know you were such a great cook."

"Hey, I love food. But baking is my favorite. I baked a Red Velvet cake." Sina sat down, then jumped back up. "Oh, I almost forgot the wine. I've paired a Semillon Sauvignon Blanc with our appetizer." She walked to the refrigerator, opened it, and removed the bottle from the door. She walked over to the table, held the bottle for Rodney to view the label, then laughed. "Will you do the honors?"

Rodney poured the wine, first for Thomasine then himself. They tasted, and enjoyed the first course. Rodney stifled a chuckle.

"What?" Thomasine asked.

"You're good. Really, good. You might need to join the family business with Kimmy and me."

Sina began clearing the plates.

"Oh?"

"Yes. Kimmy has wanted her own restaurant since she was in seventh grade. I was in second grade then, and after school she would prepare food for me, plate it, and serve it to me as if I were one of her patrons."

"How fun." Thomasine checked on her mushroom burgundy sauce which was simmering on the stove, then added the fillets. In another pan, she poured a little olive oil and a pat of butter, then added chopped shallots.

"That's why she went to culinary school after she graduated from college." Rodney sipped the last of his wine. "Each Sunday she tests out a menu item on Mom and me."

"Nice." Thomasine added silverbeet to the shallots, then chopped garlic, salt, and pepper. She stirred the vegetables with a wooden spatula, and heated the mashed potatoes. "The main course will be ready in just a second." Sina turned and handed Rodney a bottle of Rothbury Estates Hunter Valley Merlot. "Will you do the honors, again?"

Thomasine plated their meals while Rodney poured the wine. She tried to mimic Rodney's description of Kimmy serving him an after-school snack when she placed his plate in front of him. Once Thomasine sat down, he looked at her, she nodded, and they both laughed. "You're so serious," Thomasine said as she cut her tenderloin, chewed it once, then took a sip of wine so that the flavors could blend in her mouth.

"This sauce is really good," Rodney's eyes were closed in pleasure.

"Just a little something I whipped up," Sina tried to make light of her endeavor. "But in all seriousness, I wanted us to have a special dinner because this is the last time we'll see each other until—Sugar Cane, when will I see you again?"

He rested his fork on his plate. "We leave for Nairobi tomorrow. Twelve games on the continent of Africa over three weeks, then after that we head to Asia. Say, what are you doing the week before Christmas?"

"I don't have any plans."

"You do now. How does Fiji sound?"

"But I don't have."

Rodney interrupted. "You don't need a visa to travel to Fiji. Your US Passport will suffice."

"In that case, nice. Very nice."

"Walks on the beach, beautiful sunsets, just you and me."

"That sounds perfect."

Rodney's heart felt light, and he felt warm inside when he saw the big smile on Thomasine's face. "Then I'll call my travel agent in the morning and have her book our tickets."

She took another sip of wine. "I hope that you've saved room for dessert."

"I certainly have, and I can't wait. I love red velvet cake."

"It's a nice night and the sun is setting. I thought we'd go outside. I have a fire pit."

"I'll start the fire," Rodney started towards the courtyard.

Lavender and coral bands extended across the sky, and intensified as they reached the rooftops. Rodney smiled, then laughed when he saw that Sina had already placed the wood in the fire pit, which made his job easy. She set a tray with two slices of red velvet cake, two mugs, an urn of coffee, and cutlery on the bistro table on the patio. "I picked up some decaf at Bay Coffee when I was there earlier in the week." She poured a cup of coffee and handed it to Rodney, then handed him a slice of cake and a fork. She joined him with her mug, and they sat in front of the fire, feeding each other the first slice, sipping their coffee, starting the second slice, and planning their future while the sun lowered completely in the sky, and the only light they had was the glow of the fire.

15

PICK YOURSELF UP

It was a sunny, but brisk late fall Saturday morning. Whispers of frost were still present in shaded areas of the field at Eckersall Stadium. An eight-lane track circled the football field. Sadly, the aluminum bleachers were sparsely filled for the championship game between the Hawks, coached by Jason, and the Eagles. There were five minutes left in the first quarter and the Eagles had the ball. The Hawks were up 7-0 when Christopher, who stood on the sidelines, heard his name, then turned around and smiled. Jason glanced over his shoulder and saw Zuri greet a man with a friendly hug. He waved to Christopher.

"The ball is snapped, the Eagles quarterback throws the ball, caught at the 15-yard line by number 85. He's wide open, on the ten, the five, he scores. The conversion is complete and the game is tied."

At half-time, the Eagles were up, 21-14. While the Eagles' cheerleaders performed a disjointed routine, out of sync and off beat, Jason gave the team a pep talk. "You are still very much in this game. There's a whole half to go. We're just an open middle, a complete pass, a solid block away from another touchdown. You can do this! I believe in you." Jason patted number 17 on the shoulder. "Now let's get on the field and win this game!"

The Hawks offense ran onto the field and huddled, "What's our name?" the quarterback asked.

"The Hawks," the players said in unison.

"Who are we?"

"The champions"

"What's our name?"

"The Hawks"

"What will we do?"

"Win this game!"

On the third play, the ball was snapped, the quarterback handed off to Christopher who saw an opening up the middle, "he takes it, he's going, going, gone." When he reached the end zone his legs became lighter and his toes barely grazed the grass. With the conversion, the game was tied at 21.

In the fourth quarter, the Hawks were up 28-21 when the Eagles quarterback threw a pass to the wide receiver in the end zone. The championship game was tied and went into overtime. Jason huddled with the team. "You are one play. Just one play away from winning this game. So, get out there, and don't stop hustling until the clock hits zero."

The ball was snapped, the quarterback handed off to Christopher. He fumbled. The ball was recovered by an Eagle who ran into the end zone and scored. The Eagles won the Youth Football championship.

The players on both teams lined up and one by one they shook hands with their opponents. The Hawks gathered together for the last time. "Guys. You gave it your all and played your hearts out. That's what I expected. I'm proud of each of you. Never give up on your dreams."

❧

MALCOLM WALKED down the stairs at Patrick and Veronica's, his eyes wide in amazement. Like his older brother, he was very impressed by the Power Rangers comforter set. Martin made his way to the bottom of the steps and he grabbed Malcolm's hand. "Come meet Miss Ronnie." Martin led the way to the kitchen, while Patrick switched between the Vanderbilt and Tennessee games. Tennessee was 6-1, their only loss of the season was to Florida. Vanderbilt was a different story. It was clear that 1997 was not their best season.

Martin returned from the kitchen with Malcolm, and gave him a tour of the downstairs of the apartment, including the photos that sat on the end table and the mantel. When he made his way to Patrick's Kindergarten picture, he told Malcolm, "Now, that looks like me, but it isn't. This is my Daddy's Kindergarten picture. I'm going to look just like him when I grow up."

Malcolm looked at the picture, then at Martin, and Patrick. "Wow! I guess I'll look like Brothaman when I grow up, then." Malcolm did not have the same feelings towards Brothaman that Martin did. In fact, he missed his Dad.

"Daddy, when the commercial comes on can you set up the table so that we can play checkers?"

Patrick turned away from the TV. "Do you remember how to play?"

"Yes, I remember. First you choose a color, red or black. Then you put the checkers on the black squares starting with the row closest to you. The two rows in the middle are empty because that's where you play. You move the checker one space sideways to the front."

"Diagonally, son."

"Diagonally," Martin repeated. "And if there is a blank space behind that checker then you can jump and you keep the piece."

"Very good." Patrick got up to remove the card table from the closet. He set the table up, and put a booster seat in Malcolm's chair, then put the checker board on the table, and Martin took over for him.

Martin instructed Malcolm on play, and then told him that the first game wouldn't count because he needed to practice first so that he could learn the game. He was such a good big brother.

"I'm thirsty," Malcolm said after the practice game.

"I'll get you some juice," Patrick said. He stood from the sofa, eyes glued to the television set, and at the end of the play, he went into the kitchen to get juice and healthy snacks for the boys.

Martin jumped Malcolm's last checker. "I won."

"Can I try again?" Malcolm asked. "And can I be black this time?"

The boys set up the checkerboard, and began play. "Look Malcolm," Martin said, pointing to the TV. "There's Uncle Rodney."

Malcolm turned and looked at the TV. "He's not our real uncle, Daddy. But he and T-Sina took us to the zoo when we were in Chicago during summer vacation."

Martin and Malcolm watched as Rodney and other IBL players from across the globe spoke out against violence against women in their respective languages, with English subtitles. Veronica came into the living room to tell them that dinner was ready when Martin read along when Rodney reappeared at the end of the Public Service Announcement. "It's not about being a hero. It's about doing what's right." She had chills up and down her spine.

"Patrick, I was thinking that maybe we could have dinner in here, instead of the dining room."

"Great idea."

Martin and Malcolm began putting their checkers away, then folded up the checkerboard. "Miss Ronnie, did you make fish sticks again?"

"No Martin. Your Mom told me that you love fried perch, spaghetti, and Cole slaw, so that's what I made."

"That's my favorite!" Malcolm shared, a broad smile spread across his face.

"I hope you enjoy it." Patrick returned with placemats, cutlery, and drinks for him and Veronica. He set a chair for himself at the table so that he could still watch the game, and one for Veronica across from him. Veronica carried the boys' plates, and Patrick followed with theirs. Patrick muted the television so that the boys could lead them in saying the grace. Veronica braced herself because, after the last dinner conversation, she didn't know what this one might reveal.

Tonight, it was much more pleasant, mostly about school. "Daddy and Miss Ronnie, will we watch a movie tonight like last time?"

"Yes," Veronica responded. "I rented *Toy Story*."

"That's my favorite too," Malcolm said. "Thank you, Miss Ronnie."

After dinner, the boys helped Veronica clear the dishes, then they all piled up on the living room sofa and watched *Toy Story*. Before long *Toy Story* was watching them. All of them. Veronica carried Malcolm, and Patrick carried Martin up to bed and tucked them in, before retiring for themselves.

੪.

RACHEL LOOKED out at the Ohio River as she set her plate on the table, and sat across from her coworker. Sonia Perkins had invited Rachel to join her for a day trip. A thin buffer of ash trees sparse with deep rust colored leaves met the water's edge. The sun was high in the sky, casting a marigold glow through the nearly bare branches. "Did you know the Kentucky state line starts where the water starts?" Sonia asked.

"No I didn't, this is my first time here. Heck, this is my first time at a casino," Rachel put salt and pepper on her meal of fried chicken, mashed potatoes, and broccoli.

"Then you'll probably have beginner's luck," Sonia shoveled a forkful of string beans into her mouth. "Always bet three credits, then you'll win more."

"But won't that cost me more?" Rachel asked.

"Don't worry about that," Sonia replied. She wiggled her ample hips in the chair to get more comfortable. "Remember you're here for a little getaway, and to have some fun. Cheap fun." Sonia said of the nominally priced roundtrip charter which included a free buffet. They were waiting for the boat to dock, and the previous group of gamblers to disembark. "Oh, and play the Double Diamond slot machine."

Sonia pushed back from the table, then stood slowly. "Can I get you anything?" she asked Rachel before making another round at the buffet.

"No, I'm good right now."

While Rachel was excited about going to the casino, truthfully, she was afraid. She was barely making ends meet with two jobs and no support from Brothaman, who was still her husband, although they were separated. While Patrick was paying court ordered support, he was in graduate school during the first three years of Martin's life, then had a post-doctoral fellowship for the next two years. He was just starting to earn a full-time salary in his career as an Assistant Professor. Rachel looked over at the river and reflected, then decided to put limits on her time at the casino. She couldn't afford to lose more than twenty dollars, and decided that she would only play for twenty minutes. If she won, she would take all her winnings home, and call it a day. That way she couldn't lose too much time or too much money, at least in her mind.

Sonia returned to the table with two plates, one of chicken wings and fries, and the other plate held the most decadent chocolate cake that Rachel had ever seen. Rachel decided to indulge, in dessert and coffee. The texture of the cake was dense, and rich. It melted in her mouth like fudge.

Rachel and Sonia walked across the sky bridge between the restaurant building and the entrance to the riverboat casino. It overlooked Riverside Drive, and cars passed underneath in both directions. Once they reached the end of the sky bridge, they took a two-story escalator down into a dark, noisy smoke filled area. It wasn't long before they heard the vocal chatter, whistles, and bells which filled the three-story casino. "Let's meet right here in about two hours," Sonia told Rachel.

Rachel walked through the maze of tables to make her way to the slots. She watched as people played blackjack, roulette, and craps. She saw a scantily clad bar waitress in flesh colored stockings walk through the crowd while balancing a tray on the palm of her hand. To the left was a stairway, and Rachel decided to try a different level that might be less crowded. On the second level, she saw a long line at the cashier, and since she didn't have any chips, she joined the others in the line. The lady in front of her had two buckets of coins, and a huge smile plastered on her face. The line moved slowly. "Congratulations," Rachel said to the portly redhead with rosy cheeks that dimpled as she chewed her gum. "This is my first time here. My friend said I should play Double Diamonds."

"Honey," she said, with a thick Kentucky accent. "You need to be on the third floor." She chewed her gum a bit then took a break, "And you don't have to stand in this line. The slot machines take cash in all denominations."

Rachel climbed to the third, less traveled level. She found a dollar slot Double Diamonds Deluxe machine and put a ten-dollar bill in. *I know Sonia said I should bet three credits, but that will only give me three spins.* Rachel studied the buttons on the machine. She bet one credit, spun the reels, and got a cherry for a two-credit win. She played a few more spins, and watched some of the diamonds on the bars move up and down in the direction of the point of the diamond. Sometimes she won five or ten credits, other times she didn't get a second or third match. A cherry here and there, sometimes bars. Ten minutes had passed and Rachel was down to four credits left. She bet one credit, spun the reels, and saw Double Diamonds in the first and second columns followed by a red seven in the third. She watched as the numbers for credits won got higher and higher. First, she saw fifty. She had not won that much combined with the cherries and bars. When the number grew to one hundred she was ready to start shouting, but it continued to grow and grow, and grow.

"Congratulations." The middle-aged man sitting next to her had salt and pepper hair and a belly that protruded over his belt. He pushed his glasses up on the bridge of his nose. "You just won three hundred-twenty dollars." He handed Rachel a bucket for her chips. She pressed the cash out button, then stood in the much shorter cashier's line than the one she saw on the second floor. She couldn't believe it when the cashier counted her winnings back to her. Rachel stuffed the cash deep in the left front pocket of her Lee jeans. The remaining ten dollars in money she allotted for gambling was in her right pocket. She decided ten more minutes at the slot was worth a chance at increasing her winnings. If she didn't win, she'd still be ahead.

Rachel walked to the opposite end of the slot floor and found a Triple Diamonds slot machine. This one was a fifty-cent machine. She grabbed a bucket from the end of the row like an old pro, and sat on the stool beside a very animated woman with toffee colored skin and a short haircut who was playing two slots at the same time.

Rachel put her ten-dollar-bill into the machine and saw her credits go up to twenty. Again, she bet only one credit at a time. Sometimes she got a mixture of bars and sometimes a cherry that allowed her to play a bit longer. Just when Rachel was down to her last credit, she spun the reels again and started backing away from the machine, in acceptance of defeat. Two triple diamonds and a yellow bar lined up across the front of the machine. She watched the numbers go up, and up, and up. When they reached three hundred-sixty they stopped growing, and she pressed the button to cash out.

Rachel won five hundred dollars on her first casino trip, and now she was hooked. On the bus ride back, Sonia told her that if she had bet three credits she would have had so much more, but Rachel was content with her winnings, especially after explaining to Sonia that if she had bet three credits she would not have been able to play long enough to win.

They got back to Nashville shortly after eight, and Rachel made it to her quiet, dark apartment. She flipped the light switch by the door up as soon as she entered, then locked and chained the door. After a quick walkthrough for peace of mind, she called Patrick and Veronica to check on the boys. Patrick answered the phone, a hint of grogginess in his voice. He told her about their evening and that the boys were asleep. Rachel ran a bath and relaxed with a glass of White Zinfandel. She hung her dress for church on the outside of her closet door, then sat in front of her television and rolled her hair while she watched the tail end of *Early Edition*. She thought about the money she won, and how much it would help her out, especially since she and Hank had been talking about visiting Sydney to meet their siblings. In the back of her mind, she heard Aunt Mary telling her "Don't forget to tithe your winnings."

"I REALLY ENJOYED THE ANNIVERSARY SERVICE," Carol Paxton told Crystal Mintor as the mass choir lined the center aisle. Reverend Mintor stepped out of the pulpit to escort his wife from the front pew to the door of the sanctuary to greet members. Crystal looked regal in her dark charcoal shantung V-neck knit dress and matching hat. Her shoes were polished impeccably. Carefully placed sequins along the high collar neckline gave the dress an elegant look. Carol sat on the pew, and waited for the overflow of members and guests to thin.

Janae took her aunt's hand and navigated her way through the crowd. Some members were making their way to the outer aisles for a speedier exit. Others moved at a snail's pace towards the center aisle to speak to Reverend and Mrs. Mintor. Martha had no idea why they were moving to the front of the church when she had started in the direction of the outer aisle towards the rear of the sanctuary.

Carol felt a sneeze erupting, so she opened her purse to look for a Kleenex. She covered her nose with the Kleenex and looked up. Janae and her Aunt Martha were standing in front of her. "Excuse me, Ms. Paxton. I heard your name called when they announced the visitors. I just wanted to say, hello and introduce you to my Aunt Martha Mitchell."

Carol extended her hand to Martha, "It's a pleasure to meet you."

"Ms. Paxton is a Vice President at First Federal."

"It's nice to meet you," Martha said. "My niece has told me so much about you. We just know that she'll be accepted into that Financial Analyst Training Program."

While Carol understood Martha's aspirations for her niece, she thought it was a bit forward of her. "I see you revised your résumé, Janae. Good job. As you are aware, applications aren't due until the end of January, so it will be a while before you hear back from us. This program is highly competitive. We usually make selections in March." Carol looked over her shoulder and saw that the crowd was thinning out. She stood, draped her coat over her arm and put her purse on her shoulder. She picked up Crystal's purse as well.

Janae started down the center aisle, her aunt was in step behind her. "Well, Janae's parents and I are really keeping our fingers crossed." Martha was directly in front of Carol. Carol smiled. She was silent.

"Hello, Mrs. Mintor," Janae hugged Crystal. "I'm really enjoying the Single's Ministry."

Crystal placed her hand on Janae's upper arms. "I'm glad to hear that. It's a great way for you to meet other fine young Christian adults." Crystal bit her lip.

"Martha Mitchell," Crystal said, "That's a pretty nice suit you have on," she said of the red knit suit Martha wore. Crystal surveyed it, "St. John's, is it?" *That suit cost more than Martha puts in church in a year.*

"Good afternoon, First Lady Mintor. It is a St. John's. I thought it would be nice to have something new for the Church Anniversary." Martha started. "Oh, and I read all about Thomasine's engagement in the papers." She emphasized the word all.

Crystal's smile was sly. "Then you'll be pleased to meet her soon-to-be mother-in-law, Carol Paxton."

"Oh!" Martha was shocked. "You're Rodney's mother?"

"I am."

"Oh."

Crystal put her hand on her hip. "Martha," she said her name fast. "You mentioned that you read all about Thomasine in the tabloids." Crystal rotated her neck forward and up when she said the word all.

"Yes." Her response was almost a whisper.

Crystal sucked her teeth softly. "Is that all you did?"

"I don't know what you're talking about." Martha replied, feigning innocence, and at the same time, acting as if she were insulted.

Crystal nodded her head up and down and shook her finger at Martha. "The more I think about it," Crystal rested her chin in the fold between her thumb and index finger, "the more that quote from the anonymous source sounds a lot like what I overheard you telling Phyllis Jones nine years ago."

Martha held her head down slightly. Guilt was ever-present on her face. Carol clinched her teeth and Janae's shoulders shrunk.

"Unbelievable," Crystal turned to face Carol. "Some people will sell their souls to Satan for a little pocket change. And to strut up in here on the church's anniversary wearing the pain she caused my daughter." Crystal shook her head. Janae was near tears.

"Martha, I just have one question. What do you have against my daughter?" Reverend Mintor touched Crystal's arm. Crystal softly shook her head from side to side in small strokes. "What has Thomasine ever done to you?"

"I, I, I'm so sorry."

"Now you're lying, and in the church at that. You're not sorry for what you said about my daughter when she was in college, because if you were, you would not have repeated it to the *International Observer*. You didn't think about anybody but yourself. And that's what's sorry." Crystal rolled her eyes. "Now get out of my presence. Immediately!"

"Aunt Martha, how could you?" Janae asked before she ran off in tears. She felt her chances for the training program were now ruined. Her aunt waddled behind her.

"Whew!" Crystal turned to Carol, "Lord, help me! That woman almost made the First Lady cuss, right here in the church. On the Church Anniversary!"

"Hey, you stood up for your child. I've had to do the same through

Rodney's high school, college, and professional careers." Carol put her arm around Crystal's shoulder. "We're gonna get along just fine."

❧

As PAINFUL AS the end of her marriage was for Hope, she had too much pride to stay in a marriage that died long ago, perhaps before it even began. But what truly amazed her is that a fourteen-year relationship could be over in almost as many minutes. The whole process felt rushed, but with no marital property or children and equal amounts of student loan debt, there wasn't anything to divide. Just like that, she was Hope Jones once again.

While Jason petitioned the divorce much to Hope's displeasure, she eventually came around. Her move to Virginia Beach gave her the time she needed to reflect on her life, and how unfulfilling her marriage was when compared to her dreams. From the moment she first saw him, Jason was that someone she always wanted to be with, but it wasn't Jason himself, but her image of him. Her fantasy of their life together. At the same time, Jason first asked Hope out as a high school freshman to get back into his mother's good graces after he had so greatly disappointed her. And just like that, they spent half of their lives, one living her own created fantasy turned nightmare, the other living to please anyone but himself.

Hope also thought about her friends, Rachel and Sina, and how strong they were. They had both overcome heartbreak, major heartbreak. But she had great hope, since Sina recently found new love. This empowered her. *I'll have a second chance too*, Hope stood in the mahogany paneled courtroom beside her attorney. Over the five-year marriage, there were a multitude of signs from both of them that marriage, at least at that time, wasn't right. Being on her own, in a new town with no friends, forced Hope to finally grow up and realize that there was so much more for her to aspire to.

Jason and Hope had already fielded questions from their attorneys establishing their residence, length of separation, and date of marriage, as well as the reasons for dissolution. "Mr. McCoy, I've reviewed the Marital Settlement Agreement signed by you and Mrs. Jones-McCoy," the judge said. "Do you think this agreement is reasonable and equitable?"

"Yes, your Honor."

"And you intend to honor the terms of this agreement."

"Yes, your Honor."

"The financial disclosure you provided to the court is accurate."

"Yes, your Honor."

The judge turned to Hope with the same line of questioning. Before the first response she took a deep breath before replying as Jason did. As the questions continued, her voice became lighter, more joyful. She could now see clearly through eyes that once fostered tears.

With a rap of the gavel, their divorce was granted. They would each receive the final decree in the mail. Jason looked over at Hope as he turned to leave the courtroom. She was talking to her attorney.

When Hope exited the courtroom doors, she saw Jason standing near a bench across the hallway. "Hope," he called to her.

Hope looked up at Jason, as people walked between them. Jason made his way over to her. "Look Hope, I just wanted to say that I really wish you the best in life. You deserve it. You deserve more than I was able to give you."

"Thank you, Jason. That's very nice of you. I wish you the best as well."

He nodded and smiled with his lips together, then hugged her and patted her left shoulder. Hope started toward the elevator then turned. "Jason," she called.

He turned around, his eyebrows raised, teeth slightly visible. "I really hope that one day we can be friends."

Jason nodded his head up and down. "Me too, Hope. Me too." She continued towards the elevator, and he went in the opposite direction, which was reminiscent of their fourteen years together.

MARTIN STEPPED inside the Shelton's split level home. He was overwhelmed by all the people there, most of them who knew him, but he had no idea who any of them were. Veronica had invited Rachel and the boys to have Thanksgiving dinner with her family and Patrick's family at her parents' home. Martin stood on the landing not knowing if he should go upstairs or downstairs. He saw Miss Ronnie in the kitchen wearing an apron, and heard what sounded like a football game coming from the basement. Patrick heard Rachel introduce herself and the boys to Mrs. Shelton and jumped up from his seat. He stood at the bottom of the steps, "Martin!" he said with a big smile on his face. Patrick walked up the stairs and gave his son a big hug. Then he hugged Malcolm. Let me introduce you to everyone.

Patrick helped Martin and Malcolm take their jackets off, then handed them to Veronica's cousin, Natalie. "Come on boys," he said, as he climbed the stairs.

"Aunt Jessie," Martin said of the one face that was familiar to him. She was setting the tables. In addition to the dining room table that seated eight, the Shelton's set another table for six in the space between the dining and living rooms so that there would be enough seating for the guests.

"Martin and Malcolm!" she gave them a group hug.

"Come here baby," Grandma Odessa sat in a recliner in the corner of the living room near the bay window right next to the fireplace.

Patrick guided the boys in her direction. "This is your great-grand-mother, Grandma Odessa."

Grandma Odessa placed her the palms of her hands on Martin's shoulders. "Let me get a good look at you." She smiled, and he smiled back. "You have your Daddy's smile," she pulled him into a tight embrace and showered him with kisses. "And you have his warm spirit too.

"And who is this?" she asked.

"This is my brother, Malcolm."

"Malcolm and Martin, my, my, my. Your mother named you after two very powerful black men." She pulled Malcolm to the other side of her lap and hugged him as well. "Where's your mother?"

"I'll go get her," Malcolm climbed down from Grandma Odessa's lap and went to find Rachel, while Patrick introduced Martin to Grandma Long and Veronica's Aunt Norma.

Malcolm found Rachel in the kitchen as she gave the store bought sweet potato pie to Mrs. Shelton, "Mommy, Mommy, come with me." He grabbed her by the hand and pulled her towards the living room.

His body leaned sideways as he pulled, his little feet were faster than his mother's.

"Hold on, Malcolm. I'm coming." Rachel saw Grandma Odessa in the corner. While she was happy to see her, like when she met Veronica for the first time she felt awkward, uncomfortable.

"Grandma Odessa!" Rachel said, not knowing if she should shake her hand or hug her.

"Come give me a hug," Grandma Odessa replied. Rachel leaned down and received a hug as warm as the one she got from Grandma Odessa on the day that she accepted Patrick's marriage proposal. "It's nice to see you again. Martin and Malcolm are such fine young boys."

Rachel felt a bit more relaxed, and sat beside her.

"Let me introduce you to your Uncle Phil," Patrick said.

"Come on Malcolm," Martin called to his younger brother. Malcolm followed Martin down the stairs.

Patrick took the boys hands and walked with them towards the leather sectional. He stood Martin in front of him, Malcolm was to his right. "This is my brother, your Uncle Phil." Martin smiled.

Phil sat still for a moment with his mouth wide open.

"Hi, Uncle Phil. This is my brother, Malcolm."

Phil hugged both of the boys. Martin sat beside Phil and Malcolm sat next to his brother. "This is your grandfather. Grandpa Long." Martin stood to hug him before he was introduced to Miss Ronnie's Dad. For the first time in years, there were three generations of Long men together in one room.

The fragrance of sage and rosemary filled the kitchen. Pans of hot macaroni and cheese, cornbread stuffing, mashed potatoes, and mixed greens lined the countertop. Veronica removed the perfectly browned turkey from the oven and placed it on top of the stove. "Dinner will be ready in about fifteen minutes, as soon as the turkey rests," she turned and saw Rachel. "Hey Rachel," Veronica kissed Rachel's cheek. "I'm so glad you and the boys made it." Veronica's cousin Natalie rolled her eyes. She was buttering the rolls for the oven.

"Thank you so much for inviting us," Rachel said. "Is there anything I can do to help?"

"No, just relax."

With the turkey perfectly carved, and the food arranged on the buffet and sideboard, the family gathered around the main table, held hands, and blessed the food. Martin held Grandma Odessa's hand to his right, and his Dad's to his left. Grandma Odessa held Rachel's hand. Mr. Shelton led them in prayer right after Martin reminded everyone to close their eyes.

They fixed their plates, Veronica helped Martin and Rachel helped Malcolm, then everyone stated what they were thankful for.

Patrick smiled as he looked around at everyone. "I'm thankful for my beautiful wife, my son, and being part of the Shelton family." He kissed Veronica's cheek, then smiled at Martin.

"I'm thankful for my loving husband and Martin who has stolen my heart." Veronica smiled at Martin.

"I'm thankful for Malcolm, Mommy, Daddy, and my Miss Ronnie Mom. Oh, and Aunt Jessie, and everyone else I met today," Martin said.

"I'm thankful that my Daddy is not in the hospital no more." Malcolm said.

"Anymore," Rachel corrected him.

"I'm thankful for my sweet sons, for the wonderful father Patrick is, and for my new friend, Veronica." Again, Natalie rolled her eyes. Her aunt gave her a don't-start-nothing stare.

After dinner, the men went back to the basement to watch football, while the women helped clear the tables. Rachel was carrying a serving tray into the kitchen when she overheard Natalie talking to her Mom, "Veronica is a better one than me," Natalie started, "Because there is no way on earth I'd be playing big happy family with Rachel if I were her. Parading in here with two kids. What kind of woman doesn't know who the father of her child is for five years?" Rachel expected something like this, but it still hurt. She stood still in her tracks, and Veronica almost bumped into her.

"Rachel. I'm so sorry Please ignore her." Veronica put the tray on the kitchen counter, then grabbed her cousin by the shoulders and took her outside on the deck to have a word with her.

Rachel went into the dining room and said goodbye to Grandma Odessa and Mrs. Long. She hugged Mrs. Shelton, and thanked her again for inviting her and the boys. "We're gonna have to leave now. I'm not sure where Natalie put our jackets."

"Oh, so soon?"

"Yes." Rachel said. She was fighting tears.

Mrs. Shelton directed Rachel to the den where the coats were stored. She returned wearing her coat and carrying the boy's jackets. Rachel reached the top of the stairs.

"You aren't leaving yet, are you?" Veronica asked as she came inside from the deck. Natalie was beside her.

"Yes. I have to go now."

"Before you go, Natalie has something to say to you."

Natalie held her head down. "Rachel, I'm sorry for what I said. I was really out of line."

Rachel looked at her. "I accept your apology." She walked towards the front door.

"Let me walk you out." Veronica followed.

"Martin, Malcolm." The boys ran to the bottom of the steps.

"Mommy, do we have to go?" Martin said when he saw their jackets in Rachel's hand.

"I don't want to leave yet." Malcolm said.

Veronica placed her hands on Rachel's shoulders. "Rachel, if it is all right with you, Patrick and I can bring them home later."

"I don't want to impose."

"We'll be happy to," Veronica said. She took the jackets from Rachel, walked halfway up the stairs. "Natalie, could you please put these back in the den with the other jackets?"

Natalie took the jackets and walked down the hallway without uttering a word.

Veronica walked Rachel to her car.

"Thank you for everything, Veronica." Rachel said. "Your dinner invitation was a real blessing. I don't have any family here in Nashville, and I haven't been in touch with my closest friends lately."

"Martin tells me that his T-Sina is in Australia. Will you get to see her when you and Hank go to meet your siblings next month?"

"I think so," Rachel replied. She hugged Veronica. "And I thank you and Patrick for taking care of the boys while Hank and I are there. I really appreciate everything you've done and how you've made me and the boys feel welcome."

"The boys are wonderful. Both Patrick and I are crazy about

Martin. He's such a charming little boy." She smiled. "Malcolm, too. They really make our lives brighter."

BROTHAMAN PULLED his skullcap down over his ears. He looked over at the woman he was drawing while her husband stood back in deep observation. They had just disembarked from a lunch time cruise. It was two days after Thanksgiving and Navy Pier was packed with local and international visitors, some taking in the tourist attractions like the Ferris wheel and merry-go-round, and others just taking pictures. Brothaman had been out of the hospital for about a month and a half, and was regaining his strength.

He had been at Navy Pier for a few hours now, setting up his portable easel in different locations based on the volume of the crowd. He needed money with Christmas coming so soon, and hoped to be able to buy presents for the boys.

The cruise boats provided a bit of a buffer from the wind on this squally afternoon. But every now and then, a gust would blow between the ships, sending a deep chill to his bones. Brothaman looked at the woman again, and placed the tip of his ebony pencil on the paper. As he lifted his hand to continue the portrait, his fingers froze. This happened to him from time to time since Dee-Mo smashed his hands, and the cold only made it worse.

Brothaman quickly adapted. He put the pencil in his mouth, and finished the drawing. The tall, middle-aged man walked closer to him and stared in amazement. When Brothaman finished, the man paid him twice his asking fee.

"Thank you, sir, but the drawings are only,"

"You are very talented," the man cut him off. "Where did you learn to do this?"

Brothaman smiled. "I've been drawing since I was a kid, and one year my Mom got a calendar with artwork done by Joni Eareckson Tada. She taught herself to paint with the brush between her teeth, so I tried it. Sometimes when I was bored I would draw pictures with the pencil in my mouth. Came in handy today. The chill off this lake is brutal and causes my joints to ache."

"I'd love to see some of your other work," the man said. His wife was now standing beside him. "Look at this honey!" He handed her the picture, she stood still in awe.

"I been on a hiatus, of sorts, from my art work," Brothaman said. "I studied Graphic Design in college, and I used to work in advertising," he picked up his pencil case. "But I'm between jobs now. I've been recovering from an illness." That would have been true if Brothaman acknowledged that his chemical dependency was an illness.

The man went into his wallet and removed a business card. "Wow. I own an advertising agency downtown, and I'd love to have you on my team." He extended his hand. "Oh, forgive me, I'm Joseph Winterveld, and this beautiful woman you captured on paper is my wife, Joan."

"Winterveld Advertising. I applied for a job at Winterveld a while back. It's nice to meet both of you."

"So why don't you give me a call on Monday, better yet, just come down on Monday morning. I'm sure we have an opportunity for you."

Brothaman smiled. "I'll be there first thing." The Wintervelds walked away, and Brothaman folded up his easel and walked to the trolley. He was so happy that he would soon be employed again. This was cause for celebration.

When Brothaman made it to the apartment he shared with Shaniqua, he flashed the bit of change he made that day. "Baby, things are about to change for us in a big way."

"That don't look too big," Shaniqua said of the money, just before she took it from him and ran out the door.

※

BROTHAMAN SCRAMBLED TO A SEATED POSITION. The sun pierced his eyes, so he shut them quickly, then opened them very slowly. He turned his head, and looked at the time on the clock on the floor beside the bed. It was already eleven-thirty. He glanced to the left. Shaniqua was out cold from the goodies she purchased with his portrait money.

Brothaman went into the kitchen and poured a glass of the juice Shaniqua bought to go with the gin. He smiled when he sat down. He was happy to have another opportunity after all he had been through.

He was also proud of himself for placing limits on his celebration, unlike Shaniqua.

Brothaman could envision giving Rachel his new business card when she came home for Christmas. He wanted her to be proud of him like she was when they first got married, and to know that he was trying to straighten his life out so that he could be a good father to his sons. *David Brown, Graphic Artist, Winterveld Advertising.* He scratched his head. That name sounded so familiar. *Hmmm. I'll figure it out later.*

Brothaman grabbed a bag of chips, sat in his living room chair, and turned on the television. Cincinnati was at Philadelphia.

Brothaman stared at the television, cheering for neither team. He was a Bears fan, and spent Thanksgiving Day watching the game, and then binging when they lost to Detroit 55-20. *Winterveld Advertising* popped into his mind again. Then he remembered. He applied for a job with them a year ago, they scheduled an interview, and a drug test.

"Oh shit, what am I gonna do?" he asked audibly just as Shaniqua began to show signs of life.

"What are you gonna do about what?"

"The job. I think they're gonna ask me to take a drug test."

"You didn't smoke that much last night." Shaniqua sat on the arm of the chair.

"But I did smoke last night, and the night before that, and Thanksgiving."

"Shoot, you worried about nothing. All you got to do is go to Dee-Mo and get a kit."

"A kit?"

"Yeah, a clean urine kit." She rolled her eyes. "Just make sure you put the heating pad on the kit right before you provide the sample. I'll page him to meet you at the spot."

Seeking out Dee-Mo was the last thing that Brothaman wanted to do, but he thought about his sons and his desire to provide for them. Brothaman grabbed his coat, hat, and gloves and went out to face the cold world.

When he turned the corner of the alley, Dee-Mo was already waiting for him. "Not your punk ass again," he said. He sucked his teeth. "Whatchoo want now?"

Brothaman wanted this exchange over as quickly as possible, and most of all, he did not want to piss Dee-Mo off. "Look I got a lead on a job."

"And your crackhead ass gon' have to pee in a cup."

"Uh, yes." This was going smoother than Brothaman anticipated. "How much for a kit?"

Dee-Mo leaned his shoulders back, pursed his lips, and looked at Brothaman. "For you, a hundred."

"I don't have."

"I don't want to hear what you don't have. That's the price, and you can pay it one way or another."

Brothaman began counting his money. For a split second, he thought about negotiating with Dee-Mo, but thought better of it. "Look man, I really need this job. This is all I have." He handed Dee-Mo the thirty dollars he had left. "I swear, this is all I have to my name. I really need this job. I want to buy my kids something for Christmas."

"So, this is for your kids?"

"Yes."

"And I bet you'll do anything for your kids."

"I will."

"Well, I heard that you were down at Navy Pier yesterday doing portraits."

"I was, that's how I found out about this job opportunity."

"And I heard you were drawing with the pencil in your mouth."

"Yes. My fingers froze and I couldn't move them."

"You want this really bad, don't you?"

"I do. I really need this job now, but I don't have--"

"Well, you can pay me in other ways."

Brothaman's heart began to race. He had no idea what Dee-Mo was going to have him do.

"I tell you what, why don't you show me just how good you are with your mouth." Dee-Mo placed his left hand on Brothaman's shoulder, unzipped his fly with his right, and pushed Brothaman to his knees. It wasn't long before Dee-Mo's eyes rolled back in his head. He had an evil grin on his face and Brothaman heard him say, "Dumb ass motherfucker."

This was the most humiliating thing Brothaman had ever done in his entire life. He closed his eyes, and saw the faces of his sons. He also made a promise to himself to never smoke crack again.

Mrs. Jackson stood in the window of her upstairs bedroom and could not believe what she was seeing in broad daylight in the alley behind her house. She looked for the business card Tommy gave her a few months earlier. This madness had to stop!

16

LOVE'S SERENADE

Thomasine was exhausted although she had slept for most of the four-hour flight from Sydney to Nadi. She was up late working and packing the night before her trip. She hardly slept at all because she was afraid of oversleeping for her flight. For weeks she had been looking forward to vacationing in Fiji with her fiancé.

When the plane touched down Thomasine woke up, renewed and rejuvenated. After exiting Customs and Immigration she went to the airport lounge per Rodney's instructions. She smiled when she saw her fiancé dozing off in an armchair. Sina walked over to him, suitcase in tow. She bent down and kissed his forehead startling him in his seat. He opened his eyes and saw those of his beloved. "Hello, Sweetie Pie," he kissed her once, twice, three times, then stretched his arms and legs. "Did you have a good flight?"

"I did. I slept most of the way. How about you?"

"Ten hours from Seoul, but I'm still exhausted. I celebrated with the team a bit last night."

"And you have good reason for celebration. Halfway through the season and undefeated. You all have swept three continents!" Sina sat in the chair to his right. "I'm so proud of you." She gazed into his eyes and her cheeks spread out into an affectionate grin.

He returned her grin, the dimple in his right cheek was

pronounced, "Thank you, Sina. It means a lot to me to hear you say those words." He glanced at his watch. "Our car should be here soon to take us to the Sun Coast." Rodney stood and stretched.

"Aren't we staying in Nadi?"

"No. We'll spend tonight in the Sun Coast. Tomorrow after breakfast we'll go to Savusavu. It's on the island of Vauna Levu. We'll be there for a few days. Then to the Yasawa Islands for a few days."

"Wow! This is such a pleasant surprise." Thomasine stood, took Rodney's hand, and together they left Nadi International Airport for the drive along Queens Road to Vuda Point.

According to Fijian legend, Vuda Point was where the first settlers arrived in Fiji by canoe nearly 3,500 years ago. They were believed to have come from Thebes, Egypt. Rodney had reserved a Beachfront Spa bure for the night.

A lush, green lawn stretched from the bure to a buffer of hedges that met the edge of the beach. A hammock large enough for two was nestled between palm trees. The duplex-style bure was made of timber and had high ceilings and a polished hardwood floor. A basket of snacks was waiting for them, along with a notice about their appointment for a couple's massage and a note congratulating them on their engagement from Rodney's travel agent.

The hour-long massage, followed by foot reflexology was exactly what Thomasine and Rodney needed. They walked hand-in-hand on the beach as the sun lowered in the sky. Thomasine paused and looked out at the ocean. This was like a dream to her. They walked over to the chaise loungers that lined the beach front and absorbed the view. A bright orange band spread across the water's surface. To the right, the bright, white light from the sun looked like it was sinking into the water, illuminating it. "Sugar Cane, if we don't do anything else this entire week, I've already had a wonderful time."

"Any time I spend with you is wonderful," Rodney squeezed Sina's hand. "And I promise you, this is only the beginning." She leaned over and kissed him. They continued to drink in the view until only a sliver of light stood at the water's surface. Rodney took Sina's hand, and they walked along the beach. He walked beside her on the ocean side.

"I'm having a great time, but I'm even more excited about our future," Thomasine said as they walked. She found the sound of the ocean's waves relaxing.

White string lights at the base of the palm trees welcomed them to the beachfront dining area. Tiki torchlights were staked into the ground throughout, providing more lighting and enhancing the atmosphere. It was a balmy evening with an intermittent gentle breeze. They enjoyed a seafood dinner with a Fijian flair, but most of all they enjoyed each other's company.

Rodney and Sina walked along the beach back to their bure. Sina looked around the room, felt the gentle breezes through the windows from the ocean, and inhaled deeply. She smiled broadly.

"What?" Rodney asked, cheesing back at her.

"This island is so beautiful. I just love this place. It's so romantic."

"Maybe we can come here on our honeymoon."

"Sugar Cane," Sina snuggled close to him. "That would be wonderful!"

And that was music to Rodney's ears.

They spent most of the evening in each other's arms, dozing on the sofa. Just after midnight, Sina tapped Rodney on the shoulder. "We should probably go to bed. If we stay curled up on the sofa all night, we'll lose all of the benefits of the massage we got this afternoon."

"You're right." Rodney stood and stretched, then grabbed a pair of pajama bottoms out of his suitcase. Sina found a sleepshirt. They climbed into bed, cuddled together, and fell fast asleep.

Shortly after five a.m. Rodney woke Sina with a kiss. "Let's go outside and watch the sunrise." Sina slid a bra on underneath her shirt and found a pair of shorts. Rodney wore his reunion T-Shirt.

Just a few steps from the front door of their bure, Rodney helped Sina into the hammock, then climbed in behind her. He wrapped his arms around her waist and kissed the back of her neck.

Thomasine placed her hand on top of Rodney's. "Sugar Cane, these past four months have been amazing, like nothing I've ever dreamed of. You're so caring, so understanding, so loving. I can't wait to become your wife."

Rodney pulled Sina closer, inhaled deeply, and kissed her cheek. "I love you so much Sweetie Pie."

§◦

AFTER AN HOUR-LONG FLIGHT on a seaplane from Nadi International Airport to Savusavu, Thomasine and Rodney reached their resort. Everything was so pristine. The turquoise blue waters of the South Pacific were crystal clear. A cabana with a row of daybeds for two lined a serenity pool. Thomasine looked around like a child in a candy store. "Rodney, this place is absolutely beautiful! It is perfect."

"Then why don't we get married here?"

"It will be a challenge getting all of our family and friends here next summer with everyone's different schedules."

"You think so?" Rodney asked.

"Hmmm. I think it'll be hard, but maybe we can pull it off if we let them know early enough."

"Yeah, maybe we can."

Rodney looked around as they walked toward the bures with thatched roofs. "You know Sweetie Pie, when we were in Cairns you said that you preferred a small, intimate wedding. We can have that," he paused. "Now."

"I really wish we could, but I'm sure we have to have a license first, and that will require a birth certificate. I don't have my birth certificate. And—"

Crystal Mintor opened the door of the first bure when Rodney knocked, joy was spread across her face. "But your mother does."

Sina's eyes teared up. She hugged her mother, and her father walked to the door. "Mama, Daddy, I'm so happy to see you."

Crystal handed Thomasine her birth certificate. "We can catch up later. You have some very important business to take care of. Now!" Reverend Mintor put his arm around his wife and they both smiled as they watched Sina and Rodney leave for the marriage registry.

When they returned to the resort in time for lunch, Sina was in tears when she looked around and saw her closest friends and relatives. Rodney had booked the entire resort and flown everyone who meant the most to them to the island. Evonne was there, as well as Abby, Sina's graduate advisor, and some of Rodney's teammates from high school, college and the Gale Force. She was overwhelmed with joy.

For the first time since the reunion, the Three Musketeers were together again. Thomasine ran over to Rachel and Hope and they shared a group hug. A tear trickled from each of their eyes. Thomasine, Rachel, and Hope's lives had changed monumentally in the four short months since the reunion, and like all growth, it had been a painful process.

During lunch, Rodney sat with Sina's friends and family, and Sina sat with Rodney's. There were others, like Jason and Hank, who has been long-time friends of both Rodney and Sina and weren't sure where to sit. Sina finally got to meet Kimmy and Mrs. Paxton, as well as Rodney's father, Stewart, stepmom, Linda, and his younger brother, Miles. It was a very comfortable, almost familiar feeling for them.

After lunch, the women whisked Thomasine away to one of the deluxe two-bedroom oceanfront bures with a huge deck on the front overlooking Savusavu Bay. Sina's eyes filled with delight when she saw the wedding gowns her Mom, Rachel, Hope, and Kelsey selected for her. She didn't know which one to choose.

"Try them on," Sina's cousin Kelsey said. Sina removed one of the gowns from its hanger. "I can't believe my little cousin is getting married, for real this time."

"I know you didn't go there!" Sina rolled her eyes at Kelsey, then laughed. "Don't just stand there. Help me. You're my matron of honor."

Sina modeled each of the gowns, then made a final selection. She had a great time sipping champagne and chatting, reconnecting with friends, and bonding with her soon-to-be sister-in-law. The afternoon rolled by and they lost track of time when they heard a light rap on the door from the Bure Mama reminding them about dinner.

The muted orange tablecloths perfectly accented the reddish-brown mahogany hardwood flooring in the open-air restaurant. Rodney stood when he saw Thomasine enter with the other ladies. He embraced her deeply, then motioned to the seat beside him. It faced the serenity pool, and just beyond it the bay and mountains in the distance.

"Are you having a good time?" he asked as the waiter served Kokoda, a Fijian ceviche made with coconut cream and served in a coconut to each of the guests.

"Do you really need to ask?" Sina tasted her fish, then closed her

eyes as the flavors blended in her mouth. "This is soooo good."
Thomasine took another bite.

There was a thick tension at the table with Hope and Jason sitting
almost across from each other. "Jason, Rodney tells me that you're
coaching a youth football team. How's that going?" Sina asked, hoping
to circumvent the awkwardness.

"We had a great season, then lost the championship game."

"Ouch," Thomasine said.

"But making it to the playoffs is huge. And the championship
game. Monumental! As for the loss, well, it helps them build
character."

"True," Sina replied.

"So, Rachel," Jason began as the waiter served the main entrée.
"How are the boys?"

"They're doing great."

"I'm surprised you didn't bring them, with Hank here. Is your
mother with them?"

"Oh no. They're staying with Martin's father."

The chatter came to an abrupt halt. "Martin's father?" echoed down
the table.

"You mean their father?" Jason asked.

"I certainly hope you didn't leave them with Brothaman after that
breakfast fire?" Hope finally spoke.

"No, definitely not him. He just started a new job at Winterveld
Advertising in downtown Chicago, so he can't take any time off
from work."

"Rachel," Hope said. "This doesn't make any sense." Thomasine
darted her eyes toward Rodney, then bit her lower lip.

"OK, everyone, I have an announcement to make," Rachel sighed
and put her fork down. She drank quite a bit of the bubbly that afternoon in the bure. She picked up her fork and tapped it on the side of
her glass. "According to DNA paternity test results, Patrick is Martin's
father?"

"The guy you were engaged to?" Jason asked. "Oh, oh, Ohhh. You
did get married pretty fast after you broke up with Patrick."

She picked her fork up and continued eating. Everyone else
stopped.

As much as Jason wanted to ask Rachel the million-dollar question —how could she not know Martin was Patrick's son for five years, he thought better of it. "How did Patrick take the news?"

"Oh, he's been great. The boys are in good hands. Veronica is a Family Nurse Practitioner." Rachel took a sip, then giggled with a squeak.

"Who is Veronica?" Hope asked.

"Patrick's wife. We had Thanksgiving dinner at her parents' home. Patrick's parents and brother came down, so Martin got to meet them for the first time. Patrick's sister, Jessie, lives in Nashville. She's a junior at Vanderbilt. For the most part, it was great." She was nonchalant.

"That had to be interesting. Veronica must be a very, uh understanding woman. How long have they been married?" Hope asked.

"Since September."

"Oh!" Hope said in a high-pitched voice. "September of this year?"

Everyone at the table looked at Rachel, then at Rodney.

"OK. I know what you're thinking. Do not go there," Sina said.

"I am one hundred percent certain that I do not have any children," Rodney answered their unasked question.

"It's all good," Rachel said. "Martin adores his Daddy. He and Malcolm visit them two weekends a month. This has truly been a blessing for me, given all that I've been through the past few months. Brothaman's coma, the news about my father, then finding out that Hank and I have a sister and two brothers in Sydney. We're visiting them right after the wedding."

"Wait," Jason said. "You found out your son has a different father, and you have three siblings in Australia! Whew!"

"Yes. We're going to Sydney to meet Heather, James, and Shane." Rachel turned to the waiter, pointed to her glass, "I'll have another."

Rodney wiped his mouth. "I think it's time for a toast."

SINA AND RODNEY caught the last rays of the setting sun over dessert at an intimate table for two at the end of the pier. "You look very happy," he said as they sipped a dessert wine.

"Are you kidding? This is better than a dream." Thomasine set her glass on the table. "I just don't know how you pulled this off. How did you get everyone here on such short notice?"

Rodney pushed his chair back from the table, then helped Sina up. They strolled along the pier, his arm around her shoulder. "All of these people really love us, Sweetie Pie, and they want to share in our happiness, particularly your parents. When I met with them to ask for your hand in marriage, they talked to me a long time, especially your father. He really wants the best for you and I'm honored that he sees me in that way."

Sina looked deeply into Rodney's eyes.

"And a few more guests will arrive tomorrow?"

"Oh, who?"

"Remember Nick from high school?"

"Yes. You all were tight?"

"He'll be here in time for the rehearsal dinner."

"Nice."

"Your Mom and I talked and she said you would want your regular stylist to do your hair, so Regina arrives in the morning."

Sina's eyes widened to match the smile that crossed her face. "So that's why she asked me questions about my hair and the updo I had at the reunion."

"She thinks it will be perfect for the wedding. But only if that's what you want."

"I think that will be beautiful."

"And Reverend Grace as well. She was scheduled to arrive today, but had eulogize a Mrs. McLaurin."

"Mrs. McLaurin was something else. Can you imagine a one-hundred-three-year-old woman getting up early every Sunday morning to help a ninety-year-old woman get ready for church?"

"Wow," Rodney laughed. "That's truly a blessing. I hope to have a long, healthy life like Mrs. McLaurin."

"And I hope, we have a long, healthy, prosperous life together."

"'Til death do us part."

"For all of eternity." They stopped, Rodney leaned down and kissed Thomasine.

"I'm really glad that we got to have dessert alone, have a little time to ourselves. So, what are your plans for the evening?" Rodney asked as they reached the front door of Sina's bure.

"I guess I'll just wait for everyone to come back from dinner or wherever they are." She made note of how dark it was inside. "How about you?"

"I'll hang out with the guys. Get to know your big, I mean my big brother a little better."

She turned to face Rodney and pulled him close. Her head rested on his chest as she held him in an embrace. He bent down to meet her lips, squeezed her more tightly, then inhaled deeply. "Mmm, I'll see you at breakfast."

Sina opened the door. Tea light candles on the floor outlined a path strewn with rose petals. She followed the trail, some red, some pink, some white which led to the rear of the bure. As Sina approached the French doors leading to the deck and courtyard she heard soft, sensual music. When she reached for the door it opened, a hand reached for hers. He was strapping. His black attire was punctuated by a red tie. He gazed at her with beguiling eyes, a diamond stud accented his left ear. His smile bloomed, displaying perfectly spaced white teeth surrounded by a neatly groomed beard. When he spoke, his voice was deep and mellow.

"Good evening, Thomasine," he said. "I'm Vincent Tyler. Tonight, I want you to relax and let your mind escape," he led her to the chaise underneath the pavilion. In front of it was a well-lit serenity pool surrounded by most of the ladies who came to celebrate. Her Mom and Carol Paxton decided to sit this one out. "Tonight, I'm going to take you on a sensual journey of passion and enchantment. So, listen carefully, to the voice of romance." Vincent Tyler thrilled every woman there through his performance of erotic poetry from his forthcoming book *I Thought About You Today*.

AFTER BREAKFAST, Sina and Rodney joined their parents and siblings on a Medicine Walk offered by the resort. This was an interest of Reverend Mintor who majored in biology in college and had long been curious about the medicinal properties of plants. Kimmy also had an interest, but from a culinary perspective. During the two-hour long journey, they were introduced to over twenty specimens of plants native to Fiji from Totodro, to Moli, and Layalaya, which cured a variety of ailments.

The afternoon was spent in leisure as well. Sina and the ladies explored Savusavu's marine life through a glass bottom boat tour. While dolphins danced in front of their boat, they saw colorful coral reefs, and schools of orange and white clownfish, blue sergeant fish, grouper, iridescent parrotfish, and giant clams.

The happy couple met with Reverend Grace before dinner on the beach with their families and the wedding party. Rodney and Sina took turns sinking in their seats as their friends and relatives roasted them. And after everyone had spoken, Rodney and Sina stood and thanked everyone for their years of love and support, and for taking time out of their schedules to fly halfway across the globe to join them in their celebration of love.

🍋

REGINA HAD STYLED Sina's hair in a lovely updo. Her makeup highlighted her natural beauty. Sina looked regal in her A-line gown with a portrait neckline. Swarovski crystals outlined the neckline and perfectly accented designs on the lace overlay. She wore her grandmother's cultured pearl necklace, which her mother gave to her along with the same advice she received with her mother's pearls on her wedding day.

There was a rap at the door. Four warriors in grass skirts had arrived to escort Thomasine. They guided her to her chariot, which they carried to the water's edge. It floated on a raft decorated with local flowers and braided palm fronds. Sina sat underneath a decorated arch. A bouquet of red ginger flowers was in her hand. Anticipation built as they slowly floated on the bay. This felt surreal for Sina. A bright, sunny day on clear, turquoise waters in what she called paradise. Sina felt warm and fuzzy inside. Her heart was melting. She savored every second as she moved closer and closer to her guests, and saw her father standing on the beach waiting for her. Another Fijian warrior was there to greet her. He blew the davui, a conch shell, to signal the procession of the bride. Of Sina. Rodney took one look at his bride and became full, emotional, his lips spread into a big smile through tear-filled eyes.

The warriors lifted her chariot from the raft and carried her to her father, then lowered the chariot so that her father could walk her down the aisle behind the Fijian flower girl.

Tears began to fall from Rodney's eyes as Sina came closer and closer. Reverend Grace looked at the happy couple and beamed with joy and pride. When they reached the marriage altar of palm fronds and tropical flowers, Reverend Mintor shook Rodney's hand, removed the veil from Sina's face, then kissed his daughter's cheek. With his right hand, he removed Sina's right hand from his left arm and placed it in Rodney's left hand. "Who gives this woman to be married to this man?" Reverend Grace asked.

"I do," Reverend Mintor replied, tears of joy in his eyes. He took the seat next to his wife, then held her hand.

"Dearly beloved, we are gathered here today in this celebration of love for Rodney Joshua Paxton Harris and Thomasine Elizabeth Mintor. For we are not here to witness a beginning, but rather a continuation of what already is! Each of you here today is very special and important to Rodney and Sina, and they have asked that you join them in this celebration of the love that has already occurred in their lives, and this commitment they make today. The couple has chosen to write their own vows."

Rodney looked more deeply into Sina's eyes. He had not taken his eyes off her since he first saw her chariot arrive. The palm trees gently swayed with the light breeze. "Thomasine Mintor, my Sweetie Pie, I've had a crush on you for a really long time. Since we were juniors in high school. And I'm overjoyed to have found you again. I love you dearly and deeply, and I cherish each moment with you. You are an accomplished, amazing woman, and I want to share what's left of this life with you, loving you, cherishing you, building and living our dreams together. Starting and ending our days together.

"I love the way your face lights up when we share joys, and the way we hold each other close when we face challenges. I promise to always be there for you through the good times and bad.

"I'm so glad we've reconnected, and I know with absolute certainty that this is our time. I can't promise that our life together will be easy, but I can promise you that I will always love you and be right by your side on this journey.

"Thomasine, I love you. I appreciate you. I thank you for all the happiness you bring to me. You make each day worth living."

A tear fell from Sina's eyes. "Rodney, when you proposed to me, you said that when you went to the reunion, you weren't expecting this, I certainly wasn't expecting to find the love of my life, but I'm elated that I have. You bring me peace and joy like I've never experienced, and happiness to brighten each day, and I love you.

"Sugar Cane, you're strong, wise and courageous, and what I love most about you is your decision making. You always do what's best.

"I promise to be your biggest cheerleader in life, and work with you as we attain our dreams and goals. With you by my side, I know that we'll reach any goal we desire.

"You empower me. You uplift me. You've healed me.

"Rodney, you've shown me what real love is, and you've taught me that I deserve the best. You know me well. Very well. This. I thought I was just going on vacation, but this! Your attention to detail. This pleasant surprise, which I would have planned the exact same way.

"Rodney, I love you immensely and I always will. Each day I start and end with thoughts of you. We have a whole lifetime ahead of us. And you are the one I look forward to sharing each day with."

After they exchanged the rings, Reverend Grace pronounced them husband and wife. They continued the wedding in Fijian tradition, a Kava ceremony and a performance by a Fijian quartet.

Just a stone's throw from the wedding altar, the sun peeked through the row of palm trees which lined the beach. The head table was adjacent. Round tables dressed in white linens and covered chairs with red bows matching the bridesmaid's dresses held the guests who just witnessed Rodney and Sina's Celebration of Love. To the right, a wooden walkway led to the mahogany portable dance floor.

As Sina and Rodney finished taking photos with their bridal party, they walked arm-in-arm to join their guests. After their introduction and a blessing, the newly married couple made their way from table to table greeting everyone while waiters passed hors d'oeuvres. They sat briefly at the head table and had a quick bite, when the DJ began playing a new song both Rodney and Sina had fallen in love with, Ramsey Lewis' *Love's Serenade*. During the light percussion in the introduction, Rodney led Sina down the wooden walkway to the dance floor for their first dance as husband and wife.

Her focus was fixed on his. The first notes of the bass were their cue. They moved in rhythm with the music. Sina smiled at Rodney and sang her own loving lyrics in perfect pitch along with the piano melody. He spun her, then dipped her as the song reached a crescendo. As the motif recurred, they resumed their slow dance. Their gaze was constant, consistent, caring. Sina looked deeply into the eyes of her beloved, her Sugar Cane, and gave thanks.

After Sina danced with her father to Nat King Cole and Natalie Cole's version of *Unforgettable,* and Rodney had a memorable dance with his mother to *You are the Sunshine of my Life* the wait staff resumed the food service.

Jason stood from his seat. "French author and poet Victor Hugo once said, 'The greatest happiness in life is the conviction that we are loved.' I think that we can all agree that this celebration we have each flown halfway across the world to witness, is a prime example of that happiness. Most of all, we can clearly see how much they love each other. All I have to say is, Rodney, Thomasine. It's about time. I've known Rodney almost twenty years. We first met when we played on the same youth football team. We were kids, just nine years old. A few years later we reconnected at Piney Hill, and I met Thomasine our freshman year. Man, you all should have seen how Rodney cheesed every time he saw Thomasine walk past his locker between classes. I was like, Man, why don't you ask her out. Take her to the movie. Take her to see *Nightmare on Elm Street 2* so that she'll squeeze your hand tight on the scary parts."

Rodney and Thomasine laughed, along with the rest of their guests.

"I thought by senior year you'd get the courage, but that prom thing didn't quite work out."

Rodney and Sina looked at each other with eyebrows raised, shrugged their shoulders, then smiled.

"I always knew you and Thomasine were the perfect match. I've been dropping you hints for over the years. Thomasine's doing a radio show. Thomasine just got her Ph.D. Thomasine's coming to Chicago next week.

"But when I caught a glimpse of the two of you dancing to that Luther Vandross and Gregory Hines tune at the reunion, I thought just maybe this is the start of something magnificent. Then when you told me you just up and got on a plane and flew to Sydney just to let her know you cared, I thought, this brother is in love. Really, in love. That night we watched the Broncos and Patriots game, and you told me you were going to propose when you got back to Sydney, I was thrilled for you man. You both deserve the best. You are two amazing people who I'm fortunate to call friends and I wish you the greatest happiness life and love have to offer."

With the remainder of the traditional wedding reception festivities complete, the cake cutting, bouquet toss, and garter toss, the happy couple and their guests filled the dance floor to the Electric Slide. Rodney eased his way over to the DJ and asked him to lower the music. He walked over to Thomasine and took her hand. "Thomasine and I would like to thank each of you for joining us as we start our life together. I hope that you each enjoy the rest of your time on Savusavu. My beautiful wife and I are off to our honeymoon. We love each of you so much. You mean the world to us."

Rodney and Sina walked along the beach towards the bures. "So, we're honeymooning on the, what was it?"

"Yasawa Islands, Turtle Island in particular."

"Oh."

"It's a couples only island. And they only allow fourteen couples at the most on the island at one time."

"Nice. What time does our plane leave? I have to pack."

"It's a charter, so we'll be good." He bent down and kissed his bride. "Wear something comfortable. We're having dinner on a pontoon."

She reached the knob of the door on the bure where she was staying. "Wait a minute!" Rodney said. He swept her in his arms and carried her over the threshold, then gently put her feet on the floor, supporting her back until she was upright. Sina looked up at him with starry eyes.

"This is the first time I'm alone with my husband." She caressed the

side of his face, then kissed him passionately, feverishly, and fully. Sina
outlined his shoulders with her fingertips while he pulled her close, his
hands resting on her lower back.

"At the rate we're going, we'll never make it to Turtle Island." He
kissed her again.

"You're right." Rodney turned towards the door. "But before you
go darling, I need your help." He turned to face her and she turned
around, then pointed to her zipper. He served as her able assistant and
helped his new wife out of the dress.

He stood back and looked at her. "I think I'd better go, now,
before I."

"Yeah. We'll never make it if you don't."

"I'll meet you back here shortly." He carefully closed the door
behind him.

Sina felt joy rising inside her. She was Mrs. Rodney Harris. She
chose a strapless red dress for the evening, then carefully packed her
clothing and toiletries in her suitcase. She looked down at the diamond
band on her finger. *This is really happening to me.* She closed her eyes
and savored the moment, the feeling, the joy.

WHEN THEY ARRIVED on Turtle Island they stopped to carve their own
message into a paving stone on one of the resort's walkways. *Sugar
Cane & Sweetie Pie, 12-18-97.* They checked into Vonu Point, a stone
villa with floor to ceiling windows offering panoramic views of the
lagoon and neighboring islands.

The sun had fully set when they made their way to the beach for
dinner. The flicker of candlelight from soft lanterns surrounded the
table for two in the center of the floating dock. The air was light, the
waves were subtle as they drifted very slowly from the shore over a
dinner of fresh caught Pacific green lobster and champagne. Turtle
Island specialized in fresh, local food picked just minutes before it is
served.

Sina was full of emotion. She inhaled deeply, lips pursed, cheeks in
full bloom. She looked across the table at her husband, soft candlelight

illuminating his face, and saw a reflection of her immense happiness. They both found the dinner and each other delectable.

The moon was waning and darkness enveloped them as they relaxed in the in-ground spa of their villa. The floor-to-ceiling windows of the sunroom offered a spectacular view. The starry sky was breathtaking. Rodney pulled Sina close, and became intoxicated from the champagne, the view, and his beloved.

17

MAIDEN VOYAGE

Heather had barely let go of Rachel's hand since she and Hank arrived. Along with James and Shane, she welcomed their long-lost siblings with open arms at baggage claim at Sydney Kingsford Smith Airport. After their brief stay in Fiji, Rachel and Hank felt like old pros going through customs on their first trip abroad. When Heather first laid eyes on her older half-siblings, she encased them in her arms. "Rachel, Hank," she rocked from side-to-side as she squeezed them tighter, "I'm so happy you're here." She exhaled the word "so" out of her mouth very slowly. Heather was almost possessive of them, barely letting James and Shane get a good look at them.

James tapped Heather on the shoulder. "Ease up Heather," he said. "Can I at least say G'day, eh?"

Heather stepped back, and they all chuckled. Shane grabbed Rachel's bag, and they made their way to the parking lot. "Sit next to me, love," Heather told Rachel as she got behind the wheel. Shane opened the left front door for Rachel. "The fellas can sit in the back."

The auto dealerships and shops that lined O'Riordan Street reminded her of suburban Chicago. From what she could see, Sydney didn't look much different from the place she called home. They turned left onto Wyndham and continued onto Gibbons. That area reminded Rachel of the Piney Hill High neighborhood with big, open urban green space. Once they turned onto Lawson, she saw a vast difference. The area seemed more compact. Row houses lined one side of the street while the train station was on the other. They turned onto a very narrow street, and Heather parked across from the colorful and crowded homes with filigree wrought iron railings on the second-floor balconies.

"I'll get your bags," Shane said after he opened the door for Rachel. They followed Heather to a Victorian Era sandstone terrace home. The exterior had been painted a butterscotch yellow. In the living room, a Christmas tree with ceramic ornaments hand painted with traditional Aboriginal dot art stood in front of the window in the center of the front wall. A black angel adorned the top of the tree. Just above Rachel's eye level, there was an oval ornament of the Aboriginal flag. To the right hung a kangaroo with a Santa hat. "I'll take your bags up to the room where you'll be staying," Shane said to Rachel. James showed Hank to his temporary quarters, just beyond the living room.

The walls of the living room were painted a terracotta red and a beige sectional sofa consumed most of the room. Above the sofa, a display of photos of Heather, James, and Shane, and traditional Aboriginal dot paintings hung neatly. Heather looked at her watch. "We have time for a cuppa before dinner. I made us reservations at Fish at the Rocks." Rachel and Hank followed her down to the kitchen and they enjoyed the sunny summer afternoon on the brick courtyard.

PENCIL SKETCHES of sailboats adorned the viridian green walls of Fish at the Rocks. The sun was slightly visible through the blinds of the packed restaurant. The siblings were seated at a table in the center of the room. Hank sat at the head, and Heather and Rachel sat side-by-side. James and Shane were across from them. They left the seat with the back to the door empty. It was something their Dad always did. "This was Dad's favorite restaurant." Heather shared.

"Yeah, we came here every year for his birthday," Shane said as the waitress brought them glasses of water, then removed the extra chair.

"And he always ordered the Cajun shrimp," James added.

Rachel smiled. "Wow. I'm not surprised. He grew up in New

Orleans." Rachel sipped her water and perused the menu. "The architecture of the homes in your neighborhood reminds me a lot of New Orleans. I can see how he would have felt at home here. It makes sense." It was the first time Rachel said anything about her father since she arrived in Sydney, but as he had been missing since she was an infant, there wasn't much that she knew about him, at least not first-hand. She hoped through meeting her Indigenous Australian siblings that she and Hank could fill in the gaps. "What's a Moreton Bay Bug?" she asked.

Heather chuckled. "It's a tiny lobster. You should give it a burl, eh." Rachel had a puzzled look on her face.

"She means you should try it," James said. "You should try stuff you can't get back in the States."

"Order all you want to try," Shane said laughing. "James is paying for it all. He just got a big job in engineering."

"And don't worry," Heather said. "If you don't like it, Shane'll eat it. He'll eat anything."

Rachel took Heather's advice, and found what she knew as an appetizer, but the Australians considered an entrée, of Moreton Bay bug tails with a sweet chili sauce, quite tasty. Both she and Hank particularly enjoyed the Barramundi stuffed with prawns, vegetables, and red curry sauce. Rachel and Heather decided to take dessert to go, while their brothers headed over to Kings Cross to pub hop.

"PUT YOUR FEET UP." Heather told Rachel, just before she grabbed the tray with their tea and dessert. Rachel walked through the French doors which led from the dining area to the courtyard. A gas grill rested against the sandstone fence, painted butterscotch yellow like the house. Rachel relaxed on a chaise lounge, and Heather placed the tray with their goodies on the table beside her.

"So how did Dad meet your Mum?" Heather asked Rachel.

Rachel smiled. "They were high school sweethearts. He was born in New Orleans in 1950 and raised by a single mom."

"What about his Dad?"

"As far as I know, it was just him and his mother. I really don't know anything about our grandfather. I got to visit our grandmother a few times, but I was very young when she died."

"Did he have any siblings?"

"No, he was his mother's only child, but I don't know if he had any siblings through his Dad."

"Were his parents ever married?"

"No. Curtis was his mother's maiden name. I guess if I got his birth certificate I could find out his father's name. I don't know, I guess he could still be alive."

"Who knows, he could be quite delighted to learn he has five accomplished grandchildren, eh."

"He might be." Rachel sipped her tea, then smiled broadly. "My Mom often told me stories about when they first met. It was freshman year of high school. Mom said that Dad told her when he first met her that she would be his wife."

"How sweet?"

"After high school Mom went to Chicago to go to college. She lived with her Aunt Mary and commuted to Roosevelt University. That's in downtown Chicago. Dad followed her and went to work in a factory on the west side of Chicago. Eight months later, they got married. I was born a year later."

"Wow." Heather took a bite of her tart. "Is your mother still alive?"

"Yes," Rachel replied. "She eventually remarried. She was pregnant with Hank when she learned that Dad was missing. She was so young and had what we now know as post-partum depression. Her Aunt Mary and Uncle Charlie raised us. But they've both passed on. Uncle Charlie died my sophomore year of college, and Aunt Mary died from cancer right after I graduated from college."

"My Mum died from cancer, when I was fifteen. Poor Shane was only eight."

"That's so sad. I'm so sorry to hear that."

"It was really hard on us. All of our Auntys and Uncles stepped in and helped us out."

"How many brothers and sisters did your Mom have?"

"She had a sis' n two brothers, but none of them lived in New South Wales. They were separated from their Mum and from each other when they were young. Bloody Stolen Generations! Mum said she was from a small area near Cairns in Queensland." Heather sipped her tea. "In my culture, we have a great deal of respect for the elders in our community. We call them our Auntys and Uncles."

"Ok. What we call extended family in the US," Rachel yawned and stretched. The sun had completely lowered in the sky offering relief from the near ninety-degree heat of the day. A soft breeze made the late Spring evening perfect. Summer solstice was two days away.

"It's getting kind of late, you've had a long day with the flight from Fiji. We can go inside."

Rachel reached for the tray. "Hands off, I've got it," Heather said, "I want you to relax and enjoy your time here. Go up to the second floor and turn right. Your room is on the front of the house. I'll be up in a minute with something a little stronger. We can chat on the balcony until you're ready to go to sleep."

"Thank you, Heather."

"No worries, Sis." Heather loved saying that almost as much as she loved having a sister.

Rachel smiled, changed into shorts and a T-shirt, then sat in a chair at the small bistro set on the wrought iron balcony. She waved to one of Heather's neighbors she saw walking on the narrow sidewalk of the narrow street.

"I brought something a little stronger than tea," Heather said when she joined Rachel, in her lounging clothes. Rachel took a sip, then posed a question.

"Say, how did Dad meet your mother?"

Heather smiled, then made a clicking sound with her teeth. "You know, Rachel, it all makes sense now. They met in 1971 at an anti-Vietnam Moratorium rally in Hyde Park."

Rachel bit her bottom lip and smiled. "Given what we both know now about Dad, that's not surprising."

"Mum was quite the activist. I think that is what Dad found so attractive. Paul Coe, he's one of our Black activists, was giving a speech, and Mum was among the ten thousand cheering for him. That's when she caught Dad's attention. Mum told me and our brothers how moved she was by Paul's speech over and over again. He said, '*You raped our women, you stole our land, you massacred our ancestors, you destroyed our culture, and now—when we refused to die out as you expected—you want to kill us with your hypocrisy.'* Mum was very active in the beginnings of the Black Power Movement, until I came along, then James, and then Shane.

"She helped out when she could, but put her kids first. She was a wonderful Mum and he was the best Dad in the world. I'm sad that he's gone, but happy that he died surrounded by James, Shane, and me."

Rachel sniffled. "Heather, it gives me great relief to hear that. All my life I imagined that he had a horrific and gruesome death as a prisoner of war. I'm so happy to hear that he was surrounded by loved ones when he took his last breath." Rachel smiled through tear-filled eyes, then took another sip of her liquor. "I just wish I remembered something about him."

"He loved James, Shane, and me the same, but I was really a Daddy's girl. I had Dad wrapped around my little finger."

"My Mom told me I did as well." They both laughed.

"When I was at university and came home for breaks, Dad used to cook me a big brekkie, and we sat out back and ate it while James and Shane were at school. And he was always there, for every school play, every recital, every, everything.

"And when I started dating as a teen he sat me down and said to me, 'Heather, always remember that you are the prize. Never let a bloke treat you like you aren't.'"

"That's advice I needed to hear as a teen."

"Not so lucky in love, eh?"

Inspired by liquid courage, Rachel opened up to her sister about the triumphs, but mostly the travails of her love life.

"Sorry to hear about Calvin. He's a wanker! And your husband's addiction! I'm so sorry you are going through that love, but I understand where you are right now. Just remember that he can beat his addiction when he makes the decision to. It won't be easy. It can be done, but he has to want it for himself."

Rachel sighed deeply.

"So how did he take the news that Martin isn't his son?"

"I haven't told him yet."

"Rachel!" Heather exclaimed. "You have to tell him."

"Heather, I couldn't do it over the phone, especially since he had just gotten out of a coma when I found out," she turned up her cup and finished her drink. "But when Hank and I fly back home, we will stop over in St. Louis and meet Patrick and Veronica with the boys during our layover, then fly to Chicago. I will tell him as soon as I see him face-to-face."

NESTLED on a picnic rug among the tens of thousands who joined together to ring in the holiday season, the siblings spent their last night together in Sydney at the annual *Carols in the Domain* concert in the Royal Botanic Gardens. It had been a family tradition ever since Heather could remember watching the concert from her Dad's shoulders. "Maybe you can bring your boys next year, eh," Heather said to her sister as a tear streamed from her eye. While she was elated to be with her newfound siblings, it was the first time in her memory she attended without her Dad, and it would be her first Christmas without him. For Rachel and Hank, it was the perfect way to usher in the holiday after their whirlwind tour of the South Pacific.

HANK TILTED the tree slightly to the left. "Is it straight now?" he asked his nephews.

"Yes, Uncle Hank," they said, almost in unison. Snowflakes fell lightly from the sky, joining the white blanket which already covered the grassy areas. As exhausted as Hank was from the trip and long flight, he shoveled the walkway of the previous day's snow before he went out to find the perfect tree.

Hank stood back and looked at the tree he placed in front of the bay window. "It's perfect." He walked over to the box of Christmas decorations and pulled out a string of white lights. He handed Martin the end with the plug, then stretched the lights out. Hank took the end of the lights, picked Malcolm up, and handed it to him. "We'll start at the top," he said as he and the boys walked towards the tree. "Martin, hold that end up. I'll let you put the next string of lights on, and Malcolm can hold the plug." The boys took turns stringing white lights around the tree, before they added metallic gold garland.

"Uncle Hank, how will Santa know we're in Chicago?" Malcolm asked.

"Mommy sent him a letter before she went to T-Sina and Uncle Rodney's wedding. He knows you and Martin are here." Rachel said as she walked down the stairs. When she reached the bottom landing cheer spread across her face. "It's beautiful," she told her sons, who by then had begun to hang ornaments on the tree. She wore a denim dress and boots. Her hair was still in the updo from Sina's wedding with extra bobby pins to hold the pieces of hair that had fallen astray. Her makeup was flawless. She walked to the closet and put on her coat, then stood by her sons and admired the tree once again. "Hmmm, something's missing." She walked over to the sofa, then unzipped her carry-on bag. "Boys," she pulled out a kangaroo ornament with a Santa hat. "Your Aunty Heather sent this to you from Australia. She's Mommy and Uncle Hank's sister."

"Your real sister, not like T-Sina and T-Hope?" Malcolm asked.

"Yes, our real sister. We have the same father. You also have two real uncles, James and Shane. They live in Australia."

"Wow! Did T-Sina find them for you?" Martin asked.

"No, Martin. We found each other."

"I guess you and Aunty Heather are like me and Malcolm. We don't have the same father, but we have the same mother, so that makes us brothers."

"Yes, it does."

The boys debated briefly over where to hang their Australian orna-ment. They chose a spot at their eye level, then stood back and admired it. "Great job!" Rachel told her sons. She bent down and planted a kiss on each of their foreheads. "Mommy will be back later. I have an errand to run."

Rachel picked up her purse and Hank's car keys off the table near the front door. The engine was still slightly warm from Hank's tree purchase. Rachel brushed the light dusting of snow from the windows, and drove off, even more full of anxiety than she was the day she took Martin to meet Patrick.

She turned right to head west on 95th Street. The traffic was moderate for the holiday season and the road was a little slick due to the mix of oil and freshly fallen snow. From the glow of her headlights she could see the dirty snow that had piled up along the curb, with well-worn areas at corners for pedestrians to cross the street or board the bus. She crossed Ashland, and as usual streetlights had been decorated for the holiday season in Beverly. The median held trees illuminated by white string lights. If Rachel thought contacting Patrick to tell him he had a five-year-old son was hard, having to tell her estranged husband that he is not the biological father of the little boy born less than a year after their marriage was even more difficult. Addiction aside, he was a man who had been there for her when Aunt Mary died. She still loved him, but not what he had become.

She was thankful to find a space in the small parking lot of *Pepe's*. She found a little comfort in the restaurant she and her friends spent so many weekend evenings at during their youth. It felt as much like home as a restaurant could. Rachel ordered a margarita on the rocks while she waited for Brothaman to arrive.

With her face in her palms, she rubbed her fingertips across her eyes, then her temples. A votive candle provided a hint of light on the table of the booth where she sat in the dimly lit restaurant. The décor was simple. Wham!'s *Careless Whisper* played on the jukebox. Rachel took a sip of her drink, then glanced at her watch. She breathed deeply.

"Rachel," she heard the familiar voice of the man she still had feelings for.

She turned her head, looked over her shoulder at him, then tilted it to the side. "David?" The top of Brothaman's jacket was unzipped, revealing the knot of his tie. His hair was neatly cut and his chin sported a goatee. In a nutshell that brother looked fine, finer than the day she married him. In his left hand, he carried a shopping bag, and when he sat it on the seat of the booth across from where she was sitting, then removed his jacket, Rachel noticed he was wearing his wedding band on his healing, but still mangled hand. He bent down to hug her.

"I hope you haven't been waiting too long. When I got to 95th and Dan Ryan, I had to wait in line for a bus."

"I haven't been here very long," Rachel took another sip of her drink.

Brothaman sat across the table from her. The waitress came to take their orders.

He smiled at his wife. "So how have you been?" Admiration was in his eyes.

"I've been good considering. I've had a lot going on lately."

"I have too, Rachel." He took a sip of his water. "But first I need to apologize to you, Hank, and especially the boys for all the mistakes I've made. I know I made your life a living hell. But I've been clean now for almost a month. Three weeks and two days to be exact." He beamed with pride at this accomplishment. "This job at Winterveld Advertising has given me a new lease on life.

"Rachel, I've been going to Narcotics Anonymous meetings, and right now I'm getting back on my feet. This new job I have is wonderful, just wonderful! The benefits—wow. When I make it past ninety days on the job I'll be eligible for tuition reimbursement. Once I get back on my feet, I'm going to go back to school and get a master's degree. I'm not sure what I'll get it in yet, but free tuition. I have to take advantage of that." He couldn't stop talking and barely paused to take a breath.

"Hey, I got this for you." Brothaman took a flat, square jewelry box from the shopping bag. "It's a Christmas gift, but I really want to give it to you now."

Rachel opened the box. Inside there was a heart-shaped pendant with small diamonds on a fourteen-karat gold chain. "I bought it at an actual jewelry store, not off the street. I'm done with that. With all of that. I really hope that you'll consider giving me another chance. I want to make it up to you and the boys. I really do.

"Rachel," he took her hand. "You know that until you came into my life, it was just me and my Mom. Just the two of us. When she was diagnosed with cancer when I was fifteen, I started getting high to ease the fear and pain of possibly losing her. The cancer went into remission and she lived long enough to see me graduate from Columbia College. She was my biggest cheerleader, then the cancer came back. She died and you came into my life. You have given me so much that I took for granted, but no more. I have to be honest, when Martin was born, as happy as I was, it was scary at the same time. I was afraid that I would not be a good father because I did not know how. You know I've never seen my father. He left my Mom when she told him she was pregnant. I did not want to be like that, but I didn't have an example of what a good father should be. It scared me. I should have been honest with you about what was going on with me emotionally, instead of turning to drugs."

Rachel looked into Brothaman's eyes. Her tears matched his.

"Rachel, they are a demonic force that ruined my life and nearly took it. I almost died in that alley, but I've learned my lesson. I want to make things right with you, with the boys. I want us to be a family again. I'm saving up so that when the school year ends you and the boys can move back to Chicago and we can be together again. Maybe we can buy a house." He took her hand. "And I promise to be the man I told you I would be when I asked you to marry me. Rachel, will you please give me a second chance?"

The waitress placed their hot plates in front of them as Rachel erupted in tears. "David," she squeezed out between her deep sobs, "I have something to tell you that you're not going to like, and I don't know how."

"What is it?" there was urgency in his voice. "It's okay. After everything I've been through I can handle anything."

Rachel held her head down, "David," she sighed deeply, "I found out a few months ago through DNA testing, that Martin is not your son. He's Patrick's son."

"What? How?" Brothaman closed his eyes and listened while Rachel recounted the story of her discovery, and explained that this was something she felt she owed to share with him face-to-face. A mélange of emotions consumed Brothaman. His chest felt like it would burst, while an intense pain developed in the pit of his stomach. It was a mixture of anger, disappointment, and a deep wound to the ego.

"So, I can't leave Nashville. The boys are settled there, and they spend two weekends a month with Patrick. Martin has missed out on the first five years of his life with his father. I can't take him away now." Brothaman's heart began to race even faster. He rubbed his hands down the sides of his face, his eyes burned a hole in Rachel's face.

"I just lost my appetite." Brothaman placed cash on the table to cover the bill and left the restaurant without uttering another word.

He crossed the street and paced back and forth at the bus stop. *She can't take him away from his father. I don't believe this.* To the right was a pay phone. Brothaman put a quarter in the phone and as much as he hated to, he paged Dee-Mo. His cheeks filled with air and he externally exhaled deeply, as if he was blowing dozens of candles off a birthday cake. A few blocks away, he saw the bus coming. He walked closer to the curb only to have the bus, full of shoppers from Evergreen Plaza, pass him by.

Inside the restaurant, Rachel finished her margarita and asked the waitress to box the food. She loved Pepe's and wasn't willing to let the food go to waste. "Say, have you ever been to the casinos in Indiana," she asked the waitress when she brought back their food.

"Yes. I go to the Empress all of the time."

"How far is it?"

"Not far at all. Just go east on 95th as far as it goes, then make a right onto Ewing to Indianapolis Boulevard, then make a left. You'll see it a few miles down on your right."

JASON SLOWED to find a parking space. To his right, he saw Zuri out shoveling the snow. He pulled to the curb, jumped out of the car, and took the shovel from her. "Go inside," he told her. "I'll take care of this." Jason cleared the sidewalk in front of her house and the walkway to the curb, before tackling the porch. Zuri sprinkled salt on the landing of the porch, before Jason assumed that responsibility on the sidewalk, driveway, and walkway for her. He walked back to his car and removed the shopping bag of gifts from his trunk.

Zuri had hot cocoa ready for him when he stepped into her foyer, placed his bag beside the door, removed his boots, and sat on the sofa. "Thank you for shoveling the snow," she sat beside him. "Christopher had been handling that for me, but he's with is Dad for Christmas."

Jason warmed his hands with the mug, then looked over at Zuri and smiled. "I just picked up a few gifts for Christopher. He reminds me so much of myself when I was his age," he sipped the sweet cocoa. "He's such a good kid."

"That's so nice of you," Zuri smiled. Jason stood and walked across

the room to retrieve the bag. He took some of the gifts from the bag
and put them underneath the tree.

"And there's something for you too," Jason said as he handed the
long, flat box to Zuri.

"Oh, you didn't have to," Zuri said. "Thanks." She smiled. "I hope
you don't mind if I wait until Christmas to open it."

Jason sat beside her. "I don't mind at all." He took another sip of his
cocoa. "Zuri, I have a personal question to ask you."

She turned and looked at him. "How personal?"

"Are you single?" he asked.

"I am."

"You're a really nice lady Zuri, and I really like you. Maybe I could
take you out to dinner sometime, that is if you're interested."

Zuri smiled at him. "Jason, I'm really flattered." She sipped her
cocoa, then placed the mug back on the table. "I like you too, but I
have a personal question for you."

Jason rested his chin on his left thumb, his index finger just below
his nose. He placed his other hand on his lap, his face began to spread,
lips parted slightly revealing a hint of his pearly whites. "Sure."

"Are you fully available to me?"

"Yes, I'm single."

"That's not what I asked you." She put her mug on the table.
"Jason, are you fully available to me."

"I am. My divorce was final six weeks ago."

"And how long were you married?"

"For five years."

"And how long did you and your ex-wife date?"

"Nine years. Since freshman year of high school."

Zuri stood and shook her head. "You don't get it."

"Get what?"

"Jason, you just ended a relationship you were in for fourteen
years. You spent about half of your life with your ex-wife. You haven't
had a chance to heal. You need time and space for that."

Jason rested his elbows on his thighs, folded his hands together
with fingers pointing downward, and rested his chin on the tips of his
thumbs. The look of defeat was on his face.

"You have a lot to process, and it'll take some time." Her fingertips grazed his shoulder. "But, I'm sure that you'll agree with me that a happy, healthy relationship, built on friendship is best, and that's where I'd like for us to start."

&

BROTHAMAN PULLED the collar of his jacket up to cover his earlobes as he walked briskly after getting off the bus. The tops of his ears were beet red from the cold. He hoped Dee-Mo was still there since his journey took longer than expected. Two more buses filled with Christmas shoppers passed him before he was able to board one with standing room only.

Brothaman crossed the street, he was now a half-block from the alley. A police car turned from the alley and Brothaman could see the silhouette of an arrestee in the backseat. As he made his way to the mouth of the dead-end alley, he could hear the hum of the engine and see the red lights of the ambulance. An area was roped off with crime scene tape. An officer approached him.

"Hey, what happened here?" Brothaman asked the detective.

Tommy looked at Brothaman, then down at his hands. "We responded to a call about a fight in the alley."

Brothaman looked down the alley at the body on the ground. "It doesn't look good."

"It isn't. But we caught the perpetrator in the act," Tommy responded, then looked into Brothaman's eyes. "This time."

Brothaman shook his head, and expelled white smoke from his mouth as he exhaled in the near freezing temperature. "Oh man. I'm so sorry to hear that." He bit his lower lip.

"Say, do you live around here?" Tommy asked.

"No, just passing through. I'm on the way to visit a friend. He lives two blocks over. Why do you ask?"

"Because we're cleaning up this neighborhood, thanks to community involvement. Four months ago, we got a call from one of the residents of this community about a similar beating in this same alley. Fortunately, we arrived in time to save that guy's life. We weren't so lucky this time."

"Wow," was all that Brothaman could say.

"And if I were a gambling man, I would say that it was the same perp, who is off the streets for good."

"Man, this is just crazy, and so close to Christmas."

"It is crazy."

"Oh man," Brothaman closed his eyes and shook his head. "I feel so bad for his family. They'll be devastated. It makes me count my blessings." Tommy nodded in response.

Brothaman really counted his blessings, and in a few hours, he would be three weeks and three days clean. He looked at his watch, "I really hate that this happened," he told Tommy.

"Yeah, me too." Tommy patted him on the shoulder, and Brothaman turned to walk towards his imaginary friend's house. In that split second, he made the decision to drown his sorrows not in a controlled substance, but in his artistic gift.

&

RACHEL RETURNED from her riverboat expedition penniless. She couldn't believe she had gambled away the money she planned to use to buy the boys Christmas gifts. She set the shopping bag on the floor by the front door, then sighed as she hung her coat in the closet. She admired the decorated tree in front of the bay window. The blinking white lights bounced the shimmer of the gold garland on the ceiling, illuminating the dark living room. The house was quiet, and the sweet scent of fresh baked cookies hung in the air, which meant that after a bedtime snack Hank had put the boys to bed, and was catching up on his rest himself.

Rachel went into the kitchen and poured herself a drink. She racked her brain trying to figure out how she would get money to buy the boys gifts. Although Hank would do anything for his nephews, she didn't want to ask him and she absolutely could not ask Patrick. He and Veronica had just put earnest money on a home they were building. Honeymooning Sina was out as well.

Hmmm. She sipped her vodka and orange juice, then opened her purse, and removed her small phone book. Hope had written her new address and number in it. Rachel walked across the room to get the phone on the end table. She also picked up the shopping bag so that she could put the boys' presents underneath the tree.

Rachel dialed Hope. She took another sip of liquid courage as the phone rang. She looked at her watch. It was only ten in Virginia Beach, not too late she hoped.

"Hello," she answered.

"Hope, this is Rachel. I need a HUGE favor."

"What is it?"

Anxiety built inside Rachel. Although they reconnected at Thomasine's wedding, Rachel felt awkward only calling Hope when she needed something.

"My life is just a big mess."

"What happened?"

"I met Brothaman at *Pepe's*. I wanted to tell him about the DNA test face-to-face."

"Yes. I think that's the best way. You shouldn't do it over the phone."

"Hope, you should have seen him. He looked better than he did when I first met him. Clean shaven. He even wore a tie. Said he's been clean for almost a month. And I believe him this time."

"Rachel, did you sleep with him?"

"No Hope, I didn't sleep with him. He was different. I think it's this new job. He even brought presents for the boys, and gave me a necklace, from an actual jewelry store. It was in a box," Rachel reached into the bag to retrieve it and felt an envelope. She opened it and there was a card with a note from her estranged husband. *I know this doesn't make up for all of the time I did not contribute to help with the boys, but I hope this little bit helps.* The little bit was five one-hundred dollar bills. Rachel gasped.

"What is it Rachel? What do you need?"

"Oh, I don't know. I just felt horrible telling him about the DNA test. Hope, he poured his heart out to me. Even said that he wanted us to be a family."

"You be careful Rachel. Make sure he stays off the drugs before you get involved with him again."

"I will."

"And Merry Christmas."

"Merry Christmas."

Rachel put the money in her purse then put it on her shoulder. She picked up her glass, walked across the living room to put the cordless phone in its cradle on the end table, and unplugged the Christmas lights. As she climbed the stairs to the bedroom she and Brothaman once shared, she made a solemn promise to herself to never use the money for the boys at the casino. She never wanted to be in a penniless position again.

RODNEY KISSED Thomasine's forehead which rested on his shoulder as they rode to Haberfield from Sydney Kingsford Smith Airport. They felt absolutely serene after their vacation, wedding, and honeymoon in Fiji. It was early evening, the summer sun had yet to set on what was one of the longest days of sunlight in the Southern hemisphere.

"Wake up, we're home," Rodney told Sina when the driver parked. He got out of the car first and Sina walked ahead of him while he retrieved their bags. She opened the gate and walked toward the door of the home. The courtyard was just beyond her.

"Wait," Rodney said to Thomasine as she turned the key in the lock. He ran, a light, wobbly jog, with the handle of a wheeled suitcase in either hand. When he reached the door and stood their bags on the ground of the courtyard of Thomasine's sabbatical home, he swept her into his arms. Rodney gazed into her eyes as he carried her over the threshold of her sabbatical home in Haberfield, Sydney, New South Wales.

"A girl could really get used to this," she looked into his eyes.

"You're not a girl, you're my wife," he kissed her, before gently lowering her. Her toes, then heels were firmly planted on the floor. Rodney stepped outside the door to retrieve their bags, which he took to the bedroom.

Thomasine went to the bathroom, washed her hands, and returned to the kitchen. "Can I get you anything?" she asked her husband. Her cheeks spread and lips parted at the joy she felt. When she was last in this home, she just thought she was going on vacation with her fiancée, but came back his wife. She prepared a platter of cheese and crackers.

Sina looked out the window over the kitchen sink and smiled when she felt Rodney's arms around her waist. He bent down and kissed the back of her neck. She turned, put her hand on his left shoulder, tilted her head up, and kissed her husband. "Let's sit on the courtyard and watch the sun set." She handed the corkscrew to Rodney so that he could open the 1994 Bannockburn Pinot Noir, then carried the platter to the courtyard. Rodney followed with the bottle of wine and stem glasses.

"I should really wipe this table down," Sina said just before she set the platter on the small bistro table. It had been exposed to the elements during the week and a half they were gone. "I'll be right back." She carried the platter with her and decided to make multiple trips, first cleaning the table, then back to retrieve the platter after a pit stop to the bathroom.

"I am so pissed off," she said as she made her way back to the courtyard.

"What's wrong?" Rodney asked, after observing the look on her face.

"The red cardinal has landed early. A whole doggone week early."

"What?"

Thomasine ignored his question. "But at least I don't have cramps this time."

"Oh." Rodney said. Thomasine placed the platter on the table and sat beside him.

"I hope you aren't too disappointed," Sina said. "We only have a few more days together. Then I won't see you for two months."

"A month and a half. And no. I'm not disappointed. We have the rest of our lives together."

"Well there are other things we can do." Sina winked and Rodney's lips spread across his face.

Sina took a sip of the wine Rodney poured while she was inside the house. She looked at the bright orange sphere, now lower in the sky, then took another sip to accompany her cracker topped with cheese. She loved the way the flavors melded on her palate. "Rodney, when I come home in February, I'm going to talk to my doctor about having the myomectomy when I return in May."

"I think that's a good idea."

"Yes, the past few months have been brutal for me. I need to do this sooner, rather than later."

Rodney reached across the table and took Sina's hand. He closed his eyes, inhaled, then smiled at her. "My season will be done by May, so I'll be there to take very good care of you during the surgery and recovery."

"Then next fall we can work on starting our family. Who knows, maybe this time next year you will actually be doing endorsements for diapers and formula," Sina said. Rodney laughed, and they enjoyed the warm evening on the courtyard before retiring to bed.

THOMASINE ROLLED over and smiled with her eyes closed. "Ahhh," she stretched and woke with a frown at the empty space beside her. "Rodney," she called. Sina put her feet on the floor and slowly stood. With her eyes half-open, she trudged to the bathroom, looked in the mirror and smiled as she washed her face, then turned to face the window when she heard the front gate close. The sweet-tempered breeze on the early summer afternoon gently swayed the curtains. She couldn't believe she had slept that long, but with the travel, her iron-deficient anemia due to the fibroids, and the wine, it wasn't a surprise. Thomasine smiled as she saw her husband wearing shorts, a T-Shirt, and carrying, she wasn't quite sure what he was carrying, but his hands were full.

She quickly rinsed her mouth, wiped her face with a towel, ran to the door and opened it quickly. "What's in the box?" She held the door open for Rodney who also had a bag hanging on each bent arm.

"A Christmas tree. I really wanted to get a live one, but they're hard to find this late. It's Christmas Eve." He set the box on the floor and the bags slid down his forearm. He squatted, picked up the smaller bag, and handed it to Thomasine.

"Pine spray?"

He snickered. "Yeah, I figured that at least it could smell real." He opened the box, and put the base of the tree in the corner of the room. Sina helped him assemble the tree, then handed him the pine spray.

"Spray away baby." Sina laughed. "Hey, I'll get those ceramic ornaments we purchased in Fiji." Thomasine had double wrapped them in newspaper and placed them in her carryon to insure they arrived in tact.

When Thomasine returned, he was nearly finished lighting the tree with strings of colored lights. She hung the three ceramic ornaments, one of a Fijian coat of arms, the other two beach scenes. She stood back and looked. "That's one sadly decorated tree."

"But it's ours, and our first Christmas together. That's what makes this memorable." Rodney sat on the sofa.

"And special." Sina got her disposable camera and she and Rodney took turns posing in front of the tree. For the last exposure, Rodney held the camera up and pointed the lens down at them, then snapped. "I hope this one turns out all right when we get it developed." They sat side-by-side on the sofa.

"Oh no!"

"What Sina?"

"I need to buy groceries for Christmas dinner. Heck for breakfast too and dinner tonight."

"We'll go out to dinner tonight, I rented a car. We'd better hurry before the stores close."

❧

RODNEY STRETCHED his arms before placing his feet on the floor. He licked his lips as he smelled the aroma of bacon from the kitchen, then slid his feet into his slippers, and made the short jaunt into the living area of the home. "Good morning, Sweetie Pie."

"Merry Christmas, Sugar Cane." Sina handed Rodney a mug of coffee and kissed him quickly on his lips. He sat on the sofa and sipped it, while thumbing through the newspaper.

"Breakfast will be ready as soon as I scramble these eggs," Sina said. She sipped her ginger tea, then looked over her shoulder. "Oh, and we're on page thirty-one."

Rodney set his mug on the coffee table and flipped through the pages. "I really like this picture of us." They were standing underneath their palm frond altar. The caption read *The IBL's Rodney Harris and his*

mystery woman, Dr. Thomasine Mintor, were wed last week in a private cere-
mony in Savusavu, Fiji.

"I do too," Sina said as she seasoned the eggs. "And now I'm no longer the mystery woman who gives courtside kisses, I'm Mrs. Rodney Harris," her voice was melodious. She fixed their plates and carried them to the small dining room table.

Rodney placed the newspaper on the coffee table and walked across the room to join Thomasine. The dining table was directly across from the Christmas tree. Rodney sat in the seat facing it. "Hey! When did you?" There were five beautifully wrapped presents underneath the tree.

"I shopped before our vacation," Sina ate a forkful of eggs, and broke off the end of her bacon with her fork. "And there's one for Zack, too."

Rodney sipped his coffee. "That was nice of you to think of my dog. Our dog."

"Our dogs," Sina rested her fork on the side of her plate. "Sparky and Zack seemed to get along pretty well last summer. I guess they'll be friends for life now."

"Zack seemed very happy when I told him my plans."

"Really? How could you tell?"

"His ears perked up whenever I said your name."

"Oh?" she laughed.

"And when I told him that you and Sparky would live with us he wagged his tail."

"Cute."

"After you recuperate from the surgery, we can start looking for a bigger house in Chicago."

"Maybe I should start applying for positions at universities in Chicago."

"I thought you wanted to go up for promotion and tenure at Steeplechase. Didn't you tell me that you would be the first Black woman to be tenured in your department."

"Yes, but."

"But nothing. I think you should go for it."

"I just thought."

"Sina," Rodney chewed the last of his eggs. "One of the things that attracted me to you was your ambition and your passion for your research and students. You've worked very hard to get to this point, and the last thing I would want is for you to think that I would expect for you to give it up to be my wife. I love everything about you, and you have my full support.

"I'm on the road most of your school year. Exhibition in September, then I play on six different continents. And even when we're in North America, I'm on the road then. When we make it to the playoffs, our season ends just around the time that your classes end for the school year. Then we have our summers together, and right now, neither of us has to work."

"True. It will be just you, me, Sparky, and Zack."

"Besides," Rodney stood from the table and stacked the dishes. "This is my seventh season in the IBL. I've already accomplished most of my goals. I'll be retiring in a few years." Rodney carried the dishes to the kitchen sink.

"Rodney. Retirement? You're only twenty-eight."

"I want to leave on top of my game," he put the stopper in the sink. "I'll probably retire after the 2000 Olympics."

"That's here in Sydney."

"It is." He squeezed the dish soap into the water. "And we can have a second honeymoon and revisit all of the places where we fell in love after the games."

"I like." Sina stretched and pushed back from the table. "I'm going to hop in the shower."

"Okay, Sweetie Pie," Rodney said as he washed the dishes.

As soon as Rodney heard the water running in the shower, he went outside to retrieve Thomasine's gifts from the trunk of the rental car. He gently closed the front gate, tiptoed inside the house, and placed the gift-wrapped boxes underneath the tree. When Thomasine exited the bathroom and went into the bedroom to change, Rodney innocently thumbed through the sports section while stretched out on the living room sofa.

"This feels so weird," she said when she entered the living area in shorts and a T-shirt. "I'm not used to Christmas at the beginning of summer." She sat on his lap and turned her head slightly in his direction.

"Is this your first Christmas away from home?"

"This is my first Christmas away from Chicago." Her teeth grazed her lower lip, before they spread out into a smile. "But my home is wherever you are." Rodney pulled her closer, and rested his folded hands on her abdomen. He kissed the back of her neck.

"Let's do it."

She looked over her shoulder and uttered a throaty, "Oh?"

"Not that." Rodney removed his hands from Sina's abdomen and pointed at the tree. "I'm talking about that. Let's open our gifts." Sina jumped up from the sofa and floated to the tree. Her brief steps were long and fluid.

"You first." She handed two boxes to Rodney. "These two go together." Rodney ripped the paper off and opened the boxes. "Do you like them?" Sina asked.

Rodney held up the cashmere sweater and scarf. "Since you're going to Europe next, I thought this might keep you warm, since I won't be there." She put her arm around his waist.

"I love it, almost as much as I love you." Rodney kissed his wife, then handed her a large box.

She found the edges of the paper and carefully removed it, fully intact. "A body pillow!"

"For you to cuddle with when I'm not here."

Sina pulled Rodney close and rested her head on his chest. She looked up and kissed him. "We think alike. Thank you, Sugar Cane."

"I have another."

"So do I." She handed him another box.

"Silk boxers! I love these." Rodney handed Sina a small flat box.

She opened the paper carefully again, then looked up at Rodney with her eyes and mouth open wide. "A massage package at the Four Seasons Sydney."

When Sina gave Rodney his last present all they could both do was laugh. A pair of swimming trunks, in Carolina blue.

They spent the rest of their first holiday together watching Christmas programming, then enjoying barbecued ginger prawns for their holiday dinner at the patio table in the courtyard and making plans for their future until the sun set.

18

AC-CENT-TCHU-ATE THE POSITIVE

Hope pedaled away on the stationary bike at a very crowded *Fit & Healthy* gym. She would have preferred an elliptical, but decided to take the first available piece of cardio equipment. It was the first of the year, the time when the gym was full of new year's resolutions that lasted two weeks, a month max. As much as Hope would have preferred to ride her bicycle on the boardwalk path, the bite in the air and five p.m. sunsets guided her to the gym. She had maintained her commitment to fitness and nutrition for the most part, with a few exceptions during her trip to Fiji and over the holidays.

As Hope rode, but traveled nowhere, she flipped through the pages of the *Weekly Spectator,* a newspaper that covered the hottest entertainment venues in Hampton Roads. She increased the resistance and made note of an ad for the Hampton Jazz Festival in June. A great get together for her, Rachel, and Sina! *How much longer?* Hope wondered, pedaling harder as she climbed a virtual hill. She scanned the page and stumbled upon a blurb about an open mic at a coffee shop not far from her corporate apartment. She looked at the clock on the wall and noted that after showering and changing into attire more appropriate for an open mic, she could attend, albeit fashionably late.

When Hope arrived at *Ruminations* she could see through the floor-to-ceiling windows that the open mic was a popular event. For a

Thursday night, the place was packed. Hope clutched the journal that held her poetry close to her chest as a gentleman held the door open for her. "Thank you," she said graciously. She paid the cover charge and scanned the room for a seat in the dimly lit venue. Square tables for two or four were spread throughout the coffee shop. To the left there was a gas log fireplace surrounded by fully occupied leather sofas. A coffee table connected the guests who sat across from each other. A bar bisected *Ruminations*. Glass display cases with fresh baked goods circled one half of the bar. The wall behind the other side of the bar held shelves of liquor and syrups for lattes. Hope grabbed a seat when she saw a patron who just paid his tab leave. He held the bar stool steady while she placed her heel on the rung, then lifted herself into the seat. Once comfortably seated, he pushed her stool towards the bar. She had the perfect spot. Fifteen feet to her right, against the exposed brick walls, was a stage made of a deep, rich, dark brown hardwood flooring. At the front of the stage a woman belted out Anita Baker's *Caught Up in the Rapture*, backed by the house band consisting of a drummer, keyboard player, bassist, and guitarist. The singer, whose name she later learned was Sharon, was good, so good that Hope had reservations about signing up to perform.

"Would you like anything to drink?" the gentleman who sat beside her wore a neatly groomed beard on his deeply tanned caramel skin. His brown eyes were warm and inviting. He wore tight-fitting jeans and a crewneck sweater which complemented his trilby hat.

"No thank you," Hope said, remembering all the trouble her nightly escapades with rum and Diet Coke nearly caused.

"My name is Murray. My friends call me Buddy. I haven't seen you here before."

"It's my first time," she looked up at him and smiled. "You know, maybe I'll have a Coke." Hope had lost fifteen pounds since starting her fitness and nutrition commitment, so she felt entitled to splurge. Murray placed Hope's drink order with the bartender.

"Thanks."

"So, I take it you're a poet."

"How did you?" she looked at the journal on the bar just beneath her right hand, then up at Murray and laughed. "I wrote poetry when I was younger, and recently rediscovered my gift."

"I hope you'll share some tonight. Go on. Sign up. When the band takes a break, the poets usually perform."

"I don't know," she paused. "I've never shared my work."

He cut her off. "This is a friendly crowd. I promise they'll show you much love."

Hope took a sip of her Coke. "Are you sure?"

"Yes," Murray smiled. His bottom teeth were a little crowded, but the top row was perfectly spaced. "I'm a regular. I've been coming since my man Jerry started this open mic five years ago. The crowd will be nice to you. I promise," he scooted back in his chair. "Let me get the clipboard so that you can sign up. Don't let anyone take my seat."

Murray, or Buddy as he preferred to be called, felt familiar to Hope. Like an old friend. They laughed and chatted while they listened to a motley collection of singers and musicians. Some were fabulous, others were clearly beginners. And just like Buddy said, when the band took a break, Hope's name was called.

"New to the *Ruminations* stage, let's welcome Hope Jones." Hope set her purse in her chair and strutted to the stage like an old pro.

Jerry adjusted the mic to Hope's height and wished her well. "Good evening everyone," Hope started. "This is not just my first time here. This is my first time performing." The crowd applauded even louder. "This piece I will perform for you tonight is called 'Fighting.' I think we can all relate.

"*Words unspoken, glances revealed. Fighting our feelings and not being healed. Each wanting more, yet denying ourselves. Relying on destiny, what we hope time tells. Times of togetherness, love, happiness, and joy. Feeling the feeling, yet still being coy. But the truth is, as long as we fight. Destiny, karma, and fate stay out of our sight.*

"*So, let's call a truce, and stop all of this madness. Rewards will result, hearts full of gladness. I'll make you one promise that ends this plight. Let's surrender our feelings. Let's end this fight.*"

Hope smiled broadly when the crowd roared. She was hooked. All she thought about the next day, the next few days in fact, was writing and rehearsing more material for the next open mic. It consumed most of her weekend, and it was all she could think about at work on that Monday.

It was midafternoon when she received the call. Hope sat at her desk and looked at the gray, cloudy sky through the blinds of her office window. It terrified her even more than the broken condom from the nameless man in her hotel suite four months earlier. When she had her annual pap smear a week ago, she expected a completely clean bill of health. Hope had exercised caution since that dreadful experience. *Abnormal pap! Colposcopy and biopsy scheduled for next week.* "Oh God!" Hope said audibly. She rubbed her fingers over closed eyes and exhaled deeply. *Cervical cancer risk.* That is what scared her the most. Additionally, she had no idea how to contact the men she met while she was healing from Jason's painful rejection of her. She thought after the divorce, and how well she and Jason got along at Sina and Rodney's wedding, that everything was moving forward beautifully in her life. Now she wasn't so sure.

HOPE RELAXED on the living room sofa, this time with rum and Diet Coke, after changing out of her work clothing. Her Mom always told her to hang her clothes up as soon as she came home and the heat from her body would press them. She scratched her head. *I can't believe this is happening to me.* She looked at the clock, and decided to wait another hour or two before calling Rachel. She wanted to give her time to get home from work and get the boys settled. Then she remembered it was a holiday. The national observance of Dr. King's birthday. Hope picked up the cordless phone on her end table and dialed Rachel, who answered on the second ring.

There was excitement in Rachel's voice when she answered. Unbeknownst to Hope, Rachel had a magnificent weekend and was twenty-five hundred dollars richer after her trip to Indiana. She felt like a high roller now. Her tone and high came down a bit after she heard deep worry in Hope's voice. "What's wrong, Hope?" she asked. They had been friends since they were both in the church nursery at Front Street African Christian Church. The fear she heard in Hope's voice quickly brought her down from her gambler's high.

"I'm scared, Rachel. No, I'm terrified." Hope began to sob.

"What is it Hope?" Rachel asked, now afraid herself.

"I just got a call from my doctor. My pap smear was abnormal. I have to have tests next week to rule out cervical cancer."

"Oh," Rachel's voice was lighter. She was relieved. "Hope, please don't worry about that. I've been through that myself."

"You have?"

"Yes. I went through that this time last year," Rachel said. "You have nothing to fear. You have access to the best physicians in your area."

"That's true."

"I know it's hard because things seem uncertain right now, but I'm sure you'll be fine."

"You think so?"

"I know so," Rachel turned her lamp on. "And if you ever want to talk, you know I'm here. You can call me anytime."

"I love you, Rachel. Thank you for being such a great friend." Hope pushed her glass to the center of the coffee table. "How are the boys?"

"They're doing great. I'm getting ready to pick them up from Patrick's."

"Please tell them I said hi and that Auntie Hope loves them."

"I will." Rachel pressed the flash button to disconnect the call, then put the phone in the charging cradle. She went to the hall closet to retrieve her coat and purse and double checked to ensure that the front door was locked before she got into her car.

Though she was ambivalent she knew that asking Patrick and Veronica to keep the boys each weekend was an imposition, but she enjoyed this time to herself. She hadn't had as much fun as she was having at the riverboat since she, Sina, and Hope spent their weekend evenings at Pepe's and the theater. During the drive, she pondered the proposition back and forth in her mind.

The trees were bare, it was overcast, and droplets from a light drizzle danced on Rachel's windshield. The intermittent sway of her windshield wiper provided brief clarity, but that wasn't nearly enough. Rachel sought a balance. She loved her sons dearly, and the short getaway to Fiji was much welcomed. Although she felt great peace when she met her Australian siblings, there was still so much confusion. *Why can't I get my life together?* She turned into the visitor's parking space at Veronica and Patrick's townhome. Remnants of fallen leaves stood at the base of the Crepe Myrtle beside the front door. She rang the bell.

"Mommy!" Malcolm said when Patrick opened the door. Martin joined his brother in hugging their mother around her thighs. She bent down and kissed both of their foreheads.

"Go get your things together," Patrick instructed. "Hi Rachel. Did you have a good weekend?"

"I did," she walked over to the wing chair near the front window and sat. "Patrick. I have a big favor to ask you."

"Oh," Patrick sat across from her on the sofa. A book of photographs by Gordon Parks rested on the coffee table alongside a vase. "What is it?"

"I don't know. I don't want to impose."

"Rachel, remember what I told you. I will never view my son as an imposition."

"Do you think it would be possible for you and Veronica to keep the boys every weekend."

Patrick leaned back against the sofa, tilted his head to the side, and looked at Rachel.

"Never mind," she said immediately.

"What's going on, Rachel?" Patrick asked. She could never tell him the truth. Instead she went with this.

"I just feel so overwhelmed with everything that has happened. Malcolm's father wants us to move back to Chicago, or at least he did before I told him that you were Martin's father."

"I see. Hmmm. Maybe not every weekend, but a third weekend sometimes," Patrick said. While his job as a professor gave him the opportunity to work from home, Veronica's job didn't offer that same luxury. They were beginning to spend less and less time together. "I have to talk to Veronica first."

"Of course."

"I'm always happy to see my son and Malcolm, but you know Veronica and I are building our first home. We're scheduled to close in early April."

"Then forget it," Rachel said. "You have a lot on your plate as well."

"Daddy," Martin called from upstairs. "Can you please help us with our bags?"

Patrick stood from the sofa and climbed the stairs to carry the boys' overnight bags down for them. When the three men, two of them young and little, reached the bottom landing, Rachel was already standing by the door. "Rachel, did you ever contact Robinson?" He was a therapist Patrick recommended to Rachel when he first learned about all she had to deal with.

"No."

"You really should. I think he could help you."

"I'll do it this week." She had no plans to.

Patrick opened the door.

"Look Mommy, Miss Ronnie," Martin called. Veronica had just pulled into her parking space and was gathering her purse before getting out of her car. "Mommy, can I say goodbye to Miss Ronnie?"

"Yes," Rachel replied and watched her boys run over to greet her. Veronica wore a million-dollar smile on her face. She kissed Martin and Malcolm, then gave Rachel a hug.

"You seem very happy," Rachel said as the embrace parted.

"I am. Very happy."

Rachel and the boys walked across the parking lot and climbed into their car.

Patrick greeted his wife with a kiss as she entered their home. Veronica sat on the sofa, then giggled like a teenager. Patrick smiled in return, then tilted his head to the side. "What is it?"

"Good news," Veronica squealed. "Very good news!"

"Oh! What is it?"

"I'm pregnant!"

Patrick covered Veronica's face with kisses. "Darling, I'm so happy." He released her. A huge smile spread across his face. "I'm going to be a father." Patrick put his hand on Veronica's abdomen and smiled more broadly. "Hi there little Patrick."

"Or Patricia."

"I can't wait until you get here."

§.

THE LIGHT DUSTING of snow covering Michigan Avenue was nothing compared to the wind that whipped from Lake Michigan over Grant Park. Brothaman walked down the crowded sidewalk, and dreaded turning onto the wind tunnel on Harrison between Michigan and Wabash. The biting wind was so cold it burned his face and so strong that it nearly lifted him off the ground and carried him to the corner. Brothaman planted both feet firmly on the ground and braced himself while he watched a woman walking in the opposite direction fight to chase a paper that fell from her hand. It was nearly impossible for her. He stepped to his left. The paper landed right in the center of the front of his jacket. He struggled with gloved hands to get a grasp.

"Thank you," she said as he handed it to her. "And try to stay warm." She walked through the revolving door of the building beside her.

"Spertus Institute." Brothaman paused, then pursed his lips together. He followed her inside. He didn't actually follow her like a stalker, but he found a brief respite from the cold.

A security guard in a burgundy blazer sat atop a tall stool at a podium. With head tilted down, his spectacles had slid to the tip of his nose. He looked up. "How may I help you?"

"Hi, my name is David Brown, and I'm interested in learning more about the programs offered through Spertus Institute."

"Are you interested in Judaic Studies or our graduate program in Human Services Administration." Although he wasn't exactly sure what that was, he chose the latter. It sounded interesting. He was directed to the elevator which he took to the ninth floor.

He left Spertus Institute so elated, he could barely feel the "Hawk" whipping off the lake. This program was perfect for him! Winterveld Advertising would cover his tuition. His cohort would have class one night a week, Tuesday, Wednesday or Thursday, for eighteen months. Electives met on Mondays. He had an option of writing a research thesis, grant proposal, or organizational study for his major project.

As he boarded the bus headed to his south side home he felt more hopeful than he had since he married Rachel. This degree in human services would equip him with the skills and resources to do what was most passionate for him right now, help recovering addicts get back on their feet. He was elated to be back on his.

❧

THOMASINE LOOKED out of the window onto the main quad of the campus. A frangipani tree with clusters of star-shaped flowers with pink edges and yellow centers stood still beside a bench. A neatly trimmed row of gardenia shrubs formed a straight line behind it. A bed of kangaroo paw, Dahlias, bottle brush, and dwarf Bougainvillea created the perfect centerpiece. The copper and rosy coral tones of the Sundown Echinacea were spotlighted by the noon sun.

Thomasine completed the cover letter to accompany her article submission to the *Global Journal of Women and Culture*. She and Evonne had proofread the article multiple times. Thomasine placed blind copies of the article, along with the cover letter into a manila envelope and sealed it. She placed the stack of folders into her briefcase, and gathered her purse. It was a warm, sunny day and Sina was delighted to spend the rest of the afternoon out on her courtyard hanging out with Melba and Denise.

She locked her office door, put the envelope into outgoing mail, and checked her mailbox before she left the building. There was a letter from the agency that funded her grant. She stuffed it into her purse and headed for the train to Haberfield. It was summer break, and while some classes were in session, the campus wasn't nearly as crowded as normal.

She drank in the beauty of the day. The sun. The flowers and flowering trees. The beautiful melodies from the birds. She reached Central Station in what seemed like seconds. Her train to Haberfield would soon arrive.

It wasn't long before Thomasine opened the wrought iron gate to her quaint sabbatical home. The trip would have been much quicker in a taxi, but she enjoyed the short walk from the Haberfield station. When Thomasine entered her home, she opened the blinds on the window to the courtyard, then stood her briefcase on the floor beside her desk. She went into her bedroom. Her small suitcase was on the bed. She placed her purse beside it and delighted in the fact that she got the journal submission off before her trip home. She wanted to be work free and worry free when she reunited with her husband.

❧

"Let me help you with that," Denise said as she took a tray from Sina, then held the door open as they walked to the courtyard. They had spent the last thirty minutes marveling at Thomasine and Rodney's wedding album while waiting for Melba to arrive. Thomasine had planted marigolds and zinnias along the border of the fence in the sunny backyard.

Denise opened, then tilted the umbrella on the table while Thomasine put her hand over the coals. "They're ready," Sina said, then placed the chicken in the center.

Denise poured two glasses of iced tea, then sat and took a sip. "Whew, this is sweet."

"I hope it's not too sweet." Sina sat on the opposite side of the table.

"No, it's good. I've never had this before."

"It's a North Carolina drink. Sweet tea is popular in the American South, but not all areas of the South sweeten it this much." Sina laughed. "I remember the first time I ordered it at a restaurant when I first moved to North Carolina. I wasn't expecting that intensity of sweetness. I actually let my ice melt to dilute it a bit." Denise laughed. "But I didn't put nearly as much sugar in it as they do in the South."

"Well, this is really good," Denise took another sip. "G'Day Melba," she called from afar. Melba closed the wrought iron gate and joined her friends on the courtyard. Thomasine stood to hug Melba.

"Sorry I'm late." Melba sat across from Denise. "But I was at a meeting. I can't believe what they are doing in Redfern. Soon I won't be able to afford to live there."

"What's going on?" Sina asked.

"Another run-down terrace home is on the market for over four hundred grand."

"Wow!"

"Oh, that's nothing. The one across from the railway station sold for half a million last year. They say it will take about a hundred grand to renovate it."

"And it's all due to this bloody Olympics in two years." Melba said. "The government wants to clean up Redfern and run all the Blacks out so that when the cameras and lights come for the Olympics in 2000 the world won't see what the government calls our black ghetto. Redfern is an embarrassment to the government."

"The truth is, the government really doesn't want the world to see how awful they treat us."

Sina stood and turned the chicken. "I'm not surprised. They cleaned up areas of Chicago for the Democratic National Convention. Oh, and parts of Atlanta for the Summer Olympics summer before last."

"That's exactly what they are doing here. They did it fifteen years ago in Brisbane for the Commonwealth Games."

Denise handed Melba a glass of tea. "We need to organize. Maybe we can start a non-profit to keep some affordable housing in Redfern like they did in Pyrmont and Ultimo." She took a sip of her tea. "This is good, eh."

"Well, I'm on board." Denise said. "We must maintain our sense of community in Redfern."

Sina sat at the table. "You know, I've always enjoyed watching the Olympics, and I read articles about the so-called community improvements to prepare for the summer games in Atlanta, but I never thought about how the communities were impacted." She shook her head. "What can you do about this? How can you use the international media coverage to bring awareness? What can I do to help?"

"Sina, you'll be long gone by the Summer Olympics."

"But if Rodney makes the US team then I'll be here as a spectator. We've already talked about having a second honeymoon here after the games."

"I'll. No, we'll have to think about this. We'll have to do a lot of planning."

"And we have over two years to map it out."

ॐ

THOMASINE WAS the first to deplane when she landed at O'Hare. Rodney stood at the door to the gate, a dozen roses in his hand, a down stadium jacket was draped over his arm, and a toothy ear-to-ear smile fanned out across his face. Thomasine's pace was brisk. Her outstretched arms wrapped around his shoulders while her purse slid and its strap rested in the fold of her arm. "I'm so happy to see you Sugar Cane."

He caressed her cheek with his right hand, then kissed her quietly and deeply. "Welcome home Sweetie Pie." He handed her the roses, then helped her put on the warmer coat to prepare her for the brutal truth of February in Chicago.

Sparky and Zack nearly knocked them down when Rodney and Sina arrived at the townhome. Sina felt so loved. She was inundated with affection, especially from Sparky, who missed her the most. He jumped on Sina, his paws on her chest, then licked her face, and ran around in a circle before repeating the same action.

This all felt so weird for Thomasine. It was the first time she flew into Chicago and was not greeted at the airport by her father, Reverend Mintor. She had a new home now, a new life, and she planned to enjoy every second of it.

They climbed the stairs to the kitchen area. Zack and Sparky were on their heels. "I have some good news," Sina called to Rodney as he took her suitcase into the bedroom. She put her purse in a dining chair.

"What is it?"

"It's about my grant."

"Oh."

"Unfortunately, the agency that funded my grant is closing, so I won't have funding to stay in Australia a second year."

"I'm sorry to hear that. I thought you said you had good news."

"The good news is that I've been able to get quite a bit done on the project, and even submitted an article for publication last week."

"That's wonderful. I'm so proud of you."

"And the greatest news is that I'll be home for good at the end of April." When Sina said that, she asked herself just where was home now—Chicago or North Carolina.

"Oh Darling," Rodney hugged Sina. She looked up at her husband and smiled.

She kissed him again. A quick peck on the lips. "I need to freshen up," she said to him. "It seems I've been traveling for an eternity." Sina walked down the hallway to the master bedroom. Through the skylight, she could see the moon waxing crescent. Thomasine walked over to the luggage rack and unzipped her suitcase. She retrieved a small bag and her toiletries, went into the master bath, and turned the water on in the Jacuzzi tub. She first brushed her teeth, then climbed into the tub. She slid down so that the water covered her shoulders and was enveloped in warmth. Sina adjusted the intensity of the water flow and welcomed the gentle massage. It was much needed after being seated for twelve and a half hours from Sydney to Los Angeles, then another four hours to Chicago.

Thomasine exhaled deeply and marveled at how much her life had changed in six short months. She attended her reunion, only expecting to catch up on the lives of her high school acquaintances, and was introduced to the rest of her life. She smiled at the memory of her last time in the tub, the night before she left for Sydney right after she and Rodney first made love. Her reverie was fleeting as the water was becoming lukewarm. Thomasine stepped out of the tub and toweled off while it drained. She moisturized her skin with her thick, luxurious lotion, then cleaned the tub and its jets. Sina modeled one of her Christmas presents from Rodney for herself in the massive bathroom mirror. Back in the master bedroom, she rifled through her suitcase for the pumps Rodney bought her to go with the red dress she wore the night before he left Sydney the first time.

Long and gentle strides guided Thomasine to the dining area. Rodney stood at the kitchen island pouring two glasses of wine. Zack and Sparky were frozen in place at the sight of her. "Sugar Cane," Thomasine breathed out, softly. Her tone was rich and warm, like chocolate melting in your mouth. He turned to face her mesmerized, the wine he was pouring spilled over the top of the glass.

"Sweetie Pie," he said. He dropped a dish towel over the spill, and walked over to his beloved. His toes barely touched the floor. He grazed her cheek, then brushed her lips with his, and closed his eyes, kissing his wife deeply. His fingertips gracefully wandered down, first to the small of her back, then to her hips, then to. He lifted her, carried her to the bedroom, and closed the door behind him.

Their overnight trip to North Carolina a few days later was action-packed. The late-night flight was delayed due to weather out west. Their midnight arrival made the journey from the airport free from any traffic.

When Sina entered her River Run Estates home, she inhaled the fresh scent of wintergreen. She was pleased that she took her mother's advice to have a service clean the house monthly while she was gone. Sina walked over to the thermostat and set it to seventy-two. The late-night temperature was near freezing. The vaulted ceiling made the great room particularly cold. With Rodney's hand in hers, she guided him to the master bedroom and flipped the switch to start the gas log fireplace. After Sina gave Rodney a quick tour of the house, it was his first visit, they snuggled together underneath the crimson and gold comforter and drifted off to sleep.

They started their day at Brigs with her favorite, the B.L.T.C., an open-faced, knife and fork sandwich with mounds of cheddar-jack cheese and home fries. Rodney enjoyed the Alaskan omelet. He sipped his coffee while skimming the *Durham Herald-Sun*. Thomasine looked at her watch. "OK. I can't put it off any longer. It's time for my dreaded annual exam." Rodney signaled to the waiter, then paid the check. The OB/GYN office was just around the corner.

Her morning was long. After her annual exam, Dr. Torres ordered an ultrasound, which meant that Sina had to go through the bladder filling ritual again. One of the fibroids had grown by a half centimeter. The other diminished in size by the same amount. Myomectomy was scheduled for the day after Mother's Day. That way Sina could participate in commencement exercises. Several students she taught the previous years were graduating, and attending commencement was important to Sina. She loved to meet their parents and tell them how wonderful their children were.

Crimson and yellow pansies were planted at the entrance to Steeplechase University. Most of the red brick buildings were uniform, four stories tall with gable fronted dormers at the top level, all in the Colonial Revival architectural style. There were a few modernist buildings, namely the library and student union. The newest arrival on campus, a suite-style residence hall, unique in its presence, towered over the other buildings. In the center of campus, a bell tower chimed on the quarter hour, reminding the campus of the alma mater daily at eight am, noon, and five pm.

"Dr. Mintor!" Nikol was excited to see her favorite professor when Sina and Rodney climbed to the second floor.

"It's Dr. Mintor Harris now," Sina said, "No hyphen." She turned to an angle. "Let me introduce you to my husband, Rodney. Rodney, this is Nikol."

Rodney extended his hand. "It's nice to meet you Nikol."

"Say, aren't you in that PSA?" Rodney nodded. Nikol turned to face Sina. "I really wish you were coming back in the Fall," Nikol said. "I'm starting to look at graduate programs, and I could really use your help."

"Guess what?" Sina's grin was large.

"What?"

"I will be back in the Fall. I'm wrapping up my project in the two months. The agency that funded my grant closing, so I'm coming home."

"And I'm glad to have you back." Dr. Nestor, her department chair, overheard the conversation. She was on her way into the department office after teaching a class. "We'll be able to add your ethnography class to the fall schedule."

Sina smiled with delight, then introduced Rodney. After brief visits with her colleagues, some of whom said they were delighted to see her, she checked her mailbox, then headed to the parking lot.

As they got closer to her River Run Estates home, Sina decided to make a detour to her old stomping grounds, the UNC-Chapel Hill campus. They started at the Smith Center which was familiar to Rodney. He played there a few times during his college career. Their UNC campus tour ended at the Carolina Inn, an iconic hotel that would blend well with most of the buildings at Steeplechase University. Sina introduced Rodney to shrimp and grits, and they enjoyed an early dinner, before securing the house and catching their evening flight.

Thomasine ended her two-week trip home after the Gale Force played in Los Angeles. She attended the home games, and got to know her father-in-law and brother-in-law better at the Atlanta game. When she and Rodney attended Front Street African Christian Church for the first time as husband and wife, they were received warmly. Her parents joined them afterwards for dinner at Kimmy's. Sina delighted in her new role as wife and looked forward to waking up each morning with her husband. The next two and a half months could not come quickly enough for her.

Rodney walked his wife to her gate. His team flight to Chicago left from the same terminal. "I wish I were going home with you," Sina said. A tear formed in her eye.

Rodney pulled her close. "It won't be long Sweetie Pie." He loosened his embrace and looked lovingly into her eyes. "You'll be back home before you know it." He kissed his wife, squeezed her tight, and inhaled her scent before he made his way to his gate where his plane was boarding.

19

YOU'VE CHANGED

The sun struggled to force its intense light through the mass of clouds, curdled like cotton balls against a sea of deep cerulean blue. A gentle breeze blew from the ocean as Hope rode her bike along the Boardwalk Bike Path. It was early morning and in the low sixties. With her body temperature rising from the workout, Hope would soon need to remove her light jacket. The bike path was a bit less traveled, which she was sure would change as the hours passed and this beautiful Spring day emerged.

Hope inhaled the scent of salt on this unseasonably warm late March morning. She found it more pleasant than the putrid odor of the Bradford pear tree outside her bedroom window. The ornamental grass that lined one side of the Boardwalk path had been trimmed to a mid-calf height. Its flowering plumes gone but for a season. Hope looked ahead, then to the left. Bright, yellow daffodils and white hyacinths lined a bed in front of a hotel. Buds showed tulips waiting to be born, one of them was due today.

Hope felt light. She had now lost twenty-two pounds since beginning her fitness journey. She also let go of a heavy emotional weight she had been carrying, well most of it anyway. Through journaling and writing poetry, Hope came to realize that her food obsession stemmed from her longing. As a child, she longed for her father to be more present than his traveling job as a pharmaceutical sales rep allowed. She replaced that longing with a love that Jason was never able to share with her. Through this journey, she learned to love herself, and that love was growing to an intensity she never believed to be possible.

Hope was blessed. She had a great job, wonderful salary, and was in moderately good health. The colposcopy and biopsy revealed no cancer, and she had finally completed the TCA treatments. She found the biweekly treatments to be gruesome and wished that she could have taken a pill to treat the condition instead.

In just a week, she would also lose an hour to usher in the start of her favorite time of the year, daylight savings time. Hope was particularly excited to be in a warmer climate as spring approached. In another month, her friend Sina would be just a few hours away. Hope pedaled on. In many ways, Virginia Beach reminded her of her college days in Savannah. Only, this time around she promised herself that she would have more fun.

For the first time, Hope was okay with her singleness. She wasn't just okay, she absolutely embraced it. She was free to come and go as she pleased, and was happy to again have her bed to herself. Since she controlled everything that went into her refrigerator, Hope found it easier to focus on her wellness and her own personal growth. The harsh lessons of the past few months taught her the true value of friendship and the danger of being judgmental. She thought for a moment about Thomasine and Rodney's whirlwind romance and fairytale wedding. Then she remembered that competing with her friends is what brought her the misery she was now overcoming.

Hope rang her bell as she pedaled around a biker in front of her. Now she was in the lead, not only on the bike path, but in life. Though she didn't consider herself to be lonely, she did think it would be nice to have someone special to share with. To share meals, sunsets at the beach, and bike rides along the path. It had only been four months since her divorce, three since she received the decree. She understood the danger in starting a relationship on the rebound, and knew from her late summer encounters that it would not heal the pain she had, which was dissipating day by day.

Hope reached the end of the path. She was proud of herself for making the first three miles. She stepped from her bike, and swiped the kickstand with her left foot. Hope took her jacket off, and tied it around her waist, then stretched. Just as she began to mount her bike again, she saw a group of black women runners join her at the end of the path. Some spoke, others nodded, before turning to run the three miles back to the start of the path. Hope paused, watched them in awe, and wondered if she could join them one day. They were all shapes and sizes, some long and slender, others short like her and stout like she once was. She truly admired their tenacity. She was inspired. She watched them, until they met a bend in the road and were slightly out of her sight, then she mounted her bike and continued her leisurely ride toward the beginning of the path.

DAVID HAD RETURNED from his post office box, his Dunkin' Donuts coffee and maple frosted on the table in front of him. It had become his Saturday morning ritual. He shuffled through his stack of mail, then he eyed the envelope with the faint gray return address from Spertus Institute. He was nervous, almost afraid to open it. He relaxed his shoulders, bit his bottom lip, closed his eyes, and inhaled deeply. David didn't know why he was afraid. His coworker, Dorothy, a copy-writer, reviewed his essay before he submitted his application. It was good enough to award him an interview, which he believed went well. With the tip of his right index finger, he ripped the top of the envelope and removed the letter.

His sigh was reassuring. "I got in." He and Shaniqua had parted ways shortly after Thanksgiving, which was key in his recovery. "I'm going to get my master's degree." He said the words deliberately, giving each word its own spotlight.

David became teary eyed, then smiled as he thought how proud this moment would have made his mother. "Yes!" he shouted, then hoped that he did not disturb his next-door neighbor. He paused to read the letter in its entirety. His cohort was scheduled to start on Wednesday, June 3, 1998 with a brief orientation. The first class, a Communication Module, was scheduled to begin a week later. His lips spread broadly across his face, then grew, revealing his teeth. David shook his head and marveled at how different the last four months of his life had been. His side hustle directed him into a career that he loved, and now an opportunity to make a difference in so many lives. He hoped that he could soon make a difference for Rachel and the boys.

He picked up the phone and dialed Rachel. He was sure that she had to be up by now. "Hi Rachel, this is David. I have some really good news, and you're the first to hear it."

"Oh," she croaked out. Her voice was a bit groggy. Last night she dropped the boys off at Patrick and Veronica's apartment for the last time. The Longs were scheduled to close on their new home on Tuesday. Rachel scooted back to a seated position and knocked the empty wine glass off the night stand. She was still in bed and her blinds were closed. She cleared her throat. "What is it?"

"I got," he began as the line went dead. Rachel's phone was disconnected during the call. It was the end of the month, she had twenty dollars to her name thanks to her job as a church musician, and all she wanted to do was chase cherries on the one-armed bandit. While the end of March payday was on Monday, most of her check would go to pay off the auto title loan she got last month. She was behind on her rent, and didn't know what to do. More importantly, she was in denial. No, truthfully, she was ashamed to tell anyone how foolish she'd been and continued to be. She thought surely she would have won back the money to pay both the rent and the loan by now, but it didn't happen. Well she did win, but then she got greedy and ended up losing all her winnings, and then some. The payday loan, along with the exorbitant ATM fees at the casino left her checking account overdrawn.

Rachel looked at the clock, no time for a shower if she were to make the bus to Evansville. She sauntered to the bathroom and brushed her teeth. When she washed her face, she didn't like the reflection she saw. The figurative weight she carried was much heavier than that she carried when Aunt Mary died, than when she learned about Brothaman's addiction, and than when she had to reach out to Patrick about Martin's paternity.

Rachel squeezed into her jeans, and put on a T-Shirt. She grabbed her purse and a light jacket she hadn't worn in nearly a year. With the front door locked, she put her keys into the right pocket and felt paper. Amidst the receipts there was, much to Rachel's delight, a twenty-dollar bill. She now had forty dollars. Rather than taking this as a sign to buy fresh groceries to make a dinner for her sons, as Sunday dinner had become quite inventive in recent weeks, she considered it a sign from God for increase. That was exactly what she hoped to do as she started her car and backed out of the parking space. She set an intention to turn that forty dollars into four thousand. It was a lofty goal, but she felt she had nothing to lose.

&.

"MAN, you look like you've had some fun in the sun," Jason said to Rodney as he shook his hand, then climbed the steps to the living area of Rodney's townhome. Sparky and Zack were on their heels. "Because I know you didn't get that tan in this weather. I can't believe how cold it is here. It was freezing this morning, and it's April." Jason removed his jacket and draped it over the arm of the sofa, then sat down.

"That's what three weeks in a South American summer will do for you." The Gale Force had swept the season, completed the first round of playoffs, and had the home court advantage. They were officially North American champions for the third year in a row. In a few days, they would play a best of five series against the Asian champions. Rodney opened his fridge. "Can I get you something to drink?"

"No man, I'm good." The Chicago Bulls, first in the NBA Central Division, were playing at Houston. Rodney sat in the armchair catty corner to Jason. Sparky was beside Rodney and Zack stretched out between them.

"So how have you been?" Rodney asked. "This is the first time I've seen you since Fiji."

"Oh, I'm good. Work is great." Jason turned towards the television, then pumped his hand in the air as Ron Harper hit a three. "And I finally moved out of my mother's house."

Rodney smiled from ear-to-ear. "So, was this move inspired by a particular football Mom?"

Jason smiled, and bit his lip. "I wish, although I take her to lunch every Thursday and we meet for coffee sometimes, Zuri and I are just friends," Jason paused to watch game action. "And it's best for right now. It wouldn't be fair to her for me to date her on the rebound."

"That's true," Rodney took a sip of his pop. "So where is your new crib?"

"Chatham. I signed a twelve-month lease in February."

"Nice hood." Rodney laughed.

"Yes, I'm practically your neighbor."

"That, you are." He smiled.

"And I saw the specialist you recommended."

"That's right. Your appointment was for early April. How did it go?"

"Surgery is scheduled for June."

"That's great."

"I just hope recovery and rehab go well."

"The fact that you are in great physical shape gives you a huge advantage."

"You think so?"

"I know so."

"It's silly, but I wonder."

"What is it?" Rodney took another sip of his pop.

"Do you think football is history for me? I mean, I haven't played in eight years. Coaching this team for my firm has got me—has rekindled my love for the sport. I wish I had done this surgery years ago. Maybe I'd have a Super Bowl ring by now."

Rodney laughed.

"What's so funny?"

"I told Thomasine I'm thinking about retiring in a few years, maybe after the 2000 Summer Olympics. And you're thinking about starting a career in professional sports. You never know. It will depend on your recovery and the strength of your desire."

"Now it is official. I've just set a goal to go back to football be it arena or a making a NFL practice squad."

"You redshirted your freshman year. Don't you have a year of eligibility left?"

Jason scratched his head. "You think I should go back to school?"

"It's just one pathway to your dreams. Go for it. Life is too short not to." Rodney shook his head. "Who knows, you might be a star. Just be prepared to juggle your personal life and life in the spotlight. Keep them separate. Some of these media outlets are like vultures, circling to find the roadkill of your past mistakes. And of those you love."

"That's good advice." Jason nodded. "It seems since your wedding the tabloid fodder has cooled down."

"It has, thank God. I was really worried about the impact it would have on Thomasine."

"Speaking of Thomasine, how is she?"

Light shone in Rodney's eyes, his voice became softer. "Thomasine is great. And she'll be home for good in a few weeks."

"That's wonderful man. I'm so happy for you."

§.

PATRICK GENTLY TOOK the box from Veronica's hand. Although they moved into their home two weeks ago, they hadn't completely unpacked. He was protective of his wife, whose belly was beginning to bloom with their first children. The ultrasound revealed twins. "I don't want you to lift anything heavy," he instructed.

"This isn't that heavy."

"In that case, I don't want you to lift anything."

"Yes sir," she kissed her husband's cheek.

Their new home gave them space and options. They could dine in the kitchen nook, or in their formal dining room. The boys, who were playing in the backyard, shared a room upstairs on the west side of the home. The nursery would be greeted each morning by the rising sun. The massive master suite upstairs had a sitting area, and the finished basement offered a guest room and large recreational area.

Veronica stirred the spaghetti sauce, then pulled a spoon from the drawer to taste it. She added another dash of salt and a pinch of sugar, then stirred the boiling pasta. The oven beeped to signal that it had reached the desired temperature, and Veronica heated the garlic bread. "Martin, Malcolm. Come and wash up for dinner," she called from the screened porch.

"Okay, Miss Ronnie."

Veronica set the table, poured two glasses of juice for the boys, and placed them on the table in the kitchen nook. With the pasta drained, she plated the spaghetti, then cut it on the small plates so that it would be easier for Martin and Malcolm to eat. The brothers sat across from each other. "Patrick," Veronica called from the kitchen nook. "Dinner is ready."

As usual, they held hands, blessed the food, and then began their meals.

"So how is school?" Patrick asked.

"School is good. And Mommy makes sure that we are always on time."

"That's good. It's important for you to always be on time for school."

"She parks the car down the street from the McDonald's right by my school We go there for breakfast."

"So, Mommy isn't cooking you breakfast anymore?"

"She can't. We don't have a stove no more." Malcolm chimed in.

"Oh! Why not."

"It won't fit."

Veronica scratched her head. "I don't understand."

"He means it won't fit in the car." Martin shared.

Patrick shook his head, his forehead tight, eyebrows furrowed. "And just why would it need to fit in the car?"

Veronica's finger tips met at the center of her forehead, her thumbs rested on her jaws. "I'm afraid of the answer."

"We don't live in the apartment no more," Malcolm informed them.

"So where do you live?" Patrick asked.

"Sometimes we go to this big room with a lot of other people we don't know," Martin shared. "But most of the time we sleep in the car. Malcolm and I take turns sleeping on the back seat, and it's my turn next. It's fun."

Veronica pushed back from the table, a tear fell from her eye. "Please excuse me."

"How long has this been going on?" Patrick asked.

"Since we came home from school one day and all of our stuff was in front of the apartment. The door was locked and Mommy couldn't open it."

"Goodness grief!"

"Some of our stuff was gone too."

"Yeah," Malcolm chimed in, "Somebody stole our checkers game."

"So, Mommy put what was left in a,"

"In storage?"

"Yeah, in storage.

"She said she has to find a new place for us to live, but until then we stay in the big room some nights, but mostly in the car by McDonald's. In the morning before school we have breakfast at McDonald's and she takes us in the bathroom and we wash up. She always makes sure that we have clean clothes. We brush our teeth there too."

Patrick leaned back and closed his eyes in shock.

PATRICK HAD BEEN PACING the floor all afternoon waiting for Rachel. He could not believe what the boys had revealed. Homeless! Sleeping in the car. After he put the boys to bed, he told Veronica he wanted full custody of Martin. His wife advised him to think long and hard about that, and at least find out what was going on with Rachel first. When he heard their doorbell chime, he ran to the front door. Veronica walked briskly behind him.

"Rachel," he started. She wore a dress, black pumps, and an overcoat. Not at all like his image of a homeless person. She had just finished playing the organ at Well of Salvation. "Veronica and I need to talk to you."

"Where are the boys?" she asked. "I really need to get going."

"The boys are playing in the basement. They will be fine." Veronica said.

"Rachel," Patrick began again. "What's going on?"

"Nothing." Her ego kept her from being honest. "Everything's okay."

"Do not lie to me Rachel!" Patrick cut to the chase, his words were slow, punctuated, and emphasized. "Your phone has been disconnected for two weeks now, and Martin and Malcolm told me that you were evicted. They said they are sleeping in the car!"

Veronica saw the mixture of sadness and fear in Rachel's eyes, and her vision became blurry from the tears she was holding onto.

"Just how did this happen, Rachel?"

Rachel took a deep breath. "You know I've been going through so much lately."

"Yes Rachel, we know about everything with your estranged husband and your father," Patrick said. "Please tell me what's really going on." He placed emphasis on the word really.

Rachel sighed deeply. "When Martin and Malcolm started spending weekends with you, I wanted to relax, have some fun, like you told me to." As soon as Rachel uttered the last words, she felt guilty. Patrick was in no way responsible for Rachel's problems. "So, the first weekend my coworker invited me on a trip to Casino Aztar. It was a cheap bus ride, I got a free buffet, and came home five hundred dollars richer."

Veronica's compassion evaporated. She tilted her head to the side and stared at Rachel.

"And I was on a winning streak for months. Then it all came to a halt. Last month I had to get an auto title loan to pay my gambling debts. I thought I could win my rent money back, but I didn't. And when I got paid at the end of last month I had to pay the title loan off to keep the car. I didn't think they would really set all of our stuff outside and lock us out of the apartment," Rachel said. "But they did."

Patrick paced the floor. He clenched his jaw, his lips were rigid.

"And all I had left was the child support, which I've used for gas and to feed the boys. I promise that they haven't missed a single meal since we lost the apartment."

He sat and shook his head. "Rachel. What on earth were you thinking? You are a smart woman, or I thought you were. Those casinos are not designed for you to win."

"I won big yesterday." She reached into her purse and held out fifteen one hundred dollar bills. "This will be enough for an extended stay hotel until the end of the month. I can buy groceries too."

Patrick and Veronica shook their heads in disbelief.

"When I get paid at the end of the month, I can find another apartment for us."

"You do realize that you have to have a security deposit as well."

"I'll figure it out. I'm on a winning streak." She paused. "Now where are the boys?"

Veronica stood. "Rachel, Patrick and I have discussed this. The boys need a sense of normalcy. They already have a room here. They can stay here."

"But," Rachel started.

"And you can stay in the guest bedroom in the basement until the end of the school year. By then, we both expect you to have this figured out."

Veronica heard the oven buzzer. "I'm going to check on the roast," she turned to Patrick and Rachel. "You two can work the rest of this out."

Patrick leaned forward. His elbows on top of his thighs, chin rested in his hands. "There are conditions that come along with this arrangement."

"Patrick. I don't want to impose."

"Please stop, Rachel! My son does not deserve to spend his nights sleeping in a car and washing up in a public bathroom. And eating fast food every day. Know that Veronica and I are only doing this for him."

Rachel was quiet. She nodded.

"You have to get help, Rachel. I'd be willing to bet that you never called Robinson."

Rachel's shoulders shrank. She felt small and insignificant.

"I didn't," her voice was weak. It cracked.

"Well, here's how this deal will work. You must call him tomorrow and make an appointment. You need help, and if you don't get it, I'll be forced to sue you for full custody of Martin."

Rachel began to cry. "I've made my life such a mess."

"This is a mess that you can fix. Veronica and I truly want the best for Martin, and Malcolm. But you have to help yourself first." He pointed her in the direction of the half bath. "Now go straighten yourself up. I don't want my son to see his mother like this."

Rachel dried her tears and freshened her makeup before joining the boys in the basement while Veronica set the table. As they blessed the dinner Rachel was full, emotional, at how much she had to be thankful for. She didn't know how she could ever repay them.

Patrick volunteered to drop the boys off at school the next morning so that Rachel could make her appointment with Robinson. With the extra time she had available, she stopped by the post office box where her mail was forwarded after her eviction. There was a package in a locker. It was from Brothaman. She took it to her car, then used the ignition key to tear the shipping tape. It contained a cellular phone and a note.

RACHEL. *I'm very worried about you. I haven't been able to reach you for over a week now, and I don't know what's going on. I hope that you and the boys are well. I'm sending you this phone so that we can keep in touch. It has free long distance. I'm sure you'll use it wisely. Please call me and let me know that you got this. Kiss the boys for me, and know that I love you.*

Your husband, David.

P.S. I got into the Master of Science in Human Services Administration Program at Spertus. My classes start in June. That's what I was calling to tell you.

RACHEL QUICKLY DIALED HIM. "Look, I'm on my way to work so I can't talk long."

"Me too." David replied.

"I just wanted to let you know that I got the phone. Things have been rough. First the phone was disconnected, then we got evicted. We had a rough few weeks, but Patrick and his wife have let me move into the basement of their new home. It's temporary." Rachel spoke so fast that David could not get a word in.

He took a deep breath, disappointed that his son was having an early childhood experience similar to his. His Mom struggled to make ends meet when he was young, and they experienced a few evictions. "I'll be there this weekend."

"Where?" Rachel asked.

"Nashville. I'm heading there when I get off work on Friday." He hung up.

THE TEN-HOUR TRAIN ride put David in Nashville early on Saturday morning. Rachel picked him up at the train station and he took her to breakfast while the boys were at Cheekwood Botanical Gardens with

Veronica and Patrick. Although Veronica was apprehensive at first about inviting Brothaman into their home, she knew that it was important for Malcolm to see his father.

It was a warm and sunny afternoon when Patrick and Veronica returned home. Rachel and David were sitting on the screened porch sipping iced tea. Malcolm's eyes grew big and he smiled as he ran into his father's arms. David held his son tightly, kissed his forehead, and attempted to stifle the tears. He was unsuccessful. "I've missed you so much, son." This was the first time David had seen his son since the boys tried to cook breakfast for themselves nearly a year and a half earlier.

Martin was amazed. He almost didn't recognize the man who made his Mommy cry so much. Veronica gasped. David did not at all match the image she formed in her mind when Martin told her and Patrick about him six months earlier. Patrick didn't know how to feel. Although more than six years had passed, David was still the man responsible, in part, for his first and only major heartbreak. He didn't know if he should welcome him or punch him.

20

SOON ALL WILL KNOW

R odney took the three bottles of wine in the sealed duty-free bag, and gently placed them on their sides in the basket of the luggage cart. He pushed it closer to the carousel. Sina stood beside him, watching the other passengers from her redeye flight ride down the escalator right next to baggage claim. She stood patiently, although she was exhausted, and waited for movement on the conveyor belt. Her layover at LAX had been a lengthy seven hours. And while her twelve-and-a-half-hour flight on Qantas from Sydney offered her some comfort, she was excited and anxious about what was before her. She didn't even nod. Sina looked up at Rodney and smiled. "I'm so happy to be home," she said as the bell rang indicating the arrival of luggage. "I just wish my bags would hurry up and come. I just want to eat and sleep."

She watched as others retrieved their bags, some had ribbons on the handles to make them stand out. While her luggage wasn't the last off the plane, the wait was longer than she had anticipated. With her tote on one shoulder and her purse on the other, Sina walked beside Rodney as he pushed the cart, loaded with her luggage and everything else she picked up while in Australia, to the parking garage.

The minute Sina stepped outside the terminal, she began to sneeze.

"This always happens to me when I fly into Raleigh-Durham in the Spring," she shared with her husband. "Allergies."

They reached the hourly parking area. "Hey." Sina scanned the parking aisle. "I don't see my car. I thought you drove it from Chicago."

"About that." Rodney stopped behind a burgundy Mercedes-Benz M Class, then reached into his pocket for the key.

"Rodney, why are you stopping."

"This is your new ride."

Sina was still, a smile plastered on her face. "Rodney! Achoo."

"I thought you might need something a bit bigger, with two dogs." He pressed the remote key fob, then opened the lift gate and began to put Sina's bags inside. "Zack and Sparky seemed to enjoy the space when I drove from Chicago." He closed the lift gate. "And next summer we may be bringing our first child home.

"Do you like it?"

"Like it? I love it," Sina wrapped her arms around Rodney and stood on the tips of her toes to kiss him. He handed her the key. "Why don't you drive home? I'm so tired," Sina handed the key back to him, sneezed again, then walked to the passenger side door.

Bearded irises in a variety of purple hues greeted them when Rodney pulled into the driveway of their River Run Estates home. A hedgerow of azaleas in shades of pink and orchid bordered the front porch. A trio of peonies: Karl Rosenfield, Sarah Bernhardt, and Gardenia, brightened the opposite side of the garage in shades of pink and white. Rodney pressed the garage door opener and drove inside. "I'll take care of the bags," Rodney instructed. "Sparky and Zack will be very excited to see you."

Sina climbed the three steps to the door and heard Sparky whimper. He knew her scent. When she opened the door, she could barely get in. The dogs beat her with their tails. Sina continued down the hallway before squatting down to pet them while Rodney brought her luggage in. "What are you in the mood for?"

"Do you need to ask?" she smiled coquettishly at her husband.

"I mean lunch."

"I'd love to have some chicken fried hard, mashed potatoes, and green beans. I miss Southern food."

"I know the perfect place. Rick's Diner. It recently opened. It's on University Drive and Shannon Road."

Big band music played throughout the restaurant. A black and white tiled floor complemented the corrugated barn tin wainscoting, accented by a wooden border painted with a high-gloss black. Black and white photos were symmetrically arranged on walls painted a deep cranberry. On the opposite wall, a large blackboard listed the lunch specials. A glass display case with fresh baked desserts rested beside the cash register.

"This place is new," Sina was seated across from Rodney. "Before I left for Sydney, Harrison's was here. I loved their grilled chicken pita with Colby cheese." She perused the menu, then ordered half-sweet/half-unsweetened tea and her perfect welcome home meal she had so long desired. Rodney opted for the lunch special of salmon cakes.

SINA SPENT most of the first few days back catching up on rest and adjusting to the time change. On Tuesday morning, Rodney pushed the empty trash cart from the curb into the garage as he and Sina were leaving for her pre-op bloodwork. He was officially on trash cart duty. While she was excited about getting relief from the cramping and heavy irregular periods, Sina was very nervous about going under the knife.

"Sweetie Pie, everything is going to be all right," Rodney told her as they enjoyed an after dinner walk with Zack and Sparky. The evening was mild, the sun was beginning to lower in the sky, and the bright orange in the horizon promised a sunny tomorrow. They were happy to have a moment to themselves as the weekend had been busy, almost overwhelming.

Sina's parents had flown in on Friday and stayed in the down-stairs bedroom. Sparky was happy to see them both. Tommy and Carol Paxton arrived on the same Saturday morning flight and Tommy brought Carol to the home in the car he rented. After attending morning commencement exercises on Sunday, Sina met the group at Rick's Diner for a late breakfast, a best-kept secret. The owners recently decided to open on Sundays from seven a.m. to three p.m. This was the second week, and with four commencement ceremonies at large universities that morning they were fortunate to get a table for six. They didn't want to take a chance on finding a table for dinner.

Sina and Crystal spent the early afternoon making potato salad, baked beans, and greens to accompany the meat Rodney and Tommy grilled on the deck, while Carol made Rodney's favorite, peach cobbler. After Mother's Day dinner, they spread out in the great room and it wasn't long before the television was watching them.

When Sina and Rodney returned with the dogs, the great room was dark, and everyone had retired to their respective rooms. Sina told Sparky and Zack to sit, gave them each a treat before she showered, then joined her sleeping husband in bed.

The house was quiet and the night was still. Through her bedroom window Sina stared out at the clear sky and fixed her gaze upon a bright star. Beside her, Rodney slept peacefully. Sina was restless, anxious. "Rodney," she whispered. "What if the myomectomy becomes a hysterectomy. It happens sometimes. I'm so afraid. I would be devastated if I couldn't give you any children."

Rodney cracked his eyes, pulled her close, rested her head on his chest, and caressed her face. "I don't believe that will happen baby. And if it does, that won't change us or my feelings about you. Sweetie Pie, I love you, and I'm confident that everything will be fine."

ॐ

JUST BEFORE SUNRISE, after prayer led by Reverend Mintor, the family made the journey to UNC Memorial Hospital for Sina's surgery. Tommy had a late afternoon flight back to Chicago, so he put his luggage in the trunk of his rental vehicle.

Rodney sat in the waiting area and stared blankly into space. Although he said everything to reassure his wife, he too was nervous. He only took a few sips of the coffee Tommy and Reverend Mintor brought for the group. His mother-in-law sat beside him. "Rodney," Crystal took his hand. "Don't worry. Sina is going to be just fine. She is at one of the best hospitals with a very skilled surgeon. Over the course of my career I've seen much less skilled surgeons perform myomectomies without complications."

He looked up at his mother-in-law. Worry slowly faded from his eyes.

"Right now, you should give thanks for Thomasine's healing, and for your children who are waiting to be born."

Rodney hugged her, and when he released the embrace, he looked up to see Dr. Torres approaching the waiting area. The look on her face gave him great relief. He walked towards her.

"I'm pleased to say that everything went well. We removed two fibroids, one the size of a navel orange, the other the size of a plum, as well as several pea-sized fibroids. Your wife is in recovery, and you'll be able to see her as soon as we move her to a room."

When Sina came home on Wednesday, Crystal insisted that she stay in the downstairs bedroom for a few days, rather than climb the stairs so soon after her surgery. Her father and mother-in-law had already returned to Chicago, and Crystal had prepared a freezer full of meals to make life easier for Thomasine and Rodney over the next few weeks. When she left on Friday, Sina had to reassure Rodney that she would be fine alone for the forty-minute trip to and from the airport.

LATER THAT EVENING, Rodney and Sina were cuddled on the great room sofa watching TV. While they enjoyed spending evenings on the deck, the ninety-degree day and humidity encouraged them to seek comfort inside. Sina, nearly asleep with her head resting in the crook of Rodney's shoulder, was startled when Zack began to bark. Sparky ran to the front door. Then Sina heard a car door close.

"I'll check it out," Rodney carefully removed his arm from around Sina's shoulder and slowly got up from the sofa.

Sina heard the storm door close, and Rodney's footsteps on the front porch. Sparky ran to Sina, then back to the front door. When she heard the door close, she asked, "What's going on, Rodney?"

"I couldn't be this close to you and not come and see you," Hope said. Sina turned towards the hallway, and slowly rose from the sofa. "I came as soon as I got off work."

"Hope! What a pleasant surprise!" Sina hugged her friend. "You look fabulous!" Hope's now twenty-eight-pound weight loss was very noticeable, especially to her friend who hadn't seen her in months. "I'm so glad you're here."

"The move to Virginia Beach was the best thing for me," Hope started. "I love my job, I joined a gym, I started journaling and writing poetry. I now understand how I used food to fill my other longings, and I've changed my perspective."

Rodney carried Hope's bag into the guest bedroom, then left the life-long friends alone to catch up.

Sina was startled the next morning by the loud, shrill tone of the house alarm. Day was just beginning to break, the early morning light made its way through the French doors leading to the deck. Sina sat upright on the great room sofa, and pushed the throw someone covered her with aside.

"I'm sorry, I didn't mean to," Hope whispered.

Sina did a double look, then wiped her eyes.

"You are very serious about this fitness kick!" Hope wore shorts, a tank top, running shoes, and a sun visor.

"It's not a kick for me, it's my new way of life."

Sina walked to the keypad and disabled the alarm, just before the phone rang.

"How long have you been running?" Sina asked, once she informed the alarm company that she was safe and there was no need for the police to come.

"About six weeks now. I'm hooked."

When Hope returned from her morning run, Sina was seated on the deck with coffee, juice, and fruit, as Rodney prepared breakfast for them. Although it was a bit humid, the morning sun was at a state that was still bearable. Hope took an empty glass from the table, went into the kitchen, and filled it with water.

"Good morning, Hope," Rodney said. "How do you like your eggs?"

"I'll just have an egg white omelet."

"What kind of cheese? We have cheddar and Swiss."

"No cheese, just some of those onions and peppers."

Rodney began to separate the eggs as Hope made her way back to the deck. Sparky and Zack roamed free in the fenced backyard.

"No juice?" Sina asked Hope.

"No, too many calories," she took a gulp of water. "And after my run, I need to hydrate."

"Whoa!" Sina said. "You are seri—," Sina began when Rodney stepped onto the deck and handed her the phone.

"It's Rachel."

Glee permeated Sina's face and voice. "Hi Rachel," she paused. "Hope is here. Let me put you on speakerphone."

"Hi Rachel," Hope said. "I'm so glad you called. I haven't been able to reach you."

"How are you and the boys?" Sina interrupted.

"Things have been really rough lately."

"Hey," Sina began. "Maybe we shouldn't do this on speakerphone." She turned to Hope. "Ask Rodney for the other receiver."

Hope went to the French doors and asked Rodney for the other phone.

"Oh no!" was Sina's response to Rachel's revelation of her eviction and phone disconnection.

"What is it?" Hope asked. Sina held up her index finger.

"You're living where?"

Rodney handed Hope the phone just in time for her to hear Rachel say she was living in Patrick and Veronica's basement.

"How did all of this happen?" Sina asked. Rachel knew that facing her mistakes was key in her recovery. She told her friends all about her gambling addiction.

"I understand," Hope replied, in an effort to comfort her life-long friend. "I really do."

Thomasine turned her head quickly toward Hope, lips pursed and eyebrows furrowed. She was shocked at how Hope had changed.

"Patrick gave me an ultimatum. And he's right. I have to get myself together so that I can raise my sons."

"He's absolutely right," Sina said.

"I've been seeing a therapist for the past month. And David has been wonderful in all of this. He sent me this cell phone when my phone was disconnected."

"Oh," Hope said. "Who is David? A new love interest?"

"She means Brothaman. His real name is David."

"Oh," Hope replied. Her tone had a hint of judgementality. "Be careful."

"Hope, he's really changed. He's been clean for six months now, and just got accepted into a master's program."

"Really?" Hope asked. "Wow!"

"That's wonderful. I'm glad to see that he is turning his life around."

"He fully understands addiction. It nearly cost him his life." Rachel paused. "And he comes down once a month to see the boys."

"That's great," Sina said as Rodney placed their plates in front of them. "Speaking of the boys, maybe you can bring them for a weekend at the beach."

"Yes," Hope said after taking a bite of her egg white omelet and giving Rodney the thumbs up. "I practically live right at the beach."

"I can't make any travel commitments right now," Rachel paused, then sighed. "I'm going to a residential treatment center for my gambling addiction right after the school year ends. I'll be there for four weeks."

"Wow," Sina didn't intend to verbalize her thoughts. "Well, if there is anything we can do to help you, just let us know."

"Yes," Hope started. "If you need anything at all, just let us know. We're here for you."

21

GIANT STEPS

D avid stood beside LaTanya, a member of his cohort, and they marveled at the view from their classroom window. Spertus Institute was across the street from Grant Park, and from the window they could see the entire lakefront, even the Ferris wheel at Navy Pier.

"If you think the view is beautiful now, just wait until December. The night time view is spectacular." She placed her books on the desk, "I'm Dr. Walters, your instructor for this course, the Communication Module. I'll also be the research mentor for your cohort. Now let's start by getting to know each other. I'd like for each of you to stand, give your name, undergraduate institution and major, and your goals for this program."

David sat front and center. As they transitioned out of introductions and into the lecture, he copiously took notes and was earnest to answer questions. Never an eager student, unless it was art related, he now understood the transformative value of education. David was determined to make the most of his year and a half at Spertus.

The sun had finally begun to set on this mid-June evening, but the class time passed by almost unnoticeably. David looked at his watch. He couldn't believe three hours had passed.

"Some call it stream of consciousness writing." Dr. Walters walked to the front of her desk. "I call it the Golden Pearl.

"So, for the next twenty minutes I want you to write down whatever comes to mind. No editing." She walked between the rows of desks. "And I guarantee, that from this exercise you will get a clear vision for your major project." She perused the faces of her students.

"This exercise is important. Every assignment you complete during this module will be based on your Golden Pearl." She scanned the room again.

"Yes, LaTanya?"

"So, I'm just supposed to write whatever comes to mind?"

"Yes. Don't worry about spelling, grammar, or anything. Just jot down whatever comes to mind for the next twenty minutes or so."

"But I don't see how I'll get anything out of this."

"Trust me," she said, then looked at her watch. "And you may begin now."

David tried to have a loose grip on his pen to avoid a Swan's neck in his right index finger which happened from time to time due to his injury. Martin and Malcolm were on his mind, as well as his childhood, and what led to his addiction. Thoughts formed in his mind much faster than he could write them down.

While the students wrote, Dr. Walters sat at her desk and wrote as well. Twenty minutes and seven pages later, David not only had the mission and vision for the non-profit he intended to start, he also had the name, H.U.H.O. Short for Helping You Help Others. Though a daunting task that would require tons of grant funding, he wanted the individuals he served to go on to serve others.

❦

"THANK you for letting me stay at your house for the next few days," Zuri backed into her driveway and lined the passenger side front door of her car up with the walkway.

"Your apartment is on the third floor! You'd never make it up there." She opened the back door, pulled the crutches from the back seat, helped Jason swing his legs to the right, then helped him stand.

"Be very careful," she said as he started toward her front porch. The five steps were nothing compared to the flights he'd have to conquer had he returned to his apartment. Jason had just left the hospital after his ACL surgery, and Zuri was by his side every step of the way. She ran ahead of him, unlocked the front door, held it open for him.

Jason plopped into the mauve wingback chair in front of the picture window where the Christmas tree stood half a year earlier. Zuri pushed the ottoman in front of Jason, and elevated his leg. "I'll be right back with an ice pack," she handed him the remote.

"Thank you," Jason said. His eyes followed Zuri past the television set until she turned into the kitchen. He closed his eyes briefly, the meeting of his lips parted, cheeks spread slightly. Jason wiped his eyes, his fingers made their way down and along his cheeks before he massaged his neck. Reflected in the floor-to-ceiling mirrored wall opposite him, Jason could see Christopher, backpack on his right shoulder, standing with friends beside the maple tree in front of the house. Its bright green canopy shielded the house from the vivid rays of early summer sun. The temperature was in the low eighties, but very humid. Jason's cheeks spread wider as he saw Christopher walk up the driveway.

"Coach McCoy!" Christopher exclaimed as he walked through the front door. His backpack slid from his shoulder as he ran over to Jason. Jason's seated turn was awkward as he reached out to hug him.

"Be careful, both of you," Zuri placed the ice pack on Jason's knee. "And pick up that backpack before someone trips over it."

"Yes, Mom," Christopher retrieved his backpack, and held the bag in his hand by the haul loop. "I was so excited when Mom told me you would stay with us for a few days. I told her that you could sleep in my room."

"That's nice of you," Jason replied. Zuri smiled.

"Mom said it would be hard for you to climb steps, so I'll sleep in the guest room in the basement." Christopher stood his backpack in the small space between the end table and the sofa, then sat across from Jason.

"Thank you. I really appreciate it."

"Oh, Mom." Christopher bent down, unzipped his backpack, and retrieved his report card. "I got my math grade up this quarter. I got a B."

"That's wonderful. I'm glad that you're improving, son. I'm so proud of you."

Christopher smiled. "I'll do even better next year in fifth grade after the math camp."

"Did you start packing yet?" Zuri asked her son. "You leave in the morning."

"I packed most of my things last night when I cleaned up my room for Coach," Christopher said. "I even took my bag to the basement so that Coach won't trip over it."

"That's very thoughtful of you," Jason said. "Where are you going?"

"My Dad registered me for a summer math camp at UW-Parkside. It starts on Monday and he's coming in the morning to pick me up. You'll get to meet him."

"That's great. How long is the camp?" Jason asked, he turned the television to ESPN SportsCenter.

"Three weeks. I'll be back on July 11."

"That'll be just in time for you to go to the football camp at Duncan."

Christopher scooted to the front edge of the sofa as his Mom stood in the kitchen doorway. "Time to take the ice pack off, Jason. Twenty minutes on, sixty off."

Christopher retrieved the pack and walked towards Zuri.

"Mom, can I go to the football camp at Duncan? Please? It doesn't start until after the math camp is over."

"I'm sure that will be just fine," she said. "I made you and," she paused, "Coach a snack. Why don't you get the TV trays out of the hall closet?"

When Zuri returned to the living room with the snack, Christopher had carefully positioned the tray for Jason.

ॐ

JASON USED his upper body strength to push his body to a seated position. He stretched his arms. *Mmm.* He first inhaled the scent, then heard the sizzle of bacon cooking. Jason swung his legs over the edge of the twin-size bed, then reached for his crutches which leaned against the wall. It took him a few seconds to figure it out, but he made his way first to the bathroom, then to the kitchen as quickly as he could.

"Whoa, slow down Speedy," Zuri greeted him.

"Good morning," Jason said. He smiled at Zuri, then shifted his weight to his right leg, and reached for the stove. Zuri's hand came down like a seagull swooping for fish. Jason teetered and fell into her arms.

"See, that's what you get," Zuri said, then bit her lower lip. Jason's gaze mirrored hers, and for a moment it was as if they were the only beings in the world. Nestled safely in Zuri's arms, Jason leaned in a little further. Their lips met for the first time. With the crutch securely underneath his right arm, Jason reached up with his right hand and caressed Zuri's face. Her eyes were warm, cheeks soft and relaxed, a euphoric smile on her face.

"Mom, you made bacon!" Christopher said as he reached the top step. He carried his duffel bag on his shoulder. Jason leaned back on his crutches.

Zuri turned and hugged her son. "Special breakfast for my favorite son."

"I'm your only son."

"And you're still my favorite." The look of unconditional love spread across her face as she looked at Christopher. "I'll put this in the living room so it'll be out of the way while you help Coach to the table." She took the duffel bag from Christopher and left the room.

Christopher pulled the chair out for Jason as he hopped towards the table. "Coach, I need to have a talk with you."

"Oh?"

"Yeah. Man to man."

Jason lowered to the chair and handed the crutches to Christopher, who hooked his right arm through them. His arms folded across his chest.

"I saw what just happened."

"What?"

"The kiss. I saw it, and I want you to know that if you break my Mom's heart, you will have to deal with me." Emphasis on will. "Do you hear me loud and clear?"

"Yes sir, I do."

Jason looked up and saw Zuri turning the corner into the kitchen. She placed the platters of scrambled eggs and bacon on the table. "I hope grits are okay." After stirring the pot one last time, she put the grits in a serving bowl and placed them on the table alongside the other food.

"Christopher, why don't you get the orange juice out of the fridge?"

He scooted back from the table, opened the refrigerator, and first poured juice for his mother, then Jason, then himself.

"I didn't even ask if you wanted coffee," Zuri said to Jason as they joined hands to bless the food.

"I'm good."

Zuri sat at the end of the table, Jason was in the seat beside her which gave him more room, and Christopher sat opposite his Mom, his back to the china hutch. The side of the table across from Jason was flush with the wall.

The kitchen was so quiet at first that you couldn't even hear the hum of the fluorescent lights. Every now and then a crunch from the bacon, scrape of the fork on the plate provided the only sound. The ding dong from the doorbell interrupted the near silence. "May I be excused," Christopher asked. He pushed back from the table without awaiting a response from his mother.

Zuri looked over at Jason as he sipped his juice. She cleared the plates from the table as Gregory, Christopher's father, walked into the kitchen.

"You must be Coach McCoy." Jason tried to scoot back from the table.

"Don't bother, Bro. You just had surgery." He extended his hand. "Christopher talks about you all of the time."

"It's nice to meet you." Jason shook his hand firmly. "Christopher is a great kid. He reminds me a lot of myself when I was his age."

"Christopher says you're a great coach. Thank you for taking an interest in my son."

Jason nodded at the compliment. Awkward was how he felt, especially after the man-to-man talk he had with Christopher.

Gregory looked at his watch. "We'd better hit the road now if we want to beat the Great America and outlet mall traffic."

Zuri dried her hands on the dishtowel, pulled her son close and hugged him tightly. "I expect you to do your best at the math camp," she loosened her embrace, kissed his forehead, then turned to Gregory. "Drive safely. Tell Nina and Ashley I send my love."

Gregory turned to Jason once again. "It is really nice to meet you." He hugged Zuri and they left. Jason heard the front door close, then the car doors.

"Zuri," Jason began. "Christopher saw the kiss."

Zuri sat near Jason at the table. She rested her elbows on the table, forehead in her palms. "I wish I had known before I sent him off for three weeks."

"He let me know what he would do to me if I didn't treat you right."

"Oh," she looked up, her nose wrinkled slightly, cheeks raised and the faint freckles underneath her eyes began to spread.

"He did." Jason smiled. "He really loves his Mom."

"I have a great son." Her smile spread further across her face.

"And he has a great Mom." Jason reached for Zuri's hand. "I think he just wants to make sure you're happy."

"This may be as much about him as it is about me," Zuri started. "This is a discussion we need to have over coffee." Zuri walked over to the counter, and put a filter, then coffee into the basket before adding water to start the brew.

"Could you please hand me my crutches," Jason asked. "Little boys room."

Zuri walked over to the table and helped Jason with his crutches. "Be careful. I won't be there to catch you this time," she laughed as he hobbled out of the kitchen. "I'll set up a tray table in the living room, and make you another ice pack."

Jason found comfort once again in the mauve wingback chair by the picture window. With his leg propped up, tray table in place, Zuri served Jason coffee just how he liked it, light cream, one sugar, having observed how he preferred his coffee over their weekly meetings of the past six months. She sat on the sofa.

"So why do you say this may be as much about Christopher as it is about you?"

"Gregory is a great father to Christopher, but we split up when

Christopher was a toddler, shortly after Gregory graduated from U of I."

"That had to be devastating."

"It was for me. Christopher was so young at the time that he has no recollection of me and Gregory as a couple. I threw myself into caring for my son, completing my degree, and starting my career so that I could provide for him. My family was always there to help out as well. My younger sister, Johari, loved babysitting her nephew."

Jason smiled.

"I eventually dated again, but the relationship had to be serious, like deeply committed serious, before I let him meet my son. I didn't want a bunch of men coming in and out of his life."

"I understand that."

"When I met Kendell, we dated for months before I let him meet Christopher," She sipped her coffee, then placed the mug on the table. "We had a lengthy engagement. Christopher grew very close to Kendell. When we broke up it was as devastating for my son as it was for me."

Jason rubbed his brow. "I'll bet it was," Jason said, recalling a broken relationship his Mom had when he was in his early teens.

"Kendell reignited an old flame with his first love." She shook her head. "I can't take my son through that again. Ever," Zuri said. "I really like you Jason, and that is why I asked you if you were available to me at Christmas. If you aren't serious, don't even think about kissing me again until you are."

❦

"I THINK this is the perfect home for you," Priscilla slowed her silver Lexus RX to a stop at the subdivision's gatehouse. "We have an appointment to see the home on Tranquility Way." Priscilla was a powerhouse of a realtor and a long-time friend of Carol Paxton. She sold Rodney his first home.

The gate slid open, and Priscilla drove slowly down the paved road lined with perfectly manicured hedges. She turned left down a road of well-spaced gated homes set back from the road. Each lot had to be at least five acres. At the third home, she turned right. The two stone pillars were connected by a wrought iron gate, which was uniform with the fence surrounding the property. As they turned onto the long, winding driveway made of stone, a fountain in the center of the circular drive was perfectly aligned, at a distance, with the front door. Thomasine's eyes got big and she gasped.

"Wait until you see the inside," Priscilla said as she drove slowly into the port-cochère, a courtyard leading to the two garages, one held two cars, the other three. "Your service entrances and servant quarters are on this side of the home. The port-cochère was large enough for Priscilla to easily circle in her SUV. She slowed her car to a stop at the front door of the home.

Thomasine stood in awe at the colonial stone home. It reminded her of the manors she saw in films set in eighteenth-century England. Neatly trimmed boxwood hedges enclosed the circular fountain. Just beneath them, a bed of pink begonias offered a splash of color.

"Let's go inside," Priscilla opened the lockbox and retrieved the key.

When Thomasine stepped inside the leaded beveled glass French doors, her purse slid from her shoulder. The grand foyer with the sweeping staircase and marble tiled floor was breathtaking. The wave-like pattern on the black iron staircase railing was unlike any she had ever seen.

From the front door, the foyer extended to the rear French doors, also with leaded beveled glass. Priscilla walked them through the first floor. Most of the rooms had arched Palladian windows and each room had Dentil crown molding. Molding in the ballroom, conservatory, and great room was accented with gold leaf. Sina walked along the ball-room's parquet floor, through paned glass French doors onto a terrace overlooking the tennis court. Rodney stood behind her, his arms around her waist. She turned and tilted her head up. "This place is amazing!"

Hand in hand, across the parquet floor, they made their way into the neighboring conservatory with floor to ceiling arched Palladian windows on three sides. It led to the dining terrace. "I've always wanted a baby grand piano. This room would be perfect."

"I'll add that to the list." He kissed his wife. They followed Priscilla through the great room, then den to the west stair hall.

"You'll love this room, Thomasine," Priscilla said as she opened the French doors of the library. Tall barrister's bookcases of a rich mahogany, each beside a window of equal height, caused Thomasine to exhale deeply. The arched coffered ceiling had been painted ivory and accented with gold. The fireplace, the fifth one Sina counted on that floor, would be comforting and cozy on cold or rainy days.

Priscilla walked Sina and Rodney to the rear of the house. "Up or down?" she asked when they made their way to the elevator. Sina was excited about the first-floor guest bedrooms which may come in handy should her elderly parents ever have to live with them, especially with her parents considering retirement. But an elevator? That was beyond Sina's wildest dreams.

The master suite with his and hers bathrooms and closets, and a sitting area covered the entire west wing of the home. "Why is your closet larger than mine?" Sina asked Rodney, jokingly.

"Fair trade, your bathroom is much larger than mine. You get a tub and a large shower." A naughty thought crossed Sina's mind when her husband brought up the shower, but since they were in the company of a long-time friend of her mother-in-law, she kept that thought to herself. There were more than enough bedrooms on the second floor for their growing family, in addition to those in the service quarters just above the two-car garage.

"This house is perfect for us," Thomasine turned to Rodney. "Hope, Rachel, and her boys could visit at the same time, and everyone could have their own bedroom AND their own bathroom. All on this floor." She held his hand tight.

Priscilla took them to the lower level. Thomasine was stunned by the movie theater, wine cellar, and ample storage space. Rodney found the indoor basketball court and large exercise room with a dry sauna and massage room quite impressive. A kitchen, wet bar, and multiple recreational rooms on the lower level completely sold Rodney on this home.

He turned to his wife. "So, what do you think?"

"I think we've found our home." Thomasine smiled. "And it's going to be hard for me to go back to North Carolina with all of this."

"You haven't even seen the back of the home yet," Priscilla said.

"There's more?"

"Yes. This is the hidden gem of the south suburbs," Priscilla said as she led them to the lower foyer near the theater room, and up the stairs to the main level.

The lush carpet of Kentucky bluegrass in the back of the house led to an in-ground pool and separate whirlpool. Priscilla stood on the terrace while Sina and Rodney walked across the lawn, over to the pool, and admired the back of the home.

"Priscilla was right, this house is perfect for us."

He pulled Sina close. "It is." He kissed her cheek. "The exercise room, sauna, basketball court. I can work out here during the off-season and spend more time with you."

She kissed him back. "I'd like that, a lot!"

THE TRUNK of the cherry blossom tree stood tall in the corner of the room. To the right, Veronica hung pink letters spelling Patricia on the pegs Patrick installed on each branch. The letters to the left spelled Stephanie. Each girl would have a great-grandmother's name for her middle name. Patricia Odessa and Stephanie Vanessa.

"Perfect!" Patrick put his arm around his wife's shoulder as they stood back and admired the wall mural. The letters hung neatly over each crib.

"The nursery is shaping up nicely." Veronica took Patrick's hand and put it on her abdomen so that he could feel the twins kick.

"Two future soccer players," Patrick commented.

"Or maybe they'll study dance, like their Mama." Veronica laughed, then sat in the Vanderbilt rocking chair in the corner opposite the tree, near the window. She looked at the saplings in the front yard which did little to block the morning sun.

"We will definitely have to add a window shade or curtains."

Patrick walked over to the window. "I'll put that on my to do list." He gazed at his wife. "This is nice. Just the two of us. Alone. Finally!"

"Yes," Veronica stood. "I had reservations about David at first, but he seems to have really turned his life around. I guess he's trying to redeem himself."

"I can understand. He probably feels like he's lost time with his son. I can relate." Patrick rubbed his chin. "He has gotten his act together."

"Yes. He's been here every weekend. Work, school, he's really straightening his life out."

"He's been a big help to us since Rachel went into rehab." Patrick and Veronica began to walk towards the door of the nursery and down the hallway towards their bedroom. "I just hope she gets her act together. Those boys have had more than their share of misery in their first five years."

Veronica stood in the doorway of the master suite, her hand on her hip. "Yeah, she'd better get her act together," she said matter-of-factly, "Because she needs to be out of here long before the twins arrive."

Patrick was silent.

"This was temporary. Until the school year ended!" She sat on the side of their bed, head in her hands. "Patrick. As much as I want to be supportive for the boys' sake, I just can't take this intrusion any longer. We need to bond with our daughters, and we don't need Rachel in the way."

"She has respected our boundaries."

"Patrick! I've been a good little trooper through all of this. Put yourself in my position. I do love Martin and Malcolm, but what about us? She's got to go! One week. She has one week after she gets out of rehab to find an apartment for her and the boys."

Patrick exhaled deeply, then nodded.

"And we will go back to the original court ordered arrangement with regards to joint custody. The boys will come every other weekend, and that's after we've had time to bond with our daughters alone. They can come visit and meet the girls, but they can't stay overnight for the first two months."

Patrick sat beside his wife. "You know, that's not a bad idea. Rachel started gambling when we started keeping the boys on weekends. This will eliminate the opportunity for her to go to the casino. She should have no problem finding an apartment with the money she has saved on rent since she's been with us. I'll call her today."

&

JASON SAW the big green D from a distance. His gait was a bit slower than normal, four-weeks post op. As he got closer he stopped, his head tilted as he surveyed the building from top to bottom. When Jason stepped inside, he marveled at the transformation of the place once considered his second home while a student athlete at Duncan University, Foster Fieldhouse. Now a center for Duncan University student athletes, the Hall of Spartan Achievement welcomed visitors. The multi-storied foyer featured glass display cases offering Spartan fans a view of the rich athletic history and a walk down memory lane. Jason stopped to read the list of football conference championships the Spartans won, including those during his years as a running back.

"Jason! My man. Long time no see."

"No way! CJ!"

"Man. How have you been?" CJ Rhodes hugged Jason. CJ became the number one running back after Jason's injury. "It's been years!"

"I'm good." Jason shifted his weight to his right leg. "Just had my ACL restored."

"You've got to be kidding."

"Four weeks ago."

"Wow."

"Man. I thought you were living in Miami. I've followed your career over the years."

"I am," CJ said. "But I come back every summer to help Coach McCann with the youth football camp."

"That's cool. My lady's son is attending. I'm a little too early to pick him up. I just stopped by here to kill time after my appointment at the medical center."

"Which one?"

"Christopher. Running back. He's ten. I coached him last season."

"Christopher," CJ smiled. "I worked with him. Good kid."

"Yes, he is."

"Man, it's so good to see you. What's new?"

"I'm an attorney. I work in licensing at Zandt, Monroe, & Cates. Coaching Christopher's team last year made me realize how much I miss football."

"I hear you man. I've been blessed to be able to do what I love as a career. I know it won't last forever, but I'm riding this baby as long I can."

"I'd give anything to play again. Anything."

"Hey, you only live once, right?"

"This is going to sound crazy. But if I heal well and get back into form, I'm thinking of coming back to Duncan, maybe in the L.L.M. program. That is if I have any eligibility left."

"That doesn't sound crazy at all. Look at Chris Weinke. He was a twenty-five-year-old true freshman. You probably have one year of eligibility left at the most."

"You think I can do it?"

"You won't know if you don't try. Talk to Coach. I'm sure he'll be happy to see you." CJ looked down at his watch. "Look man, I've got to run." They hugged. "And I'll tell Naomi I ran into you."

"Naomi the Omicron Opal?"

CJ smiled. "We've been married for five years now."

22

DETOUR AHEAD

A warm, gentle breeze swirled around Sina and Rodney as they rode south on Cicero from Midway Airport in Rodney's roadster. Sina loved flying into Chicago at night and watching the city sparkle from above. The moon, waxing gibbous, was almost fully illuminated. "Did you pick up—"

"Yes, Sweetie Pie, I picked up the ovulation predictor," he interrupted her. It had been slightly more than three months since Thomasine's myomectomy. The timing was impeccable. Sina was home for a few days after starting her Fall semester at Steeplechase. It was the weekend before Rodney's training camp started, the prelude to his six-month tour around the world. Making this baby right now was a must with Rodney on the road for so long. A September conception meant a June birth. By then Sina's school year would be over and she would be able to take maternity leave during the Fall semester. That would give her more than six months to bond with her little one before she had to return to work. This well-thought plan was foolproof.

They closed on their new home almost a month ago. Robinson-Goode Interior Designs worked earnestly for Sina and Rodney. Although Sina had yet to see what they had done, Rodney was pleased with the results.

They turned onto Tranquility Way. The coach lights atop the stone fence posts shined brightly. Rodney eased his car through the gate, then moseyed over the cobblestoned driveway to the port-cochère and into the garage. Sina followed Rodney through the family room and kitchen to the elevator by the rear foyer. "Baby, I'm so exhausted," she began. "We had a faculty meeting that wore me out. Then I had to drop Sparky and Zack off for boarding. As much as I want to see everything the designers have done, I don't have the energy. I just want to crash."

He pushed the up button. "The designers will be here in the morning. They have a few things to tweak, but they're practically finished. Wait until you see our bedroom."

The elevator door opened just outside their master suite. "I really like this," was all she could muster up to say as she walked through the master sitting room. She went into her bathroom. The ovulation predictor on the counter was the first thing she saw. Sina grabbed a wash cloth, washed her face, went into her closet, slipped on her pajamas, then said "Good night, Sugar Cane," Just like that, she was down for the count.

§

RODNEY RINSED a peach in the island sink. The bright, morning sun flooded the kitchen through the wall of windows just above the larger sink. "You're up and full of energy early this morning." Thomasine had already been to the grocery store and was taking salmon cakes out of the oven.

He bit into the soft, ripe peach, a drop of its juice trickled from the corner of his mouth. Rodney walked over to the counter near the stove and grabbed a paper towel to wipe it.

Thomasine stirred the grits, then added sharp cheddar cheese as Rodney finished his fruit. She plated the breakfast, which Rodney carried over to the island. "I thought we'd eat outside," she took a pitcher of juice from the refrigerator. "It's such a beautiful morning."

"I have to head out to the team meeting shortly." He poured a glass of juice for Sina. "We live further south now, so my commute is a bit longer."

"What time are the interior designers due?" She sat at the island.

Rodney looked at the kitchen clock. "In about forty minutes." He cut the salmon cake with his fork, then sampled. "Sina." He sang her name. "These are better than I remembered."

"How long is your meeting?" She pushed her glass over slightly to the right.

"I'll probably have lunch with a few of the guys. Is that okay?"

"Of course."

"You should be done with the designers by the time I get home." Rodney took their plates to the sink and rinsed them while Sina put the juice pitcher in the fridge, then wiped down the island. "I'd better hop in the shower," Rodney said. He bent down and kissed his wife.

Sina began to walk around the first floor of their new home in amazement. The wall sconces and chandeliers were beautiful. She walked to the library and sat at the desk. It looked great in the catalog, and even better in its new home. The Palais executive desk was made just for that room. Sina loved the arrangement. The floating desk allowed her to enjoy the view from the windows and of the fireplace. The brass metal table lamp on the right corner of the desk was the perfect accent. Its ivory colored shade with gold accents matched the coffered ceiling quite well. For a moment, Sina felt warm and fuzzy. It was from the joy she felt. A little more than a year ago she questioned Rodney's intentions, until she woke up on her flight to Sydney and saw him sitting across the aisle from her. She didn't know it then, but that was just the beginning of the rest of her life.

Sina smiled, then inhaled deeply. The phone rang, only once. From a distance, she could hear Rodney walking down the stairs. She pushed back from the desk and met her husband in the den.

"Sweetie Pie, the designers just rang. They'll be here shortly. I really have to run now to get to my meeting on time, but here is a list of what they'll need to do." Rodney handed a slip of paper to his wife, then hugged her tightly and kissed her forehead. "They have a temporary code for the gate." He leaned back and looked in Sina's eyes. "I'll be back this afternoon. I'm really looking forward to—."

"Me too, Sugar Cane. Me too."

Thomasine spent the morning with the designers going over every detail. They exceeded her expectations. Her new home was beautiful beyond her imagination. Just before they left, they photographed each room to use for future advertising. Sina signed a release form which ensured that neither the address nor the names of the homeowners would be disclosed.

She sat at the kitchen counter and ate a handful of grapes. The sun was at its highest point for the day. Sina slid from the stool and opened the refrigerator. She was glad she had picked up some chicken salad as she expected the weekend to be too busy for her to cook. Sina put a scoop of chicken salad on the plate, then went to the pantry for crackers. She tore a stem from the grapes in the fruit bowl on the island and enjoyed her sustenance.

After clearing the lunch dishes, Thomasine took a glass of water with her as she climbed the grand sweeping staircase to her master suite. She walked along the balcony, paying close attention to the railing's detail, then looked down at the marble tile in the foyer which extended from the front to the rear of the home. Joy did not begin to describe what she felt, and she was excited about what was to come. By this time next year, Sina fully expected for her and Rodney to start their growing family here.

She stopped at the alcove leading to the master bedroom and admired the sculpture by Debra Hand. There was another one she'd have to talk to Rodney about purchasing. It was a seated trumpet player that would rest perfectly on the grand piano in the conservatory.

Nothing, absolutely nothing could bring Thomasine down today. Especially after she confirmed that she was indeed ovulating. She was elated. For once, everything she ever wanted was finally coming together in her life.

She picked up her cell phone from the night stand, and without thinking, called Rodney on the Nextel two-way. "Sugar Cane! Are you there, Sugar Cane?"

"Yes, Sina." She heard snickers in the background from Kenny and his other teammates. "Let me call you right back."

Rodney asked his friends to excuse him, and walked through a maze of lunchtime diners to the bank of payphones in the crowded north suburban restaurant. It was a bit quieter there. He dialed his wife's cell phone.

"Sugar Cane. How soon will you be home? Operation Baby Harris is underway. I'm ovulating." She was giddy with excitement.

Rodney looked at his watch. "I'll leave right now. It should take me an hour, forty-five minutes if there's no traffic." He put his cell phone back into its holster and walked to the table.

"Guys. It's been great. But I have to run."

"But you haven't had lunch yet," Jeremy said. "We need to catch up."

Kenny laughed so hard that he nearly spat his water out. "Rodney ain't thinking about you, man. When Sina says the O word, Rodney goes running home." Rodney ran into Kenny in the drug store when he was buying the ovulation predictor earlier in the week.

"Oh," Jeremy replied.

"I ain't mad at ya," Kenny said. "I'm really happy for you and Sina. I hope this works out for you. I really do. You deserve the best." Rodney shook his hand. "Now get home so I can have a godchild."

❧

RODNEY DROVE south on I-294 to I-57 with the top down on the beautiful, sunny afternoon. The traffic was light and the lunchtime crowd had already made their way back to work. He was thankful for I-Pass which made his trip a bit quicker since he didn't have to slow down to toss coins at the toll booths. Most of all he was glad that he didn't give up on Sina. His gentle persistence paid off after she rejected him in high school, then later during their college summer internship. This time last year he was flying back from Sydney, hopeful that he had won her over. Their Australian courtship and Fijian wedding were leading to his longtime dream. To be a dad.

Rodney exited I-57 and it seemed that he got caught by every light. He drove through the gates of his subdivision, then down the road to his home with caution. He was now even more mindful of small children at play. The excitement and new awareness of parenthood transformed Rodney in a way he never imagined. He drove along the winding driveway, then parked the car in the circular drive next to the front door. He didn't bother to put the top up, and honestly didn't care if it rained. All he cared about at the moment was how the love that he and Sina shared would create new life.

Rodney unlocked the front door. His feet barely touched the marble tile in the foyer. "Sweetie Pie," he called. Rodney climbed the stairs, taking two steps at a time. He strutted, head up, chest out, into the master suite. "Sweetie Pie," he called again.

Rodney scanned the bedroom. Through the French doors leading to their master balcony he could see Sina sitting on the upper terrace. Her shoulders were shrunken. His heart sank.

With fierce urgency, Rodney ran to the doors, then calmed himself down. He stepped onto the terrace. "Sweetie Pie," he said in that low mellow voice she so loved. "What's going on? You don't seem excited. Are you having second thoughts about the baby? About us?" He sat next to her.

She turned to face him through tear-filled eyes. "No Rodney. You know that I love you and I want nothing more than for us to start a family."

"Then what's wrong?"

"I got a call. I forwarded my home phone to the cell. I'm a match."

"A match?"

"Yes. For a child who needs a marrow transplant."

"That's great! You could potentially save someone's life, Sweetie Pie. That's nothing for you to be upset about."

"Rodney," she took his hand. "I can't donate marrow if I'm pregnant."

"Oh," his shoulders sank along with his heart.

"I didn't give them an answer because I wanted to talk to you first. You're my husband. But if I don't donate, I will forever wonder if a child died because of me." Her sobs grew louder.

Rodney pulled Sina to his lap and squeezed her tightly. "I love you, Sweetie Pie. Nothing will ever change that." He sighed and she heard a slight 'oh wow,' underneath his breath. "I support your decision. If you want to donate marrow, I'm behind you a hundred percent."

"If I agree to donate the marrow, I'll have to cut my weekend with you short. I'll have to fly to Baltimore tomorrow for medical tests. The haploidentical transplant will be done at Johns Hopkins. I don't fully understand what that means. A representative is coming here this evening to discuss this with us. Mama and Daddy will be here as well." Her shoulders shook as she cried, "I do know that the child has leukemia. He or she has probably been suffering for a while. And that has to be especially hard on the parents." He wiped her tears. "I know that you were looking forward to this weekend."

"Hey. Don't cry, Sweetie Pie." He caressed her cheek. Parenthood is in our future. The way I see it, I'll just get to have you all to myself a little longer." He pulled Thomasine close and hugged her as tightly as he could, before planting a trail of kisses down her neck.

23

IT'S ALL GOOD

"R eservation for McCoy," Jason told the maître d.
"Right this way," Zuri followed him, and Jason walked behind her admiring the grace in each of her steps and the way the hemline of her black sheath dress met the depression in the back of her knees. Her posture was erect and she oozed confidence.

They were seated at a table for two in the wood paneled dining room of Shaw's Crab House. Chrome fixtures hung from the center of each section of the exposed beam ceiling, casting light over the center of their table, and spotlighting the contrast of the floral arrangement and white linen tablecloth. Zuri perused the menu.

"What wine would you like?" Jason asked Zuri as he scanned the wine list.

She chuckled. "That's always a tough one for me. I think I'm going to have the Club Room Combination." It included a six-ounce filet, sea scallops, and garlic shrimp. "I never know whether I should pair with the beef or with the seafood."

Jason laughed.

"What's so funny?"

"I'm going to have the Filet Oscar, so I was depending strongly on you to make the wine recommendation." On most of their dates over the past three months Zuri and Jason had selected similar meals.

A huge smile spread across Zuri's face. "Maybe we should go with a red and just pair with the beef." She folded her menu and placed it on the table. "Doctors say that red wine is good for your heart."

Jason's cheeks spread. "You're what's good for my heart." Zuri blushed. "The last three months have been fabulous." The waiter came to take their orders.

With the wine presentation ritual complete, Jason raised his glass. "To your promotion to Marketing Director, and to us," their glasses met. "I'm so proud of you, Zuri."

"Thank you, Jason. And I agree with you. The last three months have been great." The waiter brought their meals and Jason blessed the food, then waited for Zuri to begin eating. She cut her medium-well filet, then took a sip of the wine so that the flavors could meld in her mouth. "Great selection," she told Jason. "This pairs perfectly."

Jason savored the blend of crabmeat, beef, and Béarnaise sauce. "Oh, I have great news."

Zuri rested her fork on her plate. "What is it?"

"I've been accepted into the LLM Program at Duncan."

Zuri's smile grew wider. "That's great. When does the program start?"

"January."

"Wow, that soon."

"It's a one-year program. This will give me an opportunity to learn the offense in the Spring and play in the Fall." Based on his rehabilitation progress, Jason was convinced that he'd be ready for Spring practice.

"That's great, Jason."

"And!"

"There's more?"

"I'm able to take a leave of absence from the firm."

"Wow. That's wonderful. I'm so proud of you for pursuing your passion, Jason."

"I'm just happy to have a second chance."

ZURI ROLLED up the window as Jason drove south on Lakeshore Drive.

He flipped through the stations, and chose the instrumental jazz on WNUA over the Saturday night house mixes of his favorite stations. "I can turn the air on."

"No," Zuri said. "I'm good. I just didn't want to mess up my hair."

"I'm so sorry. I didn't even think of that."

"This evening has been great. I'm so glad that Christopher is staying with Johari. He's crazy about his Aunt Johari. My sister is like like a second mother to him."

He glanced at her. "So that means that I have you all to myself this evening."

She looked at him with a cheeky smile, "It does."

"That's too bad."

Zuri tilted her head sideways. "What?"

"Christopher had another man-to-man talk with me. He gave me very specific rules—that I can hold your hand, and that I can kiss you, but not on the lips."

Zuri folded her arms. "Well, you broke that rule while we were waiting for the valet."

"And I intend to break the rules over, and over, and over again tonight."

೪

DAVID RAPPED LIGHTLY on the door to Dr. Walters office.

"Come in," she looked up from the stack of papers on her desk. "Hi David."

"I hope I'm not bothering you," he stepped into her sterile office, with cinderblock walls painted white and florescent lights. "But I'd like to talk to you about my major project."

"When you come to my office during my office hours, you're not bothering me. But if you call my home after eleven o'clock, that's a different story." She motioned to the chair in front of her desk. "Please have a seat."

David sat in the chair and set his briefcase on the floor beside it. Five months had passed since he started the program, and he was ending his fourth intensive course. "Dr. Walters, ever since I did that Golden Pearl exercise in your class, it has been on my mind."

She smiled. "It's interesting that you came to see me about your major project today. I'm posting a sign-up sheet for members of your cohort to schedule appointments with me in about two weeks." Dr. Walters was a part-time faculty member at the college, and was only on campus once a week. "Tell me about your project."

"Dr. Walters." David's cheeks spread from ear-to-ear. "I'm so passionate about it. I want to create a non-profit agency to help recovering addicts. Unfortunately, addiction has greatly affected my family, both substance abuse and gambling addiction."

"Hmmm," Dr. Walters pursed her lips. "The drug problem has been around forever, but with all of the new riverboat casinos in Northwest Indiana, Joliet, Elgin, and Aurora, the need is definitely there."

"Definitely. Buses leave every few hours from 87th and the Dan Ryan to go to the Northwest Indiana casinos."

"Yes. My pastor was very upset to learn that one of our church members had a business that took bus trips to the boats. Now, I think he crossed the line when he asked her for a list of church members who go to the casino."

"Wow. What did she tell him?"

"She said, 'Reverend, if you want to know who goes to the casino,'" Dr. Walters began to laugh, "'Just get on the bus!'"

David began laughing, "That's pretty funny." He sat straight, shoulders up and back. "But in all seriousness, addiction is no laughing matter. As a recovering addict, I know how hard the battle is. I lost everything. This time last year I was in a coma fighting for my life. I had been beaten by a drug dealer and left in the alley for dead."

"I'm so sorry to hear this," Dr. Walters gasped, "but I'm glad you've turned your life around."

"I do not take anything for granted any longer." David felt good sharing his story with his research mentor. "A few months later he was arrested after he beat someone to death in that same alley."

"Was this right before Christmas?"

"Yes."

Dr. Walters shook her head. "That happened right behind my mother's house." She exhaled deeply. "Wow!"

"What I want to do through my agency is start a new cycle."

"Tell me more about this."

"I want to create a model where those who make it through our program help others."

"Elaborate."

"It's really interesting how my life turned around." David told her about his day at Navy Pier sketching portraits. "That was when I got a second chance at life. When I felt that my family had given up on me, I found a complete stranger who believed in me, then offered me a job."

"And now you're four courses into your master's degree."

"Yes. And the company is paying for it."

Dr. Walters nodded her head up and down. "That's wonderful." She opened her desk drawer and retrieved a packet outlining the major project guidelines. "From what you've described to me, you can write a grant proposal or an organizational study for your major project. Either would help you as you start your agency."

"Thank you, Dr. Walters." David stood and reached across the desk to shake her hand. "I really feel empowered from talking to you."

"You are going to do well in this program, David, and with your agency. In the few months I've known you, you've shown me that you are embracing characteristics that will help you succeed. The fact that you initiated this discussion about your major project shows me how serious you are. I usually don't begin talking to students about their projects until the middle of the fifth course. But what impresses me the most is how far you've come in a year. It sounds like you've completely turned your life around."

"I have, Dr. Walters."

"I'm excited about the lives you're going to change once you're done with this program." She looked down at the cohort schedule that was taped to her desk. "This time next year you'll be getting your cap and gown for December graduation."

೫

INSTRUMENTAL JAZZ REMINISCENT of the Roaring Twenties permeated Laurell's, Rachel's favorite restaurant in Nashville. Their table was near the stainless-steel oyster bar, in the room painted an array of bright colors. Rachel sat, then hung her purse on the back of the black, slat back dining chair. "You have to try the gumbo, Heather," Rachel insisted. "Laurell's has the best, probably north of New Orleans. That's where Dad was from."

"I'll give it a burl." Heather responded.

"I think I'll get the crawfish étouffée so that you can have a taste," Rachel gave the waitress their order. "Oh, and we'll start with the hot crab dip."

Since her time in gambling rehab, Rachel had become great at saving and sticking to a budget. She was determined to never put herself in that position again. Her downsized apartment was closer to the boys' school and her job, which saved on gas. On nice days, she walked them to school, then went to work. Her new neighborhood was the ideal location, in proximity to three grocery stores. While this lunch with her sister was a splurge, it was certainly worth it after the hospitality shown to her and Hank last year in Sydney.

"I had a lovely time in Chicago with Hank. It's such a beautiful city, but it's cold," Heather said. "I don't think I could live there, at least not in the winter."

"Nashville is definitely warmer."

"Hank really wanted to come, but he has a rotation this weekend," she paused. "I'm so proud of my big bro," she smiled, a bit teary eyed, "'n' I know that Dad would be really proud of him."

"I'm sure he would," Rachel said. "How are James and Shane?"

"Shane is doing well in school, James got his own place, and got an absolutely fabulous review on his job." Heather smiled broadly.

"Is there something you aren't telling me?"

She grinned from ear-to-ear.

"Oh, I know that smile. What's his name?"

"George. We met on New Year's Eve."

"And I take by that smile that things are going very well."

Heather closed her eyes. "Very." She opened them, this time her smile was even broader. "You're gonna be an Aunty."

Rachel squealed with delight as the waitress placed the hot crab dip between them.

"When?" She picked up a pita wedge and scooped the dip.

"June," Heather's tone changed. "James and Shane are filled with joy at becoming uncles. George is excited as well. It'll be his Mum and Dad's first grandchild."

"I'm so happy for you," Rachel said, then nudged the dip into Heather's direction.

"I just wish Mum and Dad were here to meet their first grand-child." Heather sipped her water. "How are you going, love?"

"It's been a rough year, but I'm back on my feet now, and I've learned a very valuable lesson." She recounted her spring eviction, temporary residence at the Long's home, and six weeks in rehab.

"The pokies can be addictive, eh," Heather said of the slot machines. "I'm glad you got help. Good on ya."

"I had to, for the boys. Patrick threatened to sue me for full custody of Martin if I didn't, and when I got back he gave me a week to move out of his home. I realize just how lucky I am to have support from the fathers of both of my sons."

"Patrick gave you some tough love, eh." Heather took a bite of her dip-filled pita chip. "This is delicious." She wiped the dip from the corner of her mouth. "That's what was best for you and the boys. It forced you to straighten up your act."

The waitress placed their orders in front of them. Heather tasted her gumbo, then closed her eyes momentarily and smiled. "Dad used to make us prawn and chicken stew every New Year's Eve." She looked across the table at her sister. "This makes me think of him."

"I'm glad you like it." Rachel looked at her watch. "I need to stop by the store before we pick up the boys from school. I've got to pick up a sweet potato pie for the Thanksgiving dinner at Veronica's parents' home."

"Tell me more about Thanksgiving. I mean, the types of food you serve." Rachel told her sister all about the holiday and the traditional Thanksgiving fixings.

"You can't buy a pie. I'll cook something for Thanksgiving dinner with an Aussie flair. Maybe I'll make a sweet potato and chive damper, and lamingtons for dessert."

"Damper, lamingtons?" Rachel asked.

"A damper is like soda bread. The lamingtons are a dessert."

&.

HEATHER CRACKED the car door open, then took her jacket off while

Rachel went into the school to get the boys. *Much different than the weather in Chicago.*

The clouds were so thick in the sky they looked like they had been painted there with a heavy body acrylic. Trees held vestiges of what had been a beautiful summer. She smiled when she saw Rachel walking towards her with two little boys. The youngest wore a back-pack that seemed to be almost as large as he was.

Heather swung her legs towards the curb. "Oh my, what lovely boys you are!"

"This is your Aunty Heather." Malcolm stood close to his mother's legs. "G'Day. You must be Malcolm," Heather said first hugging her youngest nephew. "Your Mum tells me you're in Kindy." She pivoted toward his brother, "Martin. How are you going?"

"We're going home," Martin responded. Heather and Rachel erupted in laughter.

"She means how are you doing?" Rachel explained.

"Aunty Heather, why do you talk so funny?"

"Malcolm!" Rachel scolded.

"That's how we Aussies talk. It's English, but a different accent."

"It's kind of like how people from Nashville sound different than people from Chicago."

"Oh."

The boys climbed into the back seat of Rachel's car.

"Mommy. Does T-Sina talk like that now? She was in Australia last year."

"No, Martin. T-Sina talks like she always has."

Rachel looked over her shoulder, then eased away from the curb. When she stopped at the corner, she looked up at the sky. "It's going to storm. I'm so glad we stopped at the store after lunch."

Rachel pulled into the parking space in front of the glossy, over-painted brick red door of her townhouse apartment. Martin and Malcolm had recently resumed weekend visits since Patricia and Stephanie were born, and the boys were crazy about the twins. David now visited monthly as the demands of his graduate program had increased.

Rachel popped the trunk open, then unlocked the front door. She gave each of her boys a lightweight grocery bag to carry into the apartment. This apartment wasn't as nice as their previous home, but the neighborhood was safe and the kids loved it. Martin and Malcolm set their bags on the dining room table, as the kitchen counter was slightly out of their reach. The apartment had a galley style kitchen, living room that opened to a patio, and a half bath on the first floor. The two bedrooms and shared bath were on the second.

Rachel carried Heather's suitcase into the apartment and up the stairs to her bedroom she had prepared for her sister. She would sleep on the living room sofa.

"Where's your loo?" Heather asked her nephews.

Malcolm and Martin laughed. "What's a loo?"

"A toilet."

Malcolm took Heather's hand and guided her to the first-floor half bath. "Boys, you should always wash your hands when you come inside the pad. Keeps outside germs out."

"Pad?" Malcolm inquired.

"Your home, love."

Heather saw a tea kettle on the stove and filled it with fresh water. "A cuppa," Rachel said as she looked through the serving window, then joined her sister in the kitchen, putting some of the groceries away.

"Arvo tea." Heather smiled.

Heather made sandwiches, cut them into quarters, and then cut the crust off. "Rachel, where are your plates?"

Rachel retrieved four teacups and saucers for the tea, and plastic plates for the sandwiches. "Martin, Malcolm. Time for a snack."

Heather told her nephews about her childhood in Redfern, about their uncles James and Shane, about their grandfather, and about the importance of tea in Australia. "If you're in Australia and someone says, 'Can I fix you a cuppa?' they mean tea. You always say yes."

❦

"Granny Odessa is a gem," Heather sat in the recliner in the corner of the living room with her feet propped up. She reached to the end table to her right, picked up her mug, and sipped her chamomile tea. The afternoon with Rachel, the boys, and the Long and Shelton families at

Veronica's parents' home had been an interesting adventure. The boys had been bathed and were fast asleep.

"She really loved your damper and lamingtons."

"No, she really loved Your damper and lamingtons," Heather laughed. "Remember, you baked them."

"Well, I did cut the sponge cake and dip it into the chocolate before you rolled it in coconut." Rachel warmed her hand with the mug. "Thank you so much, Sis."

Heather smiled at being called Sis by Rachel.

"Last year Veronica's mother did look at me sideways when I brought a store-bought pie." She sipped her tea. "And the receipt may have still been in the bag." Rachel placed the mug on her coffee table and shook her head. "I'm amazed at how much I went through over the last year and a half."

Heather smiled. "You made it."

"Yes, I did. We all made it." Rachel turned the television off since neither of them was watching it. "I'm amazed at how different things are this year than last."

"How so?"

"My ex-husband has really turned his life around. This time next year he will be graduating with his master's degree. Martin has two sisters. I have a sister and two more brothers. I'm so happy to have each of you in my life."

"I'm so happy to have found you," Heather eased out of the recliner, sat next to her sister, and hugged her.

24

BEAUTIFUL FRIENDSHIP

Rodney looked across the table at his wife. She was wearing the black opal necklace and earrings, along with the red dress she wore on their dinner cruise just before he left Sydney the first time. Through the floor-to-ceiling glass windows, sapphire blue clouds floated in a clear, vivid sky. Their private dining room at the Signature Room had a Brazilian cherry hardwood floor, and was illuminated by miles and miles of gold lights reminding them that although the sun was setting, the city was still very much alive. A jazz ensemble played their favorite songs. Rodney spared no expense in celebrating. On this, the eve of their first year as husband and wife, Sweetie Pie and Sugar Cane would share dinner overlooking the most spectacular view in Chicago—a hint of Lake Michigan to the left, skyscrapers in the foreground, and an eternity of lights in the distance.

"How far south do you think we can see from here?" Sina asked. She had been back in Chicago for a week after ending her Fall semester. She felt greatly relieved, having just submitted her materials for promotion and tenure. She relaxed before Rodney's arrival by spending time with her parents and shopping with her Mom. On Sunday, she prepared dinner for her parents and her brother Tommy. Rodney arrived a few days ago after playing in Seoul, even more

exhausted than he was last year. This season was a bit more challenging than the previous two, especially the last two stops in Asia.

"From this view as far south as the city extends." Rodney sipped
his champagne.

Thomasine looked across the table at her husband and felt warm
and fuzzy inside. "What is it?" he asked.

"You just don't know how happy I am." She smiled at him. "I can
barely contain it."

"I do." He took her hand. "I share the same joy." He squeezed her
hand tightly, then raised his glass with the other. She responded in
kind. "To our past, our present, and our future."

"To us." Sina replied.

"Sweetie Pie, I want you to know how proud I am of you."

"I'm proud of you too, Sugar Cane," Sina put some horseradish on
an oyster.

"You had a difficult decision to make. I just wish I had been there to
help you recuperate after the marrow donation."

"Every time I wanted to complain about the pain, I thought about
how painful all of this was for my recipient and the family. It was
the right thing to do. The child is in remission." She ate the oyster.
"And like you said, you'll just have me all to yourself a little
longer."

"I will."

"Oh! I have good news."

"What is it?" Rodney smiled, fully focused on his wife.

"My paper got accepted to an International Women's Studies
Conference. It's in March."

"That's wonderful! Where's the conference?"

"Rio." She wiped her mouth. "I wish you could be there with me."

"We play in South America in March?"

"Really?" Sina asked as the server brought their entrees. "It would
be wonderful if I could see you play."

Rodney poured Sina another glass of champagne. "We'll definitely
plan something."

The knife glided through Sina's petite filet like a dense, rich pound
cake. She raised the fork to her mouth, and savored the flavor. "Rodney, you have to taste this. It's so good."

Her husband sampled her dish. "I'll have to order that on our second anniversary."

"Let's not rush. I'm savoring this celebration." Sina went into her bag and retrieved an envelope. Rodney's name was written on the outside in a metallic gold marker. She slid it across the table. "Happy Anniversary."

"Thank you, Sweetie Pie." He slid back from the table. "I think we should open our gifts together." He walked over to the center of the room and met the guitarist who handed him a wrapped present.

"Happy Anniversary."

Sina tore into her gift like an excited child on Christmas Day, a big contrast for one who always found the edges and used her fingertip to gently break the tape on gifts. "Rodney!" She scooted back from the table and ran to the other side to hug her husband. "It's beautiful," she said of the framed pencil sketch drawn from a photo of her on their wedding day. "I love it! The artist did such a great job capturing what I felt that day."

Rodney slid his finger across the top of the envelope. Sina had created a booklet of reusable coupons for Rodney to kick off the celebration of their first anniversary, and their life together.

LANDSCAPING lights illuminated the entrance to Tranquility Way. Front facing windows each held a candle. Bedecked with garland and white lights, the balcony spotlighted the front door. Rodney stood at the bottom of the sweeping staircase, and smiled in anticipation as Sina made the journey with slow and careful steps in her floor-length black silk sheath gown encrusted with sequins, seed beads, and bugle beads. The foyer had been trimmed in white lights. Pine garland hung from the railing. There were three twelve-foot Christmas trees, one decorated with silver and blue, another with the Gale Force colors of red and white. Near the front door, a tree decorated in burgundy and gold welcomed guests. Beside each tree was a huge box for the donations of toiletries, linen, clothing, winter coats, and unwrapped toys. They were required for admission to the holiday party. The items would be donated to an organization that provided essentials and holiday gifts for women and children living in shelters for victims of domestic abuse and sexual violence. Rodney and Sina were happy to open their home for such a cause.

"Hope, Rachel!" Sina gave her close friends a tight hug as they entered. They turned and posed for a photo together. She pulled them aside and asked if they instructed the valet to park the car in the port-cochère. Their overnight bags would be delivered to their guest quarters by staff.

"Thomasine, this house is amazing!" Rachel said.

"It is beautiful." Hope added. "I never knew there were homes like this in the south suburbs."

"We were happy to find a house close to our parents and siblings," Sina said. "Excuse me," she turned to join Rodney in welcoming the owner of the Gale Force.

Rachel and Hope were guided by the fluid, mellow sound of the tenor sax leading the melody of "The Christmas Song," in the conservatory. The piano softly accompanied, and the trumpet joined in for the chorus. It sounded like a slow dance you never wanted to end.

"Look at the detail," Rachel said of the parquet floor in the ballroom. The well-heeled crowd was scattered, socializing in hubs at reception tables on the perimeter of the room, the tables toward the center of the room were nearly empty. Waitresses in black cummerbunds and bow ties carried trays of appetizers. One handed Rachel a napkin. She took a skewered mini beef kebab wrapped in bacon. Hope followed suit. The French doors leading to the ballroom terrace were open on this unseasonably warm December evening.

"It's nice outside, let's check out the back before it gets too dark," Hope said. Rachel crossed paths with a waiter carrying a tray of champagne. She took two flutes and followed Hope to the terrace, which wrapped around the curve of the oval shaped ballroom. Three sets of French doors gave partygoers easy access.

"Here," Rachel handed Hope the glass of champagne. "I know this isn't a New Year's party, but I want to toast to 1999. May it be much better than this year was for me."

"And may I continue to grow and heal in the year to come," Hope clinked her glass with Rachel's.

"Grow? You look like you're shrinking to me," Rachel laughed.

"You look fabulous, Hope. I've known you forever, and I don't think I've ever seen you this slim."

"Thanks, Rachel. My move to Virginia Beach has been a journey of self-exploration. At first I was afraid to be there by myself, but when Jason filed for divorce I knew I had to make a go of it." She sipped her champagne. "It was hard, and I made a lot of bad choices. The pain was so intense that I tried to use the wrong things to dull it. Then I embraced it, but most of all, I embraced Hope. I got to know Hope and love her."

Rachel giggled. "Hope, you sound like a poem or something. You haven't even had that much champagne. And neither have I. I'm not ready for you to get deep on me."

"I don't believe you Rachel," Hope laughed. "I'm trying to be serious."

"You're at a party. Relax." Rachel sipped her champagne. "But on a serious note, how did you lose the weight?"

"Gym membership, personal trainer, biking on the boardwalk. In the Spring, I joined a running group and ran my first 5k in July. I just completed my first 10k at Thanksgiving."

"Whoa! You are serious—5k, 10k!"

"I finished first in my age category in my first 5k, but it was a small race."

"Wow." Rachel replied. "That's funny, considering how P.E. was your least favorite subject in high school."

"You know what's even more funny?"

"What?" Rachel asked.

"Look over there," Hope pointed to her right. "Can you believe Sina has a tennis court with her poor eye-hand coordination. Do you remember when we had badminton in P.E. sophomore year. I may not have been able to run, but I could hit a birdie. Sina couldn't even do that."

Rachel walked closer. "That is a tennis court. Too funny."

"It's getting a little chilly out here," Hope drank the rest of her champagne. "Let's go back inside."

ZURI WAS STARTLED by the beauty and majesty of the grand foyer. She stood still at first near the door, taking in the marble tile, sweeping staircase, and Christmas trees that looked like they had been decorated for a photo shoot. She wore a burgundy A-line, Princess V-neck evening dress with sequins on the cap sleeves and wished she had her camera as the tree closest to the front door complemented her dress perfectly. Zuri stepped forward, her eyes fixed on the intricacies of the railing. She'd never seen one like it.

She bumped into Thomasine. "Excuse me. I'm so sorry." She apologized profusely. "I'm Zuri Hicks."

"Thomasine Harris," she extended her hand, then tapped her husband on the shoulder.

"Excuse me," Rodney said to the guest he was speaking to. He turned around. "Jason!" he exclaimed as he saw Jason enter.

Jason dropped his donations into the box, then walked towards the center of the foyer to join them. "I see you've met." He put his arm around Zuri. "Zuri was a cheerleader at Illinois your first semester."

Rodney extended his hand to Zuri's. "It's nice to meet you. Jason talks about you all the time." Zuri glanced at Jason who bit his lip, and winked. They headed toward the ballroom.

Thomasine was suddenly having flashbacks to the reunion. Although their divorce was final and they seemed to get along well at the wedding a year ago, Thomasine was not sure how Hope would respond to seeing Jason with another woman for the first time. She was equally shocked that Rodney knew about Zuri. As her best friend, Sina felt the need to warn Hope. She turned and began to walk in the direction of the ballroom when Rodney took her hand, "Sweetie Pie, there's someone I'd like you to meet."

THE INNER CIRCLE of reception tables had begun to fill, and the crowd was denser than before. A waiter with champagne stopped in front of Jason. He retrieved a glass and handed it to Zuri, then took one for himself. He smiled at her, and clinked his glass with hers. He took a sip, then looked across the room. The glass fell from his hand.

Rachel led Hope from the terrace into the ballroom. She stopped in her tracks. "Oh shit," she said in a stage whisper.

"What is it?" Hope asked. She looked ahead. If she acted human, she would feel like a hypocrite after the 'I love Hope' speech she just gave to Rachel.

For a moment, they were all frozen in place. All of them, except for Zuri.

"Are you okay, Jason?" She asked. She looked at his eyes and followed his gaze. "What's going on?

"Jason!"

Jason turned to Zuri. "Baby, I'm so sorry. I had no idea that my ex-wife would be here. I know that she and Thomasine are best friends, but she lives in Virginia. I did not think she would be here tonight."

"Jason, it's okay. We're all adults."

"Zuri. I'm so sorry."

"What are you apologizing for?" Zuri started walking towards Hope, then thought better of it. She wasn't sure how she would feel if she were in Hope's shoes.

Jason was amazed at Hope's transformation. He noticed that Hope had lost weight at Rodney and Sina's wedding, but this. Wow!

One of us must be the adult, Hope thought. She took two steps towards Jason and his lady, then thought better of it. *She might think that I want him back. And I don't.*

Rachel shook her head. She was fuming inside. Like Sina, she too was having flashbacks of the high school reunion. She looked at Hope who was very calm and collected.

Rodney followed Sina into the ballroom. Like the others, she was frozen in place. And like the rest of them, he didn't know what to do. He took two glasses of champagne and whispered to the waiter. Within seconds the music faded. He handed a glass to Thomasine, and put his arm around her. Together they walked to the center of the ballroom. *Perfect time for a speech.*

"My beautiful wife Thomasine and I would like to welcome you and thank each of you for your generous donation. Your gifts will make the holidays brighter and life easier for women and children in the Chicagoland area.

"And this is not a solo event. Today, members of the IBL in other cities around the world are hosting similar events to raise awareness about domestic and sexual violence against women. It's a global epidemic, and it must stop. It starts with awareness." The crowd applauded.

"Each of us here today can impact change. As you leave, you will be given a pamphlet with resources you can share with someone in need." Rodney paused. "And remember, it's not about being a hero. It's about doing what's right.

"Thomasine and I want you to enjoy the rest of the evening. There's plenty of food, champagne, great music, and this beautiful dance floor."

The band began to play "Let it Snow," and he took his wife's hand. "Will you dance with me?"

The standoff continued a moment longer, then Hope approached Jason and Zuri. She extended a hand to Zuri, "I'm Hope Jones." Rachel stood back and watched from across the room at her friend's bold move. That small part of Hope that had not yet fully embraced herself wanted Jason to know that she had moved on, and detached herself from everything McCoy.

"Zuri Hicks."

"It's nice to meet you." She turned to Jason, "And how are you, Jason?"

As much as Jason wanted to compliment Hope on her transformation, with Zuri next to him, he wasn't sure exactly what he should say. It was unbelievable to him that he was so uncomfortable. Hope had been a big part of the most important years of his life. "You've lost weight, Hope." *There I said it, and I'm sure Zuri wasn't offended.*

"I'm training for my first half-marathon," she informed him.

He looked at her, eyebrows raised.

"I'm going back to school to get my L.L.M. at Duncan," he shared. "And I'm trying out for the football team." As soon as he said that, he thought about how it may have come across. He wasn't trying to one-up Hope, but it sure sounded like it.

"I wish you the best," Hope said, she joined Rachel on the other side of the room.

The request they made after their divorce hearing had been fulfilled. They were moving towards friendship. They weren't to the hanging out stage yet, and may not ever make it there, but this was a beginning.

੪ৡ

AFTER THE GUESTS LEFT, Rodney worked with the staff to sort the donations into categories. They would be delivered to the agency in the morning.

Sina joined her friends in the bedroom next to her sitting room with a quart of Daiquiri Ice and three spoons.

"I've moved on," Hope insisted. She ate a spoonful of the sorbet. "I really have."

"I'm proud of you." Rachel sat beside Hope in the king-size bed and took the quart from Sina. "I don't know if I could be so nice."

"You could," Thomasine reached for another spoonful. "Look at how you handled the situation with Patrick."

"True."

"The truth of the matter," Thomasine began, "Is that we will each be thirty next year. That officially makes us grown ass women. No time for childish, immature behavior. We do not operate like we did as teens or even twentysomethings."

Hope started laughing.

"What's so funny, Hope?" Rachel asked. "I know you don't think you're getting a buzz from this like we did when we were younger."

Hope shook her head and chuckled. "Jason told me that he's going back to school, and that he's trying out for the football team. He's almost thirty. Do you believe that?"

"That's crazy?" Rachel said.

"Maybe not. There are a few nontraditional students playing Division 1 football. Maybe Jason sees this as his last chance. What is he going to study? He already has a law degree."

"He said he was going to Duncan to get an L.L.M."

"Who knows, he could get drafted to play in the NFL in 2000."

Rachel and Hope laughed hysterically at Sina's comment. "Hey, time will tell," Rachel said.

25

I BELIEVE IN YOU

S tudents corralled out of buildings in a mad rush, on the way to their next classes with a fierce urgency. Campus seemed more crowded than Jason remembered, and like he remembered, the Hawk whipping across the lake put pep in everyone's step. Although the walkways on campus had been cleared, mountains of snow were a reminder of the record snowfall that came with the blizzard a week ago. While twenty plus inches of snow would cripple many cities, it just caused a brief pause in Chicago. If the snow weren't enough, the brutal temperatures that followed made the average Chicagoan long for a tropical vacation. Jason was grateful that classes started on Tuesday rather than Monday. The 14-degree temperature felt like a heatwave compared to the 1.4-degree temperature and minus 14-degree windchill of the day before.

Knapsacks bounced on undergraduates' backs as they walked rapidly. Some students carried musical instruments by their side. One student startled Jason as he whizzed by on a skateboard in shorts in the dead of the Chicago winter. The mere sight made his bones ache. Jason wrapped the wool scarf Zuri gave him for Christmas around his neck, and secured the top button of his overcoat. His pace was a bit slower than that of younger students. He carried a briefcase by his side.

"Excuse me, Sir," the bespectacled female student said. "Could you please direct me to Nichols Hall?"

"Nichols Hall is." Jason racked his brain. "Nichols. I don't remember a Nichols Hall."

That's when reality set in for him. He was going back to school eight years after graduating from Duncan, and the campus landscape had changed. There were new buildings, and some that existed before no longer stood.

Jason's brother Johnny thought he was crazy. His mother couldn't understand why his Juris Doctor wasn't enough. Zuri fully supported his decision, and promised to help make his life easier as he adjusted to the rigors of being a student again. Now an adult on the campus where he experienced so many firsts, he felt like he had teleported into another generation.

Jason pointed the young lady in the direction of the campus map, and decided to check one for himself so that he made it to his Intellectual Property Law course on time.

§.

PATRICK TURNED the chair around so that it faced the high chairs to his left and right. "It's lunch time, girls," he said while Patricia and Stephanie cooed, matching his pitch and tempo. The twins were six months old, and were finally sleeping through the night. Patrick placed a container of pureed carrots on the kitchen table in front of Patricia. Peas were Stephanie's favorite. While he had mastered giving the twins a bottle at the same time, Veronica usually fed one girl while he fed the other.

Patrick stirred the vegetables and shook the excess off the spoons. The carrots were in his right hand, the peas in his left. He guided the spoons carefully towards their mouths. Patricia took the spoon from his grasp, missed her mouth by a mile, and the carrots ended up just beneath her eye. She looked at Stephanie and they both laughed.

"You silly babies," Patrick laughed along with them. He put the spoons back into the containers, and got a towel from the kitchen drawer to clean Patricia's face.

"I'll be right back," he told them when he heard the doorbell.

While the twins were a lot of work for him and Veronica, he cherished every second with them, especially after having missed these developmental years with Martin.

"Hi Daddy," Martin hugged his father. "Sorry I'm late." Rachel waved as she backed the car out of the driveway. "Malcolm's father is visiting and he took us to breakfast. There were a lot of people in the restaurant, so it took a long time for us to get our food." He walked into the foyer and took off his jacket, then handed it to Patrick.

"I'm not surprised. Restaurants are usually very crowded on Saturday mornings."

"Where are the twins?" Martin loved to play with his sisters.

"In the kitchen. It's lunchtime."

"Can I help you and Miss Ronnie feed them?"

"Miss Ronnie is at the grocery store. And yes, you can help after you take your bag to your room, then wash your hands."

"Okay, Daddy."

Patrick watched as Martin walked up the stairs. He was amazed at how much Martin, who would be seven in a few months, had grown in the short time since he learned he was a father.

Stephanie and Patricia were holding hands and talking to each other in their own language when Patrick returned to the kitchen. He smiled at his daughters, then went to the kitchen sink to wet the towel with warm water. "Now let's get these carrots off your face." They were now smeared across her cheek and bib. Patrick gently wiped his daughter's face.

The babies squealed when Martin came into the kitchen. They laughed at the faces he made, and Patrick laughed with them. He felt blessed to be a father of three beautiful children. Although Veronica wanted another, they had their hands full for right now.

Patrick handed Martin the container of pureed peas. "These are for Stephanie." Martin stood next to the high chair.

"And don't put too much food on the spoon," Patrick instructed.

Martin filled the spoon halfway. "Like this, Daddy?"

"You can put just a little bit more than that on the spoon."

Working with just his left hand, Patrick fed Patricia with ease, free of mishaps.

৯

"COME RIGHT IN," Hope ushered Tammi into her office. "I'll take your coat." Tammi's wool overcoat was draped over her arm. Hope hung it on the back of her office door.

"Please have a seat," Hope motioned to the chair in front of her desk. She walked around to sit across from Tammi. "I thought I was escaping the cold when I moved to Virginia Beach, but today I feel like I'm in Chicago."

Tammi laughed, but didn't say much. "It is pretty cold today."

Hope thumbed through the stack of résumés on her desk. Her assistant's husband recently accepted a job in Dallas, so Hope would lose her to relocation. "Ok," Hope said. She placed Tammi's résumé in front of her on the desk. "I see you're a graduate of VCU, Business Management."

"Yes, Ms. Jones."

"And you have five years of experience in management," Hope nodded. "I'm impressed. You won several awards the last two years," Hope paused. "But there's no work history since 1996."

Tammi sighed. "I have to be honest with you Ms. Jones." Tammi looked Hope in the eye. "I didn't work the last three years because I was incarcerated for two years."

"But you didn't indicate that on your application."

"I know, I should have been honest. I've been looking for work for an entire year. So, this time I didn't check the box on my application." Tammi stood, then walked towards the door to retrieve her coat. "I'm sorry I wasted your time, Ms. Jones. Please forgive me."

"Have a seat, Tammi." She walked back to the chair and sat down. Hope leaned back in her chair and folded her arms. "You shouldn't give up so soon. You graduated with honors from VCU. You have experience. What happened?"

"I made some bad choices." That was something Hope found relatable. "I was raised by very loving parents. My Dad is a college professor. My Mom, a homemaker. My father was a very hard worker, because he didn't want my mother to work outside the home. He took on extra work reviewing textbooks, scoring standardized tests. I know they loved me. I was their only child. But they were strict. And I rebelled. I fell in love with a guy my senior year of high school who was all wrong for me. I was trying to make him good, he was trying to make me more like him." She took a tissue from the box on Hope's desk.

"I knew he was into some stuff, but I didn't ask any questions."

"How long were you in the relationship with him?"

"We broke up my freshman year of college, and I immersed myself in my studies. As long as I was in college and away from him I was good. I stayed on the right path. I had laser-sharp focus."

"But he came back into your life at some point."

"Yes. A few years after college I was out at a club celebrating my friend's birthday. Ms. Jones, he was my first love. We exchanged numbers. Started dating again." She shook her head. "I just can't believe that I was that naïve. I closed my eyes to what was going on and it cost me my career, maybe my life. I was with him when he got raided. I was charged with possession with intent to distribute, and I don't even know what any of that stuff was. Heck, I've never even smoked a joint."

"Neither have I," Hope smiled.

"I just want to get my life back," Tammi said. "All I need is a chance."

Hope listened intently. She thought about how much her own upbringing was like Tammi's, and what her life may have been like if she had made just one wrong decision when she was younger. She could be in the same position as Tammi.

"I'll give you a chance," Hope told Tammi. "You're hired."

26

RISE

Thomasine sat on the side of the bed and wiped her eyes. She was glad to have the paper presentation behind her, and enjoyed networking with colleagues over Caipirinhas last night. "I had one too many," she uttered as she trudged out of the bed, to the bathroom of her suite overlooking Copacabana Beach in Rio.

She turned on the water, squirted a few drops of Aveda Purifying Gel Cleanser into her hand, and applied it on her face in a circular motion. She rinsed her face, then applied hydrating lotion. Sina stretched as she made her way to her bed. Effortlessly, she sat on the edge of the bed and yawned. The jet lag, the conference. Sessions were held each day from nine in the morning until seven-thirty each evening. There were so many topics Sina wanted to hear, that choosing which sessions to attend was a challenge. All of that, along with the cocktails left her feeling sluggish.

She looked over at the clock. "Goodness. I didn't mean to sleep this late." While the conference was over and many of her global colleagues had begun returning to their host institutions, Thomasine and Rodney planned a brief, second honeymoon of sorts in between his South American games. Sina just hoped that the sun would come out today as the past few days had been full of overcast skies, scattered clouds, and rain.

She walked to the desk, and rifled through the papers in her brief-case. "Oh shoot, Rodney is already in Rio." The Gale Force played in their Brazilian city, Salvador, last night. She ran, first left, then right. Back into the bathroom. Sina started the shower and began to undress when she heard the lock in her hotel room door click. She stood in the bathroom doorway and greeted her husband in most of her glory. He was elated to see her for the first time since they brought in the new year two and a half months ago.

"What a welcome!" Rodney dropped his bag on the floor and swept his wife into his arms. His kiss was one of deep longing.

"Rodney, I was getting ready to..."

Rodney's eyes traveled slowly from her lips to her knees.

"Go ahead, Sweetie Pie. I'll join you."

Sina started into the bathroom, she turned, her head over her shoulder. "Remember what happened last time."

"Uh huh. That's what I'm depending on."

Sina winked, then slowly pranced towards the tub. She removed the rest of her clothing, then stepped into the shower. Beads of warm water danced on her back, she turned, held her head back, and welcomed the waltz across her chest.

"I've missed you so much," Rodney stepped in, kissed the back of her neck, then massaged her shoulders.

She turned to face her husband, and took a step back.

"Sweetie Pie, your hair!"

"All I care about right now is making up for lost time with you." She took another step back and let the water drench her hair. Rodney watched as it flowed down her body.

He eyed her again from head to toe as his excitement grew more intense, then pulled her closer. He kissed her slowly, wanting to savor every second in the short time they had together in Rio.

Sina squirted shower gel on a sponge. "Honey, will you wash my back?" She turned around, her back now to him. Rodney gently swept Sina's hair to her left shoulder, in a slow circular motion that felt more like a caress than a scrub, he obliged.

Sina turned to face him and scanned her husband from head to toe as he soaped his body. Her lips parted, then spread across her face slowly, her eyes bursting with a mix of love and sensuality. She stepped to the side as Rodney rinsed off, then grabbed a towel, first for her, then for him as he turned the water off.

He dried his neck, shoulder, and chest, then wrapped the towel around his waist as he held Sina's hand while she stepped from the tub. Rodney put the lid to the commode down, and sat atop, while Sina wrapped a towel around her head. Rodney then pulled his wife to his lap and began to lotion her body. When they were done moisturizing each other, they walked hand in hand towards the bed. He bent down to kiss his wife as she first shed her towel, then quickly removed his. She kissed him urgently, feverishly.

"Slow, Sweetie Pie," he pulled back a little. "Like this," his lips met with hers. His kiss was slow, long, and full of devotion. They paused.

"I've just missed you so much, Sugar Cane." Her voice became softer and slower, breathy, with each word. "You don't know how much I've missed you." She removed the towel from her head.

"Yes, I do," he brushed her hair to the side of her face, then kissed her again, soft, slow, and long. He pulled Sina close, her head resting on his chest. "I've missed you too."

Sina stepped back, took his hand, lowered herself to the bed, then pulled him to her. She arched her neck and kissed his forehead, striking the first chords of the beautiful music they made that day. Rodney continued the melody by planting kisses on Sina's face, on her chest, all over her body. Enveloped in ecstasy they reached the bridge of their original love ballad, peaking, then slowing and gradually lowering to a decrescendo. Together in harmony, they simmered to a perfect authentic cadence. Their lovemaking was beautiful, passionate, and pure.

§

"KEEP THEM OPEN," Sina said as Rodney began to close the curtains to the patio doors. The sun was beginning to set on this Brazilian summer evening. Although it was overcast the view was still great. The doors to the left revealed a peek of Sugar Loaf Mountain masked slightly by the clouds. To the right, Copacabana Beach.

"I wish it wasn't so cloudy," Rodney climbed back into bed beside his wife. "I hoped that we could spend the day on the beach. You haven't seen me in those Carolina blue swim trunks yet."

Thomasine chuckled. "I'm sure they look much better on you than the green trunks you had to substitute for underwear when you flew into Sydney." She kissed him. "And I don't care about spending the day on the beach. I'm so happy to see you. I just wish you didn't have to fly to Lima in the morning."

"I know." He kissed her forehead. "But the season will be over soon, and we can work on starting our family."

"Yes," Thomasine smiled. "Everything is working out as it should. Had we been successful in September, I would be near the end of my second trimester. I don't think I would have submitted my paper for this conference."

"Why not?"

"Travel."

"Isn't it safe to fly up until your thirty-second week?"

"Just so many factors, the radiation in the screening, certain medications that I wouldn't be able to take if I were pregnant. A lot to consider."

Rodney sat up. "I never thought about that."

"You do know that when we start a family, our lives will change drastically.

He caressed his wife's face. "I know. And I don't want to leave you at home alone with our babies."

"You're seriously thinking about retiring from the IBL."

"I am," Rodney said.

"Any thoughts as to what's next?"

"I've been pretty smart with investing. Technically neither of us ever has to work again."

Thomasine laughed. "I don't think that will work for you or me."

Rodney chuckled. "Kimmy has completed the business plan for her restaurants."

"Restaurants?"

"Yes. She has created a model that she thinks she can replicate in cities across the country. Maybe globally." Rodney swung his legs over the side of the bed. "And I'd love to tell you more about it over dinner."

&

THE VIEW from their suite was spectacular. The night time view from their dinner table was phenomenal. They ate at a Brazilian Cherrywood table on the brick patio. The blue mosaic tile inlay on the table matched the evening sky which mirrored the ocean waters. A line of twinkling lights met the water's edge in the distance.

After the Caipirinhas last night, Sina opted for water and made the same recommendation to Rodney since he had an early flight.

"I've seen some of the most beautiful sights in the world with you," Sina told Rodney as he ate his Escondidinho. She marveled again at the view while Rodney shared Kimmy's idea for fine dining establishments, and phase two, her franchisable enterprise.

27

FEELS SO GOOD

T he six-a.m. trek made Jason very glad he moved close to campus when the lease on his Chatham apartment was up at the end of January. He was a preferred walk-on, and his days were consumed with morning workouts, class, spring football practice, and study hall. The structured schedule, though grueling, was a great way for him to ease into student life after graduating from law school five years earlier.

Tulips and daffodils were in full bloom across the Duncan University campus. The green and white game, also known as the spring scrimmage, was approaching. Zuri and Christopher would attend. Since he returned to school his time with Zuri was limited to weekend dates.

"You OK Old Man?" Dennis, a sophomore tight end, lightly jabbed at Jason's arm. After three months on the team, he'd come to expect the old man jokes from his teammates, who teased him when he celebrated his birthday six weeks ago. One of his teammates jokingly asked him, "How old are you, thirty?" Jason smiled, but did not reply.

"You could learn a thing or two from this old man," Jason's jaw jutted forward a bit as he broke into a smile, then headed to the shower.

As a child, playing professional football was Jason's most ardent dream. He worked toward his dream for years, and thought his athletic scholarship at Duncan was a direct pathway to its realization. He now had one last chance, and he was determined to make the most of it. Fierce determination guided his play. There wasn't anything anyone could say to him to make him give up this time.

There were other teammates, like Al, a freshman offensive tackle, who looked up to Jason for advice. In study hall that evening Al, who was struggling with some of his classes, asked Jason for guidance. After sharing which courses he was taking, Jason offered this advice.

"You don't have a good combination of classes this semester," Jason instructed. "When I was an undergrad, I always took my most challenging classes during summer school, when I could focus solely on them."

"Wow," Al replied. "I signed up for easier classes. I wanted to double up on them so that I could graduate early."

"What's the rush, man?" Jason asked.

"I just thought—"

"Take it from someone who's been there. These are the best years of your life. Enjoy them. Don't rush them. Use this time to learn new things and strengthen skills you already have. Utilize your professor and TAs office hours, get a tutor. Do your best to in each of your classes, because if you don't, you will lose your eligibility. No eligibility, no football future."

"You're right McCoy." Some of the younger guys weren't comfortable calling him by his first name.

Jason had a small following on the team of guys who were as serious about their studies as they were about their time on the field. Others, like Dennis, spent their evening chatting with friends on Instant Messenger.

"Say McCoy," Al began. "What was it like when you were on the team before?"

Jason closed his laptop, squinted his right eye, and nodded slightly. "I think the biggest difference between then and now is that there were fewer distractions."

"What do you mean?"

"Technology. When we were in study hall, most of us did our work.

We didn't have chats with friends on computers. I don't remember any of my teammates owning a laptop."

"How did you do your work?"

"We wrote. Pen and paper. We took notes in class in a notebook. If we had a paper due, we wrote it out by hand and paid someone to type it. Heck, if we wanted to talk to our girlfriend long distance we wrote them, unless it was a special occasion, then we called. Long distance calls were expensive. Now you all have cell phones with free long distance." Jason was amazed at how much had changed in the twelve years since he was a freshman like Al.

THE PANSIES on the Steeplechase campus had been replaced with impatiens. Thomasine stuffed her office mail into her purse, then made the short walk to her car. The Spring semester was nearing an end, and although this season wasn't as successful as the last, the Gale Force was in the playoffs. She was loaded down with papers from students in her Intro to Women's Studies course. Sina was working from home for the rest of the week, and since the weather was nice, she would grade the bulk of the papers on her deck in the sun.

When she pulled into her driveway, she marveled at the Dutch irises that had been born since she left for work. The deep, rich, bluish-purple flowers were among her favorite. Sina drove into her garage, gathered her purse and tote bag. When she entered her home, Sparky greeted her warmly. Sina set the bag of papers on the bench in the mud area and bent down to pet Sparky. "Say, where's Zack?"

Sparky turned around and ran into the kitchen. The garbage can had been toppled over, and its contents were scattered across the floor. Sina didn't even have to ask. Sparky directed his nose towards the can, then towards Zack who sat in the corner, head down low.

"Zack. Did you do this?" she asked. Zack walked towards her, head low. Sina pointed to the mess. "No. Zack. Garbage. No." Sina was very happy that she put the bones from last night's chicken in a glass jar, that Zack was unable to open. She let the dogs out into the backyard, then went upstairs to change out of her work clothing so that she could clean up the mess.

Sina sat on the side of her bed, and took her work mail out of her purse. She was nervous about opening the letter in her mailbox, she didn't know why. She exhaled deeply, then slid her fingertip underneath the flap on the back of the envelope. She gently ran her finger across the length of the envelope, and slowly removed the letter. She closed her eyes, and inhaled deeply. She held on to that breath while she read the letter, joy spread across her face.

She took a pair of jogging pants and a lightweight, long sleeved shirt from her dresser drawer, changed into them, then went into the bathroom to remove her make up. As she washed her face, she stared down at the bathroom counter. "I can't wait to talk to Rodney," she said audibly, before washing and drying her hands, then heading downstairs to clean Zack's mess.

Thomasine preferred this time of the year. The days were getting longer, and she could relax in her garden planting the flower seedlings she started when she returned from Brazil. Marigolds were her favorite to plant from seed. She recalled how as a kindergarten student, she planted a marigold in a styrofoam cup to give to her mother for Mother's Day. Sina smiled at that memory before taking her trowel to begin to dig a hole. She loved how, a few days after planting the seed, a plant began to break through. *It doesn't take long for things to grow.* A mantra she applied to her life.

While the dogs stretched their legs around the backyard, Thomasine planted marigold and zinnia seedlings in a railing box on the deck. Zack came to apologize. Sina removed her gardening glove and gently petted him on his head. He knew then that he had made his way back into her good graces.

After a dinner of leftovers, Sparky and Zack took turns going for a walk. While they were obedient dogs, children were playing outside and Sina did not want to take a chance of walking them together by herself.

Sina made sure all the doors were locked, then set the alarm. She grabbed a snack and a glass of water. Sparky and Zack were at her heels. Sina propped her feet on the ottoman and turned on the playoff game. Zack watched intently, as if he knew his owner was playing. Sparky couldn't be bothered and focused his attention on Sina's snack.

Today had to be one of the happiest days of her life, only she didn't fully know it yet. Earlier in the evening, she read the letter in her load of work mail, but wanted to share that good news with her husband first. He always called her after home games. For the other, she thought it best that she and Rodney learn together.

Thomasine felt such great joy and peace that she drifted off to sleep while sitting upright on the sofa. Her feet were still propped on the ottoman when the loud, ringing phone startled her. Sina looked up to see the game score on the evening news as she reached for the phone. She couldn't believe she fell asleep on the game.

"That was a great game tonight," Sina told Rodney when he called. The Gale Force led the series.

"It was a total team effort."

"Sugar Cane, you're talking to your wife. You just gave me a soundbite."

Rodney laughed. "I didn't mean to. How's everything in NC?"

"The best it could possibly be."

"Oh?"

"Yes. I got my letter today. You are speaking to one of Steeplechase University's newest tenured associate professors."

"That's such great news! Congratulations. I'm so proud of you. You've worked so hard for this. We have to celebrate." Sina could feel the energy of his smile through the phone.

"We do, but we can't celebrate too much."

"Oh?"

"Since you got so mad at me last time, I'm bringing you along on every step of this journey."

"What journey?"

"I'm late."

"Late?" Rodney paused. "Oh! You are?"

"I took a pregnancy test this morning."

"And?" He interrupted.

"I haven't looked at the results yet."

"Why not?"

"I thought that we should find out at the same time."

"Okay. So?"

"I'm downstairs." Sina smiled. "The test is in the master bath."

"Well go look at it." Rodney chuckled.

Sina walked upstairs to her bedroom, then into her bathroom. "Okay. I'm in the bathroom." She put the lid of the toilet down and sat, then picked up the test on the counter beside her.

"Well?"

"Do you prefer Daddy or Papa?"

28

BREEZIN'

T he street light in front of *Talk of the Town* broke through the hazy mist on the July evening. It was the first girls' night out for them in ages. Hope asked Sina about open mics in her area, so she looked through the *Independent Weekly* and found *Brett's Wednesday Night Open Mic with the Usual Suspects*. It was the perfect way to start their extended weekend together.

Booths lined the front window and adjacent wall in an "L" shape across from the bar. In the front corner, patrons huddled in a mean game of bid whist. In the back, close-up paintings of musicians' fingers on musical instruments hung on the exposed brick walls at the back of the stage in the shotgun bar. To the side of the stage, the trio chose a table that seated four.

Thomasine snapped her fingers and swayed in her seat along with the *Usual Suspects* rendition of Van Morrison's "Moondance."

"The band is pretty good." Sina sipped her ginger ale while her friends enjoyed adult beverages.

Hope put her hand on Sina's abdomen and sighed excitedly. "Sina's gonna be a Mommy."

"It's about time," Rachel laughed. Then stopped abruptly at her memory of Sina's college pregnancy.

"Good evening and welcome to the Wednesday Night Open Mic."

The drummer stepped toward the front of the stage with hardwood flooring. It had a high gloss stain. "I'm Brett Chambers, your host." He was tall, bald, beard neatly groomed, and engaged the crowd with the house rules. "Rule Number One?"

"Have fun," the crowd shouted to him.

And that's just what the trio did that evening. Sina and Rachel talked about signing up to perform, and they were amazed when Hope graced the stage with her poetry. The bass player and a guest drummer backed her up.

"I'm Hope Jones, native Chicagoan visiting from Virginia. The piece I'm going to perform for you tonight is titled 'I Hear.'

"*I hear your rhythms in the midst of deep silence. I hear your voice when you're a thousand miles away. I hear your smile in the sweet scent of flowers. I hear your prayer when I need it most. I hear your walk in the steady beat of rain on the pavement. I hear your presence in the silence of a dark night. I hear your anger when your boundaries are broken. I hear your sadness in your sleepy morning eyes. I hear your joy when you embrace me. I hear what you want to say when you cannot utter it. I hear what you're saying although no one is speaking. I hear what's in your heart through the distant echoes of your breathing. I hear what you are feeling when I look at your face. I hear your desires when no one else believes them. I hear what your soul longs for with every breath I take. I hear you. I hear. You. I. Hear. I.*"

Her friends were astonished. They didn't know Hope was so deep. So poetic.

❧

THOMASINE WAS grateful that the waters were calm. After a late night at the open mic, she and Rachel slept in while Hope went for a morning run before the temperature and humidity got too high. They ate brunch, then hit the road for the three-hour trek to Southport. Although the ferry ride from Southport, North Carolina to Bald Head Island was only twenty minutes, Thomasine found this voyage peaceful compared to the choppy waters of her last ferry ride. She and Rodney had spent several summer weekends in their new vacation home on the barrier island of beaches, maritime forest, freshwater lagoons, and a salt marsh preserve. She leaned back, stretched her arms to the side, bathed in the warmth of the afternoon sun, and looked fixedly at the water. A single seagull flew ahead of them as if it was guiding the ferry by its caws.

Hope looked out at the lighthouse on the island, known as Old Baldy, as the ferry pulled towards the dock in the marina. The Harbourside Pavilion was awaiting a bride, her groom, and their guests.

Thomasine instructed her friends to retrieve the luggage, while she went to the tram assignment booth.

Rachel and Hope had their luggage and the plastic bin which carried their smaller items in a neat line when the tram driver pulled up to retrieve their belongings. They turned onto North Bald Wynd and Rachel marveled at the cabbage palmetto trees as they rode past a few holes on the golf course. "This place is beautiful. I see why you and Rodney love to come here."

Sina pointed to the golf course. "That's exactly where Rodney would be if he wasn't in Florida shooting a commercial."

The house set back from the road on the half-acre lot, and backed up to the maritime forest. The tram driver drove down the long driveway of the wooded lot and parked in front of the garage. It held Sina and Rodney's electric golf cart—the only transportation, aside from trams and bicycles, permitted on the island.

Rachel carried the plastic tub along the wooden walkway to the covered wrap-around porch. They were required to put smaller items in the container for baggage check. Sina fumbled through her purse for the key, then unlocked the door.

Rachel entered first, heard a squeak, then nearly tripped over one of Sparky and Zack's toys.

"I'm so sorry," Thomasine picked up the toys and put them in the basket near the door. "Sometimes we bring the dogs when we come here." Sina placed her keys on the breakfast bar of the galley style kitchen.

The living area was light and airy. Skylights in the vaulted ceiling brightened the earth-toned décor. Throw pillows on the sofa, and the vibrant oil paintings gave the room life. A built-in bookcase above the television held pottery Sina purchased in Brazil. A trio of double hung windows in front of the dining table offered a view of the maritime forest. A single pillar candle in hurricane glass rested in the center of the table for six. To the right, more windows displayed the rattan furniture on the screened porch.

"What kind of bird is that?" Rachel asked.

"White ibis," Hope and Sina replied simultaneously.

"Your bedrooms and bathrooms are on this floor." Thomasine pointed her friends into the direction of the bedrooms before taking her stuff up to her bedroom.

The trio chose an early dinner at the Pilot River Café, and on the way to the house, they stopped at the store to pick up a few groceries.

They ended their first day on the screened porch over a game of Uno. Hope sipped her Diet Coke while Rachel enjoyed rum on the rocks.

"I can't believe you're still drinking Diet Coke." Rachel matched Thomasine's red two with a yellow two.

"I can't believe she isn't drinking water." Thomasine looked through her hand as Hope played a yellow seven. "Other than last night, I've only seen Hope drink water lately.

"So, Hope," Sina asked. "What's up with that poem you performed last night?"

"Yeah," Rachel added as she sipped her drink. "It sounds like you wrote it for someone."

"I did."

"Ooh," Rachel asked. "Who?"

"Jason."

"Jason?" Thomasine was puzzled. She played a wild card.

"Yeah, and when I wrote that poem, I realized that although I heard him, I didn't actually listen."

"You know," Thomasine ate a cracker, "When you sent that poem to congratulate Rodney and me on our engagement, I thought it was a one-time thing—your poetry."

"Writing poetry is what helped me make it through my divorce."

"I know that had to be hard," Rachel played a blue three.

"Yeah. Jason was your first love."

"Your only love," Rachel sipped her drink. "The only man you ever. Wait. There was the guy you tutored in college. What was his name?"

"Dana," Sina recalled.

"Would you believe he works at the hospital? We had lunch once. He's a happily married psychiatry resident."

"Did anything ever happen between the two of you?" Sina asked. "Back in college, I mean."

"I certainly hope something did, because Jason had."

Thomasine pinched Rachel.

"Jason had what?"

"Wasn't Dana crazy about you?" Sina tried to change the direction of the conversation.

"Rachel. What exactly did Jason have?"

"Rachel!" Thomasine exclaimed. "I'm cutting you off." Sina pulled the bottle of rum to her side of the table.

Rachel giggled. After drinks before dinner, drinks and dinner, and now this rum on the rocks, Rachel was very open. "He studied more than books with his study partner."

Thomasine cut her eyes at Rachel.

"Hey, didn't your father always say, 'the truth shall set you free.'"

"Don't bring my father into this." Sina insisted.

The joy left Hope's voice. "Rachel. I thought you were my friend. You knew this and didn't tell me?"

Thomasine intervened. "Think about it Hope. You were both very young, and you were at least a thousand miles away from each other. I'm not surprised he had someone at Duncan."

"It's not like we had Internet chats back then either. We either had to call or write letters. And we really couldn't afford to call."

"He had a very busy schedule as a football player at Duncan so even if he had the money to fly to Savannah, his schedule didn't allow it."

Tension covered Hope's face. Her words were stern and punctuated. "How would you feel if you found out ten years from now that Rodney had a woman in another country where he plays?"

"Hope," Rachel interjected. "I can't believe you went there."

Thomasine turned to Rachel. "I can't believe you went there." She placed emphasis on you, then looked at Hope. "That's a fair question, but remember Rodney pursued me relentlessly. He flew across the globe to let me know how serious he was. He met with my parents, asked them for my hand in marriage, took time away from his work schedule to visit me, showed me he cared genuinely about my welfare and well-being when he took me to the doctor in Sydney. Then there's the proposal, the wedding he planned with my parents. He rented the entire resort and flew everyone there. We honeymooned on a semi-private island. I know with absolute certainty that Rodney loves me. I'm the woman he married, not some nameless, non-existent woman in another country."

Hope threw her cards on the table. "I'm going to bed!" she uttered through a quivering voice and teary eyes.

❧

THOMASINE EASED the golf cart out of the garage. The morning sun peeked through her wooded yard. Rachel was still fast asleep, and although Hope was nowhere to be found in the house, her overnight bag was in the bedroom. Sina was halfway to the end of the driveway when she heard the low gurgling call of the male Brown-headed cowbird. At the end of the drive she ran into Hope. Well she didn't run into her with the golf cart, but Hope nearly ran into her.

"How was your run?"

Through heavy panting breaths, "Sina. There are alligators here!"

"There are. Foxes too. They won't bother you if you don't bother them."

"Sina, that thing chased me."

"How big was that thing?"

Hope held out her arms until they were about three-feet wide.

"Aw, that was just a baby gator." Sina informed her.

"You mean there are bigger ones?"

"Yes," Thomasine replied. "More than twice as big as that."

"Oh, my goodness," Hope said. "I'm going inside and I'm not coming back out." Thomasine turned, her right arm rested on the back of the front seat of the golf cart. She watched as Hope walked quickly toward the front door, like someone who had to use the bathroom.

"I'm going to the store," Sina yelled. "Do you want me to get you anything?"

"No," Hope replied as she scurried inside the house.

Part of the reason for the morning jaunt to the store was for Sina to clear her mind. She was certain of Rodney's love for her, but last night's conversation put a lot on her mind.

WHEN THOMASINE RETURNED, the tension was thicker than ever. She whipped up a spinach and feta breakfast quiche, while Hope watched TV in the great room. After Thomasine washed dishes, then lowered the oven temperature, she went to join Hope on the sofa.

"Good morning," Rachel said as she finally came to life. Hope took one look at Rachel, then looked to her left at Sina who was lowering herself to the sofa, and stormed off into her room.

Rachel sat on the sofa and sighed. "I feel horrible, Sina. I never should have brought up Jason and Naomi."

Thomasine reached for the remote on the coffee table, then turned the television off. "No, you shouldn't have. Put yourself in her shoes."

"But she and Jason are over. You saw how calm she was when she saw Jason and his woman at the holiday party."

"Think about it, Rachel. Hope was on a stage then. There were over a hundred people there that night. There was no way she was going to cause a scene in front of Jason, and his new lady." Thomasine folded her arms across her chest. "Absolutely no way."

"Do you think she's over Jason?"

"I think that Hope has moved on. Ponder this. She started dating Jason when they were only fourteen. Fourteen, Rachel! She was with him for half of her life." Thomasine pursed her lips. "But I don't think this is about Jason at all.

"If you had told her when we were in college, she probably would have felt more betrayed by Jason than she does now. I think she mostly feels betrayed by you. It hurts her that she painted this perfect picture of her and Jason and all along you knew that he wasn't true to her. I know that would hurt me deeply."

"You're right, Sina." Rachel scooted to the edge of the sofa. "I have to talk to Hope." Rachel walked across the living area and knocked on Hope's door.

Thomasine busied herself cutting fruit and then cleaning the kitchen. When Hope and Rachel emerged, Thomasine had set the dining room table with a breakfast spread. "I made appointments for us to have facials at the spa today, I also made us reservations for a late lunch. Maybe we can go shopping afterwards." She joined hands with her friends to bless the food, "Oh, and we have a photo shoot this evening."

"A photo shoot?" Hope asked.

"What will I wear?"

"I've already taken care of that."

With flawless makeup and hair, Thomasine, Rachel, and Hope posed for a variety of photos. Each wore a tank dress, Hope in blue, Rachel in orange, and Sina in crimson. Some of the photos, such as the one of them riding rental bicycles while parallel to each other were fun. Others, such as the photo of them on the grass dunes after sunset were more serious.

"I had so much fun today," Hope said as she sat at the breakfast bar in the kitchen.

Thomasine washed her hands in the kitchen sink, then went into the refrigerator. She handed Rachel a package of ground beef. "Spaghetti."

She opened the cabinet and removed the grater and a bowl which she handed to Hope. "Cole slaw."

"I guess that means you'll handle the fish." Rachel said. "That perch you made before the reunion sure looked good. I wish we could have had some." Thomasine smiled at the memory of the spark that lit the flame for her and Rodney.

"I don't have perch. Is flounder okay?"

"I've never had it." Rachel said.

"You'll love it."

The friends enjoyed a late dinner of great food and fellowship before retiring to the screened porch. "I'm a little hesitant to come out here after last night," Thomasine said as she sat.

"It's okay," Hope said. She set her glass of Diet Coke on the table in front of her.

"I'm just having one," Rachel said. "I promise." She poured rum into her glass. "A stiff one, but just one."

Thomasine pulled out the Uno cards.

"No cards tonight," Hope said. "Let's just talk."

"I'll go first," Rachel took a quick sip of her drink. "Is it crazy that I wish David would move to Nashville?"

Thomasine leaned back and turned her head to the side so that her ear nearly rested on her shoulder. "Oh?"

"I'm tired of the back and forth. I want both of my sons to have their fathers more present in their lives."

"I can understand that," Hope swirled the ice in the glass.

"When I met with David to tell him he wasn't Martin's father, he was so different. I was amazed at how much he had straightened himself out." She closed her eyes. "And he was so fine. He looked more like the man I fell in love with. He wanted me to move back to Chicago and said that he was saving money to buy a house."

"Have you thought about getting back together with him?"

She nodded. "I have."

"Wow." Hope said.

"But my job is in Nashville, and Patrick missed out on so much of Martin's life. If I talked about moving to Chicago, Patrick would probably take Martin away from me."

"Do you think Veronica would let that happen? Especially with twin babies?" Thomasine asked. She got up from the table to flip the switch for the ceiling fan.

"I don't know. Things would be much easier if David would just move to Nashville."

"But isn't he in school right now?"

"Yes. He graduates with his master's degree in December." Rachel paused. "It has to be tough for him too, because Winterveldt Advertising paid his tuition all through graduate school. I'm sure he feels an obligation to work for them for a while longer."

"Yes, he must."

"Do you still love him?" Hope asked.

Rachel nodded. "I do."

"Have you told him? Isn't he there like once a month?"

"I haven't, and he is."

"You have quite a dilemma."

"I do." Rachel sighed, her shoulders shrunk, and she leaned back into her chair.

"I owe both of you an apology." Hope started.

"For what?" Thomasine asked.

"For the way I judged you and competed with you."

"What?"

"I was so darn self-righteous," Hope said, then sipped her Diet Coke. "And jealous."

"When were you jealous?" Rachel asked.

"Remember, you were engaged before me. I was so jealous that Patrick proposed to you at your graduation, and Jason and I had been together for so long. I expected a proposal from Jason that day. That's why I bought the ring. I seduced Jason after making him wait for so long," Thomasine gaped at Hope. "I'm not surprised he had a relationship with Naomi at Duncan. I knew that night that it wasn't his first time. He was too confident, too smooth. But all I cared about at the time was that he put the ring I bought on my finger and went along with my program."

"Wow," Thomasine put her hand on her tummy. "If I wasn't pregnant. I'd need some of that." She pointed to the bottle of rum.

"So," Rachel asked, "Is Jason the only man you ever had sex with?"

"No!" Hope replied

Rachel shook her head. "No way!"

"When?"

"When I had some of that," she pointed to the bottle of rum, "in some of this," she pointed to the Diet Coke. "It was right after Jason and I separated."

"I'm still scratching my head. No wonder you lost weight. Oh, my goodness."

"Who?"

"Shoot, I don't even know their names. Well not their last names anyway. Some of them were in Kalamazoo, and some were in Virginia Beach."

Rachel slammed her hands on the table.

"Where?" Rachel asked.

"How many?" Sina followed up.

"You don't even want to know. That hurt brought out the freak in me."

"Hope, is this how you're embracing your singleness?'

"Not anymore."

"So, you got it out of your system?"

"Yes. Nearly nameless man, broken condom."

"Oh." Rachel said. "I'm gonna to leave that alone." She turned to Sina. "Do you ever think about her? Your daughter."

Thomasine closed her eyes and bit her lip. "I do, all of the time."

"Do you regret giving her up for adoption?"

"That I don't regret."

"I've always wondered." Rachel started. "That weekend I came to your school and discovered you were pregnant, you said that Conrad wasn't the father. Who was the father?"

"I lied then. It was Conrad," she sighed deeply, a tear trickled down her cheek. "I was so ashamed, because he raped me."

Rachel and Hope got up from the table and put their arms around their friend, and they cried together.

THEY SLEPT IN, then finished the quiche, and Sina cleaned the kitchen while Rachel and Hope took their baggage outside for the tram driver. Thomasine insisted that they leave on Saturday so that Hope could be rested for work on Monday and Rachel would have plenty of time to catch her Sunday afternoon flight. They returned to Sina's Durham home closer than they had been in years.

"Welcome home, Sweetie Pie," Rodney hugged his wife.

"Welcome home to you." She kissed him.

"Did you all have a good time at the beach?"

"We did," Hope said.

It was late Saturday afternoon, and after the ferry ride and three-hour drive, the trio was famished. "Rodney, would you mind picking up dinner?"

"That would be wonderful," Rachel said. "I'm too tired to go anywhere."

"And I'm too tired to cook," Thomasine said.

"You threw down on that fish last night," Hope told Sina.

"No, we all threw down on dinner last night."

"I'll be glad to pick up something. What do you want?"

"How about Rick's Diner." Thomasine retrieved the menu from the kitchen drawer and shared it with her friends.

"You know what I want."

"Chicken fried hard,"

"You've got it."

Rachel and Hope gave Rodney their preferences and he called in the order. They sat on the sofa and watched TV.

"Oh," he turned to Sina before he left. "Your mail is on the counter."

"Thank you, Sugar Cane." She stood on her tiptoes and kissed Rodney.

Thomasine took the stack of mail, sat at the table in her kitchen nook, and sorted it. She put junk mail in one pile, preapproved credit card applications in another. There was one that stood alone. It was from the marrow donation organization. Thomasine slid her finger underneath the back of the envelope, then unfolded the letter which had been forwarded to her.

"Great news," she told her friends after she read the first paragraph. "My marrow recipient is in full remission, and thriving."

"Oh, that's great." Hope said.

Thomasine continued to read silently. "They want to meet me," she read. "Oh, Lord!" Thomasine put her hand on her abdomen, then Hope and Rachel heard a thump.

Hope looked across the room and saw Thomasine lying on the floor. "Rachel," Hope pointed to Sina. Rachel ran over to Sina while Hope used the phone on the end table to call 911.

"Thomasine," she shook her. "Thomasine." Rachel grabbed her wrist to check for a pulse. The letter Thomasine was reading was just beside her hand.

"Is she breathing?" Hope asked.

"She is, and she has a pulse," Rachel felt she was intruding, but had to know what caused her friend to pass out. "Oh, my goodness, Hope!"

"What is it?"

"I'm reading this letter from the mother of the marrow recipient. Hope, the little girl will turn eleven on August 13."

"So?"

"She was adopted, which is why the mother is so grateful that Thomasine's marrow saved her life."

"Eleven, that means she was born in 1988. August 13, 1988. No way!"

When Rodney pulled into the driveway with their dinner orders, the paramedics were wheeling Sina out of the front door.

29

LULLABY OF THE LEAVES

Hints of red and rust began to color the lush green landscape of the Duncan University campus. Jason had not only excelled in his law courses, he excelled on the field. The morning workouts, summer strength and conditioning training, and summer camp put Jason near the top of his game. Once again, he was donning a green and white Spartan uniform. While he wasn't the team's number one running back, as in his younger days, he had played in every game thus far this season, and was starting in the second home game. It was also the first conference game against the Lake Effect Bobcats.

Jason loved the fanfare of the band and cheerleaders greeting them as they disembarked the team buses on their way to the locker room. Fans came out each week to show their support. Zuri wore a big smile when she saw Jason wearing the tie she gave him for his birthday. He called it his lucky tie for several reasons. Seeing Zuri empowered him. She and Christopher were usually able to make it out to the victory walk before the afternoon games. Christopher still played youth football on Saturday mornings, and had improved his game from last year. He had also become much more trusting of Jason with his mother.

Harding Memorial Stadium was packed for the nationally televised game. A sea of green and white, from older alumni who played the game thirty years earlier, to little girls in Duncan University cheer-leading uniforms filled the stands. In the end zone, a group of shirtless male students wore green and white body paint in the first row to the left, while the band filled the center. Lake Effect had a loyal following, but their fans were greatly outnumbered.

Over the last eight months, Jason had proven himself to his team-mates. While they sometimes joked about his age, they no longer saw him as an old man wannabe, but as part of their pack. Jason watched as the wide receiver caught the ball at kickoff. With a few good block-ers, he made it to the Spartans 47-yard line.

Jason put his helmet on and ran onto the field with the offense. The ball was snapped the quarterback faked to Jason, then threw a long pass that was incomplete. Second and ten.

On the next play, the Spartans gained four yards when the quarter-back slid to avoid a sack. Third and six.

Jason closed his eyes as he walked to his position. The feel of the ground underneath his cleats, the smell of the grass. He was attuned to everything Spartan. He got into position. He didn't hear the band play-ing, he didn't hear the crowd. All he heard was that the quarterback was counting on him for the six yards they needed for a first down. He intended to give him that and more. The ball was snapped on the Bobcats 49-yard line, the quarterback handed off to Jason, who found an opening. With the ball securely tucked in Jason's arms, he focused on the familiar feeling, of his feet beating the turf, ten yards to the 39-yard line, to the 30. A mere four seconds later Jason crossed the goal line to put Duncan on the board first.

Jason netted 199 yards on 19 carries for an average of 10.4 yards per carry in the Duncan University nail-biter. With only five seconds left on the clock, Jason rushed for eleven yards to score a touchdown and bring the Spartans to victory.

After an eight-year hiatus, the Real McCoy was back in the game.

§.

THOMASINE REACHED for the snooze button. She scooted to a seated position in her bed and wiped her eyes. Glimmers of sunlight slid through the slats of the blinds in her guest bedroom. It had become her new home since her hospital visit over the summer. Her doctor told her she had to take it easy in order to have a healthy baby, and put her on bed rest. Rodney didn't want Thomasine to lift anything and hired dog walkers to help with Sparky and Zack a few times a day. He didn't even want her climbing stairs, which is why they moved to the downstairs bedroom.

Rodney stopped through in between exhibition games to check on his wife, but she was in the capable hands of her mother, Crystal Mintor, a retired registered nurse. She was a big help now that Rodney's regular season had started and he was overseas.

Dr. Nestor, Thomasine's department chair, was very supportive, and allowed Thomasine to teach her class online through a new online course management system Steeplechase University just adopted called Blackboard.

Thomasine walked over to the desk Rodney set up in the guest bedroom. The computer was connected to the extra phone line. Beside it was the photo of Thomasine, Rachel, and Hope at the grass dunes in Bald Head Island. She logged onto Blackboard and graded her students' discussion board assignments.

There was a light rap on her bedroom door. "Good morning, Sina," Crystal walked into the room and stood behind her daughter.

"Good morning, Mama." Sina rested her head on her mother's arm.

"I just let Sparky and Zack out. Why don't you come into the kitchen and eat some breakfast?"

Sina logged out of Blackboard and pushed back from her desk.

"I'll check your blood pressure."

Sina sat at the table across from the French doors to the deck. She watched Zack and Sparky chase each other through the yard. Crystal put the cuff on Sina's arm and measured. "You're good today," Crystal wrapped the manometer and bulb around the cuff. "I guess you can have a piece of the bacon I fried."

"I'm so glad you're here with me, Mama."

"Me too, baby. I'm so glad I retired last year. That freed me up to be here for you."

Thomasine tore the end of her bacon, then ate a forkful of scrambled eggs. "I'm so fortunate to have you, Rodney, and a department chair who worked with me this semester so that I can also have my semester of medical leave once the baby is born."

Crystal sipped her coffee. "I'm glad that you have a chair who cares about you and not just how you can advance the department."

"Mama, I'm thinking about leaving Steeplechase."

"Oh?"

"Not right away, but I want Rodney, this baby, and me to be a family, in one place, under one roof."

"What will you do?"

"Hopefully I can get a position at Duncan or Northwestern, now that I have tenure. What do you think?"

"I would love to have you close to home, baby, so your Daddy and I can be near our grandbabies."

"I'm just having one, Mom." Thomasine took a bite of her toast.

"You're just having one, right now. Besides, your brother, Rodney's Mom, and sister are all in Chicago. And you all have that beautiful home. Might as well enjoy it."

"You're right."

Thomasine looked out into the yard at the dogs.

"Mama?"

"Yes, Sina."

"Do you think I should meet the recipient?"

"I think you should focus on having a healthy baby right now. You can make that decision later."

"It has been bothering me since I got that letter."

"And that letter got you sent to the hospital by ambulance."

"I feel in my gut that she's my daughter." Thomasine put her hand on her growing belly and felt her baby kick. "What if she looks just like me? I'm sure she knows that she's adopted and this was a closed adoption."

Crystal reached for her daughter's hand. "You don't have to make that decision right now, and it's something you need to discuss with Rodney. Besides, you're about to have your hands full for a while with this baby. Focus on the baby that you're carrying right now. The rest will unfold as it should."

❧

"DAVID BROWN," Dean Weissman called his name, and he proudly walked across the small stage at the ceremony held specifically for his fifteen-member cohort. David shook Dean Weissman's hand, and paused while the photographer took a photo.

"Get a little closer," Rachel instructed as she took a photo of David and Dr. Walters with her point and shoot camera after the ceremony. David felt like he was floating, full of excitement about his future. Dr. Walters offered great feedback on his grant proposal, as well as some possible funding sources for Helping You Help Others. When he presented his major project to his cohort a month earlier, a few of his classmates had experience as substance abuse counselors, and were very interested in partnering with him to make his vision a reality.

It wasn't just graduation that had him so excited. Rachel took him to dinner last night and poured her heart out to him. She didn't know how they would do it with her in Nashville and him in Chicago, but she was willing to give their love another chance. E-mail and Internet chat made long distance relationships an easier prospect than they were during her college days when couples had to rely on the telephone and letters.

Martin and Malcolm sat in chairs in the lobby drinking punch and eating the graduation sheet cake. They looked around at the people in funny robes. Most of them had little slits that their arms went through with a long flap that hung to the side.

Martin looked at Dr. Walters robe and said to Malcolm. "My Daddy has one like that, except his is gold," he said of the gown he saw in Patrick's graduation photo.

"Dr. Walters, thank you for all of your help," David said, near tears.

She hugged him, then stepped back. She looked directly into his eyes to share inspiring words. "I'm so proud of you, David. You've come a long way. You have a long way to go, but you are fully equipped for the journey."

David hugged her even tighter, then felt a tug at the end of the closed sleeve on his robe the boys called flaps.

"Malcolm," David put his arm around his son's shoulder and pulled him close to his leg.

"Daddy, I'm so proud of you. I want to get a master's degree when I grow up so that I can help people."

David broke down in tears.

His life wasn't just back on track, it was spectacular. And this was merely the beginning.

30

IN THE WEE SMALL HOURS OF THE MORNING

As much as he wanted to bring in the new millennium with Zuri, Jason knew if he got caught not following Coach McCann's orders, he wouldn't play in the Fanfare Bowl tomorrow. It was the end of a great season, and after his start in the second home game of the season, with each game Jason's play was even better. While there were some bumps in the season, the Duncan University Spartans were 11-1 for the season and undefeated in conference play. The Real McCoy made national headlines at the end of the season when he announced his intent to register for the NFL draft.

Jason sat in the chair near the window of his Orlando hotel room and looked at his watch. He took his cell phone out of his holster clip, then dialed the numbers that had become so familiar to him over the past year and a half.

"Jason," Zuri said, soft and melodious like a joyful smile.

"Hey Baby," Jason replied. "I really wish I could be there to kiss you as the ball drops." Zuri was staying down the street from the team hotel. "But you know Coach McCann wants us to be focused."

"Darling, don't worry about being with me on this one New Year's Eve."

"But it's a big one," Jason rubbed his chin. "Not just a new year, but a new millennium."

"I'd love to be there with you, but this trip is all about your dream. You are going to be on a national stage tomorrow that will have a big impact on your future. We can ring in the new year when we're back in Chicago. Hey, I'll let you be the first to walk into my house."

Jason chuckled. "Deal."

"And I'll see you tomorrow, on your team's victory walk before the game."

"I'll try to sneak one to you then."

"Deal. Happy New Year, Jason."

Jason looked at the television, "Not quite yet." He started counting backwards.

"Ten, nine, eight."

❧

"Now which box did I put my journals in?" Hope thought aloud. She weaved her way through the maze of boxes in her townhome, a new construction located a stone's throw away from the beach and Boardwalk Bike Path. She went from the living room into the dining room, a wide archway anchored by columns welcomed her. Hope couldn't wait until her dining room furniture arrived in a few days. She rifled through one box, put it on the floor then looked into another. "Here it is."

Hope tucked her journal underneath her arm. She took a few steps, then stopped and admired the five-inch oak hardwood floor throughout her home. No carpeting anywhere.

She walked into the gourmet kitchen. A built-in wine rack met her at the entrance. "Ah, not many people get to see the dawning of a new millennium." She opened a drawer, and found a corkscrew. Hope retrieved a wine glass from her cabinet, and poured herself a glass of 1997 Blackstone Merlot. She started towards the steps, then remembered that she needed a pen. After retrieving one from the pencil cup on the kitchen counter, she made her way up the steps, to the partial landing, next up the second set of steps to her master suite. She set the wine glass and pen on her night stand, the journal on her bed, and switched the channel to ABC.

Hope went into her ensuite to brush her teeth. She rinsed her mouth, then turned the water off on the sink on the left. The counter in between the sinks would serve perfectly as a vanity. She needed to add a small bench to her list of things to purchase.

Hope closed the blinds in her sitting area, made certain her balcony doors were secure, and flipped the switch on her gas log fireplace, before she climbed into bed. She took a sip of the merlot, then began counting, "Seven, six, five."

~

"THIS HAS BEEN AN AMAZING YEAR," Patrick said as he, Veronica, Rachel, and David sat in the living room of the time share. Martin, Malcolm, and the fifteen-month-old twins were fast asleep, drained of every drop of energy after a day at Disney.

"It certainly has," David replied.

"I've never been happier," Veronica smiled at Patrick. "It's almost time."

Patrick got up from the sofa, ran to the refrigerator, and got a bottle of champagne. He popped the cork.

"None for me," David said. "I'm sticking with this sparkling cider."

"Me too," Rachel said.

David put his arm around his reunited wife, and looked intently into her eyes.

Patrick handed Veronica a flute and sat to her left. He raised the glass in his left hand in anticipation.

"Four, three, two." They counted in unison.

~

ONE.

"It's a girl!" Dr. Torres held the wailing baby up for Sina and Rodney to see. She entered this world, crying in a high soprano voice like her mother.

The nurse cleaned the baby up, then handed her to her mother. Sina held her carefully, looked at her, and smiled through tear-filled eyes. "Rodney, we did it!"

Rodney kissed his wife's sweaty forehead, and stared in awe at

Crystal Kimberly Harris, the first baby born in Raleigh-Durham in the new millennium.